HEART
OF A
PRINCESS

HEART
OF A
PRINCESS

HANNAH CURRIE

This is a work of fiction. All characters and events portrayed in this novel are either fictitious or used fictitiously.

HEART OF A PRINCESS

WhiteSpark Publishing, a division of WhiteFire Publishing
13607 Bedford Rd NE
Cumberland, MD 21502

ISBNs:
978-1-946531-84-1 (paperback)
978-1-946531-86-5 (hardcover)
978-1-946531-85-8 (digital)

For Georgia

Because you inspire me with your courage,
your beauty, your strength, your character, and your smile.

So tired of being someone else,
So sick of trying to be perfect,
I come.
You didn't ask for perfection
You're not looking for someone else
Just me.
Broken, bent, tired and far from perfect
I come to you
Kneeling, crawling, it's all I can do.

I look up, expecting to see rejection again
Only to see you reaching out
Smile on your face.
Waiting, you've been waiting
For me.

You open your arms wide
Invite me in
You pick me up—hurt, broken, imperfect—
All the pieces that so shame me
You hold me close, whisper love in my ear
You sing me a song you wrote
Just for me.
I look into your eyes and see what I long for—
Acceptance, love, pride, joy.
You are pleased I came.

And in that moment, all the pain falls away
I don't remember why I hurt
Because in the arms of God I have found
Who I am and always want to be
And here I want to stay
Forever.

ONE

I traced a finger over my mother's face, her perfect smile captured for all time in the photograph, and wished for the thousandth time that I might have known her. Though the palace archives were filled with her pictures and I only had to ask and they would be in my hands, it would never be enough. No number of photographs could tell you how a person smelled.

I flicked backward through the album on my lap, the photos as familiar as the ache they produced—Mother's twenty-fifth birthday, her holding Thoraben as a baby, smiling as she waved to a crowd, wedding photos, her official engagement portrait and, there, the one I'd opened the album to find. Her eighteenth birthday. Standing beside the prince who would soon be her husband, she radiated beauty.

Today, I celebrated the same birthday. Eighteen years since the day I was born.

Eighteen years since the day Mother died.

Giving birth to me.

Mama, I'm sorry. So sorry. I wish you'd lived. You were so loved, so beautiful, so perfect, so—

Everything I wasn't. Oh, the people loved me too, called me their beauty and the darling of Peverell—I'd made sure of it, making myself into the perfect princess—but inside...

Cry, and you'll ruin your makeup, Alina. You don't have time to redo it.

The deep breath I took stilled my tears but not my aching

heart. It wasn't fair. None of this was. It shouldn't have been one life or the other. If only we'd both lived. She would have been by my side to celebrate with me today and tell me she was proud of me, that everything was going to be okay. I'd long since stopped believing it when anyone else told me that, but from her, the woman with the smile so bright and a peace I envied in her eyes, I may have believed it.

The door to my suite swung open, Milenne almost hidden by the long garment bag she carried. I closed the album, tucking it back into the top drawer of my desk, glad I hadn't allowed the tears pricking my eyes to fall. The last thing I needed today was my maid or anyone else trying to comfort me with words that only made it worse. *I know just how you feel. We all lost someone special that day.* They didn't know. How could they? They'd lost a queen. I'd all but killed my mother. Before I'd even had the chance to know her. Even Thoraben had had three years.

"The car is waiting and—Oh, Alina, you're not even dressed."

Milenne dropped the bag over the back of a chair and rushed to my giant walk-in-wardrobe. I wondered if it was too much to hope she'd get lost in there. Then I could claim the need to go in and fight the thousands of pieces of clothing, shoes, and accessories to find her. Anything to get out of going into town today.

Of course, ordered as my maids kept the wardrobe, she was out again in seconds, a pair of jeans and a cotton shirt slung over one arm, canvas shoes balanced in the other. All of them unworn, as they would stay. Mother never wore jeans so neither would I.

You're the princess. Be the princess.

I stood and rolled back my shoulders, breathing in the reminder like the oxygen it was. I could do this. Two and a half hours in town, shake a few hundred hands, accept some flowers, smile through the comments, laugh a little, flirt a lot, leave the people in no doubt that there was nowhere else I'd rather be. Lie, fake, pretend, hide—the act had become more natural than the truth. Especially since Thoraben and Kenna's wedding.

Nothing happened between the two of them. Sure. I'll believe that the same day I start wearing jeans.

A single glance in the floor-length mirror was enough to assure me my hair, makeup, and outfit were still as perfect as when I'd dressed an hour ago, but I kept looking anyway, coveting the few extra moments to compose myself. Had the choice been mine, I would have spent the day hiding out in the living area of my suite, a tub of dark chocolate ice-cream dripping with caramel sauce my one companion as I wallowed in the unfairness of it all. Unfortunately, it wasn't my choice. Few things ever were. The same, apparently, couldn't be said for Kenna, who had more say in the running of Peverell than any traitor should have—princess or otherwise. Only she would think inviting everyone in the kingdom to come and help paint and furnish the newly-built Community Center a good way to celebrate her birthday. The fact that Father had agreed to it—and decreed the entire royal family would be in attendance—only added to my frustration. Lunch would be catered by the palace, but Kenna had volunteered our family to serve it.

Of course.

Breathe in. Breathe out. It's just another engagement. Another day in the life of a princess. Nothing you haven't done before.

When I turned to face Milenne, my smile was back in place. I waved aside the clothing she tried to pass me. "Thank you, but I'm ready."

The woman paused, her gaze taking in the tailored white jacket and pale pink dress I wore before dropping to my matching three-inch heels. "Are you certain that outfit is appropriate?"

A giddy laugh bubbled up my throat. Appropriate? For walking through dirt, painting brick walls, and sitting in the dust to eat with commoners? Of course it wasn't appropriate. But neither was spending the day doing charity work on my birthday. The day which would have been my wedding day, if not for—

"It's fine."

"But Princess Mackenna said to wear—"

A short wave of my hand stopped Milenne before she could complete her sentence. Or perhaps it was the narrowing of my eyes and wild anger I wasn't fast enough to hide. My words came out clipped. I took pride in the fact that they weren't screaming.

"Mackenna may be married to my brother, but she isn't the queen yet. If she wishes to wear such clothing in public, that is her choice, but it is not—and will never—be mine." Especially not today. If I had to face our people today, standing beside my brother and his new wife—and Father had decreed it so—I would take all the confidence my shaking fingers could grasp at. And that included every inch of extra height my heels afforded me. "Thank you for your concern, but I will go in this."

I grabbed a silver clutch from a side table and walked out the door, saving Milenne the trouble of finding the right argument to change my mind. It would have been a fool's errand anyway, just like trying to talk my way out of today had been.

My heels clicked on the white marble as I descended the palace's grand central staircase. No one stood at the bottom watching in appreciation or waited to escort me to the car or even wish me happy birthday as I passed. Not even the palace's elderly doorkeeper—as much a part of the palace as the front door itself—was present, having been given the day off by the wonder couple themselves to attend the public relations stunt today. As if Rebels might not at any moment come and attack the palace while we were all off effusing false happiness. The hall was as empty as my dreams had become, dashed to nothingness in the course of one night.

Pull it together, Alina. You can do this. All you have to do is walk out the door, get in the car, smile at the driver, breathe...

The air I sucked into my lungs wasn't nearly enough to fortify me for what lay ahead, but it would have to do. I'd already delayed as long as I dared.

You're the princess, be the—

I flung open the front door, striding down the steps and tucking myself into the back seat of the waiting black car before fear had the chance to convince me otherwise. Childbirth might have taken my mother and Mackenna my wedding, but no one could take my pride.

What little I had left of it.

A short word from Father to the driver set us in motion. I settled into the seat and did my best to ignore the racing of my heart. If Father disapproved of my outfit or tardiness, he didn't mention it. We were halfway to town before he spoke to me at all, reminding me again of the importance of today for our family.

I nodded, the weight of emotion sitting on my chest too much to allow for speech. I'd go today because I was part of the royal family and our people needed a show of unity, but even Father knew better than to ask me to enjoy it.

"It is in times like these when we pull together as a country and prove to the rest of the world what we are made of. Infrastructure may collapse around us, but we, the people, stand strong. We are Peverell—steeped in tradition, bound by a hope for the future."

Though my head angled toward Father at his lectern, the gaze beneath my sunglasses wandered around the assembled crowd, wilting in the heat. Their faces, like mine, showed complete attentiveness, but the niggles gave them away. They probably thought they were hiding them but from here, on the podium, they were all too clear. Shuffling feet, shushing of young children, rapid blinking—or those forgetting to blink at all, glazed over as they were—stretching necks, smothered yawns. If Father's speech went much longer, I wouldn't have to do any work at all.

"Sixty years ago, when my father, King Rafael, took up the crown and saved our great nation, he vowed it would be a place of peace, of loyalty, of courage, and of hope. He transcribed them on our Coat of Arms, and ever since we have endeavored to carry out those fidelities.

"The whirlwind took its toll on our land. It destroyed houses, businesses, and—for some of our farmers—livelihoods. But what we must remember and rejoice in is this—it didn't take a single life. Not one person was lost to its wrath. Houses, businesses, crops—they can all be rebuilt, but our people..."

Father's deep breath, the slow shake of his head as he let the sentence fall to silence, was planned, practiced, and effective. Tired backs straightened, determined nods tipped out tears, arms reached for loved ones as a mix of fierce loyalty and tenderness washed the exhaustion from the crowd. Even I felt myself sitting straighter, pulled in by Father's words and the gratitude they produced.

"Sixty years ago, we rebuilt this nation. We will do it again. Already we have begun. What you have pulled together to do in the weeks since the whirlwind has been nothing short of remarkable. Looking around this marketplace today, one would never guess it was near rubble a mere seven weeks ago. But there is more to do. We can't stop here. We will not stop here."

Father looked behind him, beckoning Thoraben, Kenna, and me forward. We stood by his sides, as we had so many times before. Hand in hand, a unified front.

"Thoraben, Mackenna, Alina, and I, we stand before you today, not as rulers but as friends. Family. Fellow workers in the building of this small but beautiful country of ours. As one, we stand. As one, we fight. As one, we care. As one, we will rebuild.

"Without further ado, let us begin."

The applause was deafening. I smiled first at the crowd, then Father, grinned at Thoraben, hugged Kenna, all the while pushing down the voice inside me screaming that it was lies on top of lies. We weren't unified. Not as a family. Not anymore. Not since the night of the whirlwind, when my brother and former best friend betrayed us all.

And unlike the land, not everything could be rebuilt.

TWO

An hour and sixteen minutes later, I placed one final plate on the Community Center's kitchen shelves and washed my hands, drying them on a hand towel, doing my best to ignore the dubious brown stain on its edge. Serving lunch had taken longer and been messier than I thought it would be—as evidenced by the drip of pork fat on my skirt and the stain of gravy gracing my left shoe, gifts from a particularly rambunctious young boy—but it had kept me away from the worst of the dirt and paint, so for that I was thankful.

Twelve minutes until I could go home.

A glance around the room, full of stainless-steel counters and glistening white walls lined with cooking implements, told me there was little else I could do in here, but I grabbed a wet cloth all the same and began wiping down counters a second time, claiming every minute of silence I could. My eyes drifted shut as I focused on the soothing motion of the cloth—forward, back, forward, back—and let everything else fade into the distance. The whirlwind's destruction, the lingering smell of meat fat, opinions I couldn't change, questions I couldn't answer...

It wasn't that I didn't love the people. I did. Truly. But some days were more difficult than others, and there were only so many times a person could smile, nod, and change the subject before they looked like an incompetent fool. The gravy on my shoe? The spot of pork fat on the bottom of my dress? None of that came even close to demoralizing me as much as the outspoken opinions of too many people who I wished had kept their mouths shut.

"When's the wedding to be, Princess Alina?"

"Where is Prince Marcos today? Shouldn't your fiancé be by your side?"

"Aren't Princess Mackenna and your brother sweet together? To think they gave up their honeymoon to help rebuild Peverell. And Princess Mackenna, spending her eighteenth birthday painting when she could have been celebrating. Gems, the both of them."

Smile, nod. Hold it together.

"Oh, but it's your birthday too, of course."

Of course.

That was the moment I'd excused myself and come to hide in the kitchen. Thoraben and Kenna had enough smiles to cover for me. And a few thousand other people as well. I glanced through the door at the two of them painting a wall on the other side of the center, their movements so effortlessly synchronized they might as well have been waltzing at a ball.

Kenna giggled in response to something Thoraben said before tapping him on the shoulder with her wet brush. Thoraben's retaliation was instant, flicking a glob of white paint right back at her before dropping his roller and capturing her wrists, pulling her close. He wouldn't kiss her, not here in front of so many of our people, but the expression on his face left no secret to the fact that he wanted to. I looked away before the bitterness burning my stomach could spill out.

If only Marcos *had* been here. He would have known what to say to the people. He always knew what to say. But he wasn't here. Hadn't been since Father postponed our wedding last week, stating that two royal weddings so close to each other on top of the toll the whirlwind had taken was simply too much for the palace to handle. Marcos had left for Hodenia the same day, despite my begging him to stay. A new date hadn't been set.

Unfair didn't even come close to describing it.

Forward, back, forward, back...

The cloth skimmed its way across another already-clean benchtop. If only I could wipe the frustration from my mind as easily. *Forget it, Alina. He's not here and no amount of wishing any different will make it so.* At least he was coming back in time for the dinner tonight. Whether he'd agreed because he wanted to come or simply to get me to stop begging—and I liked to think it was the former—he'd be here for my birthday. Part of it, anyway.

"Alina? Are you in here?"

"Wenderley." I breathed out her name, thankful for the distraction. This friend's company I could handle. Would welcome, even. "I didn't know you'd be here today."

The hair playing escapee from her ponytail made me smile, as did the colorful bracelets lined up her left wrist. Lady Wenderley Davis had come a long way from the scruffy tomboy of a child I'd been thrown into friendship with as a six-year-old, but—alongside the designer clothes and practiced poise—hints of that carefree child peeked through.

"Of course, I came. Half the kingdom is out there, bringing Peverell back to its glory. It's so sweet of you and Kenna to give up your birthdays to help."

Sweet. Sure. "Kenna's choice, not mine."

"You're still angry at her?"

"Aren't you?" If any other person had a right to be, it was Wenderley. Her dream had been crushed the day Thoraben and Kenna married too.

"No."

"Really? You don't hate her, even a little?"

"No."

"I thought you'd be on my side."

"There are no sides. It's not us or them. It's just...life. People fall in love, circumstances change, life moves on. We move on with it or we get trampled while everyone else does."

I scrubbed at an invisible mark, rethinking my decision to welcome Wenderley in, wondering if she could truly be as accepting of the situation as she seemed, hoping she wasn't. "You loved Thoraben." Everyone knew it. She'd made no secret of the fact, beaming up at him whenever they danced, clinging to his side, unashamedly telling everyone close enough to listen. She'd been in love with him as long as I could remember, wishing down the days till he declared himself.

"I did."

"You wanted to marry him."

"Yes."

"And he married Kenna."

Wenderley shrugged, the pain on her face not as well hidden as she probably thought. "She's good for him."

Though I opened my mouth to tell Wenderley exactly what I thought of that ridiculous comment, she beat me to it. "Let it go, Alina. What's done is done."

"But—"

"Did you meet Joha yet?"

The change in conversation topic was about as subtle as a rose in a bouquet of daisies, but I welcomed it all the same. My brother and his wife were far from my favorite topic of conversation. "Who?"

"Joha Samson. He's a friend of Thoraben's. Came all the way from Hodenia to help out today. I sat with him and his mother, Malisa, at lunch."

"I handed out meals to a few hundred people in the marketplace today." And did my best to blank out every single one of them. "Unless he was the particularly messy boy who left half his lunch on my outfit, I don't remember. Why do you ask?"

"Because he's cute. And he's all man." She grinned, adding a wink for emphasis. I shook my head, tempted to roll my eyes despite the admonitions of my old deportment teacher never to do such a thing.

"Really, Wenderley? I'm engaged."

"So? Doesn't mean you can't make another friend. He's really nice. I could introduce you, if you like."

I shook my head again. "Thanks, but no." The last thing I needed today was another friend of Thoraben's gushing over how wonderful it was to see him so happy and what a great king he'd make one day. If only they knew. The whirlwind hadn't opened Thoraben's eyes to the depth of his love for Kenna and the fact that he couldn't live another day without her like the rumors still circulating claimed. The speed of their wedding was due to necessity and necessity alone. They had to marry. Of course, no one would believe that, what with the way the two newlyweds were acting.

I checked the time, relieved to see thirteen minutes had passed on the kitchen's wall clock since I last looked. "Sorry, Wenderley, but it's time for me to leave. It was nice to see you."

"You too. Maybe you could come riding with Kenna and me tomorrow. We're planning on going early."

Not likely. "Thanks. I'll check my schedule."

"And make sure you're busy."

I shrugged. We both knew it was true.

"Sooner or later, you're going to have to forgive her, you know. She's your sister."

I'd thought Wenderley understood, maybe even just a little. I couldn't have been further from the truth.

"Not anymore."

THREE

Icould see the headlines already—PRINCESS SHINES RESPLEN-DENT IN ROSE. A giddy excitement welled up inside me, tickling my throat as it tugged out a smile. Just because the first half of my birthday had been a dismal disappointment didn't mean the rest had to be. I would finish this day in style. It might not be a wedding gown—something I might eventually forgive Father for—but I would still be the belle of the ball. Or state dinner, at least.

"Show me, show me," I begged Milenne, all but pushing her and the other two maids out of the way as I tore at the garment bag's zipper. Today had been long, to say the least. My head still ached from the drain of too many questions and not enough answers, but this would make up for every bit of that discomfort. I breathed in the smell of new fabric, closing my eyes for just a moment to prolong the excitement.

It had been four days since I'd seen the gown last, standing here in my suite, unable to look away from the full-length mirror propped up in front of me as Mrs. Rosina made her final adjustments. I could just feel the silkiness of the fabric slipping through my hands, dancing around my ankles as I—

I took a half-step back. Opened my eyes. Blinked twice. Pushed the black satin aside, searching for something behind it. There was nothing. Certainly not the gown I'd been dreaming about all week. The one that made me look just like Mother. I tucked the fabric back in, zipping up the bag. "That's not my gown. You've brought the wrong one."

I was halfway to my dressing table when Milenne's quiet words reached me.

"No, this is yours."

I stopped. Turned. Considered the humorless plea on her heart-shaped face, the same expression mirrored in the faces of Tayma and Christi. They wanted me to agree, but I couldn't do it. Maybe this gown was mine—Mrs. Rosina often created extra gowns for me, as spares or options in case I changed my mind on the night—but it wasn't the one I wanted.

"My gown is pink." Ruffled sleeves which sat off my shoulders, corseted bodice sparkling with hundreds of crystals, full skirt with layer upon layer of darkening pinks falling to the floor. Glorious, magnificent, exactly like the sketch I'd fallen in love with the instant Mrs. Rosina had opened her notebook.

"It's no mistake, Your Highness," Tayma said. "Your father sent the order through for this gown himself two days ago, deeming it more appropriate for the function than the original. I've never seen Mrs. Rosina so excited, babbling on about its striking simplicity and what an honor it was to create it and how the lines will flatter your curves and the color make your aquamarine eyes sparkle."

Father had done this? He'd never taken an interest in what I wore before.

Christi pulled the gown forward, releasing it from the bag. Black, the whole gown. Black, like the gaping, growing hole where my lungs should have been. Black like the dots dancing around my vision.

Breathe, Alina. Take a breath. This is controllable. You can fix this.

A simple misunderstanding. That's all it was. Milenne could go pick up my pink gown from Mrs. Rosina's while Laure did my hair and Christi my makeup. We'd be cutting it close, but it wouldn't be the first time I'd turned up late to an event. Father would understand. He knew I always wore pink, even if he didn't understand its significance.

"Milenne, take this gown back and kindly ask Mrs. Rosina for my pink gown, please."

Instead of nodding and walking to the door, Milenne hesitated.

"What is it now?" I asked, the dots beginning their dance again. Why couldn't anything go my way today? "Milenne?"

"Your pink gown isn't ready."

"What do you mean?"

"Mrs. Rosina didn't finish it. She was so busy working on this one and your father said you wouldn't need the pink one and—Alina, are you okay?"

I reached for the vanity beside me, fingers grasping at the polished wood like it was a lifeboat in the middle of a storm at sea. It might as well have been. Though I stood in my perfectly dry suite at the palace, my lungs burnt for air, the weight of panic pressing down on me like breakers in a storm, threatening any second to send me under and hold me there.

But my maids couldn't know that. I had to be strong. I was the princess. Princesses didn't fall apart in front of their maids. They didn't fall apart in front of anyone.

"I'm fine." The black gown looked down on me from its hanger, mocking me and my lies and the hope slipping through my fingers. "I won't wear it. I can't."

"Of course, you can. Here, let me help you with—"

I took a step sideways, dodging Tayma's hand. Pretending control was the one thing holding me together. If she touched me, the shaking would give away in an instant how close I was to falling apart. I couldn't fall apart. Not today. I sucked in a breath, focusing on filling my lungs to capacity before letting them deflate again. *Breathe in, hold, breathe out. Breathe in, hold, breathe out. You can do this. You're the princess. Be the princess.* My world slowly shifted back into focus, Tayma's concerned face along with it. I lifted my chin and pushed back the panic.

"The gown I wore last year to the ballet then."

I rarely wore a gown more than once but, given the circumstances, I would make an exception on this occasion. With more flowers than a florist shop dancing across the full magenta skirt, Kenna would call it inappropriate for a formal dinner like the one this evening, but I no longer cared what Kenna thought.

"I'm afraid that gown isn't available either."

My forced bravado tumbled. "Not available? How could it be unavailable?"

Milenne looked at Christi, who was looking at Tayma, who steadily refused to look any higher than the carpet in front of my toes. They all knew something I didn't. And not one of them wanted to tell me what it was. With dinner in less than two hours, my hair needing dressing and the gown I would wear missing, I had neither the time nor the patience to watch them flounder.

"Tell me. Now. Why can't I wear that gown?"

Again, that hesitation. I crossed my arms and stared each of them down until Christi finally answered. "King Everson ordered that you weren't to wear pink to the dinner this evening. On his explicit order, all your pink gowns have been removed."

"All my pink? But that is almost my entire wardrobe! Why would Father do that?"

"I'm afraid I don't know, Your Highness. Perhaps you could ask him."

"I will. Right now. And in the meantime, the three of you will either retrieve the gown I wore to the ballet or find me another that is pink, for I will not wear that colorless monstrosity of a gown right there. And find Laure," I said of my fourth maid. "As soon as I return from Father's office, she can begin my hair."

"Yes, Your Highness." The three of them scuttled out of the room, the black gown flying out behind Tayma like a cape. It wasn't the ugliest gown I'd ever seen—to be honest, it had the potential to be quite beautiful with its black bodice and flowing skirt—but it wasn't pink. Were it any other night, I might have considered wearing it, but not tonight. Tonight, it had to be pink. I'd speak with Father. He'd understand. He never denied me anything.

Two minutes later, he denied me entry.

"What do you mean, he's busy? Too busy for his only daughter? It's urgent that I see him."

The guard standing at the door to Father's study was apologetic but unmoving. "Sorry, Your Highness, but the king said he was not to be disturbed by anyone."

"But I'm his *daughter*. And this is important." I spoke slowly, as if it might change the man's mind. It didn't. All it got me was a small shake of his head and another apology.

Who was this man anyway? I thought I knew all the guards in the palace, by face if not by name. How was I supposed to know how to coerce him if I'd never met him before? Would bribery work? Flirtation? The dumb princess routine? I didn't have time to find out. I had to speak to Father now.

I went with the element of surprise, ducking past the guard and opening the study door before he could work out how to appropriately stop me. Father sat at his desk, two other men in chairs across from him. A third empty chair belonged to the tall man standing near the fireplace.

All four of them turned to face me. Three wore startled expressions, the fourth—Father—frowned so deep his eyes almost disappeared. I ignored the first three, focusing entirely on Father.

"I have to speak with you."

"I have company, Alina."

I crossed my arms, planting my heels into the thick navy carpet. If he wanted me out, he'd have to forcibly remove me, something I knew he wouldn't do. I smiled at each of the men in turn. "Excuse us, gentlemen, but I have business with my father which cannot be postponed. It won't take long. If you wouldn't mind waiting outside until we're finished?" I swept my hand toward the door I'd just entered, gratified when all three nodded and left. I waited only until the door had once again closed before turning back to Father. "Now, you don't."

He wasn't impressed. Standing behind his desk, thick arms crossed over his chest, I was almost certain smoke would come out his ears.

"Leave. Now."

I flinched at his anger, wondering if maybe I'd pushed him too far already but stood my ground. This was important.

"The gown Mrs. Rosina sent for me to wear this evening is black."

"Good."

"Good? *Good*?" He couldn't be serious. "I won't wear it."

"You will wear it and you will stop this nonsense right now. Tonight's dinner is a serious matter, and I won't have you flitting about in an overly bright, inappropriate gown, distracting my men, even if it is your birthday. It was sweet when you were a child, but you're not a child anymore. You're about to be a married woman and will one day be Hodenia's queen."

"Will I? Truly, Father? If I recall, you canceled my wedding."

"I postponed it. There is a difference."

The difference between "postponed indefinitely" and "canceled" was so inconsequential I was surprised he even made the contrast.

"Prince Marcos would let me wear pink," I countered. He'd sent across oceans for the rare pink diamond which graced my engagement ring. No man would go to that effort nor justify such an expense unless they appreciated the color. Or the woman who wore it.

"He's not here."

"No, not yet. But he will be."

"Not anymore. King Dorien has fallen ill, so Prince Marcos has stepped in to cover his father's engagements. Prince Marcos sent his apologies yesterday."

"He told you but not me? Why didn't he tell me? I'm going to be his wife."

"Perhaps he didn't think you'd handle the news."

He'd have been right about that. "But—"

"Alina, the terms I am negotiating with those men you so rudely sent from the room are a matter of national security and have the potential to change the future of Peverell. Despite what you may think, your wardrobe will not."

Marcos wasn't coming. Father wasn't bending. This day was going from bad to worse. Tears began pricking at the backs of my eyes. I blinked them away.

Strength, Alina. You can do this. Try again. Change his mind. Tell him why it's so much more than just a gown...

"But it's my birthday. My *eighteenth* birthday. Mother wore—"

His hands came down, thumping the desk with enough force to send one of the papers flying to the floor. "Your mother knew how to behave. Something you have, apparently, forgotten. You will wear the gown I ordered and you *will* be dressed and in the formal dining room at seven sharp. Do I make myself clear?"

"But I—"

"Do I make myself clear?"

I ducked my head. "Yes, Father."

Spinning on my pink heels, I stalked from the room, slamming the door shut behind me. My nails bit into the soft skin of my palms as I acknowledged the men standing there and thanked them for their time. They smiled, assuring me it was fine. I fled before they saw I was anything but.

Hold it together, Alina. Breathe in, breathe out. Keep moving. You can't fall apart here.

Closed doors flew past me as I walked down the hallway as fast as I dared, my shoes clattering on the marble tiles. I focused on the noise they made, refusing to let the despair grabbing at me take hold. Click-click, click-click, smile at the maid dusting portrait frames, click-click, click-click, wave to one of the gardener's assistants bringing in fresh bouquets, click-click, click-click. One more corner and I'd be at her room. My refuge. The one place I could let the masquerade drop. No one ever came here.

I stopped, the sob caught in my throat nothing compared to the volcano threatening to erupt. "Thoraben."

Thoraben turned, guilt written across his face. If my head hadn't been pounding in time with my heart, I might have asked what he was doing hiding here, deep in conversation with a bearded man I didn't recognize. As it was, I only cared about getting past.

"Alina, I didn't expect to see you here."

Move Thoraben. And take that man with you. The one who's looking at me like he can see past the mask. "I always visit Mother's suite on my birthday." *And every other day.*

"This is Joha, a good friend of mine. You met—"

"Nice to meet you." *Go away. I don't want to talk.* I gritted my teeth together in a desperate attempt to hold back the tears threatening any second to spill. "If you'll excuse me."

I didn't wait for their permission, pushing past them into Mother's suite, closing the door behind me, leaning back against it. My shoulders shook as the sobbing took hold, my stomach clenching with pain. I wrapped my arms around my waist and let the tears come.

FOUR

I cried until the tears dried out. Though it left me feeling as wilted as the flowers I'd brought in here six days ago, experience had taught me it was the only way to dull the pain. I washed my face at Mother's bathroom sink before taking a seat at her desk, my favorite place in the palace. There was nothing special about it, the one in my own room being almost an exact replica, but she'd sat here. The woman I'd never known but ached with every breath to remember.

I had pictures of her, people's recollections, even a few of her favorite jewels, but nothing that was truly her. It was a silly thing, but I wanted to know what she smelled like. What she felt like to embrace. What it sounded like when she really, no-holds-back laughed. Was it a tinkle of a giggle? A full-throated guffaw? A delicate sigh of a laugh?

But more than that, deeper than that, I wanted to know her heart. Did she like being queen? Did she love the people as much as they claimed? Or was she, like me, ever putting on an act? Desperate to hide who she truly was and what she felt inside.

She'd given her life for me. Hundreds of people over the years had told me it wasn't my fault, but I couldn't deny the guilt or the wondering if her sacrifice had been worth it. I wanted to believe it was, that I was enough, but when the crowds went away and the lights went out each night, the doubts returned. Every year when I was little, my birthday wish had been to know my mother. I'd grown out of that by my eleventh birthday when I realized wishes were as fanciful as dreams. At least dreams you could enjoy for a moment. Wishes were only good for heartache.

I knew exactly what gown I wanted to wear tonight—the one Mother wore to her eighteenth birthday celebration. The night Father proposed to her. She'd already been the darling of Peverell, the tiny country having fallen in love with her right alongside Father. From the tales people told, it had been a night like no other. Dressed in a floor-length, pink gown sprinkled with crystals and a single silk rose, she'd looked like the princess she was about to become.

The dress itself was long gone, like most everything else of hers. Packed away in a fit of grief following her death, spoken of but never seen. The pink I wore daily reminded me of her, made her feel closer, somehow. As if she was standing beside me or I was wrapped in her embrace. Pink roses, pink gowns, pink shoes. It was more than a favorite color—it was part of her.

How could Father have refused me that gown? He hadn't even listened, sending me from his office in disgrace like one of the kingdom's Rebels he was so fond of exiling. I was no Rebel. I was his daughter. His only daughter. The image of the woman he'd adored.

I had to wear pink tonight. No matter what Father said. I just had to.

The door to Mother's suite creaked open. I stood so fast the chair tipped backward—fortunately for me, not falling. I didn't have enough time to pick up a chair and compose myself. I took a deep breath and held it, wondering who had found me, hoping it wasn't my maids come to tell me I was late for dinner. Or worse, Father. Especially after his ultimatum that I be there on time.

"Alina, honey? Are you in here?"

The breath flew out in a rush of relief. Mrs. Adeline. Kenna's mother, though for all intents and purposes she might as well have been mine. She'd cared for us both since the day we were born. Her influence and authority reached to the heart of who I was, but she wouldn't come in here even if I invited her, having far too much respect for her late queen to do so.

"Just a minute."

I tucked the chair back in its place at the desk and looked around the suite one last time before walking out. Mrs. Adeline waited at a bench in the hall under a large picture window. She patted the cushion beside her, inviting me to join her.

I shook my head. "I should go back to my room. My maids will be wondering where I am."

"They are."

"They called you?"

"They were worried about you. Milenne said something about a black gown and when Thoraben stopped by earlier, he mentioned you were here." She patted the chair again. "Tell me what's going on."

I wavered for a moment, considering. Thanks to my extended crying fit, there was little chance of me breaking down again, but did I want to risk it? Already the anger was swelling in my throat, recalling the callous way Father had sent me from his study. If I talked about it—

"Alina, honey?"

I walked the three steps to the bench and sat down. My legs were having trouble holding me anyway. The instant her arm came around me, the words began spilling out.

"Father won't let me wear pink to the dinner tonight. He says it's too immature. He thinks I'm immature. He told Mrs. Rosina to stop making the gown I designed and ordered a black one instead. I tried to change his mind, but he wouldn't even listen. I don't understand why he's being so stubborn about this. It's just a color. Plenty of people wear pink. Mother wore pink to her eighteenth birthday celebration."

"And you want to be just like her."

Mrs. Adeline used her free hand to tuck a strand of my hair back behind my shoulder, like she'd done so often when I was a child. I felt myself calming just being beside her. If there was one person's devotion I could still count on, it was this woman's.

"You already are, you know," she said. "Looking at you is like seeing her all over again. The same beautiful blonde hair and aqua eyes with those long dark lashes. You even have the same smile. I think the only part you got of your father is his stubbornness."

Not quite enough though, since he'd still beaten me.

"I can't believe my girls are eighteen already. It seems like just yesterday you were babies, snuggled in my arms, and yet here, it's been eighteen years since I first saw you." She nodded toward Mother's suite. "First saw this place."

"Thank you for coming."

"Oh sweetie, how could I not? We all loved your mother, and the whole kingdom was excitedly anticipating your birth. I couldn't believe it when those palace guards came to my house that afternoon, telling Nate and me the queen had died, and asking if I'd come care for you. I thought it was the exhaustion of birthing Mackenna taking over my common sense. The queen had died? I couldn't believe it. Our queen? Gone? Just like that? When we'd seen her only two days before? She wasn't supposed to give birth for another month. It was their tears that finally convinced me. I swaddled Mackenna as best I knew how and went with them.

"And there you were, this tiny thing in a huge palace, red face scrunched up and skinny arms shaking as you cried your little lungs out. There were so many people around you—maids, nurses, staff, even Thoraben, who'd snuck in a side door to see what all the fuss was about. They handed you to me as soon as I walked through the door. You stopped crying instantly. Your little mouth started opening and closing as you tucked your head under my shoulder, all but burying yourself inside me.

"I knew then and there that, no matter what happened after that night, you would always hold a part of my heart. I spent that first night—and many after—sitting in a chair, you in one arm and Kenna in the other, marveling at the miracle of not one but two tiny girls I held so close."

I'd heard the story a thousand times, but it always made me smile. Someone in this ridiculously large palace loved me.

"You have no idea the privilege it's been watching you grow

up. You couldn't have been more precious to me if I'd given birth to you myself. I am so proud of you." Her words soothed my temper like silk over hessian.

"Thank you."

"Now, tell me. Color aside, did you like the gown your father chose at all?"

"Well..." It was difficult to tell the fit without having tried it on, but the fabric had felt like silk the way it fell across my hands. The silver overlay in the skirt had been pretty too.

Standing, Mrs. Adeline pulled me up beside her. "Come on. You have a dinner to prepare for and a gown to try on." She grinned, winking. "We might even be able to find a way to add just the tiniest bit of pink to it. After all, your father said no pink gowns or clothing. He never said anything about accessories."

At 7:02 PM, I walked into the dining room, dressed head to toe and looking like the resplendent princess everyone knew me to be. My smile was genuine—and genuinely defiant as I stared Father down.

Beneath the striking black and silver floor-length gown—which, much as I hated to admit, was gorgeous—I wore my brightest, glariest, tallest pink heels. Though neither he nor anyone else would ever see them, I knew they were there.

Mrs. Adeline had also added a dark pink ribbon around the waist of the gown while Laure tucked miniature pink roses into my hair. It wasn't much, certainly not the profusion of pink I'd wanted to be gowned in, but it was something.

My victory was dimmed somewhat by the fact that no one but Father noticed my arrival. I should have risked his ire and waited another twenty minutes as I usually did so that every eye in the room would have been on me, but Father was in the most peculiar of moods and I didn't dare. There would be time later to charm the room. If I even wanted to. One glance around the chamber made me wonder if it would even be worth the effort.

Politicians, dignitaries, and ambassadors. With the exception of Thoraben and Kenna, there wasn't a single person here under the age of sixty. The Minister of Agriculture had brought along his dour wife but other than her, Kenna and I were the only women present. I wondered why I'd even bothered dressing up. It wasn't as if any of these men appreciated fashion, if they could even see past their hairy eyebrows or the reading glasses perpetually perched on their noses. Who needed glasses to eat dinner anyway?

"You're late," Father told me, his rebuke hidden from the rest of the room by the glass he raised to his mouth.

By two minutes. Practically early for me.

"Thoraben said you were in your mother's room."

I sent an angry glance in Thoraben's direction. Had he gone directly from seeing me to telling everyone in the palace where I'd gone? All I'd wanted was a few moments of privacy in a world where nothing was sacred. It appeared I couldn't even have that.

Father nodded his welcome to the Minister of Defense walking through the door, continuing to work the room despite the quiet conversation he was having under his breath with me. "What were you doing in there?"

Falling apart. Not that he needed to know that. "It's my birthday. I wanted to be near her."

"She's gone. And I don't want you in there again."

"What?" He couldn't do that. "No, Father. Please, I need—"

"To remember your place. I am the king and you will do what I say. Do not go in there again. Ah, Georgio. How nice to see you this evening."

I turned away from the man who could rebuke me with the same breath he used to bestow welcome upon a guest. As if he hadn't just taken away my entire world. I schooled my face into a passive expression, careful to hide the seething deep inside. How dare he. First my gown, then my wardrobe, now the one place I had in the palace where I could be myself. I needed that room. I crossed my arms and gritted my teeth behind my smile. This was all Thoraben's fault.

Father had doted on me until the day Thoraben defied him and married Mackenna. Everything I'd ever wanted had been mine—clothes, jewels, his absolute devotion. And then, in the space of one night, everything changed. It was as if Father realized he couldn't control Thoraben anymore and determined to control me instead. My clothes, my outings, my activities. My wedding.

That was Thoraben's fault too. I glared at his back and took two chicken concoctions from a passing server, stuffing them both in my mouth before anyone could tell me otherwise. *I* wasn't the one who'd defied Father in front of a room full of witnesses.

"Princess Alina, may I offer you my heartfelt—"

"Dinner is served."

I smiled into the room, all too happy to have been saved from a conversation with the simpering Mr. Lellanc. For the first time today, something had gone my way. It wasn't much, but I'd take it. My smile dimmed, however, as I walked into the dining room, the extent of tonight's décor summed up in the place cards.

Black printing on a white card. No fancy lettering. No border. Not even a flounce or sketch. I sighed as a manservant pulled my seat out for me. Kenna was seated on my right with Thoraben beside her. The Minister of Agriculture's wife claimed my other side.

The men across from me started up a conversation regarding the importance of coal in our country's economy. I fiddled with the stem of my water glass and wondered how long it was going to take for Lord Capper to realize the glasses he was looking for were on his nose. It was going to be a long night.

FIVE

Long was an understatement. By partway through the third of eight courses, the mental list I was creating of all the things I'd rather be doing was longer than the table we sat at.

Feed sharks with my bare hands.

Clean my own bathroom.

Look through Kenna and Thoraben's wedding photos and pick out all the ones I'd ruined with a frown.

Sleep with rollers in my hair.

Weed a cactus garden.

Wear black for an entire week. Including my shoes.

"Are you going to ignore me the entire meal?"

Would answering Kenna's whispered question negate the need for it? "I planned to."

"Why?"

I couldn't believe she had to ask. "You seduced my brother, forced him to marry you, ripped apart my family, all but canceled my wedding, and you wonder why I don't want to talk to you?"

All that and she also had the nerve to frown. "That's hardly fair, Alina."

"Fair? You dare talk to me about what's *fair*?"

"I've told you before, nothing happened between Ben and me the night of the whirlwind. I fell asleep beside him, that's all. You and a hundred other people were in the hall too, you know. Do you truly think either of us could have done what you're insinuating with that many witnesses?"

"Then he married you for no reason? Impossible. He was supposed to marry a princess, or, at the very least, nobility with something to offer and strengthen Peverell. Not a commoner like you."

"Your brother married me because he loved me, as you once did too."

"Yes, well, apparently, I was as much a fool as him, since you turned right back around and took advantage of every gift we'd ever given you. After all Father gave you. The prestige, an education befitting a princess, the finest gowns and foods. A place at his own table. This is how you repay him? Repay us? He should have paid your mother in jewels for caring for me and left you out of his gratitude altogether."

Picking up my fork, I speared my fish with enough force to have caught it soundly, were it still alive and swimming rather than drowning in sauce on my plate. The poor fish didn't stand a chance.

"Can't we just be friends, Alina? We used to be so close."

Ha. Not likely. If Mackenna wanted to hold on to the naïve assumption that I would turn around and forgive her, that was her delusion. I had no intentions of doing so.

"You might be a real princess now, but you will *never* again be my friend."

Silence met my whispered declaration. I looked up from my plate to see Kenna swallowing back tears, but it was my brother's expression over her shoulder which held my gaze. He was angry. Thoraben was never angry. He was kind, compassionate, patient, agreeable to a fault, but never angry. With one statement, I'd changed that.

He laid a hand on Kenna's shoulder briefly before pushing his chair back and standing. The temptation to ignore the hand he offered me was strong, but I refused to back down. I'd meant what I said, and if I had to defend those opinions to my brother then so be it. I'd been walked over all day. I was in the mood for a fight.

And the fish on my plate was disgusting anyway.

The farther we walked from the dining hall, the more trouble I knew I was in. Thoraben didn't only want to be out of sight of the dinner guests, he wanted to be well out of hearing distance too. We were almost to the west wing of the palace before he stopped. When he turned around, he was livid. I crossed my arms, leaned back against the wall, and waited for him to explode. It didn't take long.

"How dare you speak to Kenna like that? You rude, self-centered, bitter—Do you have any idea how much you've hurt her?"

"She deserves it."

"Deserves what? Your bitterness? Your selfish opinion that you are the only person in this world who matters? Truly? If you want to continue to hold on to the ridiculous notion that Kenna somehow seduced me in the middle of a whirlwind surrounded by a few hundred people then go ahead and do so, but stop taking your anger out on her. She has done nothing wrong, and you know it. You have abused her, belittled her, called her a liar, shunned her, and been nothing but cruel to her ever since that night and she *still* cries over you and the loss of your friendship.

"I thought, if we gave you time, you would see the truth, but I'm starting to wonder if that's even possible anymore. The whirlwind changed us all, but in your case, it wasn't for the better."

"Oh, sure, take her side."

"Of course I'll take her side. Not only is she the woman I love, but she's my wife! And you'd do well to remember it. Her position outranks yours now. Mackenna could send you away from the palace and you would have to obey. Any more trouble from you and I give you my word, I'll send you away myself. I love you, Alina, but I will not stand by and watch you hurt my wife."

Bluster and threats. Thoraben would never send me away. Neither of them would. They were too kind to do anything like that. The fact that Kenna still cried over the loss of my friendship—and held on to the hope that we might one day reconcile—proved how spineless she was. Conniving, but spineless. And Thoraben had married her.

"Peverell is a small country and you know its people look to us as their royal family for leadership and strength. We have to stick together."

"Maybe you should have thought of that before spending the night with that traitor."

"Alina."

"What? It's true."

"Apologize to Kenna."

"Not a chance."

"Don't bother coming back to dinner until you can."

"You can't stop me from eating dinner."

"I can and I will. Apologize, Alina."

"No."

Thoraben dropped his arms to his sides, closing his eyes as he did so. The expression of disappointment in them when he opened them shook me deeper than his anger ever could, though I refused to let it show. His anger I could fight. His disappointment tore me open. This man, my brother who I'd looked up to my whole life, was disappointed in me.

"I wish I could help you. You used to be so full of joy and kindness, but lately...I don't know. It's like you've turned into a different person. You were downright rude to Joha this afternoon and now this."

Joha? Who was—Oh. He must have been the man Thoraben had been speaking with in the hall. The one I'd walked right by. I hadn't meant to be rude. But to explain that, I'd have to admit how close I was to falling apart and no one, not even my brother, could know that.

He held out a hand. "Come back with me. I know a lot has changed in the last few months, but we can work this out. We want you in our lives."

For the smallest of moments, I considered taking his hand and accepting the offer of peace. Much as I hated Kenna, I missed my best friend and hated even more to have Thoraben disappointed in me. My hand twitched at my side before I crossed my arms, stubborn pride squelching down the longing. "No."

His words when he spoke were quiet, as close to begging as I'd ever heard. "I hope you reconsider. For your sake, as much as hers."

He strode back to the dining room without a single glance back to see if I followed. I told myself I wouldn't cry. I might have succeeded had the anger pulsing through me not pushed a few tears out.

How dare he! How dare they! My father, Marcos, Thoraben, Kenna. This was supposed to be my night. My long-awaited eighteenth birthday. I didn't even know who I was most angry with—Father for postponing my wedding in favor of a political dinner, Marcos for not being here, or Thoraben and Kenna for pretending they understood how I felt when there was no way they could have.

Ever.

They were happy. Blissfully so. In the course of a single night, all their dreams had come true. In one single night, all mine had been crushed.

They got the wedding.

They got the people's devotion.

They got their happily ever after.

I got a lecture from Father and told to grow up.

This was *not* what I'd planned for my eighteenth birthday party. And Father knew it. It was like he was punishing me. For Thoraben's insolence. All my life, I'd been the dutiful daughter, and this was how he rewarded me. With a state dinner. No dancing, no music, no gifts or decorations, no one even close to my own age.

Happy birthday to me...

SIX

I stomped up the hall. Away from the dining room. I didn't have any destination in mind, only the certainty that I had no intention whatsoever of sitting around listening to dull conversation for the rest of the night. Father could berate me later. No doubt Thoraben would tell him every detail of what had occurred, if he hadn't already.

The terrace was in sight when my heel caught in the skirt of my gown and tripped me, sending me sprawling to the ground in a graceless swirl of black fabric. The howl I let out had nothing to do with the pain of hitting the cold marble and everything to do with the fact that this day was quickly becoming the worst day ever.

I sat up but didn't bother standing. What was the use? It wasn't as if I had anywhere to go. Maybe a maid or one of the other hundreds of palace staff would come by and give me some sympathy. It would be more than anyone else had given me today.

"Are you okay, miss?"

I flung my head up, searching for the man who belonged to such a deep voice. There. Against the wall, near the terrace door. My frustration had probably hidden him from my view as much as the shadows had. I stood before he could offer to help me. It was enough that he'd seen me fall.

"I'm fine." I brushed aside his concern with a wave of my hand. I thought he'd leave. He didn't, walking toward me instead. Stopping a respectful two feet away. Was that appreciation I saw in his dark gaze? Affection? I drank it in, ignoring the voice inside telling me I should send him away. He was a stranger in the palace and a man at that, but I was too emotional to be wise. "Actually, no. I'm not fine. It's my birthday. Did you know that?"

"No, miss. Happy birthday."

"Thank you. And it's Princess, not Miss. Princess Alina Ciera Georgia May the First, daughter of King Everson and the late Queen Ciera of Peverell."

"Forgive me, Your Highness. I didn't recognize you. Photos don't do you justice, and I've never before had the honor of meeting you in person."

His words and deep bow both charmed and confused me. Who was this man? A nobleman? A guard out of uniform? His clothing was too fine to be a servant's but too simple to be a noble. Plain white shirt, pure linen if I didn't miss my guess. Plain black pants, fitting him to perfection. Shoes polished to a shine but also too nondescript to give any clue to his identity.

"Who are you?"

"Sir Gray Nichols at your service, my princess."

His name wasn't any more familiar than his face. I searched my mind for anything I could think of to place him. "Your accent. You're Hodenian?"

"Born and raised."

"Will you tell me about it?"

"Hodenia?" I nodded. He waved my question aside with a flick of his hand. "Oh, my descriptions would only bore you. You'll see it soon enough for yourself. When is the wedding to be?"

I frowned. "You don't know?"

"Forgive me. I've been away for a time, but I thought a date had been set. Did something happen?"

"You could say that."

"Oh?" Interest pulled him half a step closer.

"I was supposed to marry Prince Marcos. Today, in fact. But then my brother, Crown Prince Thoraben, married Mackenna, the girl who used to be *my companion*, in what might as well have been a shotgun wedding, and suddenly my wedding wasn't all that important anymore. Instead of a wedding to celebrate my coming of age, I get a boring dinner. Dignitaries. Ministers. Dull men with even duller conversations. Some birthday this has been. And Prince Marcos isn't even here."

"No?"

"He went home after our wedding was postponed but was supposed to return for the dinner tonight, only King Dorien is sick so Marcos is covering his engagements. Apparently. Of course, he couldn't even find the time to tell me himself. *Father* had to tell me. Did Marcos think I would overreact if I knew? Be the immature child Father thinks I am? They're wrong. I'm mature. I'll be a great queen. And I'll wear as much pink as I want."

"I'm sorry your day hasn't turned out the way you hoped."

I shrugged. I should have known better than to hope. "That's being a princess for you. Everyone thinks it's all glamor and smiles, but it's a whole lot of acting happy while doing what you're told. *Do this, meet this person, stand up straight, wear this, and for goodness' sake, don't forget to smile.*" I huffed. "As if, after eighteen years of being told, I didn't know." I pasted on my crowd smile, the one I'd been using all too often of late, to prove to Sir Gray how fake it truly was.

"You play the act well. I had no idea you were so discontented in your role."

I shrugged again. "It has its good moments, of course, though they've been few and far between lately. Since Thoraben married Mackenna and Father got all grumpy with me. As if *I* was the one to defy him in front of everyone instead of Thoraben."

"Prince Thoraben defied your father?"

"You really have been away, haven't you."

His smile was almost as charming as his earlier bow had been—and sent a shock of warmth through me. "Again, forgive me. I had no idea I'd missed so much."

"Only a lifetime."

"I beg your pardon?"

I sighed, doing my best to explain.

"Seven weeks ago, there was a terrible whirlwind. The force of it tore apart much of the kingdom. This palace was one of the few places sturdy enough to withstand it. Only, rather than staying within its shelter, Thoraben took it upon himself to go and rescue Mackenna and her mother, who were living in one of the nearby cottages. Father forbade Thoraben to go but he was adamant and went out into the storm anyway. He eventually brought her back, but instead of returning to us, he defied Father again by staying with her amongst the crowd in the Great Hall.

"I was back in my suite the next morning when I heard the news. Kenna had seduced Thoraben and despite Father's adamant objections and her lack of any noble blood, the old law would be upheld and they would marry. Immediately. I'll leave you to imagine what occurred that such drastic measures were required. Though she grew up in the palace, Mackenna Sparrow was just a servant in a pretty dress. Prince Thoraben, heir to the throne of Peverell, married a glorified servant girl.

"They break the law and I'm the one who pays for it. We couldn't possibly have *two* royal weddings within such a short time so, of course, my wedding is 'postponed indefinitely' and Prince Thoraben and the new Princess Mackenna go off and live happily ever after."

"Princess Alina, I had no idea."

"Of course you didn't. The royal publicists aren't paid to let a scandal like this reach the masses. We can't have anyone thinking Peverell's royal family are anything less than perfect now, can we?" I shook my head. What a load of rubbish. If only they all knew. Thoraben and I yelling at each other in the halls, me hiding in Mother's suite like a lost child, Kenna crying herself to sleep, Father furious at us all.

"And yet, here you stand, perfection itself."

Was he flirting with me? Furthermore, did I want him to? "You're not a guard, are you." He was patient enough to be one but would have told me off already for being alone with a stranger if he was.

"No."

"A dinner guest?"

"Tonight, I am simply a friend."

A friend. *That* I could appreciate. "Well, friend, it was nice to meet you, and I thank you for listening. I feel better already. I should go, but I'll see you again, I hope."

Sir Gray bowed, grinning as he stood tall again. "I'll look forward to it. Happy birthday, Princess Alina."

My smile as I walked toward my suite bloomed from a place deep inside me and was every bit as genuine as the gown swishing around my bright pink shoes. Perhaps my birthday hadn't turned out so terribly after all.

SEVEN

My hair jerked in Laure's hand the next morning as the door to my suite flung open, thudding against the wall before being caught by an overly apologetic maid. I was surprised it didn't hit her in the head. "Forgive me, Your Highness, but your Father wishes to speak with you immediately."

A summons from Father? That didn't happen very often. I might have worried had I actually cared. Even twelve hours later, anger still simmered inside me at the way he'd sent me from his office yesterday, disgraced in front of his dignitaries who were there to, apparently, save the world. As if my world didn't even matter anymore. And then to ban me from Mother's room? I leaned back in my chair, letting Laure continue her styling.

"Thank you. You may tell him I'll come when I'm ready." Tomorrow, perhaps. Or next week. Sooner, if he groveled. Part one complete, Laure put the straightener down and picked up a comb, dividing my hair into two sections, clipping one aside.

"King Dorien and Prince Marcos were there too, Your Highness."

This time the hard tug of my hair was my own fault as I flung my head around. "Marcos? He's here?" She should have started with that information. I pulled the clip from my hair, wincing as it ripped several strands out, and hurried toward Father's office, thankful I'd already dressed for the day.

There he was, standing outside Father's closed door, tall and handsome as ever. The man who held my heart and every hope

I had for the future. Married to one of the most powerful men in the world, and certainly the most eligible, I'd never have to worry again about whether I was good enough. The status that came with the title "queen" ensured that.

"Marcos."

I couldn't believe it. He'd come back after all. Had he realized how much I missed him already? Had he missed me too much to stay away? *Oh, I hope so.*

Father's reasons for summoning me, Thoraben's disappointment, my anger at Kenna, and intrigue regarding Sir Gray—I left them behind as I ran toward Marcos and threw myself into his arms, laughing as he took a step backward to catch his balance. Two kings waited for me behind that closed door, but I couldn't find it in myself to care. Not with the steady thump of Marcos's heartbeat pressed against my ear.

He extricated himself from my arms, taking a large step back and ending my moment of bliss long before I was ready. I opened my mouth to tease him about being such a stickler for propriety but closed it when I saw his face. Eyes glaring, mouth clenched shut, that was *not* the face of a man pleased to see me.

"Marcos?" I reached out a hand to touch his arm, dropping it when he took another deliberate step away. He might as well have slapped me.

"I thought I could trust you," he bit out.

"I beg your pardon?"

"Don't you know better than to speak with the press about sensitive matters? You grew up in a palace, for goodness' sake. Father's had people imprisoned for less."

The press? "I didn't talk to the press."

He opened the door before I could ask any more questions, standing aside, ever the gentleman, as he waited for me to walk through. I wasn't so sure I wanted to. If the perpetually calm Marcos was this angry...My heart thudded against my chest, coursing fear throughout my body. What had I done?

The glowers of the two kings standing waiting had me hovering a step inside the door. Fight? Flight? Or fall apart. The latter was seeming most probable. King Dorien was clearly unwell with his red nose and handkerchief clutched in his hand, and yet he'd come, all this way, to say something. I swallowed the bile rising in my throat as Marcos closed the door, blocking my escape. There was nothing for it but to face my mistake. Whatever it was. I clasped my hands behind my back and forced my gaze up.

"Princess Alina, the engagement between you and my son is, as of this moment, terminated."

"No." The shocked whisper tore from my mouth, lost in the sound of Father's fist hitting his desk.

"That is *not* what we agreed to, Dorien."

"I agreed to my son marrying a princess, not a temperamental girl who doesn't know how to keep her mouth shut. It not only shows a lack of decorum, it's a complete lack of respect. Princess Alina is beautiful, of that there is no doubt, but Hodenia deserves a queen who can act like it and *she*—" His chin thrust toward me, in case there was any doubt who he was speaking about. "—is a liability."

A liability? Temperamental? Terminate the engagement? But—No—My heart thudded in my throat, blocking the air I tried to gasp. I had to marry Marcos. It was everything.

"She is my daughter and I will not have you speaking that way about her. It hasn't even been proven it was her yet."

"Oh don't be a fool, Everson. How could it be anyone else? Every one of those papers has direct quotes which could only have come from her."

King Dorien swiped a pile of newspapers across the desk and onto the floor. My face stared back at me from the top one, the headline MARCOS DOESN'T TELL ME ANYTHING effectively stopping my heart. I didn't want to touch them, didn't want to see what the rest of them said but, like flies to a stench, I couldn't stay away. I knelt by Father's desk and opened the paper, skimming its pages, as desperate for a moment to compose myself as I was to know what I was being blamed for. The exclusive promised on the cover didn't disappoint. My stomach clenched tighter with every word I read of it. The other papers were no better.

DULL MEN WITH EVEN DULLER CONVERSATIONS.

KING CAN'T KEEP HIS OWN CHILDREN IN LINE, HOW WILL HE CONTROL THE COUNTRY?

WHAT REALLY HAPPENED THE NIGHT OF THE WHIRLWIND?

I wouldn't throw up. I wouldn't cry. Not here. Not with King Dorien glaring at me and Marcos not saying a single word in my defense. Did he want to dissolve our engagement too?

No...please...

They couldn't. I had to fix this. Somehow. Marrying Prince Marcos was my future. It meant security, status, and the chance to prove to everyone that I could be just as good a queen as my mother had been. I could do it, I knew I could. I had to. Her sacrifice couldn't be for nothing.

"What did you do, sell your frustrations to the highest bidder?" King Dorien asked me, his fury barely controlled. "Call a press conference? All the papers are quoting you. Who did you speak with?"

I shook my head, blinking back tears. *Control, Alina. He already thinks you're a child. Don't prove him right.*

"I didn't. Truly."

"You must have spoken with someone."

"I didn't!" The only person I'd spoken with at all last night was—"Sir Gray." I breathed out the name. He hadn't looked like a reporter, nor acted like one but—words came back to me, ones I'd said in anger as I ranted about the dismal state of my life—I had said those things. Every one of them. Had he been a reporter?

Marcos took my arm, wrenching me to my feet. "What did you say?"

"There was a man. Sir Gray Nichols, he said his name was. I ran into him in the hall after I left dinner last night."

"And proceeded to blurt out every thought you'd ever had about your life and the lives of every other person in the royal families of both Peverell and Hodenia, apparently."

"I didn't know he was a reporter."

"It shouldn't have mattered *who* he was," King Dorien blustered. "You live in a royal family, you keep your mouth shut. Any fool knows that."

"I'm sorry." The two words caught in my throat on their way out, sounding more garbled than sincere. I cleared my throat, faced King Dorien and tried again. "I'm sorry. I should never have said anything. Please don't cancel the wedding. I'll do better. I promise, I will."

I reached for Marcos's hand. He crossed his arms.

"Please."

My plea hung in the tension-charged office. I willed myself not to burst into tears or kneel on the floor and beg. Even though we'd only officially been engaged since Prince Marcos proposed at the Midsummer's Ball three months ago, I'd been unofficially betrothed to Marcos since birth. If not before. I was going to be Marcos's wife and the next queen of Hodenia. They couldn't take that away from me. Not here. Not now. Not due to a simple—I looked down at the papers again, my stomach looping over itself at the sight of them. Fine. So, it wasn't such a simple mistake, but it was an honest one.

When the men finally did stop glaring and start talking, they left me out of the conversation entirely.

"A retraction needs to be written as soon as possible," King Dorien said, "before people start believing this. Within hours, if we can. A full press conference, the right media. Princess Alina will have to make the speech, unfortunately, but get someone versed in diplomacy to write it for her."

He might not have called me a fool to my face, but I felt the barb as painfully as if he had.

Father gestured over one of his advisors. The man already had his notebook out, pen flying across the pages. "Watts, a retraction speech, a press conference, the right media—see to it."

"Right away, Your Majesty."

"And find out how this Sir Gray person bypassed security. I will *not* have the privacy of my family violated. Alina, you may leave. Go back to your room directly and stay there until I call for you."

"What about the engagement? Are we still..."

I held my breath while Father and King Dorien considered one another. Though no words were spoken, plenty was being said. The question was, who was saying what and would it be enough to save me?

There were no smiles when they turned to me, no sign of affection in any of their expressions, but the words King Dorien offered gave me the smallest bit of hope.

"For now."

EIGHT

The glare of the sun, blinding as it was, had nothing on the intensity on the faces of the reporters in front of me. Holding out all manner of recording devices, they arched forward, vying for that singular soundbite which made their story the most damning, the juiciest, the best.

It was far from the first time I'd addressed a crowd. It *was* the first time I'd addressed one so hungry for a story. The princess who didn't believe in her country. Her father. Her fiancé. The fact that we'd called a press conference at all when normally we'd ignore such claims as gossip spoke volumes.

I clasped my sweaty hands together and smiled at those I knew—Damin Tunney from the *Peverellian Times*, Priscilla Parson from *News Alive*, Harriet Jones from the *Royal Review*—but there were so many I didn't. Did Peverell even have this many papers? Did Hodenia? How far had Sir Gray, or whatever his real name was, spread my shame? Peverell was a tiny country, its royal family respected within its borders but hardly newsworthy outside of them. We were the adored much younger cousin of the rest of the world—a child bumbling its way through life in a way that provided amusement and a peaceful way of life to sigh over but was hardly worth fretting about.

Of course, what we lacked in resources and authority, Hodenia offered in spades. It was the reason my marriage to Prince Marcos was so important for Peverell, to keep the peace with our closest neighbor. They were our greatest ally. The sooner the ceremony took place, the better. I had to convince these reporters, and every reader they had, that all those things I'd said were lies. Even if the vast majority of them were true. Thoraben had been right about one thing—our people needed a show of unity from our family.

"Ready?"

I nodded to Mr. Bowe, doing last minute checks of the microphone. Another lie, but then, wasn't most of my life? Bright smiles brimming with confidence while I cowered inside?

"You'll do great. You always do."

I looked down at the notes in front of me on the lectern, ignoring the shaking of the hands that held them. It was one thing to make a speech at the opening of a hospital or sporting event, but another entirely to have to face up to a crowd of reporters in an attempt to reclaim my reputation after the papers had pulled it to shreds. Still, if it saved my marriage...

Breathe. Just breathe.

"People of Peverell, thank you for coming today. I count it a true honor to stand before you, my people, and be given the chance to speak from the heart.

"Being a princess is far more than a title for me. It's my job, my privilege, and my life. It's who I am. It's not a life I chose, but it is the life I cherish."

My family hadn't come. It shouldn't have surprised me. I'd disappointed Father, disgusted Marcos, and all but forced Thoraben and Kenna from my life, but somewhere deep within me, I'd expected them to be here. If Mother had lived, would she have come? I liked to imagine she would have, that she would have been by my side no matter what, but I had no way of knowing.

"With regards to the sentiments reported recently in the papers, I would like to state right from the start that they are wrong. I have nothing but respect for the Kingdom of Peverell, its people, and the royal family I am a part of. And I am very, very honored to be marrying Prince Marcos."

Wait, was that—It was! Thoraben, there at the edge of the crowd. He'd come after all. My heart lifted, bolstered by his support. I didn't have the luxury of pondering right now why that meant so much to me when I didn't like him at the moment anyway, but a real smile broke through the fake one I'd been using since Father's advisors had ushered me toward the lectern. I forced my attention back to the crowd in front of me, working on making eye contact with each of them in turn. Speeches weren't my favorite—it was much more difficult to work a large crowd than a single person—but my elocution tutor had spent hundreds of hours over the years ensuring I was more than proficient.

"My father once told me that to be a princess is to be the heart and life of the people. Where kings and princes are tasked with the responsibility of seeing to a kingdom's logistics and loyalties, my role was to be its heart. To encourage, to strengthen, and to find beauty in every person we have the privilege of serving as royals. Since the day my father told me that, I have endeavored to be not only the best princess I could be for you, but the best person."

I glanced over at Thoraben again, faltering when I saw he'd turned his back to me. Was he talking to someone? Likely, given the way his hands were moving. He could have at least pretended to pay attention to me. If he was going to ignore me so blatantly, it would have been kinder if he hadn't come at all. I looked down at my notes again, taking a moment to remind myself why I was here. The people. Not for Thoraben or whoever he was speaking with, not even for Father. I was here because the people needed to know I was still on their side.

"Soon, I will marry Prince Marcos, and subsequently have the honor of serving not only Peverell but also the kingdom of Hodenia. This was my choice, and one I would make again given the option. Believe me when I say I am very much looking forward to being Prince Marcos's wife." I delivered the line with a grin, pleased to hear a twittering of laughs from the crowd in response. Was Father purposely watching from inside? Knowing that, were he to come out, the people's focus would be divided between us rather than solely on me?

"A new date for the wedding is still in negotiations but you can be assured, the moment it is decided upon, you will be alerted to it."

The crowd of reporters surged forward, one of them pushing the main camera to the side. The words on my autocue bounced, blurring them in my vision. I paused, hoping thoughtfulness and contemplation came across to those listening rather than the confusion and nausea I felt. *Smile, Alina.* I would have made a joke or admonished the crowd if not for the strict instruction both Father and Marcos had given me to say what was on the prompt and not a single word more. This was my one chance to make things right. I couldn't risk ruining it.

"With regards to the matter of Prince Thoraben and Princess Mackenna, they are—"

"Tell us what you really think," yelled a voice from the crowd. "Are you being forced to marry Prince Marcos?"

"—very much in love and enjoying their new marriage despite what I was quoted as—"

"Is Princess Mackenna pregnant?"

"—saying in the papers this morning."

The cameraman was pushed to the ground along with the autocue. My hand flew to my mouth as the crowd continued to surge forward. More guards appeared, to my left and right, their arms linked as they attempted to hold the crowd of reporters at bay.

I looked down at my notes, searching for calm as much as what I was supposed to be saying. The papers had been more a prop than a requirement to this point but, with my autocue gone, they were my last resort.

"It is hoped that—"

Words fled as I hit the ground, pushed aside by a guard intent on protecting me. Black spots pricked at my eyes as another stood on the hand I put out to catch my balance. I pulled the hand in against my chest, cradling it as the shakes began. All around me was shouting—the guards, the reporters, the growing crowd. One minute, I'd been calmly standing on the palace steps, my words clear as I addressed the press, and the next I was pushed to the ground and stood on as an angry mob raged around me.

Somewhere in my fear-filled mind, I knew I should stand—run, even—but that same mind told me my legs would never hold me. Not shaking like they were. My breath came in gasps as I leaned back against the lectern and closed my eyes to the fray.

The Rebels, it had to be them, come to destroy what was left of Peverell's royal family. All my life, Father had been fighting against them and their animosity toward us. What better way to finish us off than to come while we were already down and vulnerable?

"Alina! Alina!"

Amidst the ruckus, I was almost certain I heard my name, but when I opened my eyes, all I saw were the tall, black boots of far too many guards. I curled up in as tiny a ball as I could and faced the truth—no one was coming to save me.

NINE

I lay with my eyes shut, terrified at what I would find should I open them. I knew one thing already—the bed was too rough to be mine. My sheets and pillows at home were the smoothest of satin. These were cotton, at best. And there was something more. My mind skittered around, testing and taunting until I finally grasped the wisp of a realization.

Silence. The room was silent.

Whether it was the footsteps of my maids, the lilting lullaby of music they played in my suite or the not-too-distant sound of guards out exercising their horses, I never woke to silence.

Opening my eyes confirmed what I already knew. Though every muscle in my far-too-tense body protested at the movement, I sat up. My head spun with the effort.

I wouldn't panic. I couldn't panic. I was a princess. As long as I could remember and likely before, I'd been taught to handle every situation with grace and aplomb. Nothing could faze me. Not even waking up in an unfamiliar room with no memory of how I got there. Or even where "there" was.

My hands started shaking. A sharp sob cut its way out of my throat.

Calm down, Alina. You're fine. Truly.

My heartbeat thudded so loud in my ears that I was certain it would deafen me. Another dry sob escaped. The harder I tried to hold myself together, the more I fell apart. Where were my maids?

Breathe, Alina. In. Out. Focus. I made myself look around the room, my gaze pinning one piece of furniture at a time.

Breathe in. One bed, single sized, blue and white comforter, white sheets. *Breathe out.* Bedside table, white wood with a white lamp on top of it. *Breathe in.* Single wardrobe, white like the bedside table, mismatched knobs on the doors, gray scuff mark near the bottom. *Breathe out.* Framed photo of some type of purple flowers on the wall. Pretty enough, basic as it was. *Breathe in.* One large window bracketed with pale blue curtains. Narrow table and chair beneath it. Meant to be a desk perhaps? *Breathe out.* Dark blue carpet, well-worn, no rug. Simple dome light fixture in the middle of the roof.

Light shone through the window, but its view of clear sky gave me no indication of where I was, nor the time. Was it morning? Afternoon? How long had I been asleep? My head spun again, taking my balance with it. I closed my eyes, willing away the nightmare. Still hoping it was one.

It wasn't. No matter how many times I closed and opened my eyes, the tiny room remained.

The Rebels. They'd abducted me. I wasn't bound, nor did the room look anything like a prison, and yet, why else would I be waking up in a room not my own with no recollection of how I got there? Had they drugged me? That would likely account for the head spin. Were they coming back to torture me next for information on how to finally destroy Peverell's royal family like they'd been threatening all my life to do? I might as well have walked up to their front door and handed them everything they wanted, what with the way those articles had screamed to the world that I was the weakest link in our defense. King Dorien was right, I was a liability. *Ask Alina, she'll tell you everything you could ever want to know.*

A knock at the door had me scuttling to compose myself. Letting the panic get the best of me in private was one thing. I would never forgive myself if anyone witnessed it.

Stand tall. Keep your mouth shut. Don't tell them anything.

"Princess Alina?"

A woman's voice. I almost fell off the side of the bed in my hurry to stand. The pillow I clutched to my chest as the door eased open made a poor weapon but it was the best I had.

"Oh good, you're awake."

The middle-aged woman who walked through the door didn't look anything like I would have imagined a Rebel or kidnapper to look like. Short, overweight, smelling of spices, and dressed in jeans and a tan, cable-knit sweater two decades out of fashion, she reminded me of a cinnamon roll.

I hated cinnamon rolls.

She walked over and sat on the bed, tapping the cover beside her, inviting me to sit. I crossed my arms tighter over the pillow and took two steps backward. She stopped tapping and stared at me, her eyes softening into a compassion I didn't want to see. I looked at the floor and wondered again what time it was. If I could just find out that one piece of information, I felt like my world might begin to make sense again. Perhaps even that was too much to hope.

"Are you feeling any better, sweetie?"

Better? Than what, exactly? Not knowing how to answer, I stared at her instead. Father would be horrified at my lack of manners but, with all my strength going to holding myself upright, I had nothing left for artifice. She stared right back, no fear or trembling in her. But then, why would there be? She had the upper hand here. She knew where she was, who she was, who I was, the time. I knew nothing. The silence stretched until I could take it no more. The questions inside me tumbled out almost faster than I could enunciate.

"Where am I? What am I doing here? Who are you?"

"You don't remember?"

Memories so foggy I wasn't certain they were even real wavered in my mind. Father's anger, people pushing, blinding white clouds... I closed my eyes and wound back the memories, watching them, willing them to clarify. Not one of them explained why I was here, nor why this cinnamon roll of a woman was still looking at me. My heartbeat climbed higher, pushing the breath from my lungs. What was I supposed to remember? Was she a Rebel after all? Was this the start of her interrogation? Asking what I knew?

"You were knocked over when the crowd got too close at the press conference. The guards were so busy trying to save you from the wall of oncoming reporters that I don't think they noticed you'd gone down. Ben was the first to see you were missing. We pushed our way through the crowd to find you curled up tight at the base of the lectern."

It was as if she was talking about someone else's life. Hard as I tried to remember, I couldn't make any of what she said feel real.

"Ben picked you up and carried you out of the fray, buckled you into my car and told me to bring you here. You cried yourself to sleep within minutes of the three-hour drive, poor sweetie. I thought you were waking when we arrived but, after assuring us you were fine, went right back to sleep. You've been asleep ever since."

"Three hours?" A wave of dizziness assaulted me, threatening to tip me sideways. I pressed my fingers against the wall behind me, clinging to the fragile knowledge that as long as my hand stayed still, so did my body. "We're not in Peverell?"

"No. It's a poor introduction, I'll admit, but welcome to Hodenia."

"The palace?" I looked around the room again, taking in the simplicity of its furnishings. This couldn't be my new suite, but perhaps they'd put me in a different room. I'd been unconscious for some time, apparently. Was this a recovery room? But then, where were the machines? The nurses?

"No, not the palace. Our home. A refuge, of sorts, just across the border from Peverell. We call it The Well. It's been a stopping point for lots of people over the years. Yourself included. I thought you'd recognize it. You came here, once, as a child. The last time this happened. You stayed in this room then, too. You'd stand on that chair there and look out the window. It was your favorite view. You liked the way the green fields went on and on forever."

She was lying. I'd never been here before in my life. I would have known.

Wouldn't I?

But then, I had no recollection of how I'd gotten here, and nothing certain from the moment I'd started speaking at the press conference.

Breathe, Alina, breathe. In, out, in, out. It's lies. She's trying to trick you, break you, even. You have to calm down. You have to— "I can't." The words were a strangled whisper as I battled the panic for peace.

"Oh, honey. Are you okay?"

My head pounded, my lungs ached, my heart thudded in my throat, every muscle in my body shook so much it was a wonder I still stood, and any second I was going to explode into a sobbing mess of tears. No, I wasn't okay. Not even close.

"I'm fine. I'd like to go home now." I didn't relish the idea of three hours in a car with this woman, but it was faster than sending for someone to come and get me.

"You can't."

"Can't? Of course, I can. I have to. I'm the princess."

"You need to stay here."

"I don't think you understand. I can't be away from Peverell right now. I have responsibilities, appearances, meetings, a wedding to plan..." Not to mention a reputation to rebuild. They'd think I was hiding or worse, running away.

"Ben said—"

"*Thoraben* is not my father nor is he my fiancé. He has no right to decide what I do."

"He cares about you. You should have seen how upset he was about what happened and heard him going on about how you'd hate him for sending you here. I assured him you'd understand. He wants you to be well. We all do. He's not the only one who's been worried about you recently."

"I told you, I'm fine. And if Thoraben cared for me at all, he would have taken me home." Mrs. Adeline would have embraced me and sent for hot chocolate. My maids would have drawn me a bath and wrapped me in my softest pink robe and slippers when I'd finished. I could have been relaxing in my suite right now. "I can rest perfectly well there."

"With all those engagements and responsibilities and press watching everything you do? That's not rest. Ben will sort out the details with your father and the press. For now, your job is to relax and let yourself recover."

My hand pressed harder against the wall, its strength the only reason I was still standing. If the wall fell, I'd fall with it. Who needed Rebels to destroy your life when your own brother could do it perfectly well? He'd done it. He'd sent me away. I willed my legs to hold me steady as the shaking started again. Another wave of dizziness tilted my consciousness.

"Let me go," I said again, the whisper barely making it past the bile rising in my throat. I couldn't fall apart in front of her. "Please."

Ms. Cinnamon Roll shook her head. "Give it time, sweetie. You've been under so much stress lately. You need rest. You'll love it here. I promise."

"No." The word rushed out of me with a sense of unreality, as if someone else had spoken it. Someone with the fortitude to both face and fight the betrayal she'd been served rather than the battered princess cowering against the wall, begging it not to fall.

The woman was still staring at me. I wished she'd go away and leave me to fall apart in peace. I didn't need her. Not her protection, not her house, and certainly not her sympathy.

"How long?" I didn't want to know. Not really. Even asking the question felt like surrender, but if it was just for one day, maybe I would take it. The way my head pounded, I didn't relish the idea of getting back into a car right now, or any form of transport. It would be a relief to sleep for a few more hours, even on cotton sheets.

I saw the apology written across her face before she said the words. Felt my heart sink to the tips of my stockinged toes.

"Two weeks, maybe more."

Don't cry, Alina. She'll see it as proof. Hold it together. Just a bit longer. You can do this.

"My maids? My clothes?"

"I told Ben not to worry about them. Your gowns and fancy clothes are gorgeous, but they'd just get wrecked around here. I went through the donation boxes while you were asleep and found quite a few outfits your size. They're in the wardrobe waiting for you."

The polite thing to do—what Father would expect me to do—would be to thank her, but I couldn't do it. That would involve being able to breathe. Secondhand clothing? Never once in the entirety of my eighteen years had I ever worn secondhand clothing, and I had no plans to start now. I had to get out of here. And not cuddled up beside that woman as if we were best friends.

"I'm afraid we didn't have any shoes your size. I'll see to that as soon as possible."

She kept talking. I stopped listening. Thoraben might have sent me away, but I had no plans on staying. People adored me. I'd burst my way into their hearts the day I was born and cemented that place the older and more like my mother I looked. This stubborn woman aside, people would do anything for me. If I could just get out of her presence, I knew I could find my way home, even with a pounding headache. And every step of the way, I would find more ways to make Thoraben pay. But first, to get past the cinnamon roll.

I walked to the bed and sat on the edge of the mattress, allowing myself a slight sway toward her as I did so. Her hand was instantly on my arm. I covered it with my own, looking up at her with a well-practiced smile.

"My head..."

"Oh sweetie. What can I get you? Water? Something to dull the pain? Tea, perhaps?"

"Thank you, but I think I need to lie down for a while. You understand."

"Of course. I'll get a book and sit myself over there in the corner so you won't feel so alone."

"No!" She frowned. I gentled my panicked voice back to a normal pitch. "That is, I'm certain you have better things to do than sit and watch me sleep."

"If you're sure?"

"I am." I lay back against the pillow, trying to look as weak as possible. It didn't take much effort.

"Very well then. I do need to get on to dinner. Come down to the kitchen when you're ready. It's down the stairs and to the left. You'll find it."

"Thank you."

I smiled again as she turned at the door to check on me, reassuring her that though I was weak, I would be well. She smiled back and shut the door. The instant she closed it, I sat up. Rubbing the feeling of her hand on my arm off with the edge of the cotton sheet, I stood. I'd give it a few minutes, long enough for the cinnamon roll to be engrossed in whatever dinner she was preparing and my head to stop spinning, and then I'd make my move.

It was time to go home.

TEN

Every tiptoed step I took through the house the woman had named The Well confirmed my decision to leave. The carpet was worn, the walls clad in hideous wallpaper which I doubted had ever been in style, and the furniture had probably been nice twenty years ago but was in desperate need of an update. Every mismatched piece of it. It might as well have been a museum, albeit a poorly furnished one.

It even smelled old. I'd reached out a finger at one point to touch the top of one of the lounges before thinking better of it. Who knew how many years of dirt hid amongst its synthetic fibers? The sooner I got out of this place, the better. Already I felt the need for an hour-long soak in my favorite lavender-scented bath to wash the stench from my hair and skin.

The sound of humming, no doubt from the cinnamon woman, came from one end of the house's lower floor. I walked in the opposite direction, looking for a door outside. It didn't take long to find one, though the lock had me baffled for long enough to wonder if, despite the woman's words, I truly was her prisoner. It was with no small amount of relief that I finally felt the lock click and the door slide open. I breathed in the fresh air like I was taking my first breath—and told myself to stop being melodramatic and hurry up.

The door opened to an arbor of trees. Though I'd never seen one so close to a building before, their camouflage suited my needs perfectly. I wouldn't have to worry about being spotted as

I escaped if I kept the trees between myself and the end of the house the humming had come from.

Walking out onto the grass, I stopped only long enough to put on the three-inch heels I'd been carrying. They sank into the grass with each step I took and threatened to toss me to the ground, but I refused to be done in by them. They were all that stood between me and who knew what awful bugs and dirt—and they were pink, satin, and studded with tiny diamonds. Counted among my favorites, I could no more leave them behind then I could my own heart.

"Going somewhere?"

Said heart all but leapt out of my chest along with a screech which could have rivaled an angry monkey. I grabbed at the closest tree to keep my precarious balance. The man had already scared me out of my wits. I had no desire to fall on my face in front of him as well.

Turning, I got my first good look at the man who'd rudely interrupted my escape. It was no wonder I hadn't spotted him, with as much dirt as he was covered in. His button-up shirt might have been blue once but was so dusty I wasn't certain. His jeans were threadbare in places and his dirt-scuffed boots looked as if they could tell enough tales to fill a novel. One even had its tongue sticking out. Had the man even tied them before deciding to scare the brains out of passing travelers?

I didn't know what color his eyes were underneath that old cowboy hat, but it wouldn't have mattered if they were the most captivating turquoise or intriguing brown given his beard took away any chance he might have had at being the slightest bit attractive.

He was also still waiting for an answer.

"As a matter of fact, I am. If you'll excuse me, I'll be on my way."

He picked a piece of bark off one of the trees, rolling it between his fingers before dropping it to the ground. "Sorry. Can't do that."

Growing up a princess in a palace full of guards, I was well accustomed to being told what to do by men. They, however, had the authority to do so. This man, whoever he was, did not. "I don't believe the choice is yours to make." I took two steps forward before he blocked my path, arms crossed.

"Nor yours."

He looked directly at me, recognition hitting like a fist to the stomach. This was no old man, as I'd first thought. He was young. Likely only a few years older than me. And I'd seen him before.

"You were at the palace."

"Surprised you noticed, quick as you snubbed me." He stuck out a hand. "Joha Samson, since apparently you've forgotten." I ignored the hand, wishing I could ignore him just as easily.

"Well, Joha Samson, I am leaving, so if you'll kindly move."

"Nope."

"You can't say no to me."

"Sure, I can. Because, like it or not, you're not the boss around here."

"Do you know who I am?" I asked him.

"Sure. You're Alina, the girl who's supposed to be inside the house staying out of trouble."

I drew myself up to my whole height of five feet, nine inches—heels included—and gave him a glare which had gotten my way more times than it should have. "I am Princess Alina Ciera Georgia May of Peverell, daughter of King Everson and Queen Ciera of Peverell, fiancée of Prince Marcos, heir to the throne of Hodenia. I have more power in a sneeze than you could possibly have in your entire life."

The infuriating man shrugged, taking his time considering a branch of the tree above him, as if he wasn't talking to his future queen. "Like I said, Alina."

"How dare you!"

"Look, I know you don't want to be here, but Ben is not only a prince but my friend. And he's asked that you stay here for a time, so you're staying. Now, please, go back inside."

"Why should I listen to you?"

"Because you're not in any position to be able to make demands. Of anyone."

"What would you know? You don't even know how to wash yourself."

He adjusted his dirt-encrusted hat before crossing his arms and leaning back against a tree trunk, as if he had all day to annoy me. "September seventeenth, the night of your eighteenth birthday, you left a dinner with your brother and, after a heated discussion between the two of you, failed to return with him. Instead, you came across a man near the east terrace of the palace and spoke with him at great length about not only your frustrations with your family but the very role of being a princess."

My heart found its rhythm but raced faster with each word Joha spoke as fear took hold of me. "How do you know this?" No one was supposed to know. King Dorien had made that more than clear as he stalked out of the palace, Marcos two steps behind him and only marginally less irate.

"Did it cross your mind even once to think about protocol or wonder who he was and what he was doing there before blurting out all your issues?"

"*He* was a gentleman." Even if he hadn't told me who he was.

Joha snorted. "He was a reporter who broke into the palace hoping for a good story, and you gave him far more than he could have ever dreamed. Even facing criminal charges, he's probably counting himself the luckiest reporter alive. It's a wonder anyone tells you anything the way you talk.

"Now, why don't you go back inside like the good little obedient princess everyone thinks you are and leave me to my work?"

Infuriating was seeming more and more like an understatement. "Why should I listen to you? I don't even know you."

"Actually, you do. Or did. You even called me your friend last time you were here. Something, apparently, you've forgotten. Not that it matters. Ben trusts me, and that should be enough."

It would have been, three months ago, when I trusted Thoraben with my life and respected his opinion more than my own. Before he, and every other person it seemed, had betrayed me.

Including my own memory, if Joha and the cinnamon woman were to be believed. Had I really been here before?

"Stop calling him Ben. His name is Prince Thoraben. Only family are allowed to call him by his nickname." Not that I did very often.

"I am family."

I let out a bitter laugh. "I think I would know if you were related to me."

"Yeah, well, there's a lot you don't know." He uncrossed his arms, gesturing with a swirling hand for me to turn around. I was still wondering how offended to be by his comment about my naiveté when he placed his grubby hands on my arms and physically turned me, pushing me toward the house. "Go on, princess. Go back to the safety of your room so the rest of us can clean up this mess you've made."

I stomped to the house, letting myself in the same door I'd thought I escaped from, telling myself that my return had nothing to do with Joha's order and everything to do with getting out of his maddening presence. If I never saw him again in my life, I would be more than content.

Two hours later, I was still fuming. If one could call it that. Laure would have called it sulking—behind my back, of course—but a princess never sulked. And the room assigned me was too small to sulk in. Seven steps. That was all it took to get from one side of the room to the other. Four, if I walked the length of it instead, my bed taking up a full third of the room. How was one supposed to stalk from one end of the room to the other when they only had seven steps? The bathroom in my suite at home was twice this room's size.

You're the princess. Be the—

I scuffed my foot across the carpet, catching my heel, wishing I could have let out the scream in my chest begging for release. I couldn't do this. Not the strangers, not the tiny room with its one window which apparently I'd loved once but didn't remember a single inch of, not the second-hand clothing I knew would break me if I opened the wardrobe. I'd ignored it till this point, but I'd have to face it some time.

I didn't even have the words in my vocabulary to express what I thought of Thoraben at this moment. I suppose I should have given him credit for handing me off to someone else instead of standing back and letting me get crushed by the crowd. If that's really what he did. For all I knew, it was yet another lie. I certainly had no memory of it. But how dare he think he could run my life and decide what was best for me?

A knock at the door had me flinging it open with far more force than necessary. An eggshell blue towel and a wrapped cake of soap were thrust at me before I could close the door in Joha's face.

"Mom sent these up. She forgot them earlier. Said to let her know if you needed more soap or anything."

The tiniest bit of my anger drizzled out, draining away at the thought of a long soak in some soap-perfumed water. It wouldn't take away any of my current problems, but it might make them easier to deal with. Against my better judgment, I felt my animosity toward the man in front of me softening. Of course, that might have had something to do with the fact that he'd washed and changed into clothes that didn't smell like a dung-ridden mud puddle. The beard still needed work, if not a complete shave altogether, and he'd never be classed as handsome, short as he was, but he looked presentable.

"Thank you. Where's the bath?"

"The bath*room* is that one there—" He pointed to a closed door halfway down the hall. "—but it has no bath. Only a shower. Good spray though. Feels like a pounding on your back. Just what you want after a long day's work."

My dreams of luxury thudded somewhere around my toes. "I have to *share* a bathroom? And a—" My stomach clenched, threatening to retch— "shower?" I tried not to think about all the germs swimming their way around the shower floor. What if it had mold on the walls? "With you?"

Joha rolled his eyes. "It's not like we'll be in there at the same time, princess."

The blush covering my cheeks was instant, and as mortifying as his insinuation. That was not what I'd meant and, from the grin peeking out through that scruff of a beard, I was certain he knew it.

"The apartment above the stables doesn't come with a shower so yes, I use this one. But hey, if you don't like that idea, there's always the hose outside. Or there's a creek down in the back paddock. It's cold and pretty muddy, but you might come out cleaner. Maybe."

I slammed the door in his smirking face, the moment of gratitude I'd felt toward him dissipating in a wave of furor. How dare he think he could tell me what to do? How dare he make fun of my name and my title? Had he no respect whatsoever for his rulers? And that woman. In all her attempts at explanations, she'd neglected to tell me her name. Rude and uncivilized, both of them. I threw the towel and soap on the floor and stomped the seven steps back to the bed.

Thoraben wouldn't take me back, not given the way I'd treated him and Kenna the night of my birthday. Father might, though his reaction very much depended on what tale of woe Thoraben had spun him. If Father believed I was safe, he'd likely leave me here, especially given the public relations mess I'd left at home. I couldn't count on Father's assistance. But Marcos, perhaps he would help me. Only I had no way of getting word to him, not without talking with either Joha or the woman again, something I planned to put off as long as possible.

I sat on the bed, head on my arms as the helplessness of my situation overwhelmed me. They might as well have taken my name. They'd taken everything else.

My stomach growled, reminding me again how long it had been since I'd fed it. I opened my mouth to call for my maids before remembering they weren't here. If I wanted food, I'd have to get it myself. If I couldn't find a way to get home today, I'd have to shower here as well. My already roiling stomach protested again at the thought. I couldn't do it. They didn't understand if they thought I could. An uninvited tear dribbled its way down my cheek. Another followed. I let them come, not even bothering to wipe them away. What did it matter? There was no one here to see me cry.

I lay back in bed, curled up in a ball, and let the sobs come. If Joha or the woman heard, I didn't care. If they came to check on me, I didn't notice. The next time I opened my eyes, it was morning.

ELEVEN

A full night's sleep worked wonders for my overanxious brain, something I would have appreciated far more if it hadn't also convinced me of three things. One, my behavior yesterday was inexcusably rude, two, I needed to apologize, and three, skipping a full day's meals had been a terrible idea. Something my screaming stomach was not going to let me forget any time soon.

Also, I needed information. A lot of it.

Unfortunately, all those added up to the fact that I now had no choice but to face the communal bathroom, and the contents of the chipped wardrobe, both of which had me tensing with dread. The wardrobe seemed the lesser of two evils so I tried it first, telling myself it couldn't be as bad as I was making it out to be in my mind.

It was. If not worse.

They expect me to wear these clothes?

I riffled through the few outfits hanging there. Three t-shirts in various colors, one white blouse, a gray-and-black-striped skirt with all the shapeliness of a blanket, a bright orange and blue sundress, two pairs of jeans, and a dusky pink skirt, long out of fashion but my only hope of looking somewhat like myself. Albeit a much-faded version. I took the pink skirt out along with the white blouse and closed the door on the rest.

I can do this. I can do this.

The mantra echoed in my head with each step I took along

the hall to the room Joha had indicated. Still, my hand trembled on the handle as I pushed open the door.

The bathroom was cleaner than I'd expected, but no less menacing. It smelled of bleach and something else, something I couldn't place. Berries? In a bathroom? Was it an air freshener or something? My breath caught as I looked at the shower itself and the water clinging in droplets to the door. Puddling on the floor. Someone else had recently showered. Someone's grime still sat in those puddles.

Bile rushed up my throat in the place of air, causing me to gag. I put a trembling hand to my mouth, closing my eyes as I sucked in breath after shuddery breath. It was too much. They asked too much of me. I couldn't do this. I just couldn't. I wanted to run to Mother's suite and hide myself there until the horror of this day passed—only they'd taken that from me too.

A rogue tear dripped onto my skirt, landing beside a crooked crease stretching the length of the skirt's front. Another crossed it near the bottom, horribly marring what had, just yesterday, been perfection. I looked as pitiful as I felt.

Shower, Alina. Get in, wash yourself, and get out. You can do this. Do you really want to find out if Joha was joking about the hose outside?

I took a deep breath and focused on fueling my anger against Joha with all the ways he'd wronged me, whether or not he was to blame. The more anger I felt, the less room fear had to consume me. *I will not wash in a stream, Joha Samson. And those clothes? Horrible. Demeaning. Not even a beggar would wear them. But then, that's what I am to you, isn't it? A beggar. An imposter. Well, Joha Samson, it's your fault I'm here. You could have let me go, but no, you had to stop me. Horrible man.*

At least the towel was clean, and warm, since it had been sitting on a patch of sunlit floor when I'd woken this morning. *Take that, Joha Samson.*

It was, by far, the fastest shower I'd ever taken but, two minutes later, towel wrapped around me, I leaned against the sink and breathed a sigh of relief. I'd done it. The scalding water might have turned my skin red for the rest of my life, but I was clean. My chest heaved like I'd faced down a ten-thousand strong army instead of an empty shower, but I claimed the victory all the same. And chose not to think about the fact that I'd have to do it all over again tomorrow. Perhaps it would get easier.

And perhaps my entire wardrobe from the palace would be delivered to my room by the time I returned there.

My breath hitched again as I stared at the towel-clad girl in the foggy mirror, wondering how I'd fallen so low. Three months ago, my life had been perfect. The envy of every girl in Peverell, if not the world, and rightly so. I had it all. A wardrobe of design-er clothing, four personal maids at my beck and call, and a whole palace full of others to order about, a father who doted on me, a brother I adored, a best friend who might as well have been my twin sister we were so inseparable. I smiled and people cheered. I paid them the smallest bit of attention and they recounted the story for the rest of their lives.

And if all that weren't enough, I was engaged to Prince Mar-cos—tall, dark haired, take-your-breath-away handsome with a smile that made my insides dance every time he bestowed it. Prince Marcos, heir to the throne of Hodenia. Marriage to him would make me queen one day, the darling of not just one king-dom but two.

And here I stood, stripped of it all. No power, no title, no one to hold me together. Forced to wash in a communal bathroom and wear borrowed clothes. My stomach heaved again, convul-sions tearing at my throat despite the fact that there was nothing there to expel. The mirror's fog had almost cleared by the time I could look up again. And then, I wished it hadn't.

Curls. Popping up everywhere. My blonde hair hadn't been curly since my eighth birthday when a reporter had called my curls "adorable." I didn't want to be adorable. I wanted to be stun-ning, beautiful, flawless. Laure had straightened my hair every day since.

Laure, what am I going to do?

The answer came as quickly as the question.

You're the princess. Be the princess.

Every time she finished my hair. Every time a hurtful comment surfaced about me in the papers. Every time I complained about the rigidity of my schedule. Every time I left for a ball or function, Laure said that to me. Sometimes it was offered as advice, sometimes encouragement, sometimes admonishment. Always, out of love. Even however many miles she was away from here, Laure's strength still held me together.

I tucked a curl behind my ear and nodded at my reflection. *Very well, Laure, I'll do it.*

If there was one thing I knew how to do, it was to be a princess.

"Why did Joha say he was family?"

The cinnamon woman might have changed her clothes overnight, but these were just as tasteless. Had she updated her wardrobe even once in the past twenty years? It was hard to believe any cardigan could have been worse than the one she wore yesterday but, knitted from chunky dark orange wool with a large pink pocket either side of her, this one beat it by a mile.

"Alina. How are you feeling this morning? Did you sleep well? Here, take a seat. Would you like a cup of tea? I've just boiled the kettle."

"No, thank you. I don't like tea." The chair she gestured to sat ignored as I stayed in the doorway. "I'd rather some answers. Who are you? What is this place? Why would Thoraben send me here? Because you're family or something, like Joha claimed? Is that it? You're my long-lost cousins?" *Oh, please, don't let it be true.* The last thing I needed right now was to be related to this woman. Or worse, Joha.

The woman frowned and wiped her messy hands on her equally messy apron. She might as well have left the apron off. Food on that horrid cardigan would be an improvement.

"You spoke with Joha? Oh, wait, that's right. I sent him up

with the towel yesterday. You found the bathroom, I see. I'm glad the clothes fit."

I crossed my arms over the blouse which wasn't even close to fitting, loose as it was around the waist, and swallowed back the response I wanted to give. *Be kind, Alina. Respectful.*

"Thank you for them," I lied, schooling my expression into what I hoped she'd see as gratitude. It probably shocked her to see the flawless, fun-loving, frivolous princess had a human side and thrilled her to be able to help the royal family by caring for me in my "time of need." As if I was broken.

Shattered was far closer to the truth. All my life, I'd held the pieces together, every tiny shard, even when they left me cut and bleeding. A smile here, a tinkle of a laugh there, a wave, and gown after beautiful gown. I knew the right things to say. I'd practiced the lies so often they fit me better than the truth.

I might have been in the spotlight more often than not, but that didn't mean anyone actually knew me. I chose what the spotlight saw, and very little of it was personal. I'd come down here to get answers, and so far she'd asked more questions than she answered. If I had to demand them of her, I would. If I had to starve myself, so be—

Were those waffles she was making that smelled so good? I watched, mesmerized as she placed two on a plate and drizzled chocolate over the top of them.

No, I couldn't get distracted, and I wasn't supposed to eat waffles anyway. My figure already teetered on the edge of what was considered an acceptable weight. Waffles would push me over the edge entirely. Information. I needed information. I had to know why...why... A handful of raspberries followed the chocolate. *Focus, Alina!*

"Are you my relations?"

"No."

Right. Good. One worry out of the way.

"Not really. Not to you, anyway. I'm Kenna's aunt. Adeline is my sister."

The first information she'd offered, and it was an outright lie. "You can't be. Kenna doesn't have any aunts."

"She didn't know about us until recently."

"How recently?"

"Ben introduced us yesterday. Before the press conference."

The plate of waffles landed on the table, a knife and fork close behind. I did my best to ignore the smell of warm chocolate wafting across the room.

"You were the woman talking to Thoraben at the edge of the crowd." Though most of the memory of yesterday's press conference still hid behind a thick layer of fog, here and there patches poked through. The irritation I'd felt at Thoraben's lack of attention was one of them. "But, if you're really Kenna's aunt, why was Thoraben the one introducing you to her? Why would he know you when Kenna doesn't? Who are you? I don't even know your name."

"I didn't tell you my name? Oh, I'm so sorry, sweetie. Malisa Samson. My husband, Pat, and I own this place."

"And you're Mrs. Adeline's sister?"

Malisa nodded. "Older by four years." She shuffled over to the fridge, peering at what seemed like hundreds of photos of people on the front before picking one off and holding it out. It was sun-damaged and old—maybe even older than me—but clearly Mrs. Adeline and Malisa, arms around each other as they grinned. Even if they weren't sisters, here was proof they knew each other well.

Like I'd thought I knew Kenna. Mrs. Adeline too. They'd never had any other family. And now, suddenly, they did? It was almost too much to take in.

"She never said anything. Why did she never talk about you?" All this time, Mrs. Adeline had mothered me, guided me, loved me, and never once mentioned she had a sister? Not even to Kenna?

"Life is complicated. Families even more so."

Now that I could believe, although it was far from an explanation. "So, Thoraben sent me here because you're Kenna's aunt?"

"Thoraben sent you here because it worked last time."

No... Breathe, Alina. In, out. You're the princess. You're in control. Don't let her see you tremble. Stand tall.

"You're lying. I've never been here before."

The compassion in her eyes almost broke me. "You were five when the panic attacks started. At first, Adeline thought it was a stage you were going through, given you'd just started school. Any new situation, you'd work yourself into a panic, usually ending up ill from the strain. But then, you started blacking out.

"Physically, there was nothing wrong with you. Your father had numerous doctors check. They claimed you simply needed rest and to be out of the spotlight, something virtually impossible for the longed-for princess Peverell had come to love. After you blacked out three times one particular week, Mrs. Adeline pulled rank and brought you here, to The Well. You spent two months here before going back to the palace."

My legs threatened to give way, shock ripping through my system. I wedged myself tighter against the doorframe, hating that I needed its support. Hating even more that this woman was witnessing it.

"I don't remember."

She nodded. "Panic has a way of doing that to people, and you were still quite young. The public were told you were traveling abroad as part of your schooling. There were only a few of us who knew the truth."

"Two months?"

"We couldn't keep you hidden here forever. When you went home, it was with the understanding that you were always welcome here, anytime, should you need the space again."

"But I never came back?"

"The panic attacks stopped. You never needed to."

They hadn't stopped. I'd just learnt to hide them. Probably because of the fuss it caused the first time. If it even did. Nothing she said brought back even the faintest of memories, nor did any of this place seem familiar. She could have been talking about someone else's life.

Sure, Malisa had given me a room for the night, clothes, and proof she knew Adeline, but that didn't mean I could trust her. What if she was just spinning stories to get me to play right into her scheme? For all I knew, she could still be a Rebel and this place their base of operations. Even if she did know Adeline.

And Thoraben.

And was somehow related to Joha, who had definitely been at the palace yesterday at Thoraben's invitation, and knew way more about my interactions with Sir Gray than anyone should have.

It's real. She's telling the truth. But that means...she knows... no...

I had to get out of here. Back to the palace, where I was Princess Alina Ciera Georgia May, perfection personified. Where I knew how to play the part and what was expected of me. Where no one knew me as the girl who panicked to the point of passing out. I wasn't that person anymore. Not to them, anyway. Certainly not to Marcos, who'd never marry me if he knew.

Find the door. Open it. Run.

"Alina!"

I wasn't stopping. I didn't have to stay. I'd run as far as I could and then plead for someone to take me home from there. I was the princess. They'd take me.

"Alina, come back!"

I kept running, ignoring the pain in my side and the legs threatening to ground me with every step, certain if I could just get beyond that fence in the distance, I could make it home. I was fifty feet from escape when a man's arm grabbed me around my waist, its strength more than I could fight. Though I kicked at his shins and threw my head back against his chest, he didn't let go, instead holding my arms in tight against me as he crooned quiet words of calm in my ear. "Quiet, little one. You're safe here. No one can hurt you."

His voice I couldn't place, but the kindness did me in.

"Pat, oh, thank God you caught her."

My breath came in stops and starts as I tried to gain control of it. The man let go of my arms only long enough for Malisa to claim me in an embrace strong enough to start a person's heart again. She turned me around just enough to introduce the tall, white-haired older man who'd caught me. "This is Pat, my husband. You didn't get the chance to meet him yesterday."

I blinked at the wetness in my eyes, blurring Pat's outstretched hand.

Yesterday, when my world had come crashing down like my body now felt like doing. When everything I'd known had been taken from me. I'd thought being sent here was the extent of the betrayal. If anything Malisa had said was true, it was only the beginning.

"I'm not that little girl anymore. I don't need you to save me."

"Of course not, honey. But everyone deserves a break, now and then."

"Why should I trust you?"

She glanced at Pat before turning her all-too-patient eyes back to me. "Because I'm not only Adeline's sister, I was your mother's best friend."

TWELVE

N o." I fought against Malisa's answer as hard as I'd fought Pat for escape. "My mother's best friend was a woman named Emily. I heard Thoraben mention her once or twice."

"He called her Emily?"

"No, Em. Auntie Em."

"That's me. M." She wrote the letter in the air with her finger. "M for Malisa."

I didn't want to believe her. I didn't want to believe any of this. All I wanted was to be back in my room at the palace, gowned in my favorite pink day dress with its floaty chiffon skirt, going over details of my wedding as Laure brushed my sleek, straight hair. Yet here I was. In the middle of some sort of barnyard, dressed in faded, borrowed clothes, the bun I'd pulled my hair into giving me the beginnings of a headache while I vacillated between horror and hope. What if she had known Mother as well as she claimed?

Back when I was twelve, I'd seen mentioned briefly in a book the close friendship Mother had had with her best friend. Until that moment, I hadn't even known Mother had friends, as none of them were ever mentioned. I'd asked Thoraben about it. He'd called her Auntie Em, describing her to be beautiful and kind. When I'd asked him if we could go visit her, he'd said she was gone. I'd cried myself to sleep that night, feeling as if the one connection I might have had to the mother I'd never known had been taken from me as suddenly as Mother had.

And now, here she was in front of me. I wanted to call her a liar as much as I wanted it to be the truth.

"Did you never wonder why Adeline in particular was chosen to care for you?" Malisa asked.

"The guards my Father sent to town found her. She'd just given birth to Kenna and, as such, had the, uh, resources to care for me too."

"The guards didn't have to search far. Your mother told them exactly where to go and who to ask. She knew Adeline had given birth. I'd told her myself that morning. Her first and last decision as your mother was to choose who would care for you."

I stared at the ground, blinking back more emotions than I could put a name to. Mother had loved me. The proof had been there all along, I simply hadn't known what to look for. If Malisa told the truth—and that was still a big if—Mrs. Adeline hadn't been simply the first available woman the guards came across, she'd been chosen. By Mother. To care for me.

"Why the secrecy? Why would Thoraben call you M and not Malisa? Why did Mrs. Adeline never mention you? Even to Kenna?"

Again, that glance at Pat and moment of hesitation. The silent conversation I had no part of. The one I wasn't certain I wanted part of. My mind was already spinning with more information than I could handle.

Run?

My heart pounded against my chest in the erratic rhythm of the unknown as I waited for Malisa's answer. If she told me I had a secret sister somewhere or that Mother was actually still alive, I knew I'd break. And this time there would be no putting back together the pieces, no matter how hard I tried. Everyone would know what a disaster of a princess I truly was. They'd know without a doubt that Mother should have been the one to live.

Fight?

"It was easier that way. For everyone involved."

It was barely an answer but, for now, it was enough.

Stay.

"Breakfast?" Malisa asked. I took it as the lifeline it was.

"Yes. Thank you." Waffles wouldn't do my figure any good, but they might just help my heart. And give me the strength to prove to these people that I was more than the broken five-year-old they'd once swooped in and saved.

Strength, poise, grace—that was me.

At least, on the outside.

The waffles were as good as I'd imagined. Better, even. With each chocolate-soaked bite, my strength returned a bit more, the shaking having stopped altogether by my second waffle. If breakfast was going to be like this every morning, perhaps a few days here wouldn't be so bad. Maybe Malisa could even tell me a few stories about Mother.

Two days, you can do that. How difficult can it be?

"After you finish eating, I thought you might like a tour of the property," Malisa said, pouring more juice into my glass. "Joha will take you around."

"Joha? Doesn't he have work or..." What did normal people do during the day? "...something?" Surely he had better things to do than show me around The Well. I certainly did. Like lying on my bed and staring at the ceiling. Or counting how many leaves there were on the tree outside my bedroom window. Or, well, anything.

"I know you didn't want to come here, but I think you'll like it if you give it a chance. It was a refuge for you once, maybe it will be again. I'd show you the place myself, but I have to go into town this morning."

I didn't need a place of refuge. What I needed was to go home. *Two days...*

"I'll come with you," I countered instead. Anything to avoid spending more time with the man who treated me with the same respect I did a piece of dirt. "The Well will still be here when we return, you could show me then."

"I'm sorry, sweetie. Until we hear from the palace otherwise,

I think it best you stay on the property. Don't worry, Joha will look after you. He knows this place better than anyone."

It wasn't his knowledge of the place I was worried about.

"Oh, I almost forgot." Malisa walked out of the room, coming back a moment later with a notebook and pen. "This is for you."

The book was lined but as empty as my expectation of getting home again any time soon. She called this place a refuge. Prison would have been a far better description. And Joha was my jailer.

No, you're in control. You hold the power here. They answer to you.

Even if it felt like the exact opposite.

"It's a journal," Malisa said as I stared at the book. "Your mother used to love journaling. She said it helped clear her thoughts to write them down. I thought maybe it might help you too, with all that's happening in your life right now."

"I don't think a book is going to fix that." I held it out to her. She didn't take it.

"Keep it. Maybe you'll change your mind."

There was little chance of that happening—I'd never been a big writer nor kept a journal of any kind—but I tucked it under my arm as I walked back up the stairs to my tiny room. It made a nice thump as I dumped it on the bedside table. What did she expect me to write? What I actually thought of this place and the high-handedness of the man who'd sent me here? My deepest secrets?

Not a chance.

I didn't admit them to anyone. Not even myself, if I could avoid it. What was Thoraben thinking, claiming I needed rest? Who was he to judge me? And what made him think sending me to a museum of a house in the middle of nowhere with its antiquated plumbing and musty smell would help anyway? Even if Malisa could cook better than most of the chefs at the palace.

With nothing else to do, I sat on the bed and rued the man who'd sent me here. Malisa claimed he'd done it for my own good, but I knew better. It was punishment, pure and simple.

I grabbed the book and opened it, finding I had something to say after all.

> *Dear Thoraben,*
> *I hate you.*

"Can you ride a horse?"

Less than a minute with the man and already I was glaring. Did he have to treat me like a child? "Of course, I can. I'm a princess, not an invalid." I'd even been in stables before, though none quite as rustic as the one I currently stood in, clean as it was.

"Good to hear. This is Deborah. She's a real sweetie, aren't you, girl." He stroked down the horse's nose, earning himself a huff of air. "You'll ride her while I ride Knight." His mouth quirked up almost into a smile as he gently butted his shoulder against the huge, black horse he'd already saddled.

"We're riding horses around the property? Don't you have a car or something?" Horses, beautiful as they were, meant sweat and dust and the stench of manure. All of which would mean facing that shower for the second time in a day. Once had been more than enough.

"The horses need exercise, we need transport." He said it with a shrug, as if that explained everything. I wondered if the rest of the "tour" was going to be as informative. Why had I agreed to go with him again? It wasn't as if I needed the tour. I'd be gone, back to my palace tomorrow, never to have to think nor care about Joha Samson ever again. He wasn't *my* relative, by blood or marriage. Neither was he cute enough for me to want to impress.

And yet, here I was, standing in a clean but musty stable, a foot from the flank of a horse, watching Joha Samson throw a saddle over it. His shirt was so baggy, I couldn't even enjoy the sight of muscles straining across his shoulders as he did. If he even had muscles. Surely, they were reserved for the handsome men like Marcos who could do them justice.

"Okay. Use that box to mount her."

Of course, he wouldn't offer to help me himself. That would involve a level of gentility, of which Joha had none. I held my long skirt out of the way with one hand while stepping up onto the box.

"Stop."

I sighed. "What now?"

"You can't ride a horse in those." Joha pointed at my pink diamond-studded heels, catching just enough sunlight to throw rainbows across the straw.

"I don't have anything else." I certainly wasn't going to ride a horse barefoot. Germs in the shower were bad enough. There was no way I was letting my feet touch the dirt of this stable. Who knew how many years of manure had laid there, even swept clean as it was.

"Nothing? Seriously?"

"Oh, I'm sorry. Next time I get myself abducted, I'll be sure to make the kidnappers bring my entire wardrobe."

Calm, Alina. Don't let him get to you.

Easier said than done.

"You weren't abduct—Oh, whatever." He looked around the stable, spotting the old pair of boots in the corner about the same time I did. "Here, wear these."

He plonked them down at my feet. A bug scurried out the top of one. Joha stomped on it right about the same time I squealed. The layer of dried mud covering the boots was so thick I couldn't even tell their original color. Even without trying them on, I could tell they were at least two sizes too big.

"Not a chance."

"Put them on."

Absolutely not. "I am a princess, engaged to your future king. Marcos would never make me wear something so disgusting."

"You're a—" A deep breath cut off whatever he'd been about to call me. "Just put them on so we can go."

"I am not putting my feet anywhere near them."

"Unlike some people, I have work to do."

"So, do it. No one asked you to babysit me." What was it about this man that got me so riled up? I barely knew him and yet just being with him made me want to scream.

"Actually, Ben did."

Of course, he did. "What, so you're my bodyguard or something?"

"Not by choice."

"Let me guess, you're one of those rare men who'd rather look after a horse than spend time with a princess."

"Horses do what they're told, and they don't complain about it." He kicked the boots closer to me, setting another bug scurrying. "Just put the boots on."

"No way."

"Fine." Without another word, he stalked out the door, leaving me standing beside two horses, only one of which was tethered.

"Joha?" The big horse turned its head toward me, as if I'd spoken his name instead. I swallowed back the squeak of fright as he stepped toward me. "Joha?" It was barely a whisper this time. Had he left me here? Alone? I'd never had a fear of horses—before today. Deborah huffed, blowing the hair on my neck. I couldn't move. Horses didn't bite people, did they?

I could have kissed Joha when he walked back in a minute later. It would have been the worst kiss of my life with that scruffy beard, but I would have done it. Out of gratitude. Something that dissipated as quickly as it had sprung up when another pair of boots landed at my feet.

"Are these better?"

They were smaller than the first pair and in possession of far less dirt, but still scuffed around the toes. At least these ones didn't look like they'd been commandeered as a nest for rats. I kicked at them with my toe, moving them around so I could see each angle, giving any bugs within them one last chance to exit. Nothing. "Marginally."

Joha crossed his arms, his mouth a thin line of irritation. "Last chance, Alina."

I picked them up, resigned to reality. "There's nowhere to sit."

"Don't be such a princess."

"I am a princess."

"Yes, you are."

I don't think he meant it as a good thing.

THIRTEEN

Much as I tried to stay impartial, it was impossible not to be captivated by the land, especially once we left behind the stench of the stables. Alternating between orchards of trees and long, flat fields, it boasted every shade of green I could imagine and far more than I could name. Peverell's palace was set amidst hills. Green also, but rolling. So different from the flat expansiveness of The Well. Had someone tried to describe it to me, I would have thought it was boring. But there was nothing boring about the way the sky domed above us from one horizon to the other.

The land was beautiful. The animals, on the other hand...

"How many ducks did you say you had here?"

"Close to fifty now, though most of them don't come near the house so you're not likely to see them often. Except Feathers. She's got character, that one. Thinks she's a dog or something the way she follows Mom around."

"Horses?"

"Six."

"And cows?"

"Only two cows at present—Tessa and Leigh—and their two calves, yet to be named. You ever milked a cow?"

"No." And I didn't plan on it either.

"No worries. Mom will show you how. With Dad and me bringing in the corn for the next couple of weeks, she'll appreciate the help."

"I'm not touching a cow."

"Scared?"

"No. They're messy and big and smell. I am a princess. Princesses don't milk cows."

"Around here, everyone pitches in."

"Not me."

"You think you're better than the rest of us?"

"Marcos would never make me milk a cow."

"Of course not."

Up till now, Joha had been, while not chatty, a wealth of information about The Well, what grew in each of the fields and how the day-to-day worked. With one comment, that was all gone. I refused to let it bother me. So what if I didn't want to milk a cow? What was it to him? I hadn't come here to be a servant or do menial work like a maid. I hadn't asked to come here at all.

We rode for another ten minutes in silence, Joha staring straight ahead while I let my gaze wander around the extensive land. Occasionally I heard a bird cry, but mostly it was just silence. I'd never liked silence. It gave my mind too much space to think, and the more it thought, the more it betrayed me with all the reasons I should be afraid. It was the reason I woke each morning to music. I didn't like Joha, but I hated the silence more.

The trees to my left stopped, leaving a clearing where two men pushed wheelbarrows full of bricks. A concrete slab had been laid already, wooden planks forming the outline of a building. Walls were beginning to take shape, although they were only a few bricks high.

"What's that? Over there? Is someone building a house?"

"Not a house, a chapel. For The Well."

I tugged at the reins, pulling my horse to a stop. A chapel? "Why would The Well need a chapel? Doesn't Hodenia already have one?"

Peverell did. It was a grand old brick building with spires reaching so high I could see them from my palace window despite it being miles away. Thoraben's wedding had been the first and only time I'd been in it, given it was only used for royal weddings, coronations, and funerals. One day my wedding would be held there too. If Father and King Dorien ever set a date.

"Hodenia has lots. But they're a long way from here. We've used the barn as a meeting place in the past, but it has always been my father's dream—and mine—to build a proper one on the property. We've been putting aside money and materials for years and finally have enough to start."

"Do you have a lot of weddings here at The Well?" I couldn't understand why else they'd want their own chapel.

"No."

"Then why build a chapel?"

Joha smiled. Actually smiled. It was amazing how it transformed his face. He looked almost friendly. "I forgot how Peverellian you are."

So much for friendship. "What's that supposed to mean?"

"Oh, don't get all offended. I only meant that, to you, a chapel is a fancy building used for official events. For us, it's...more."

"What do you mean, more? Look, if you're trying to hide something..."

"I'm not hiding anything. You wouldn't understand."

"You think I'm stupid?"

"I didn't say that."

He might as well have. I sent my most haughty glare in his direction, something that would have been far more effective if he'd been looking my way instead of waving to one of the workers.

"Then what? Tell me, Joha Samson. What makes that building so important that it would be not only a dream of your father's but also yours?"

He was silent long enough for me to think he was ignoring me. I was halfway through coming up with a scathing retort when he spoke.

"Because it's more than a building. It's a place for us to meet together and remember who we are." His voice was quiet, thoughtful, even if he still refused to look my way. "It's a place to go when life is tough and hard to take and we need the encouragement of others who've been there before. A place to remind us that, no matter how dark the world may look at times, all will be well. A place to share impossible dreams and rejoice together in them becoming realities. It's a shelter, a refuge, an encouragement, a reminder, a monument, a testimony."

"All that in just a pile of bricks?" It sounded too good to be true.

"It's not about the structure. It's about the people. Broken, hurting people coming together and finding forgiveness, grace, faith, hope, and healing. The building itself doesn't matter so much as the people who meet there."

He was speaking in riddles. First the building was important, now it didn't matter? He was right, much as I hated to admit it. I didn't understand. But, to my surprise—and shame—I wanted to.

"Why build it then? Why not continue to use the barn as a meeting place?"

He shrugged. "Mostly because it's not big enough anymore. With all the people coming these days, we've run out of room. But also..."

He broke off and finally looked at me, considering, searching for something, though I had no idea what. Interest? Revulsion? Boredom? Fatigue? I stared back, hoping my expression didn't give away how desperately I wanted him to continue. *It's just a chapel, Alina. A pile of bricks. You're going home soon anyway. It doesn't matter.*

And yet...Shelter. Refuge. Encouragement.

"Also?" I asked.

Another shrug. A slight tip of his head. A tiny smile as he looked back at the site.

"A chapel is special. It's like a beacon almost. People see it and know it's a place they can come where they'll be safe. Think of it like a lighthouse. The lighthouse itself isn't important. Take the light out of it, and it's just a tall building. What makes it special is that it houses the light. People look at a lighthouse and know it's a safe place from the storm. I like to think of our chapel like that. I hope people will see it and know it's a place they can come where they'll be safe and welcomed, no matter who they are."

He spoke with such passion. As far as I could tell, despite his adamancy otherwise, it was still just a brick building. Not grand like Peverell's chapel with its tall stained-glass windows, soaring eaves, and centuries of history, but common brick like was used in most of the houses in Peverell.

And yet, I wanted to go inside with a desperation that felt like hunger, which was ridiculous given the chapel currently stood only as high as my knees. I wanted that welcome Joha spoke of, to be able to go somewhere and simply be Alina. Not princess, not perfect, not the poor girl who never knew her mother or the one frequently paralyzed by her own mind. Just Alina.

But the option wasn't there. Not only because Joha had already turned his horse and headed back to the house but because it would take a strength I knew I didn't have. It took one kind of strength to hide my weakness but another, far more powerful and terrifying entirely, to show it.

"Coming?"

Joha's question cut through my yearning. I tugged on Deborah's reins, pulling her around to follow Joha before my aching heart got the better of me. It was just a building. Not even that. A big slab of concrete in need of a lot of work. That's what it was. Not a lighthouse, not a chapel, certainly not a place a fraud like me would ever be welcome.

"Right behind you."

FOURTEEN

"You decided to help yet, princess?"

I burrowed deeper into my pillow, refusing to let Joha's grating voice pull me from the dream I'd been having. He'd go away soon enough. He always did. For a whole week, I'd managed to ignore his pre-dawn summonings. No, I was not going to milk a cow or feed the calves. No, I was not going to help bring in the corn. Whatever that involved. Dirt, no doubt. And sweat. A lot of it. And no, I was definitely *not* going anywhere near the ducks. Feathers was terrifying enough. A whole flock of them? No thank you. Had he seen how sharp their beaks were? And those claws! Slice a person open in an instant.

"Fine. Have it your way."

His footsteps were overly loud as he clomped down the hall, no doubt one last ditch attempt to annoy me before disappearing for the day. It worked, not that he needed to know that. I'd never get back to sleep now.

I rolled onto my back and stared at the ceiling. I'd dreamed about the chapel, the one Joha had shown me on our tour. Only it had been complete. I'd walked right in, as if I belonged there. People had greeted me, not with the awe of royalty come to visit but with the camaraderie of friends, embracing me, welcoming me. I'd smiled, chatted for a time, and then walked to a seat at the back, sitting alone and as far from the spotlight as possible as music began to swirl around us. Music and something else I couldn't put a name to now I was awake. Peace? Joy? Love? All three, somehow, in one? It filled me, bursting forth in a smile so wide I was certain my face would break apart with the joy of it. I'd closed my eyes, tipping my face upwards as if the sun itself blessed me with its warmth.

A man had come and sat beside me, putting his arm around the back of my chair, kissing my cheek, whispering an apology for being late. I'd tucked my head in against his shoulder, wondering if this was the meaning of bliss—to sit in this chapel, my husband's arm around me as we listened—

The memory jerked. Husband? Had Marcos been there with me in that little chapel? I closed my eyes, blocking out the room and everything but the rapidly fading dream. *"Sorry, I'm late."* The voice. It hadn't sounded like Marcos, and yet who else would it have been? *It's just a dream, Alina. It doesn't matter. It could have been anyone.*

But the music, that feeling. My mouth curved in a smile as I let the remnants swirl around me. One hour spent in such bliss could bolster me for a week. There'd been no fear, no wondering if I belonged or what people were thinking, no battle raging between who I was and wanted to be, only peace. Acceptance. If only I could hold onto it forever. Already it had begun to fade.

A sigh escaped as I threw back the covers and stood. A hope-fueled dream, that's all it was. My subconscious yet again aching for a place to belong. The chapel wasn't even close to being complete. Nor would I be around to see it when it finally was.

The palace at Hodenia, that was where I belonged. Not in this place.

Although...I pulled back the curtain, holding it aside as I stared out at the green fields stretching out to meet the sky. It was beautiful. I couldn't see the sun from this window but the streaks of light it sent out were visible across the entire expanse of sky. Wisps of cloud turned yellow, their undersides gold. One by one, treetops lit up as if anointed by the sun itself. Was it like this every morning? What would it be like to stand in an open field, caught up in the glow of an entire sky filled with light instead of just seeing a glimpse, framed through a window?

Was that what Joha was seeing, right now? Maybe I should have gone.

Don't be silly, Alina. What if he asked you to do something you couldn't? There's nowhere to hide out there if you panic.

The story of my life. Ever hiding, ever protecting myself from what might be. The sooner I married Prince Marcos, the better. I wouldn't have to try so hard then. Everyone would know I was good enough. Including me. Prince Marcos of Hodenia didn't just marry any girl.

Marcos. My prince in more ways than just one.

So tall the top of my head wouldn't have reached his shoulders if not for the heels I always wore. Strong chin, always clean-shaven. Dark eyes with a slight crinkle at the side when he smiled. Dark hair, perpetually neat. I'd fantasized more than once about mussing it as we kissed, wondering what it would feel like between my fingers. Not that we'd kissed. Not even once. Surprising, given how many times I'd offered. *Patience,* he'd tell me. *Wait until we're married.* He could have passed for a medieval knight with that code of honor. Still, I couldn't fault him for it. Not when he treated me like the greatest prize any man could hope to win.

The ring he'd given me the day he proposed caught the light, sending rainbows across the wall. Marcos might not have kissed me yet, but he had given me the most beautiful piece of jewelry I'd ever owned, made of pink diamonds, no less. I couldn't have imagined a more stunning piece, nor been more proud to wear it.

Marcos, where are you? Why haven't you come to save me?

I looked around the room, my gaze landing on the journal Malisa had given me. It wasn't monogrammed stationery, that's for certain, but it would do. I tore out a page as neatly as I could and sat down to write.

> *Dear Marcos,*
> *I know you had to leave as quickly as you came the morning after my birthday, because of all the engagements you had at home, but I really wish*

*you'd stayed. At least for the press conference.
Then, maybe I wouldn't have fallen and hit my
head and had Thoraben swoop in while I was unconscious and send me away like a child too stupid
to decide anything for herself. Not that I blame
you for any of this mess, of course.*

I rolled my eyes, and scrunched that piece of paper up before
starting again. None of this was Marcos's fault.

*Dear Marcos,
I assume by now you know that I'm not in Peverell. I'm in Hodenia, though, obviously, not at
the palace. Thoraben sent me here. He probably
told you I chose to come because I needed the time
away to recuperate from all the pressure I've been
under. Knowing the palace and their insatiable
need to keep the reality of our lives from the public, I'm sure that's what they've told the rest of our
people. It's not true. I am fine. Or, at least, I was
before I arrived at this place.
They call this place The Well and say it's a
refuge, but really, it's just a big farm. Pretty, but
hardly the first place on anyone's list of top holiday destinations. The way it smells, I'd be surprised if it was last on anyone's list either. More
likely crossed off entirely. I hate it here. Please
come and save me. I can't do this anymore.*

No, that wasn't right either. Too whiny and desperate. Princess Alina of Peverell was no beggar. And really, this place wasn't
so bad. Malisa and Pat were kind enough and Malisa's cooking
divine. If I could have ignored the dismal lack of amenities, the
constant bellowing from the calves, Feathers and the way she
strutted about the place, the smell of dirt every time I walked

outside, and Joha's continual need to point out how useless I was, I might have thought I actually was on a holiday.

I'd even found a favorite place. A little white gazebo, framed by trees on all but the side facing the house. Upwind of the stables, it was one of the few places at The Well that didn't stink. Add in the fact that it was within sight of the main house, negating the need for a guard of any type, and it was almost like a fairyland hideaway.

Maybe I could tell Marcos about the gazebo and the hours I whiled away there. Although that might give him the idea that I wanted to stay, and that was definitely not the case.

Oh, what did it matter? It wasn't as if I could send him a letter anyway. If Malisa wasn't going to let me leave The Well even to go to town, then there was no way she'd allow a letter to the palace, begging for them to rescue me. For all I knew, Marcos would probably throw it out without reading it anyway, given the way he'd stalked away last time I'd seen him. Had he forgiven me yet? If only I could have spent more time with him that day, before he left. I could have made him smile again.

My pen went to paper one more time, the shortest but most honest message in my heart.

Dear Marcos,
I miss you.

Pushing aside the melancholy, I dressed as quickly as I could, pulling on an apricot shirt and jeans, rolling the hems up so I didn't trip, trying not to think about how I looked like a vagrant. No one else in this house seemed to care about their appearance, so they likely weren't judging mine, but it still galled me. At least the shower didn't make me gag every time I used it anymore. Clenching my eyes shut and refusing to think might have had something to do with that. And my stubborn avoidance of the mirror.

My hair, I pulled back in a ponytail so tight I'm certain my eyes moved sideways. I'd have a headache by the end of the day, but at least no one could see my curls. Not once I twirled and tucked the length of the ponytail into a bun.

Then all that was left was my shoes. I picked up first the left then the right, examining every inch of them for mud, flicking aside a bit of dust, rubbing my finger over the diamonds. How long would they stay clean in this dusty, muddy place? I hated that they were getting dirty but the alternative, walking barefoot in that muck, was far too much to even consider.

Breathe, Alina. You can do this.

"Alina? Is that you?"

I almost laughed at Malisa's ridiculous question. As if it would be anyone else up here, given Joha and Pat had already left for the day. Did she think it was Feathers, taken control of my bedroom?

"Coming," I called back, taking a final glance at my shoes before putting them on and walking down to the kitchen. Malisa was standing at the stove flipping pancakes. A tower of them already sat steaming on a plate beside her. She turned when I entered.

"Morning, sweetie. Sleep well?"

"Yes, thank you."

"Good. Now, two pancakes? Three?" She piled three on my plate before I could answer, pushing butter, syrup, and a plate of bacon toward me.

"Thank you." I helped myself to a piece of bacon, relishing the crunch of salt bursting in my mouth as I bit into it.

"Also, I forgot to tell you, we're having a gathering here this evening."

It was the tone of Malisa's voice which set me on edge far more than her words. Uncertain, as if she wasn't quite sure how I'd react. I set down my fork, clasping suddenly shaky hands in my lap. I didn't even know why I was nervous, except that she was.

"A gathering? Of people?"

Her amusement was short-lived but there. "Yes, of people.

Good friends of ours." And there went the smile, hidden once again behind flickering uncertainty. But why, unless—

"You don't want me to come."

"Actually, you're very welcome to join us it's just...well, it'll be a lot of people—forty or so—and with all you've been through lately, I thought..."

She was uninviting me. She wouldn't say it, not directly, as that would be rude, but the inference was there. I could have hugged her for it. Facing forty complete strangers with less than a day to prepare, dressed in clothes which barely fit and with so many questions still unanswered, sounded worse than torture. Social suicide at best.

"I'll stay in my room."

"You don't have to hide. We'll be in the barn, then having a campfire. You could come to the fire later, if you like. It'll be so dark by then that no one will notice you."

"Thank you, but I don't like fire."

"Well, the invitation is there if you change your mind."

"I'll think about it." About as much as I would Thoraben and Kenna's love life. Which was not at all. One day, I would rule the people of Hodenia as their queen, but there was no way I was meeting any of them without my hair done. And a decent amount of makeup.

People had been arriving all afternoon. My room might not have been large, but it afforded me an unobstructed view of the southern paddock, where people were parking their cars before wandering over to greet Malisa at the barn and writing on a piece of paper. Signing their names, perhaps? It made sense that the Samsons would want to know who was here in case of, well, something.

It was strange to find that I was thankful for them, these people I'd not even met. I didn't know their names or anything about them, but I was glad they were here. It would be nice to have the buffer of a few scores of people between Joha and me. They'd keep him busy for certain, and I'd be able to lounge about the house to my heart's content, without his snippy comments about my being lazy. I might not have known much about the running of a farm, but I did know what relaxation was, and in no way did it involve milking smelly animals, cleaning this disaster of a house, or getting covered in concrete muck helping to build a new one.

Malisa had been vague on the details of what the gathering was about. I hadn't asked more questions than I needed, not wanting to appear interested, but I had been plastered to my bedroom window since the first car arrived sometime around four.

A family wandered over toward the barn, the mother holding a baby on her hip and the hand of another child who looked to be around five or six. They were sweet, the way they walked together. Mrs. Adeline used to hold my hand like that when we went for walks in the garden. We'd look for ladybugs on the fruit trees. She taught me how to put my finger beside the little bug so it would crawl into my hand. I used to love looking at ladybugs, although she never let me keep them, saying they were made to live outside, not in the palace.

I pushed my face closer to the glass, shielding my eyes from the slight glare to see better. The man walking with them looked familiar. A little like—I squinted before closing my eyes, forcing my mind to think. Who did he remind me of? I'd seen whoever it was recently. At...at...*where was it?* I gulped, almost choking as the answer hit me. The palace. Walking out of the throne room. *Linock Gillespie.* Renowned Rebel leader. He'd faced trial for being a Rebel earlier this year. I wouldn't have even remembered his name except for the fuss his capture had caused. Everyone had been talking about it—the leader of the Rebels caught and sentenced. But surely it wasn't him. I'd only seen Linock briefly. Perhaps this man just looked like the Rebel leader.

Yes, that must have been it. Malisa and Pat would never have invited actual Rebels to The Well. Especially while protecting me. Unless...

No. Don't even think it. You've been here a whole week already, and they've been nothing but nice. Malisa and Pat anyway. There's no way they're Rebels.

Malisa came over to embrace the woman and Linock-looka-like, tapping the baby on its nose and bending down as much as her wide girth allowed to chat with the child. No, it definitely wasn't Linock. Everyone knew he was a criminal.

I turned my attention back to other arrivals, watching children run around, Feathers strut about as if she owned the place, Malisa and Pat welcome people, and Joha laugh and clap a couple of men his age on the shoulder. Did Mr. Grump himself actually have friends? Surely not. Not human ones anyway. Horses were much more his style. Stubborn and temperamental.

Another car drove in. I told myself I was seeing things when the door opened and a man who could have been Jorel Kent's twin stepped out. It wasn't Jorel. It couldn't be. Except...

Abandoning my spy station, I ran downstairs and out the door to Malisa's side, wrenching the list of names from her, scanning frantically for the one I didn't want to be there.

Except it was. Halfway down the page, right beside his wife's. Linock Gillespie.

No.

My heart took up its drum, panic pounding it against my ribs. Linock and Jorel weren't the only ones. I recognized almost half the names on the list. And not because they'd won awards.

"Alina, honey?"

The pounding moved to my throat.

Rebels. Every one of them. Converging like bugs to a beacon. Filling the place with their laughter and happy greetings, as if they hadn't come today with the express purpose of destroying me.

"Alina? You're shaking. Are you okay?"

And Malisa. She was the worst of them all. Smiling, welcoming, feeding me hope with every meal. I should have known better.

Malisa moved closer. I dropped the list and ran. Back to the house. Through the door. Up the stairs. Into my borrowed room where I slammed the door shut and leaned against it, gasping for breath.

I was the beacon, the reason they were all here.

For a week now, I'd let myself be taken in by their care. What a fool I'd been. She didn't care. Joha certainly didn't. I'd been right to be terrified when I woke that first day. The riot at the press conference. It was just as I'd feared. It hadn't been an accident. It had been a diversion, to capture me. Had I even passed out from the panic, like she'd said? I still didn't remember it. For all I knew, they'd set off some kind of sleeping gas to knock me out.

I sank to the floor, head cradled on my arms. Did Thoraben even know I was here? Did Marcos? They would be frantic. Father too. Why hadn't I asked for proof that Thoraben really had sent me? A whole week I'd been here, and my family likely had no idea. What must they be thinking? Had the Rebels asked for a ransom? Made demands of any kind? Had Father paid it? Marcos?

"Alina? You okay, sweetie?" Malisa called up the stairs. I shrank further into myself, blocking out her voice.

All my life, Father had warned me of the danger the Rebels posed to me and our family. These were not only Rebels, they were the worst of the worst. Every one of them exiled by my father. And here, they had me captured. Helpless, guard-less, completely at their mercy.

"Alina?"

She was there. On the other side of the door. The handle twisted.

FIFTEEN

I pushed my back harder against the door, determined to keep at least that one barrier between us. For as long as I could anyway. I doubted it would be for long. A gathering? Of friends? *Fool.* This was no gathering, it was an ambush.

An hour passed, then two. The sky darkened to black through my window. I stayed in that curled up ball until my fingers went numb, my heart along with it. After Malisa's cajoling received no response from me, she tried begging. Pat's voice and accompanying knock had come next. Joha's sometime later. I'd ignored them all, refusing to answer or move.

There had been other voices, some talking to me, others quieter. I'd barely heard them through the voices arguing in my mind.

Fool.

No, not a fool.

They lied to you.

What if it was the truth? What if Thoraben really did send me? What if Malisa really was Mother's best friend?

You have to get out of here.

Maybe I can trust them.

Fool.

Round and round it went until my head pounded with the pressure, my throat raw from swallowing back tears. At least the shaking had finally stopped.

The knocking began again. Quieter this time. Hesitant almost.

"Ali?"

My heart found a rhythm as tentative as the knock, a foolish scrap of hope peeking out past the wall of fear keeping me captive. My breath caught as the woman's voice called again. "Ali?" I hadn't been called that name for years, and only ever by one person. "Ali? It's Nicola."

Nicola.

It was her. Five years ago, she'd been one of my closest friends. Five years ago, she'd gained kingdom-wide notoriety becoming the youngest Rebel ever to be exiled.

"Can I come in?"

The day after Marcos had asked me to marry him in front of everyone at the Midsummer's Ball, I'd begged Father to let me name Nicola as one of my bridesmaids. It had been optimism at its best, but I had thought he'd at least consider the question, given he knew how devastated I'd been to have our friendship torn apart. A convicted criminal at only thirteen. The request had been barely out of my mouth before he'd denied it. I'd reconciled myself to the fact that I'd never see her again.

And here, only the width of a door separated us. Less—nothing—if I chose to open it. But I couldn't trust her. Could I? She was a Rebel, just like all the others.

You thought you could trust her to stand with you at your wedding...

Yes, but you also trusted Malisa. And look how well that turned out for you.

"Please, Alina?"

You can't stay in here forever. Do, and they've already won. You're the princess. Be the princess. Don't let them see you cower.

I stretched out my legs, wincing at the pain, before slowly pushing myself to my feet. The doorknob shook in my hand. *One breath, two breaths.*

I barely got a glance at Nicola's face before she wrapped me in a hug, my head tucked tight against her shoulder.

"It's so good to see you," she said, her voice muffled by my hair. "I couldn't believe it when Joha said you were here. At The Well, of all places."

I didn't want to cry. I'd done far too much of it in the past few days. But it appeared, as with everything else, that I didn't have a choice. Hot tears eked out despite my attempts to hold them back. Nicola pulled away, her hands still wrapped around mine.

Tears wet her cheeks too, but her face shone with happiness, her smile tremulous but wide. "I've missed you. Are you coming down? I'd love to introduce you to everyone. Especially Arden, my boyfriend. We've been together for almost a year now. He's such a sweetie. Don't tell him I told you that though." She laughed at that, wiggling her eyebrows up and down in a move so familiar it was like being transported back in time. To that last moment I saw her. Walking out of her trial. Flanked either side by guards. An enormous grin on her face. Peverell's youngest exile.

My face scrunched into an unattractive ball of sobs as I stumbled my way toward the bed.

"Ali?"

"You don't understand. I can't go down there. They're Rebels," I said, the accusation barely making it past the hiccups defacing my pride. "All of them. If they see me, they'll—" My voice broke, even the thought of ending that sentence too much to consider.

"What? No." The mattress sank further as Nicola sat beside me, her arm resting across my shoulders. "Wait, you still believe that? That's why you were hiding? But you're here. At The Well."

I looked up at the sound of a chair being moved. Malisa. I should have known she wouldn't have been far away. She pulled the chair to the edge of the bed before lowering herself into it. At least she didn't touch me.

"Alina needed to get away from the palace for a while," Malisa told Nicola. "Ben thought The Well the perfect solution."

"Then she's not a Follower?" Nicola asked.

Malisa shook her head. I didn't ask what they meant. I really didn't want to know.

"Well, it's good to see you all the same." Nicola grinned at me again, bumping her shoulder against mine, either ignoring or completely oblivious to my fear. "Ben's kept in contact, of course, but his factual letters are nothing compared to the conversations we used to have. Tell me everything!"

"Thoraben sent you letters?" How? Why? When?

"Sure. He sends out newsletters every couple of months to all of us to keep us up to date and encourage us."

"Your family?"

"The Followers. Or Rebels, as you call us."

Thoraben wrote to the Rebels. It should have surprised, no, *floored* me, but it didn't. Once a traitor, always a traitor, and the truth was, Thoraben had never been comfortable with the way Father treated the Rebels. He'd told me once that it didn't seem fair.

When I'd sided with Father, pointing out what a threat they were to our family and the future of Peverell, Thoraben never spoke of it again. I should have known he wouldn't leave it at that. With the resources at his disposal, he probably had the whole lot of them tracked down. After all, he'd betrayed me, why not Father too?

"You still choose that life then."

"I never stopped."

Nicola's words burnt like acid through my heart. For a moment, I'd dared to hope that she'd changed. That, maybe, she'd missed me and the life she'd once had and realized her childish alliances were as dangerous as they were foolish. But she hadn't changed. She still clung to her traitorous beliefs.

I stared blindly at the floor as my mind churned, fear and fury at war with uncertainty. Rebels. Followers. Newsletters. Ben. And these two women, sitting calmly beside my bed as I tried desperately to pull the ragged pieces of my world back together. Pieces that no longer fit, stretched and twisted as they were.

You're the princess. Be the princess. Come on, Alina. Take back control.

If, by some crazy chance, you can.

No. Be strong. Be confident. Be the princess. Be—

"You lied to me," I accused Malisa. "You said this was a safe place and that I was here for my protection."

"You are."

I pointed at the window behind me. "Your *safe place* is full of criminals."

"They're no—"

"You think I'm that naïve? I watched them leave Peverell. 'Traitor' might as well have been stamped across their foreheads. Jorel Kent, Linock Gillespie, Gene and Downey Bensley—criminals, every one of them. And you—" I shrugged off Nicola's arm. "Did they send you in as the first wave of attack? Are you here to kill me too?"

"Of course not. Do you really think I could hurt you? Any of us could? You're our princess. The daughter of our king. There's no way."

"You're accusing my father of lying to me?"

"I think he's told himself the lie so many times now that he believes it to be the truth."

A shout of laughter filtered through my window from outside followed by the unmistakable scent of smoke and several cheers. They must have started up the campfire Malisa mentioned. How nice of them to enjoy themselves while I was stuck in a world of terror. All because of them. How long would they stay? Would I ever feel safe to walk outside this room?

Nicola reached out a hand to try and take mine. I shrank back, too afraid to trust any of them. Even her.

"Get out."

"Alina, please—"

I shook my head, clenching my eyes shut so tight black dots swam. It was all too much. I couldn't deal with their treachery for another second. Nor their compassion. "Out. Both of you."

Thankfully, they obeyed. Hot tears dribbled my cheeks as I pulled out the journal Malisa had given me, tearing out a page.

Marcos, you have to save me. They're traitors.
Every single one of them.

My wet hand smudged the words, my eyes too full of tears

to make sense of them anyway. It didn't matter. Marcos couldn't save me. No one could.

The bed creaked as I stood, wandering over to the window, desperate for something, though I couldn't have put into words what it was. Hope, perhaps? Comfort? Someone to remind me I still mattered? A star to wish on? But the stars, too, hid their faces. I told myself that my eyes needed to adjust, that if I waited long enough, they'd appear. They didn't. For over an hour I waited, but the night sky remained as black as my mood.

I was about to walk back to my bed when I heard the music. The gentle strumming of a guitar. Desperate for a connection with someone, even an unknown musician, even a Rebel, I opened the window further and welcomed it in.

I'd heard music my whole life—Father brought the best musicians from around the world to the palace to serenade us—but none of their music had ever moved me to tears with its beauty. It was as if each note bypassed my ears and tiptoed straight to my heart.

I sat on the floor, my back to the wall letting the music wash over me as it flowed through the window. It was sad, melancholy, and yet hopeful somehow at the same time. I related all too well. I hated being here at The Well, and yet, there was something about it that, against all logic, drew me in and made me want to stay. The thought that maybe I could find peace here.

It was a foolish thought. Peace wasn't found in a place, it was found within. Through conquering my fears and settling with my imperfections. Mr. Galler had drilled that into me during his hours of philosophy lectures. Only in all the fighting and settling, I still hadn't found it. I hadn't even felt as if I'd come close, until The Well. Could it be he'd been wrong? Could it be peace in its truest form had nothing to do with me?

Sooner than I wished for, the last note danced away, and the crickets once again took up the night symphony. I stayed there, in my place on the floor, for ten more minutes, hoping it would begin again, but it didn't. I could have run down the stairs, looking for the talented musician. Instead, I turned off the light and crept into bed. There were Rebels out there and, somehow, the mystery only added to the beauty.

Tomorrow, I promised myself as I drifted off to sleep. *Tomorrow I'll be brave. Tomorrow I'll face them again. Tomorrow I'll be the woman who'll one day stand beside their king as his queen. Tomorrow I'll show them how strong I can be.*

Tomorrow...

SIXTEEN

The rattle in my stomach woke me long before dawn, and though I willed it to quiet, it wouldn't be appeased. There was nothing for it. I'd have to go to the kitchen and find some food. No one in their right mind would be up this early, but I'd seen some apples sitting in a bowl on the bench yesterday. One of those would suffice until breakfast was served. I hoped.

I dressed quickly, wincing as my hair elastic snagged, wrenching several strands of hair out in the process. My stomach moved from rattling to groaning as I put on my shoes and crept down the stairs to the kitchen.

"Morning."

I yelped, hand jerking first to my heart then my mouth as I turned from the kitchen bench to see Joha sitting at the table.

"Good. You're up," he said, oblivious to the fact that he'd all but yanked my heart from my chest. "It's about time you pitched in. Come on, I'll show you how to milk the cows before I start work."

"What makes you think I'd ever want to milk a cow?" Nope. Not now, not ever. Not even for Father and the reputation of Peverell would I touch that part of a cow's anatomy. Or a cow at all. Horrid, smelly, huge creatures that they were. Horses were bad enough.

"You're here. At dawn. Why else would you be up now unless you were here to help?"

I held up the apple, wishing he'd go away so I could eat it in peace. "I'm hungry. I missed dinner." Malisa had left a plate of fruit and toast outside my door last night, but I'd been too afraid of being ambushed by Nicola or Jorel or another Rebel to claim it. There was no way I was falling for that again. She must have come back to collect it after I'd finally fallen asleep because it wasn't there when I came out this morning.

Joha threw me one of the two granola bars sitting on the table in front of him. Out of habit more than thought, I caught it. "There. Fruit and granola. You can eat on the way." He tucked his chair back in, grabbed his hat, and started toward the door. I didn't move, not even when he opened the door for me. Though it was gratifying to see he had some level of gallantry in him.

"I'm not going anywhere with you, and I'm certainly not milking a cow. I don't like animals."

The door swung shut. "Fine. Help inside the house then. Vacuum, wash dishes."

And touch someone else's mess? It took me a good twenty minutes each day for my stomach to settle after using the shared bathroom. "No way. Marcos would never make me do something like that."

"Cook then, if cleaning is so far beneath you."

"I don't know how."

"Learn. I'm sure Mom would love to teach you."

"I live in a palace. I have a whole kitchen full of chefs preparing me food. When I marry Marcos, I'll have even more. Learning would be a waste of everyone's time."

"Look, you've had a whole week to sit around and be waited on. It's time you started pulling your weight. Around here, everyone helps. You included. Don't help and you don't eat. It's the way farms work."

"It's not the way I work."

"Then I guess you'll just have to starve." He grabbed for the granola bar. I held it above my head, our faces close as we stared each other down. I should have looked away, I don't know why I didn't, except that something in that moment made me want to stay. Maybe even forever. Which was just ridiculous given how much Joha hated me, and I him. I took a deliberate step backward, crossing my arms.

"Don't go getting any ideas, farmer. I might be stuck in this hovel with you, but I am engaged to Prince Marcos."

His laugh was as incredulous as it was patronizing. "It's a *haven*, not a hovel. I guess they didn't teach you the difference between those at princess school. And Marcos can have you. Believe me, you're not my type."

"Oh? And who is? No, don't tell me. A plain girl. Nose a bit too big for her face, hands not quite sure whether to flutter or hang against the side of her style-less but practical clothes. But with a heart of gold, of course, and a personality which would like nothing better than to acquiesce to your every will as she follows you around for the rest of your life."

"You think you know me so well."

"I don't have to know you personally to know your type."

"I don't have a *type*, as you so eloquently put it."

I shrugged. "Each to their own."

He swiped the granola bar from my hand, putting it in his pocket with the other one before pushing me out of the kitchen. "Enjoy your solitude, princess."

I wasn't sure what incensed me more—that he'd sent me away or that, once again, he'd put his hands on me to do it. How dare he touch me without my permission! I was a princess and he was...was...nothing. Joha Samson was nothing. Not even a servant. Servants got paid. And he'd had the nerve to touch me. He wouldn't have done that if Marcos had been here.

Fine. I'd go back to my room. Of my own accord. I certainly wasn't doing it because a nobody like Joha had thrown me out of the kitchen. My stomach let out another loud protest. I ran up the stairs before Joha could comment on that too. What made him think he could rule my life?

Fury painted my cheeks red. What made me let him?

"Alina?" Not waiting for a reply, Nicola opened my door a crack and peered through. Spotting me on what was now my bed, she walked the rest of the way in. Pride told me to send her away. Hunger took one whiff of the food-filled tray she held and welcomed her with open arms. "Malisa said you didn't come down for breakfast, and that you missed dinner last night. She's worried about you. You have to eat."

At least someone cared. I took the plate gratefully, scents of bacon and scrambled eggs appeasing my battered spirit. Nicola put the rest of the tray down on the desk, making herself comfortable on the room's one chair. One chair, I was almost embarrassed to offer it. At home, my suite had a full sitting room, despite the fact that I rarely had visitors.

"Does Joha know you're bringing me food?" I asked between bites. Ones far too large to be ladylike but there was no way I was letting anyone take this plate back before I'd cleaned it spotless. Who knew when I'd have to go into hiding again? Three meals—four?—I'd already missed since arriving at The Well. My weight might thank me for missing them. My stomach, not so much.

"Why would it matter to him?"

Because he'd taken it upon himself to make my life even more miserable than it already was. Forget the Rebels, Joha was taking me down all on his own. "I came down to get some food early this morning. Joha was there. He told me to starve. Said if I don't help, I don't eat and threw me out of the kitchen."

"Really? That doesn't sound like him. Although, it's true, they do live by that code around here. But I'm sure he didn't mean for you to starve. He knows as well as everyone how tough you've had it lately."

"Like he'd care."

"Sure, he cares. Joha's one of the nicest, sweetest guys I've ever met—Arden included."

"Could have fooled me." I swallowed another bite of crispy bacon, washing it down with a sip of juice.

"Did you know he gives riding lessons to kids whose families couldn't otherwise afford it? Says every kid should know how to ride a horse, so he spends a few hours each week in amongst everything else he does teaching them."

Were we still talking about Joha? "How magnanimous of him."

"No, you don't understand. It's so much more than teaching kids to ride. He believes in them, jokes around with them, and makes them feel like they matter. He's like a mentor to them or a big brother. He's loyal, caring, passionate, gifted. You know, he doesn't even have a house yet because everything he earns goes into the chapel? He lives in that cramped apartment above the stables rather than build his own house because he said the chapel is more important."

"You sound like you're in love with him."

"No, we're just friends. He was one of the first friends I made in Hodenia. My family came and stayed here when we were first exiled. I was lonely for you and Kenna, and he gave me his teddy bear. Told me he was too old for it anyway. I'm pretty sure I adored him from that moment on. I did wonder once if maybe there might be something between us but then he fell for Erynn and I met Arden and, well, that was the end of that."

"Joha has a girlfriend?"

"What? Oh, Erynn. No, they broke up. Well, he...she..." She wrinkled her nose. "Anyway, my point is, he's really nice."

I cut my second piece of bacon into bite-sized pieces, stabbing four with my fork, filling my mouth so Nicola wouldn't expect an answer. When it came to Joha Samson, Nicola and I would have to agree to disagree. She might have considered him a knight in shining armor, but I could only go by what I'd seen—and none of it was flattering to the man.

"I'm sure you'd like him if you got to know him better."

I nodded, refusing to commit myself to any more than that. She might be right. Perhaps he was kind to everyone else and it was just me he hated. In which case, I was in trouble because I had no idea why or what I'd done to garner such censure. He'd been short with me from the moment I arrived at The Well.

"Anyway, I'm glad you're dressed. I thought it would be nice to go on a picnic this morning. Malisa has it all ready for us. We can go as soon as you finish breakfast."

A picnic? No animals, no questions, no Rebels—Nicola excluded—and no irritating men with nothing better to do than point out all my faults? A picnic sounded like the perfect way to spend a morning. I put the last of the scrambled egg in my mouth, leaving behind the now-soggy toast, and placed my knife and fork on the plate. "All done. Let me brush my teeth and we can go."

"You're wearing those shoes?" Nicola eyed my pink heels with disdain. "Don't you have any others?"

Sure. Lime green flats, some lace-up canvas shoes with a dubious stain, and that horrible pair of boots Joha had made me wear on our ride. No, thank you. Plus, I needed the extra height and none of those had heels. "These are fine."

"You're sure? It's a twenty-minute trek to the river."

"They're fine."

Ten minutes, and only two potentially neck-breaking stumbles later, we were on our way. Stench of the stables aside, it was a beautiful day to be outside. The perfect day for a picnic. One of those mornings which was so clear, the air almost glistened.

"So, tell me about the wedding," Nicola said as we walked along the path away from the house and, thankfully, the stench of the stable. "I wish I could have been there to see it, Ben and Kenna all dressed up in their finery, pledging their lives to each other. It must have been so romantic."

Of all the things we could have talked about, it had to be the one I wished I could forget forever. Perhaps staying in my room wouldn't have been so bad after all.

SEVENTEEN

Romantic?" I huffed. Nicola's idealistic view of my brother's nuptials was as ridiculous as the dreamy expression on her face. "Hardly. It was a farce at best. Rushed, awkward—Kenna seduced him, you know. They didn't report that bit in the papers. Conveniently left out the part that the wedding was required because of what happened the night of the whirlwind. She seduced him, forced a marriage, tore apart our family, betrayed Peverell. Oh sure, very romantic."

I shouldn't have been so negative. Father would have been horrified. He'd been as angry as me about the events which had necessitated Thoraben's wedding but, unlike me, he'd hidden it well, knowing how much the royal family's image meant to our people. He'd smiled while I'd frowned.

"Sorry," I grumbled, my voice low and frustrated. I peeked a look at Nicola to see her smiling despite the hand over her mouth to try to cover it. She would have had to cover her whole face to hide the delight dancing across it. "I'm glad someone finds this amusing."

"It's not that. It's just...I can't believe you didn't know. You lived with them both. You were closer to them than anyone."

"Know what?"

She smiled. "That Ben loved her."

"No, I told you, the papers had it wrong. A sensationalized story to satisfy the masses. Any love you think was there was simply an act for the cameras."

"It wasn't an act."

"I think I would know. Like you said, I was there."

She ducked under a tree branch. I followed, though far less gracefully. She was right about my heels. They were a complete menace, the way they tried to kill me. Every hole, every rock, every shiny leaf. If they weren't getting stuck, they were sliding or making new holes of their own. At this rate, I'd fall and break my neck long before we made it to the picnic site.

Of course, the alternative—taking them off and walking barefoot—was worse.

"You might have been there, but you're sadly lacking in the details. Ben has loved Kenna for years. He'd been biding his time, waiting for her to be old enough to declare himself. The whirlwind fiasco merely sped up the process. The wedding might have been a surprise to the rest of Peverell and even Mackenna herself, but it wasn't a mistake. Whether the whirlwind happened or not, he was always going to marry her."

On second thought, maybe breaking a neck was a good idea. At least then Nicola would stop.

"You really didn't know."

"What would you know anyway?" I muttered.

"A lot more than you, it seems."

I hit a dangling leaf with my hand, allowing myself that tiny evidence of the growing frustration I felt. I would have kicked the tree if Nicola hadn't been with me. Even at the risk of destroying my favorite pair of shoes. I could always buy more. When—if—I ever got home. Something that was looking less likely with every passing minute.

"Why does everyone keep saying that to me? First Joha, then Malisa, now you. Do you all think I'm stupid? I get it, there is this grand mystery, you're part of the Thoraben Fan Club I have no intention of joining, but you can stop it, okay? I might be Alina, young and naïve, but I'm also a member of the royal family, and that demands respect."

"I respect you."

I huffed. She certainly didn't show it.

"No really, I do. As, I'm certain, do Malisa, Pat, and Joha. There's just so much more to life than what you know."

"Like what, your Rebel ways?" Her silence was answer enough. "Look, I'm thrilled you're here. I really am. It'll be great to spend time with you. I've missed that. But I'm not a criminal."

"Neither are—"

"Can we talk about something else? Tell me about Arden. How did you two meet?"

Her smile was instant. "Here. I was visiting with Malisa when he and Joha walked into the kitchen looking for food. I think I stared at him for a whole minute in absolute silence before offering him the pear I was holding. The one with a bite already gone from one side. Either he was hungrier than he cared to admit or simply felt sorry for the twit of a girl staring at him because he ate it without even commenting."

"And yet you're together."

"Sure are. I knew the second he walked through that door that I'd marry him one day. I spent quite a lot of time visiting Malisa over the next few months, making sure I was there whenever Arden was. I'd probably be embarrassed at what a nuisance I made of myself if I wasn't so thrilled it worked. Seven months from the day I met him, Arden asked me to be his girlfriend. We'll have been together ten months next week."

"Congratulations."

"What about Prince Marcos? What's the story between the two of you?"

I opened my mouth to answer before closing it again. Me and Marcos? We were Marcos and Alina. Prince and princess. The perfect couple. The question shouldn't have stumped me like it did. I loved Marcos. I loved everything about him from his height to his broad shoulders to the way his clothing never had a stitch out of place. The Midsummer's Ball, the night he'd proposed to me and made our engagement official, had been the happiest night of my life. So why did none of that seem worth telling? "Oh, I'm sure you know everything there is to know about the two of us. Everyone else seems to."

"Tell me anyway. What's he like as a man? We all know him as the prince, but what's he really like? How are the wedding preparations going? I guess they're probably all done, right? Since you were supposed to be married last week. Are you excited? Nervous?" She put a hand on my arm. "Ali, are you okay? You're looking kind of pale. Sorry, too many questions."

"I'm fine," I lied. "The heat's getting to me. That and the smell of the cows."

Nicola grinned. "Trust you to faint from the smell of a couple of cows. Can you really still smell them? This far away? I can't. Must be used to it, I guess."

I smiled back, happy to let her believe it.

Pull it together, Alina. You love Marcos. Of course you do. He's the perfect man—and a future king to boot—and you're perfect for him. Every girl in two kingdoms wishes they were the one marrying him, and you actually are. When Father and King Dorien finally decided on a date.

I picked at a speck of something brown on my jeans, wondering how long it had been there, hoping it was only dirt and not something more sinister.

What about you and Prince Marcos?

What about us? Was there even an us? I had to believe there was. "For now," King Dorien had said.

"We're here."

I stopped short of the clearing, surprised to be here already. Shaded by trees, a river rushing along beside it, the grassy clearing was as perfect a place for a picnic as Nicola had said, except for one thing—it was already occupied. By three men.

Just what I needed.

"Nicola."

She ignored me, or, at least, the note of warning in my voice, instead walking over to the two men who'd stood on our arrival, putting her arm around the dark-haired one's waist.

"Alina, let me introduce you to my boyfriend, Arden, and our friend Darrick."

I nodded to each of them in turn, taking in their appearance along with their easygoing smiles.

Arden was classically handsome, the kind of man Father commandeered to escort Kenna and me to events when we traveled. Dark hair, long enough to show its fullness but short enough to be neat, tidy clothing, respectful manners. Similar in ways to Marcos, though without the brooding eyes which had women the world over aflutter.

Darrick, in almost direct contrast, had blond hair almost to his shoulders—whether natural or assisted I couldn't tell. Nor could I tell whether the blue tinging the ends of it was supposed to be there or he'd forgotten to tie it back while leaning over some paints and accidentally colored it. He looked like a painter or artist of some type in his t-shirt and ripped jeans. Fun, carefree, the type of man Father warned me against lest my perfect reputation be spun the wrong way.

And then there was the man with the scruffy brown beard and battered cowboy hat. The one who'd thrown me out of the kitchen this morning.

"What's he doing here?"

Joha looked up at my question but didn't move otherwise. Had the other two men not been there, watching in interest, I would have turned around and walked straight back to the house, blistered heels and all. I still might.

"I invited him," Nicola answered without the slightest bit of apology.

"Why?"

"Because he has a terrible habit of forgetting to eat, and I thought it would be fun for us to all picnic together. At least, I did when I invited them. Before breakfast when you told me, uh..." She shrugged, clearly too kind to tell Joha what I'd actually said about him. From the half-smirk on his face, he probably guessed. I rolled my shoulders back and refused to look ashamed. He deserved every bit of censure I sent his way. And more. Horrible man.

"You could have warned me." Twenty minutes walking together and not once had she even hinted that our picnic would be anyone but the two of us. Had she felt even the slightest bit guilty listening to me talk about how much I disliked Joha this morning, knowing he'd be here? No wonder she'd tried so hard to convince me of his good points.

"You wouldn't have come."

She was right about that.

"Come on, Ali. You're two of my best friends. Can't you give him another chance?"

Anyone else—any other day—and I might have. "He hates me."

Joha finally stood, brushing dirt off the back of his pants as he walked over to us, ignoring Darrick's snicker. "I don't hate you."

"No? Then it's normal for you to tell people that they are childish, immature nuisances and refuse them food if they don't do what you demand?"

"Joha Samson! You said what?" Nicola asked, incredulous. Arden's eyebrows shot up too, though his eyes sparkled with amusement. Darrick didn't even bother to hide his reaction, slapping a hand against his leg as he filled the clearing with laughter.

Joha shrugged. "I only say what I see."

"No wonder she thinks you hate her."

I crossed my arms, gratified no end to have Nicola on my side.

"I told you, I don't hate her—you," he said, looking my way again. "I just... That first day, when we rode, I thought I saw something in you. I thought maybe... Anyway, I was wrong. You've done nothing but prove how arrogant you are ever since. You don't help around the house or anywhere else for that matter and use Prince Marcos as an excuse for your laziness. *Marcos this, Marcos that.* This place is incredible, but you're so scared of getting a little dirt under your perfect fingernails that you're missing its beauty."

I wanted to lash out at him with the truth. I couldn't do any of those things he wanted me to do. Did he have any idea how stupid it made me feel? To be a woman on the cusp of marriage and not even know how to turn a vacuum cleaner on? Or be so frightened of a cow that I couldn't breathe? Or spend every hour of every day so terrified I'd make a mistake and everyone would know what a complete failure I was that every single muscle I had ached by the time I collapsed into bed each night? Had *he* ever fought his own mind to the point of losing consciousness?

Breathe, Alina. Ignore him. Let him think you're arrogant. It's better than the truth.

Easier said than done.

"You think I'm scared of dirt?"

"Are you?"

The way he looked at me, at my heels, that glint of challenge in his eyes, half smirk on his face—he knew he was right. The first day I'd met him, outside Mother's suite at the palace, I'd felt like he could see right through me. It was the same now. And I hated him for it.

"Of course not." *Liar.*

"No? Prove it. Walk across that log."

EIGHTEEN

My stomach dropped, as if one of the black boulders sitting in the river had lodged itself in there. The log he'd pointed out stretched across the river, bridging one side with the other. It was thick enough to walk over, certainly, but if I were to fall...

I should have walked away the second I saw Joha sitting there. Or after he'd confirmed he thought I was a nuisance. Certainly before I opened my mouth and walked myself right into that challenge like the complete fool he thought I was. Now, I had no choice but to prove him wrong. "Fine."

I walked to the end of the log, nudging it with the toe of my shoe. It seemed sturdy enough. I could do it. Years of dance and deportment classes had given me the balance. Easing my feet out of my shoes, I closed my eyes, taking in a deep breath before opening them and stepping up. The log might not have wobbled, but my legs did. I stood as upright as I could and pretended I stood in one of the many drawing rooms at home, book on my head as I practiced my posture.

One step forward, two, three. I was over halfway across before my foot slipped on a wet leaf sitting there. Though I caught my balance just as quickly, the damage was done, the motion jerking me from the calm picture I'd built in my mind. I froze, the water rushing beneath the log taunting me.

You're a fool. You can't do it. You'll fall in. What did you think you were doing? Showing off? Trying to impress him? One more wrong step and you'll fall. You think he'll care then? He'll laugh. Laugh at the poor princess who couldn't even cross a log.

No. I could do this. I wouldn't think about how deep the water was in the middle or whether rocks hid beneath it. Four more steps and I'd have made it to the other side.

Four more than I could take when I couldn't find the courage to move at all.

No. Think about the drawing room. The polished wooden floors. The huge windows. The chairs, ramrod straight and uncomfortable but so regal in their stance. My foot moved an inch. *The chandeliers—the largest in the middle of the ceiling with smaller versions bracketed around the walls.* Another inch. I was doing it. Moving forward. It might take a hundred more tiny steps, but I'd get there. *The ornamental rugs—their colors so vibrant one could almost smell the hues. During dance lessons, they'd be rolled back, tucked out of range of—*

It was a knob on the bark which defeated me. I saw it as my body pitched sideways, arms grappling for a hold but finding only air. Water filled my mouth and nose, forcing me to gulp. Sky, where was the sky? Above me? Or had I twisted as I fell? My lungs burned for lack of breath. Light, dark, water, shadow—they melded together in a horrifying confusion. Where were the rocks? Any second I would hit them. My bones smashed to pieces as they dragged me from the river.

There! Something solid. I grabbed at it with my hand an instant before being hauled into someone's arms. I coughed out water, gasping at air. Not finding enough. Above the water, but still drowning.

Air. Breathe. Think. Lungs. Drowning.

"Hey, easy there, girl. You're okay. I've got you."

I clung to the strong arms that held me, my head tucked tight in against my rescuer's shoulder as I fought for control.

"That's it, breathe. In, out, in, out."

"Joha?" Fog gave way to reality. I pulled my head back just enough to see his face, inches from my own. "*You* saved me?"

"Were you hoping for someone else?"

I could almost feel the water sizzling off my heated cheeks. Arrogant man.

"Put me down."

Though the water only reached my waist, I misjudged how strong the river's current was, or perhaps simply how weak my legs. I would have gone under again had Joha not caught my arm, pulling me in against him, his back to the rushing water. I felt sheltered there, and something else. Something that pulled me stronger than the current and terrified me just as much. I hoped he'd put my breathlessness down to the remnants of fear left by my fall and didn't think it was anything to do with him. Because it wasn't. At all. If someone would pass that message on to my heart...

"Alina—"

"What?" I said, my voice barely audible over the river still rushing past us.

He looked down at me, his face too close for my comfort. I took a step backward, incensed by the way I teetered again.

"Nothing. Come on." One arm tight around my waist, the other holding my arm, he started walking toward the bank. I stumbled along beside him, trying not to think about how I must look. Waterlogged, my appearance a complete mess, my heart pounding so hard and fast, I was certain any moment my eardrums would burst.

"There's nothing to be embarrassed about, you know. The log gets slippery when it's wet. Everyone's fallen there once or twice. It's a rite of passage around here."

A rite of passage I could have happily avoided. I tripped again.

Without another word, Joha hauled me back up into his arms. My face heated again as I tried not to think about what he must think of me. The pathetic princess who not only fell off a simple log but couldn't even make it out of the waist-deep water on her own. I gritted my teeth together, jaw aching with the effort it took to keep my face from scrunching into a mess of tears.

Three men watching, and it had to be the one I hated who

saved me. The one who smelled like sawdust and hay and safety. I struggled out of his arms the instant we reached the bank and stumbled into the picnic blanket Nicola wrapped around my shoulders, its warmth as welcome as its concealment.

"Hot chocolate? Banana pecan muffin? Mmmm, still warm."

Nicola offered food like nothing had happened while I sat, clutching at the blanket and the tiniest bit of dignity I had remaining. Joha accepted a muffin, thanking Nicola, asking if she had water instead. As if he wasn't dripping with enough of it already.

"Alina? How about you? Want anything?"

Yes, to go home. To my palace in Peverell. Where people bowed to me and catered to my whims rather than pushing me to be someone stronger than I was. Hot streaks of salty tears mingled with the water trickling down my face. At least they wouldn't be obvious.

From years of training rather than any inner strength or will, I found a smile for Nicola. "Thanks, but if you don't mind, I'd like to go back to the house and change." I squeezed the sleeve of my shirt, releasing a gush of water onto the ground. "I'm a little, uh, wet." My playful ploy worked, making them all laugh, diffusing what might have been an awkward moment.

"You're sure? You'll be dry in no time sitting in the sun there, and I really wanted you to get to know the guys."

Dry, perhaps, but still dirty and disheveled. I could already feel my hair slipping from its bun. While it was wet, it would hang straight, but the curls would return, of that I had no doubt. I had to get away—especially if Joha was going to continue to look at me in that way he did. I'd had more scrutiny than I could face already from him today.

"Another time." Maybe. "I'd rather change. Perhaps lie down for a bit."

"Of course. I'll walk back with you. The guys can take the food with them. I'm sure it'll be gone before we're even home."

My short laugh sounded as strangled as it was forced. I didn't bother to wait and see if any of them noticed. I didn't wait for

Nicola to walk with me either, grabbing my shoes and thrusting my feet into them mud and all before starting back the way we'd come without her. I might have been waterlogged and weary from what felt like a near-death experience, but I was still the princess—and Father would expect no less from me than that I act like one.

By the time Nicola caught up with me, the tears were gone. By the time we reached the house, I'd even managed to get the taunting voice inside me under control and my breathing back to a normal pace. If there was one thing I knew how to do, it was be a princess.

"Oh good, you're back. Did Pat find—" Malisa's words cut off as she turned her eyes on me. Eyes which widened in surprise as she took in my soggy clothes. "What happened to you?"

"Fell off a log," I mumbled, not loud enough for Malisa to catch since she turned instead to Nicola for an explanation.

"She was crossing the log bridge at the river and slipped. Went for a bit of an impromptu swim before Joha caught her."

She made it sound like I was a fish. I wanted to run up the stairs and escape Malisa's scrutiny as I'd done more times than I cared to claim already, but now that I'd stopped, finding the strength to move again was proving difficult. Perhaps impossible.

"What were you saying about Pat?" Nicola asked.

"Oh. He was looking for you. Wanted to ask your opinion on the song list for the next gathering. I told him where you were. I'm surprised you didn't run into him on your way back."

"Knowing him, he probably got distracted and went to check on the chapel instead. I'll head that way. Arden was going there after our picnic anyway. Thanks."

She was out the door before I could muster any sort of goodbye, standing there, mute as I was. Malisa's gaze turned back to me.

"Oh, sweetie."

The last thing I wanted to do in front of this woman was cry again, especially when I'd spent the past twenty minutes doggedly holding myself together, but the tears wouldn't stay away. They burst out of my eyes, gliding their way down my cheeks with no thought for the mortification I felt.

Without another word, arms wrapped around me, and I found my head tucked in against an apron smelling of gingerbread and spice. Malisa didn't ask if she could hold me, something I was thankful for since I would have said no. And then I would have had to cry alone.

The sobs came hard as the ache split my heart in two. I couldn't have even said exactly why I was crying—perhaps it was one thing, perhaps everything together. Reason flew aside as I stood there, in that outdated kitchen, wetting the apron of this woman I never thought I'd know.

"Your mom struggled with fitting in."

A tissue appeared in my hand, pulled from Malisa's sleeve like a seasoned magician. I barely registered her assurance that it was clean before rubbing it across my face. She pulled back just enough to grab the whole box from a little table near the wall. I took more gratefully, thankful the sobs were beginning to abate.

"It wasn't easy for her, moving into the palace. She loved your dad incredibly, but the palace life was a struggle. She spent a lot of time that first year crying at my kitchen table too."

"Really?" It was the first I'd ever heard of her being anything but the perfect queen. I might not have believed Malisa, yet something in her steady, unflinching gaze belied the truth. I sat at the table, my discomfort at being wet pushed aside by the incessant need to know the woman who'd birthed me. "Will you tell me about her?"

"Sure. What would you like to know?"

"Anything. Everything. What was she like? I have photos and recordings and all that but what was she really like?"

Malisa smiled as she took a seat on the chair beside mine. Flour turned glue stuck to her dark apron, streaks of something else splayed across the pocket. I should have been repulsed, but under the mess was a woman who'd known my mother like no one else. The clutter of the kitchen faded away as she began to talk.

"She was absolutely beautiful, as you'd know from the photos, but shy. Shyer than you'd imagine a queen being. She loved people but hated being the center of attention. She was far more comfortable playing with kids or writing speeches than standing out in the front delivering them. I wondered if marrying your father was the right choice for her, given how much it would throw her in the spotlight, but while she struggled with the shyness, I think it was that lack of pretentiousness which made the people care so much for her."

The sobs had abated but my heart still felt raw, as if someone had taken a hammer to it and pounded it flat. I ached with the pain. "I wish I'd known her."

"She would have wished that too. She was so excited to find out she was having a daughter."

"She told you that?"

"Actually, she screamed it. I had to ask her three times to repeat what she'd said because she was so excited she couldn't get the words out in the right order. All that deportment training trounced in an instant by one word from a doctor."

The beeping alarm on one of the appliances made me jump. And remember who I was. Had I truly just cried all over this woman? While looking like a half-drowned peasant? Heat suffused my cheeks as I stood, the chair squeaking backward on the tiles. What was I thinking, letting myself fall apart like that? Letting her feel my tears.

I threw out a quick thank you as I ran from the room. I'd found out more about Mother, but at what cost to my own pride? Malisa had seen me cry. No one ever saw me cry, not even my maids.

With a burst of energy, I flew up the stairs, stopping just short of slamming the bedroom door behind me. The bed called me, but I was too wet still to sit on it. I grabbed the first outfit I found from the wardrobe and locked myself in the bathroom instead, blasting the shower with enough hot water to fill the room with steam. It wasn't a lavender-scented spa by any stretch of the imagination, but it was warm and private. No one would bother me here. *Come on, Alina. You can't let that happen again. You're the princess. Be the princess. You have to be more careful.*

I couldn't let them see the girl inside.

NINETEEN

A small pile of books sat on the floor outside my door when I returned from the shower, my name clearly printed on the note atop them.

> *Alina,*
>
> *These were your mother's. I think she would want you to have them. I hope they give you the answers you're looking for. Remember as you read them that she was first a woman before she was ever a queen. And that she was a mother, most of all.*
>
> *Malisa*

The hardcover books had no titles, something that baffled me until I opened the first one. My breath caught as the first handwritten lines seared themselves in my heart.

> *March 1*
>
> *Today was cold, rainy—and utterly perfect. Because today, Everson, the man I love more than I could have ever imagined loving another person, asked me to marry him.*

I flicked open the second and third books, page upon page of writing and dates confirming the fragile hope flickering to life inside me. They weren't merely books, they were journals. Mother's journals. All these years I'd ached to know her and here, in my hand, I held her very heart.

I threw my wet clothes into the room and ran back down the stairs to the kitchen, books clutched to my chest.

"Malisa."

She turned from the sink, hands dripping, uncertainty in her eyes. I dropped the books on the table and rushed to hug her. "Thank you."

She patted my back, sighing into my hair. I relished it, not even caring whether her hands left wet patches on my shirt. "Oh, sweetie. I hope they help you. Maybe even give you some of the answers you've been looking for."

How could I tell her they already had? Even without reading beyond the first two lines, I knew Mother better. She was a writer. She felt things deeply. She loved Father.

"Have you read them?"

Malisa pulled back, shaking her head. "I couldn't. I don't think anyone has."

"Not Thoraben? Or my father?"

"No. But I think she would have wanted you to. Just promise me you'll remember these are her journals, her innermost thoughts. This was likely the one place she could vent and release the emotions she could never show to the public."

I knew what she showed the public. I had record of it—hundreds of photos and recordings. What I ached for was the person she was beneath that. "I will."

Though privacy beckoned, I couldn't stand the thought of more time in my bedroom, instead rushing out to the gazebo, hoping no one would bother me there.

Curling my legs up underneath me, I opened again to the first page and began reading.

> *Today was cold, rainy—and utterly perfect. Be-*
> *cause today, Everson, the man I love more than I*

could have ever imagined loving another person, asked me to marry him.

I knew this day was coming. Or, at least, I had hoped, but to hear his words, that question, to feel his ring on my finger. Some men promise their fiancée a kingdom—Everson actually has one. But I'm not marrying him for that. In all honesty, I'd probably prefer he wasn't the future king. I'm not certain I'm ready to carry the weight of that responsibility, heavy as I know it'll be. But, though I struggle with the future, I know I love Everson.

I still can't quite believe it's true. I keep playing the proposal over and over like a recording in my mind lest I forget a single word or moment of it. The way he stood before me, holding my hands and telling me how much I meant to him. The way he knelt down on the grass beneath that oak tree I've always thought so grand and asked me if I'd marry him. The way his hands shook so badly he almost dropped the ring before managing to get it on to my finger. The tear at the corner of his eye which he tried to brush off as being from the glare even though there was none.

Prince Marcos hadn't cried when he proposed to me. Nor had he mentioned love. Respect, yes. Admiration, certainly. But not love. Did he love me? Did I love him? Did it even matter? We were destined to marry regardless. And he was handsome. By his side, I would be the envy of every woman in both kingdoms. A queen. Just like my mother. With power and beauty and influence. That was what mattered.

Time flew past like the breeze playing around the garden as I sat there reading about wedding plans, the official announcement of their engagement and the way Malisa's squeal of delight at the news made her horse rear, almost unsaddling her in the process.

The wedding is in two days now. I know I've made the right choice, loving Everson, but I have so many doubts about whether I can be a princess. If only they were exclusive of each other. Everson keeps telling me it will all be fine and that I will make a wonderful princess, but I struggle to believe him. What if it all gets too much and I need time alone to recoup? What if I don't remember all the right ways to address everyone? I know I love Everson the man, but what if I can't be the woman Everson the prince needs? What if I'm about to make the biggest mistake of my life?

I move into the palace tomorrow, to the Princess Suite. My heart pounds in equal parts excitement and terror at the thought. I have to keep coming back to the fact that I love Everson. While I may doubt everything else, I have never once doubted our love or the fact that I want to be the woman who stands by his side and loves him for the rest of his life. Even if that means being Peverell's queen one day, maybe even sooner than either of us have planned given the king's precarious health.

The entry continued, but my eyes were too blurred with tears to keep reading. The reasons piled on top of each other as the tears fell.

Because I'd been given a glimpse into Mother's life.

Because her fear and doubts echoed mine.

Because she, too, struggled with the anxiety of not being enough.

Because I missed the palace.

Because the same Princess Suite Mother had moved to was now occupied by Kenna and, while I still didn't know if I could forgive her, I really wished she was here to talk to right now.

Tears dripped their way down my cheeks as if I hadn't already used up more than my share today. I let them fall. I missed Kenna, my wardrobe full of clothing which actually fit, my maids, Thoraben, and Father. I even missed my ridiculous schedule. There was too much time to think in this place.

"Alina?" I heard Joha call.

I quickly scrubbed the tears off my face. Maybe if I stayed quiet enough, he'd go away.

He didn't.

Leaves crunched under his feet as Joha walked along the path toward me. "Alina?"

"Go away."

"Fine." He turned to walk back the way he'd come.

"No, wait. Don't." I didn't like him, but there was no one else here, and I was tired of being alone. "Stay."

"Orders, Alina? You're not the boss here, you know."

"I know." Annoyed as I was with him, I was glad when he walked into the gazebo, leaning back against one of the posts.

"You're crying."

Smart man. "Again. I know."

"Why?"

He might have been obnoxious, annoying, short, lacking in finesse, and in so many ways just lacking—and potentially one of my greatest enemies—but he was here. Now. And that was better than nothing.

"It wasn't supposed to be like this."

"Life rarely is."

"I was supposed to be married and have people fawning over me. Maids to serve me, entertainers to charm me. I was supposed to be living in a palace. Instead, I'm here."

"And that's such a bad thing?"

I looked at him, wondering if he was serious. It was difficult to tell with his face hidden behind that scruff of a beard. He couldn't really think The Well compared to a palace, could he?

"You could be grateful, you know."

I held back a laugh. Barely. "For what? The scratchy clothes I'm wearing? A house full of enemies? Your stellar company?"

"That you're alive."

"Oh yay. I'm alive. To serve my life sentence in this dump."

"First, it's not a life sentence. You'll be back in your palace soon enough. And second, you are the most selfish human being I have ever known. You're rude, ungrateful, immature—"

"Don't sugar-coat it."

"Oh, don't worry. I won't. You could help, you know, instead of looking down your nose pretending you're better than the rest of us."

And here we were, back to this again. "I don't do that."

"No? Then you'll help with the milking tomorrow?"

Don't get angry. Hold it together. He's just trying to rile you.

"Why did you even bother saving me earlier?" I asked instead. All it earned me was a shrug.

"It's what family does."

"I'm not family."

"While you live in this house, you are. And I already told you, I don't hate you. Far from it."

It would take a whole lot more than his saying it for me to believe it. "Look, do you need something? Is that why you're here?"

"I wanted to check you were okay, after your soaking and all. You seemed a bit shaken up by it."

"I'm fine."

"Good." He pulled an envelope from his pocket, holding it out. "This arrived for you."

I snatched it from his hand, noting the Hodenian crest gracing one corner as I tucked it under the books on my lap. I thought Joha would leave. He didn't, continuing to stand there as if he had nothing better to do than invade my privacy. "Was there something else?"

"A polite person would say thank you."

"Thank you."

He shook his head. "You know, for a long time, I thought the two of us—" He stopped, staring at some place above my head. I waited, hoping he'd finish the thought. He didn't.

"Would what?"

His sigh could have set a bird to flight. For the first time, I wished I could see his eyes clear and unshaded by the hat he wore everywhere but inside the house. I wondered if they held the same sad note as his voice. "Never mind. Read your letter. It looks important." This time, he left, stalking back down the path like a man on a mission. To get away from me. The girl he denied hating but loathed with every breath he took. Well, what of it? I didn't care for him anyway.

I opened the envelope with more force than necessary, ripping out the single folded sheet, willing my mind to forget Joha and focus on the words in front of me.

> *Princess Alina,*
>   *Your brother, Thoraben, told me how he secreted you away during the press conference and—*

Infuriating man. What had Joha been about to say? I had half a mind to stalk after him and demand he tell me, only he already thought me demanding enough. I thought the two of us would what? Be friends? More than friends? Ugh. I certainly hoped not. Imagine, kissing a man with a beard. It would be all scratchy and just—I didn't even want to think about it. But that couldn't have been it anyway given everyone knew I'd been unofficially betrothed to Marcos since the day I was born. *Focus, Alina!* I ran my finger down the page, finding where I'd stopped.

> *—his reasons for doing so. As your fiancé, I would have preferred to have been consulted in the matter, however I understand it was a matter of urgency and think it a wise decision given the circumstances. I am certain you will agree.*

I didn't agree. Not that that was a question. More of an order. Would Joha order his fiancée around like that? *Alina!*

> *For the next month at least, I think it best you stay where you are, out of the public eye. The people have been told that you are stepping back from*

*public engagements in order to prepare for our
wedding. Again, I think it best. We cannot have
them thinking you are in danger nor unfit to carry
out your royal duties.*

I should have been incensed by the fact that the people had
been told I wasn't good enough to carry out my duties *and* plan
a wedding, and that I had to stay at The Well for another month.
I also should have read the rest of the letter, but all I could think
about was Joha and the thought he'd left unspoken.

What had he been about to say?

TWENTY

"What about Alina?"

Pat's voice was quiet, as always, but he might as well have shouted the way my ears picked up my name. I stopped, three steps shy of the kitchen, my desire for a drink of water not seeming so dire anymore.

"She can come too," Malisa said. "It would be good for her."

"Will she think that?"

A pause, the sound of something being poured, Malisa's footsteps across the room. I walked a careful step closer, willing my thudding heart to quiet as I hid outside the door.

"She needs to know the truth about the Rebels and here, we have the chance to tell her. You should have seen her last night, Pat. The poor girl was terrified. And then this morning, when she asked me about Ciera? She wants to know. Even if she doesn't know it yet."

The journals shook in my hand, Marcos's letter falling to the ground. I didn't pick it up.

"Yes, but too much too soon and she'll close off like Everson did. Patience, Mal. The time will come. You've waited eighteen years. You can wait a few more days. Give her that much. Don't forget how new this all is to her. The service isn't for two weeks. There's still plenty of time."

"I know, but doesn't it wreck you to be with her every day and not say anything?"

Any answer Pat might have given was blocked out by the

thudding pulse in my ears. The black spots dancing around the edges of my vision didn't help my concentration any either.

Breathe, Alina. Focus.

But on what? Their faded lounge? The carpet long since flattened by an abundance of foot traffic? The scuff along the edge of my shoe which I hadn't been able to get off no matter how many times I wiped it? Their *truth*?

Not a chance. I didn't want their truth. Not their home, not their family, certainly not their Rebel friends who they were definitely talking about. It was all too much already.

But did I really have a choice? It seemed Thoraben had taken that from me the moment he put me in Malisa's car. Thoraben, the Rebel sympathizer.

I could walk away now. Go to my room or back out to the gazebo, pretend I hadn't eavesdropped on their conversation and rebut any attempts they made for the next few days to talk to me. Or I could face them. Confront them. Take control of the situation like Father would rather than the cowering child I felt like.

A battle ensued inside me as I stood frozen there in the musty living room. Stay or go? Confront or cower? The truth or more secrets? And was it even the truth? It seemed Father didn't think so, if he'd walked away from them as they'd said. Or had it been because the truth was more than even he, as king, could handle? In which case, battered as I already felt, I certainly couldn't take it.

"Alina?"

A strangled gasp caught in my throat. I'd waited too long. In that moment of being spotted, the answer came to me.

I should have run.

"Pat, I—" What? Heard you? Have to leave? Am considering curling up in the corner and ignoring the world and everyone in it for as long as it takes for me to find any measure of peace again? Which might be a lifetime. "I was just coming in for a drink of water but I...I don't..." *Think, Alina. You can do better than that. Walk away. Show him your strength.*

"You heard all that, didn't you," Pat said. I stood, silent as my mind screamed at me to flee. That I could still escape this all, even though I knew it wasn't true. Pat put a gentle hand on my shoulder. "Come and sit down before you fall over."

I let him lead me into the kitchen and sat at the chair he pulled out. When he poured cold water into the glass in front of me, I drank it, almost choking on the throb of my heartbeat still sitting in my throat. Malisa turned from the stove, her face a confusing mix of emotions. Surprise, guilt, hope...

"She was out in the—"

"Tell me."

Though the words came from my mouth, they lacked any authority. Father would have grilled them both on the spot, demanding explanations before likely locking them away to wait trial. I sat in a chair trying not to spill water all over me and whispered my plea like the broken child I felt like.

Malisa turned back to the stove, switching it off, moving the saucepan she'd been stirring aside. The spoon went into the sink where she washed her hands and dried them before sitting across from me. I took another tiny sip of water.

"What do you want to know?" Malisa asked.

Everything. Nothing. Could I really do this? Ignore the rational ninety-nine percent of me and give in to the hope?

"You're Rebels too." They both nodded, confirming what I'd already known was true. The irony of the two of them sitting calmly as they admitted to Peverell's greatest crime while I was the one sweating fear wasn't lost on me.

Breathe, Alina. In, out.

I placed both hands on the table, steadying myself, forcing myself to look up at the two people who'd fed me, clothed me, and welcomed me into their home—all the while carrying a secret which threatened my future.

Maybe.

"And this place, it's where they meet."

"One of many," Malisa said, "but yes. For a lot of them, this was the first place they stayed after leaving Peverell. It's a halfway house, of sorts, until they find a new home and get back on their feet. That's why we called it The Well, because we wanted it to be a place of refreshment for them in the midst of what they were going through. And because we believe that all will be well."

"Those people weren't all staying here." It was just Malisa, Pat, and me in the house, with Joha in his apartment or whatever it was above the stables. Trust him to want to stay with his beloved animals. Not that I was complaining, given it meant he was that much further away from me. Sharing a bathroom was bad enough. I couldn't imagine ever relaxing enough to sleep if he was in the next room. He'd probably critique how many times I rolled over during the night, something half the house would be able to hear given how loud the bed creaked.

"Those who live close come back to meet up every two weeks."

"To plan their next attack?"

"To worship God."

God. Huh. I'd read about that notion. Once. In an outdated history book. Laughed incredulously at the thought that people actually believed in some invisible higher power as the source of all life. I wasn't laughing now. It was impossible to with Malisa and Pat staring at me so intently.

"God isn't real."

"Are you sure about that?"

I wasn't sure about anything right now, except for the fact that I wanted to be as far away from these people, their home, and their crazy beliefs as possible. It didn't matter anymore whether they were Rebels or Followers or right or wrong. I just wanted to be back in my room at the palace. Swaddled in pink. Maids at my beck and call. Kenna my best friend. Thoraben my greatest ally. For life to be normal again. Easy. Predictable. Controllable. When Rebels were a threat and nothing more. Not people with faces who met every two weeks to—

"You want me to meet them." The next gathering wasn't for two weeks. That's what Pat had said. That was what they'd been disagreeing about. Malisa wanted me to go. Pat thought it might be too much too soon. I agreed with Pat.

"There's a special chapel service celebrating The Well and the work it's done over the past fifteen years. I thought you might like to come."

From deeper in the house, I heard a door open and close and Joha call out that they'd be there as soon as they washed up. Whoever "they" were. Neither Malisa nor Pat called back, both of them staring at me. Waiting. For an answer, I supposed, though the question hadn't been explicitly asked.

My dream raced back, the emotions it evoked faded but certain.

Yes.

Despite my utter terror at the thought of being anywhere near the Rebels again, I wanted to go. Needed to, almost. I had to find out if anything about my dream could be true.

"The chapel isn't finished."

"Not ours, no, but there are others. We meet together in town every couple of months, meet in the barn the rest of the time."

I couldn't explain the tug I felt at the thought. Joha's fault, no doubt, for making it sound so appealing when he talked about it and my dream for building on that. Against better judgment, I felt myself capitulating.

"They're Rebels." I had to remind myself of that. I couldn't let a building sway me, certainly not an emotion. A queen was not ruled by emotion. And one day soon, I would be queen.

"They're people."

"Given the chance, they'd kill me."

"They'll do nothing of the sort. They adore you, just like they did your mother."

"Leave my mother out of this."

"I can't."

"Why?"

"Because she's the reason there are Rebels in Peverell. Her death was what started it all."

My glass tipped, water splashing across the table and onto Pat, hit by a hand I hadn't even consciously moved. Through a fog of stunned disbelief, I watched Pat grab a tea-towel to mop up the mess while Malisa threw a now-soggy magazine which had been sitting on the table into the trash.

My mother. A Rebel. But she couldn't be. It didn't make sense. She was the most revered woman in Peverell, the delight of my father's heart, still, even almost twenty years after her death.

And then there was that. Her death. It couldn't have started the Rebels. They were the ones who killed her. It was their attack on the palace which had sent her into premature labor.

"I can't—I don't—"

I shook my head, willing away the waves of panic butting me on every side. *Too much. Can't breathe. Fight it, Alina. Fight them. Run away. Hide. They lie. It's lies. All lies. Block it out. Block them out. Hold on to the truth.*

They're traitors.

They're evil.

They killed your mother.

"Mother..."

"Was one of the most ardent Followers I've ever known," Malisa said quietly. "She loved God with a passion people couldn't help but see."

"Rebels killed her."

"Not the ones you know. There were a group of insurrectionists who attacked the palace eighteen years ago, but they were found, punished, and disbanded within a week."

"Then why?" I left the question hanging, certain they'd understand what I couldn't put into words. For eighteen years, I'd lived in fear. Of a ghost? A group of people who never even existed?

Pat put his hand over Malisa's, who put her other one over mine. For a moment, we were joined, not only physically but in a deeper way. At our hearts, maybe. Their compassion just enough to keep me steady.

"Only your father can answer that."

It wasn't the answer I wanted. Not even close.

TWENTY-ONE

"Come with us."

"To a campfire? With all those people?" Nicola had to be crazy. "No, thank you. I don't like fire." Or Rebels. Much as I was starting to believe Malisa and Nicola's claims that they really were harmless. Eighteen years of fear and distrust didn't disappear overnight.

"Come on, I hate that you're missing out. The campfires around here are as much a part of The Well as the people themselves. There'll be marshmallows and stories and no doubt someone will have a guitar and start up some songs. Everyone will be there."

If that was her idea of convincing me, she had a lot to learn. Though the mention of a guitar almost swayed me. He'd been back every night, my mysterious musician, beckoning my heart with his music. I'd taken to making excuses to leave the dining room as soon as dinner finished so I could ensure I was sitting beneath my window when the magic drifted through. The Samsons never questioned my exits, probably believing I had some long beauty regime to complete before bed each night.

I'd decided it was definitely a male playing. Probably Arden's friend Darrick. The two of them often hung out at The Well long after dinner, working on the chapel by torchlight, chatting in the living room or holed up in Joha's apartment doing whatever guys did. It was all too easy to imagine Darrick with a guitar in his hand, blue-streaked blond hair drifting over the strings as he curled himself around the instrument.

"Alina?"

What? Oh, the campfire. "Marshmallows are sticky, the smell of fire is impossible to get out of clothing or hair, and I don't sing. So, no, I'm not coming. I'll be in my room."

Nicola wavered there at the door, staring at me in the hope that I'd change my mind. I wasn't going to, and to prove it, I turned on my heels and walked up the stairs to my room. With everyone at the campfire, the house would be silent—and the bathroom free. I could shower for as long as I wished, something I was begrudgingly learning to appreciate.

Ten minutes later, I was back in my room, clean, dry, and thoroughly frustrated. Showers weren't made for relaxation. No amount of steam could convince me I was luxuriating in my sunken bath. Neither had the scalding water washed away my uncertainty.

Rebels or not, it would have been nice to sit around a fire with friends. I could hear their laughter from my room, see the fire, its sparks dancing into the air.

Instead I lay on my bed, blanketed by regrets, something that happened all too frequently of late. At least I didn't have to add crying to that list of regrets this time.

Mama, I wish you were here. I wish I could sit beside you and Malisa at the fire and listen as you chat and laugh together. I wish...

But wishes were for naught. I couldn't change any of those things any more than I could allay the guilt that my birth had killed my mother.

The nights were the hardest, their loneliness smothering. The noise of the Rebels chatting and laughing together only intensified the pain. Three weeks I'd been here, three times Nicola had invited me to join them around the fire. Each time, I told her I was too tired or wanted to be alone—both outright lies. I wasn't tired, I was scared. But it wasn't the Rebels I feared as much as the part inside me, growing stronger each day, which wanted to be near them. The more I watched the Rebels together, the more alone I felt.

Back in Peverell, I'd always had my maids to talk to, staying in my room till long after I'd fallen asleep. Or Kenna, on the nights that seemed the loneliest. She'd come to my room, or I to hers, and we'd stay up chatting and laughing till exhaustion sent us to sleep.

Here, I had no one. And I felt it. The loneliness stretched out until I physically ached with it.

Go down there, join in, my heart counseled. But I couldn't do it. They'd welcome me, without a doubt, but I couldn't bear the thought that I was their project—the lone unbeliever at The Well. Or worse, that they only welcomed me because I was their princess and they had no choice but to do so.

Forget them. What do they matter anyway?

I kicked my legs around, swinging myself upright. Lying here, listening to my mind fight my heart would only give me a pounding headache. Mother's journals lay on the bedside table. I reached for the top one, certain her life would distract me from the mess I'd made of mine. Only it didn't, because though she struggled with the same things I did, she didn't deal with them alone.

She had Father. And she had her god, the one she called Faithful One. Over and over, she talked to him in the pages of her journal, moving from recounting her day to thanking him for it in what felt like the same breath. As if every entry was not only the story of her life but a letter to this god she loved. Malisa hadn't been making up stories when she told me Mother had believed in god. The proof was in front of me, on every page.

> *February 21*
> *I worry about Everson. Though he claims he be-*
> *lieves, I wonder sometimes if he truly knows you.*
> *It is as if he believes you exist and that you are*
> *King but not that you love him. Does he keep you*
> *at a distance out of fear? A lack of knowledge? Or*

has he simply never known your touch in his life?
Oh, Faithful One, I pray you would reach out and
touch his heart. Break through the pain and barri-
ers he's put up to hold you at bay and reach in
with a love he cannot ignore. The love that encom-
passes one's whole being and leaves them ever
hungry for more. I know it would only take one
glimpse of your goodness and love for him to
change him forever. One glimpse of your majesty
and he'd fall to his knees. Please, Faithful One,
may he find you. Whatever it takes, may he know
you.

I closed the book, throwing it on the bed in frustration. At Mother for dying, at myself for caring, at Thoraben for holding so much back. He didn't just sympathize with the Rebels. He was one of them. I was certain of it now. His secret meeting with Joha the morning of my birthday, his complete trust in Malisa to take me to safety, his updates to Nicola and her family—it was the only explanation which made sense. He would never have risked any of that if he hadn't believed with his whole being that it was the truth.

And yet, he'd never once said anything to me. Had he been afraid of what Father might do to him if he ever admitted it? What would Father have done? Father had exiled every single Rebel he'd found, but would he have done the same to his son? His heir?

When had it become a crime to believe in this god? Mother spoke openly of and to him in her journal, never once trying to hide her belief. More, according to her, Father believed also, or had at least claimed to. What had changed?

I groaned into the lamplit room. Too many questions, not nearly enough answers. Malisa would have the answers. And Pat. Nicola too. But could I trust them? Moreover, did I have any chance of sleeping if I didn't at least allay some of the questions?

The campfire was almost deserted by the time I found the

courage to approach it. Pat still sat there, watching the flames. Malisa stood a little further away, talking with a young woman. A couple—probably Nicola and Arden—sat on the other side of the fire, their heads close together as they whispered. I waited until Malisa had said goodbye and spotted me before letting the words piling up in my heart spill out into the night.

"Tell me about your god."

I must have been crazy. There was no other explanation for the fact that I was on my way to a meeting of Rebels—of my own volition. And I didn't even feel nervous.

The butterflies I'd long ago made peace with still fluttered about my stomach, but they didn't bat at the sides with a desperate need to escape as they usually did. They danced. With excitement.

Pat pulled up to the front of a warehouse. Plain, brick, unadorned except for a sign over the door proclaiming rugs for sale. A few of the butterflies dropped in disappointment. I'd wanted more. Something beautiful. Classic. Towering, large windows, ornate brickwork. Something which would inspire the same emotions I'd felt in that dream. Not this.

"This is it?" I asked when he opened my door to help me out. "A textile warehouse?"

"It's a central place for a lot of us and has the room."

"It's not about the building. Joha said that."

"Wise kid," Pat said, quirking his eyebrows along with his grin. "You ready?"

I looked out the window at the building, considering. Was I? I'd thought so but now that I was here, I wasn't so sure. It wouldn't have been the first time I'd allowed my emotions to rule my decisions, to both my own detriment and that of those around me. I was, quite literally, walking into a room full of my father's greatest enemies. And all because of what? A feeling in a dream? The still fragile belief that Malisa and Pat could be trusted?

It made no sense, but I had to go in. Hearing the Samsons talk about their god last night—my mother's god—made me want to meet others like them. Father hadn't allowed me or Kenna to attend the trials, claiming them too alarming for our delicate sensibilities. Could the real reason have been that he didn't want us to know the truth? That these weren't criminals at all?

Malisa certainly didn't seem like a criminal, nor the kind-hearted Pat. Joha didn't like me much but he hadn't tried to hurt me, and Nicola had been only thirteen when Father exiled her. I'd wondered all along if she'd truly been as corrupt as Father had said.

Now, crazy as it seemed, I had the chance to decide for myself. Meet some of them, if courage didn't fail me. If I ever got out of this car. *If they wanted to hurt you, they would have done so already. Remember the dream.*

"I'm ready."

Though he didn't say anything, Pat's expression of approval as he handed me out of the car was as proud as a father's would have been. It held me steady as I walked with him and Malisa through the doors, down a hall to the meeting room—which looked more like the location of a child's party than the secret headquarters of a criminal undertaking.

Balloons had been tied up in bunches at various intervals around the twirling streamers stretching the lengths of the walls. Photos of smiling people stuck beneath them, proving a source of amusement for several of the hundred or so Rebels milling about. Tables of food lined one of the walls, a two-tiered cake with the number fifteen on top of it the centerpiece. Though there were rows of chairs set up, no one sat in them, those already present preferring to wander around and chat.

I recognized Jorel, Downey, Linock, and Emmaline immediately, standing together near the front. Father had been triumphant when he'd found and sentenced them. He'd kept them in solitary confinement for two months before exiling all four of them. They'd been found at a Rebel uprising planning meeting, or so Father had said. Had it been a meeting just like this one? A simple coming together of friends?

"Would you like to meet them?" Pat asked, nodding toward the group.

I considered the question for a moment before shaking my head. "Maybe later." Right now, I just wanted to find a place to sit in obscurity. A wave of gratitude washed over me when Pat walked to the back row of seats, gesturing for me to take one before sitting beside me.

"Where's Joha? Shouldn't he be here too?"

"He'll be around somewhere. Probably tuning his guitar."

The guitar. Had he been the mystery guitar player each night? Not Darrick, with his long hair and fingers, who moved stars into place with his music? Joha seemed too brash, arrogant even, for such beautiful music. "He plays?"

"Sure. Most of the guys do. Considered starting a band once—him, Arden, Darrick, and a couple of the younger guys—but life got too busy and they gave it up. Still play together at meetings though, and around the fire at night. They sure have a talent, those boys. Lord knows, they don't get it from me."

So, all three of them played, and well. But which of them was my late-night date with bliss? My musings were cut short when Joha walked in, guitar in hand. He stood at the front, calling people to come before starting to play. Listening to him, I wasn't certain whether he was *the* guitar player whose music I'd fallen in love with or not but I did know one thing—I could have listened to him sing for hours on end. How was it a man so gruff, both in looks and manner, could sing like that? I was so captivated by the sound, I almost missed the words. He was halfway through a song when I started listening.

> *Because of him, I know*
> *No matter where I go*
> *If he's with me and I with him*
> *All will be well.*

He sang the chorus twice more—inviting the group to sing with him—before moving on to another song. While they sang, I took my time, looking around the group. It was difficult to know whether to be relieved or annoyed that no one seemed to care that I was there. There were no awed whispers behind people's hands or covert looks over their shoulders, no outright adoration or hand-picked bouquets of flowers being thrust at me. They didn't even look at me.

But, though he stood at the front of the group, very few of them looked at Joha either. They tilted their faces upward or closed their eyes, the expressions on their faces much as I imagined mine had been in my dream as I basked in the glow of that feeling. Was that what had them captivated? And if so, why couldn't I feel it?

This time, when the song ended, Joha sat down, Jorel taking his place at the front.

"Evening everyone and welcome. As you can see, we're doing things a bit different tonight.

"Seventeen years ago, all of our lives changed. Following any authority higher than the king became illegal, making many of us criminals with nowhere to go. A group of us realized the need for a halfway house of sorts and started praying for one. Fifteen years ago, that prayer was answered when Pat and Malisa bought a property and dedicated it to the ministry of helping exiled Followers find their way. Not long after, it became known as The Well, making a difference in the lives of almost two hundred people over that time.

"Instead of me bringing a message tonight, I've invited a few people to share their story of how they came to be here and what The Well means to them. Brandon? Would you start us off?"

I didn't recognize the man who stood, nor the woman with a baby on her hip and toddler in tow who stood beside him. The man glanced around the room, getting his bearings before speaking. I might not have recognized him, but the gesture I knew well—make eye contact with different people, making them feel important, while silently wrangling your nerves into submission. If you could find one person in particular in the audience to ground you, so much the better.

His wife's hand on his arm had him sharing a smile with her, and with a gentle nod, he began.

TWENTY-TWO

"Hey all, I'm Brandon and this is my wife, Jen. We left Peverell four years ago now, when Jen was eight and a half months pregnant with our oldest, Maylie. Were it not for The Well, I don't know where we would have gone. We always knew it was a risk, believing while living under the law of Peverell—and one we were willing to take—but hadn't thought much beyond that. Prince Thoraben directed us to The Well on the way out of our trial, and we came. I'd say you have no idea the welcome we found here, but I'm guessing you all do."

A twitter of laughter ran around the room along with nodding heads.

"The Samsons welcomed us in, gave us a place to sleep, and told us to stay as long as we needed to, something we very much appreciated when little Maylie decided to come that night. Here we were, first time parents not having a clue what we were doing or how we were going to provide for our tiny baby, but knowing that all would be well because we weren't alone. Within a week, Followers here in Hodenia had found us a house, donated everything we needed for Maylie, and given me a job so I could continue to provide for our new family. It was a crazy time, but one I know Jen and I will always cherish because of the overwhelming proof of God's faithfulness."

Raucous applause accompanied Brandon and his family's walk back to their seat. Though I admired his courage in standing up to share such personal information, I couldn't join in. Father had exiled a woman on the cusp of giving birth. My own father. I couldn't believe he'd been so callous. What if they hadn't found The Well? What if Jen had given birth somewhere on the road with no one to help her? What if the birth had been as traumatic as Mother's and she'd died? I tore my gaze from the two of them sitting there so contently, Brandon's arm around Jen's shoulder, wiggling his fingers to make his littlest one giggle as another man took the proverbial stage.

"Hi, I'm Lucas and I left Peverell nine years ago. The Well, for me, was a place of hope in the midst of a whole heap of pain. I left behind many of my family when I came and, as much as I wanted to be strong and face exile with grace, I was really angry. Perhaps even wondering if I'd made the right choice to stand up for my faith, if it was truly worth the cost of leaving family and home behind. I stayed here because I had nowhere else to go, but I wasn't particularly grateful those first few days.

"Pat found me one day behind the stable, pegging rocks at the wall and likely terrifying the horses inside. I thought he'd be angry, given the rocks were leaving pockmarks on the wood, but he wasn't. He walked over and handed me a couple more rocks, watching me throw them. Then, calm as ever, he gave me a pencil and told me to write the names of those I'd left behind on the stable wall, 'so I can pray for them too.'

"It was just what I needed—not someone to tell me to get over it or that I'd made the right choice but to remind me that even in my pain, there was hope. It made all the difference for me, having Pat commit to pray for them. He believed there was hope for them, that they'd one day believe, and it gave me the courage to believe also. I've had the absolute joy of coming back twice now to cross names off that list. God truly is faithful, even in our moments of doubt."

Again, that applause. The cheering and encouragement. The next person taking his place as story after story piled up, another person getting up as soon as each one was finished. Everyone else in the room was smiling. It made me almost as angry as the stories themselves. They were all so happy, talking of the faithfulness of their God amidst trial and how he'd come through for them. All I could think was how Father had ruined their lives.

I left Peverell.

They said it like it had been their choice. They hadn't *left*, they'd been thrown out and ordered never to return. By my father. And for what? Believing in god?

He'd treated them like criminals—chained their hands, kept them in isolation until their exile could be arranged, torn apart families, and ripped them from their homes. Murderers were treated with more respect. How could he have done this? And how could they not hate him for it? In that moment, I did. He'd ruined their lives. It didn't matter how many stories I listened to, all I heard was testimony after testimony of one man's reign of terror on his people's lives.

And all because of what? What had made him turn on them so cruelly? He spoke of the Rebels with contempt, claiming them a threat to the kingdom, and all my life I'd believed him. But now, having met them, I knew he was wrong. Weeds in the palace gardens were more of a threat than these people.

How could they forgive him so easily? He'd ruined their lives. Every testimony of their god's faithfulness was a story of Father's treachery. I could relate all too well to the man's story about throwing rocks. Only I wouldn't have been content with marks on a stable. I would have gone back to the palace and burned the place down.

My pulse started to race, though it was fury this time, rather than panic, which set it off. At Father. At myself. At all these people, for being resigned to a life which should never have been theirs. Why hadn't they stood up to Father? Why hadn't anyone ever told me the truth? My hands clenched the sides of the chair as emotion threatened to overwhelm me.

I had to get out of here. They could stay and listen and share stories and cake. I couldn't be part of it anymore. I should never have come.

"Excuse me," I ground out, pushing back my chair. Needing to use the bathroom would have been the most obvious excuse, except I hadn't thought to ask where they were. I headed instead to the door we'd come in, tucking myself back against a wall as I tried to control my breathing.

One, in, two, out. One, in, two, out...

I should have known Malisa would follow me.

"Alina, honey?"

The empty hall didn't offer much to hide behind, even crouched in the dark as I was. What I wouldn't give to be sitting at Mother's desk right now, tucked away in her suite where I could cry and fall apart for as long as I needed to before pulling my courage back around me and facing the world.

Any second Malisa's eyes were going to adjust to the darkness and she'd spot me. At least I wasn't crying this time. Fury didn't leave much room for tears. How could Father have done this? And more, how could they not hate him for it? Hate me. I hadn't felt like an imposter when I'd walked in tonight but now I did.

"There you are. Are you okay?"

No. I wasn't. Not even close. "Father ruined their lives."

"Oh sweetie, it's not like that at all."

"No? Then they *chose* to walk away from everything they'd known? Friends? Family? They chose heartache, of their own free will?"

"No one chooses heartache, but every one of them knew when they put their faith in God that it wouldn't be an easy road."

"Then why choose it?"

"Because when you've known a love that accepts you—every little thing about you, even the parts that shame you so much you can't even speak them aloud—how could you ever settle for anything less?"

Every little thing about you. How I ached to have someone love me like that. I'd spent my whole life hiding my flaws, fears, and struggles, all the while silently begging someone to see them. To see me.

"Come back inside. Spend some time with them. Ask them more about their stories. You'll see. Not one of them hates your father for what he did. Their lives may not have turned out the way they thought when they were younger, but they don't regret their decisions nor hold a grudge. They're the people they are today because of what happened, and I would be surprised if a single one of them regretted claiming their faith at their trial, even knowing it would result in exile."

Get to know them. My mother's friends. My father's enemies. Rebels. Love. Confusion. Peace.

What was the truth?

"I think I'd like to go home." I couldn't face them again tonight, not after I'd run from the room. Another time, perhaps. When I was stronger.

"Of course. I'll get someone to take you."

"Thank you."

Malisa was almost at the door when she turned back. "Alina?"

"Yes?"

"All will be well. You'll see."

I waited in my place under the window for hours that night, but the guitar never played. It shouldn't have bothered me as much as it did, especially knowing the mystery musician was probably still at the chapel service with everyone else, but if ever there was a night I needed peace, it was tonight. I barely held back the tears as I sat, curled up in a ball waiting, unable to shake the feeling that I'd been stood up.

The guitarist had no idea I even listened, let alone hung onto every note he played as if they were my lifeline—some days I wondered if they truly were—and I was blaming him for disappointing me. I should have become accustomed to disappointment by now, but there was something about this place which made me hope. Where, at the palace, a no was a no, here, it was like a maybe. Black and white mulling into gray.

Maybe the Rebels weren't as terrible as I'd always believed.

Maybe Mother wasn't as perfect a queen as I'd always thought.

Maybe the people here did care as much as they professed. Maybe I could trust them with the real me.

My head snapped back against the wall as I thrust that last thought from my mind. I crossed my arms tighter and glared into the dark room. No, I couldn't trust them. I couldn't let myself trust anyone.

TWENTY-THREE

The names were on the side of the stable like the man had said they were—Warren, Glenna, Kasie, Bobby, Daniel, Lissa, Red, Monie—the first and third crossed off, pockmarks around the lot of them. I didn't know why it was so important to me that I find them—especially after the way I'd fled last night—but as soon as I'd finished breakfast, I'd gone on the hunt. Perhaps it was simply that I needed something tangible to hold on to after the meeting had gone so wrong last night. I hadn't realized until it was over how much hope I'd placed in finding that feeling from my dream.

Joha had driven me home. Assured me he'd had enough festivities to last a year when I'd apologized for taking him away from the party. Though he wouldn't have been my first choice of a chauffeur, or even second, I appreciated the silence. Malisa would have talked. I had enough voices in my head already without adding another. Though I told him to go back to the party after he'd let me in to the house, he hadn't, sitting instead on one of the chairs in the garden. Far enough to give me distance, close enough to make me feel safe. My unofficial bodyguard.

"You ready?"

My unofficial bodyguard was currently talking to a young girl half his height. I turned back to the riding lesson taking place in the fenced yard beyond the stable, eager for the distraction it offered. Nicola had said Joha taught kids to ride. This was the first time I'd seen it for myself.

"Um, I think so."

The girl had courage, standing there beside the horse, holding its lead in her tightly clenched hand. Her brow wrinkled beneath the hair she kept pushing out of the way, and every time the horse moved, she flinched, but she didn't back away. I wanted to applaud her bravery, knowing firsthand how difficult it was to face one's fears, but stayed silent, not wanting Joha to send me away. If he'd even noticed me.

"Give me your foot. Let's get you up on her."

I leaned back against the stable wall and watched as he lifted the girl onto the animal, waiting for her to find her balance. If the way she clung to the saddle horn was any indication, this was her first time on a horse.

"It's so high."

Joha smiled up at her, holding the horse steady. "Do you feel like a princess up there?"

"No. I'm scared."

"Do you want to get down?"

The girl scrunched her eyebrows and pursed her lips as she pondered the question, an expression which would have looked strange on an adult but looked adorable on her. "No, I don't think so. Do you think I could just sit up here for a little bit and get used to it before she moves anywhere?"

"I think she'd love that. Wouldn't you, Bluebelle?"

The horse whinnied and nodded her head as if she understood exactly what Joha had said. The girl giggled. I wanted to smile too. Or cry. Joha was so gentle with everyone else. He'd stood beside the girl for ten minutes while she found the courage to touch the horse, not rushing her or growing angry. They'd stood there chatting about what the horse liked to eat, who named her, and whether or not she liked going on picnics while Joha slowly but deliberately moved step by step away from his place between the girl and the horse. I doubt she'd even noticed he was moving, but I had. He'd make a wonderful father one day.

"I can see the whole world from up here."

Joha laughed. "The whole world? Are you sure?"

"Yep."

"Well then, world traveler, are you ready to go?"

"Um, yes. But go slow, okay?" Bluebelle's first few steps were as small as Joha's had been, if not smaller. I couldn't tell precisely from the angle I stood but the horse may have even been walking on the spot. The girl giggled again. "Maybe a little bit faster."

Joha led the girl and her horse around the ring for almost twenty minutes. I watched every one of them, coming to accept more with each step they took how much I'd misjudged Joha.

He'd been rude to me, certainly, but maybe I'd deserved it. For a man constantly on the move, my sitting for hours on end probably did seem like laziness. It had just been easier to stay out of the way of everyone, hiding in my gazebo, than face their censure. Or worse, compassion. And, to be honest, he hadn't truly been rude, just abrupt. And he had saved me when I fell in the river, carrying me when I should have walked. Checking on me later. Not laughing at me, even once. He'd been the consummate gentleman from the second I lost my balance. Of course, I wouldn't have been on the log at all if he hadn't challenged me in the first place.

"Alina will help you."

What? My gaze collided with Joha's. Apparently, he had noticed I was here. And was now walking the horse over to me, the girl having dismounted while I considered my feelings toward him. Was the lesson over then?

"Help with what?"

"Alina, this is Kate. Her mom will be here soon but must have lost track of the time, kind of like we did. I was supposed to meet Arden ten minutes ago. You can help stable Bluebelle here, can't you? Kate's pretty excited about having a real princess help her."

What? Me? Kate looked up at me, adoration in her eyes. "But...I..." Didn't know the first thing about stabling a horse. I looked back at Joha, begging him to understand my unspoken message without me having to spell out my ineptitude in front of Kate. "Maybe you could show us both? Before you go. I mean, you're already late."

"You ride horses."

"Sure, I ride them but—" I'd never brushed one or put one away. The grooms did that. What if I missed something and left Bluebelle in pain? Or fed her the wrong thing and made her sick? A weight clamped against my chest, the responsibility of getting it right—or worse, getting it wrong—too much to bear.

"You ride horses and don't know a thing about their maintenance?"

He looked at me as if he'd seen ducks smarter than me. Having seen some of the mischief Feathers managed, he probably had. I gripped the side of my dress, wrinkling the fabric between my clenched hand as I raised my chin. "That's what the palace employs grooms for."

"You're—" He clenched his teeth together, glancing down at the girl standing beside him. He sucked in a deep breath before letting it out. "I don't have time for this or your lack. Just take her lead, would you? I'll go past the house on my way and call Mom to put her away. Can you at least do that, or would *Marcos* have something to say about that too?"

I took the rope he thrust into my hand, doing my best to ignore the disgust on his face as he spun and walked away. Bluebelle nickered, bobbing her head in his direction as if calling him to come back and save her. I straightened my shoulders, refusing to let it bother me.

"I'm Kate and I'm five."

The girl was still staring up at me, wide-eyed wonder on her face. Was I supposed to be caring for her too? I knew even less about children than I did horses. Kenna was the one who was good with kids, not me.

"I'm Alina."

"Are you really the princess?"

"I am."

"Is it fun?"

"Sure, most of the time."

"I think I'd like to be a princess and wear pretty dresses. Do you wear pretty dresses every day?"

I used to. What felt like a lifetime ago. "Usually. Do you think this one is pretty?"

She touched the skirt of my dress, running her hand down the length of it. "I think it's beautiful."

"Truly?" It was teal cotton, an awkward mid-calf length and spotted with giant orange and yellow hibiscus flowers. I'd hated it on sight, but the jeans and skirts I'd been wearing were dirty, and it was the next best thing in my wardrobe. Which wasn't saying much.

"It has flowers. I love flowers. Especially that one." She pointed to the largest of the yellow blooms. "It reminds me of a sunrise, and Mama calls me her little sunrise. Mama would probably call you a sunrise too, since you have yellow hair like me. Does your mama call you her sunrise?"

"I never knew my mother."

"Oh." Her smile dipped for a second before brightening again. "I know, you can share mine. She's really nice. She makes me cookies sometimes when I'm really sad and lets me squish them with a fork to make the lines on top. Are you sad? Is that why you were standing here by yourself for so long? I saw you when I came in, although Mr. Joha told me to ignore you and look at Bluebelle instead. Your shoes were sparkling. They're so pretty. I wish I had shoes like yours so I could be a princess too. Would you like to come over to my house and make cookies with me and Mama? I'll let you put the lines on top."

"That's very generous of you, but I think I have to stay here."

Where was Malisa? Joha said he was going straight past the house to tell her. Why wasn't she here yet? Little Kate was quickly wriggling her way into my heart, but Bluebelle was getting restless standing still.

"Oh look, there's Mama and Mrs. Samson. It must be time to go. Can I come back and see you another time when I'm not riding? I'll wear a dress so we can be beautiful together."

I couldn't help the smile that tugged at my mouth, nor the way my throat clogged with tears. She was more beautiful than she knew, even dressed in faded shorts and a shirt smudged with dirt. "I'd like that."

"Okay. Bye, Princess!"

She ran off to her mother's side before I could do more than wave. "Bye, princess." I replied, even though I knew she couldn't hear me. She'd called me beautiful. Even in this hideous dress. And, somehow, I believed her. The opinion of a child shouldn't have mattered so much, but it did. I found myself looking forward to the next time I saw the little sprite.

TWENTY-FOUR

The early morning breeze had my arms prickling with cold as I walked toward the stable. The sun hadn't even broken the horizon yet, but I had no doubt Joha would be there. He always was first thing in the morning, and in the evenings and afternoons and any time he wasn't in the fields or working on the chapel. I didn't understand his fascination with the animals, but I couldn't deny his devotion to them. Nor how badly I'd wronged him.

For the past week, I'd done my best to ignore the voice telling me I'd misjudged him.

Every morning, when he left for work before the sun was even up, and evening when he made sure all the animals were settled before coming in for his own dinner.

When he made toasted sandwiches one night for us all because Malisa wasn't feeling well, and cleaned up the entire kitchen after.

When he clapped Darrick on the back and helped him unload an entire truck bed full of timber and bricks.

When he looked with such pride on Kate, sitting atop Bluebelle.

When I turned to find him standing behind me in the kitchen one day and got such a fright, I knocked a glass vase filled with flowers onto the floor—and he didn't say a word. Just walked over to a cupboard, pulled out a dustpan, and started cleaning up the mess.

He might have dressed like a scarecrow and smelled like a stable, but under the surface, he was a good man. One I could respect, and one who deserved an apology.

We could start over. That would be nice. Be friends, even. Maybe I'd let him show me how to milk a cow.

My stomach rolled over. *Well, not a cow. Not yet, but feed one of the calves? I could start with that. Work my way up. Or, uh, down...*

I pushed open the stable door, holding a hand to my nose as the stench of horses and their byproducts hit me in the face.

You can do this, Alina. No, you have to do this. You were wrong. Don't be such a snob that you can't admit it.

My eyes watered. Was the stench always this bad first thing in the morning? Maybe I should have chosen a different place to offer my apology. But no, I wanted to speak with him alone and I might not get another chance. It had to be now.

"Joha?" My whisper sounded overly loud in the otherwise silent morning. He didn't answer. I was about to try again when I spotted the top of his hat peeking out above one of the end stalls. I fought the voice inside telling me it wasn't worth the embarrassment of apologizing and walked toward him, rehearsing in my mind what I was going to say. It was only when I got within a few feet of him that I realized he was already talking. No wonder he hadn't heard me. He was deep in discussion with someone else.

"Why do the beautiful ones have to be so shallow? She used to be so sweet as a kid, but now? It's like she's a completely different person. All but ignored me at the palace when I was there last. Barely even acknowledged I was standing there before walking away, her nose up in the air."

Was he talking about me? I ducked into an empty stall, hand clutched to my mouth lest any sound escape.

"Poor Joha." That sounded like Arden, and entirely unsympathetic. "Can't catch the attention of a princess."

I glared at the wall. They were talking about me.

"You make it sound like I want to."

"I think you do," Arden replied, his words almost drowned out by the scrape of metal on cement. Were they cleaning out the stall? That would account for the smell. "In fact, I think you like her."

"You have got to be kidding. No way am I falling for someone like *that* again."

"She's not Erynn."

Erynn? Was she the old girlfriend Nicola had mentioned? Clearly, it hadn't been an amicable split. Neither was it any of my business. The polite thing to do would be to leave, before they saw me. Only they were moving now, coming closer to where I hid. A door swung closed, the slide of a bolt locking it. Had they moved on to another stall? Were they still in the aisle?

"I know she's not Erynn."

"Do you? Because you're acting like Alina is the one who hurt you."

"Arden."

Scrape, clatter, thud. Definitely cleaning stalls. Not in the aisle then. I should really leave.

"Hey, I'm just saying, you could give her a break. From what Nicola tells me, she's been through a lot in the past few months."

Or maybe not. First these two, now Nicola. Was everyone talking about me behind my back?

"Now you sound like Mom. She keeps telling me to be nice to Alina because the poor girl is scared and hurting. Sure, she's hurting. Hurting all of us. Of all the places in the world for her to go, she had to come here. I've never met a person so lazy. You know, I feel sorry for Prince Marcos, having to marry such a self-centered woman."

My eyes narrowed, fists clenching. *Joha Samson, you're mean and horrible and you have* nothing *on Prince Marcos. He has class and style and, unlike you, something called* manners. *He'd never make fun of me behind my back.*

"At least Erynn pretended to be nice while we were together. Alina doesn't even bother with that. Too prissy to be of use to anyone and too pretty to care."

Tears stung my eyes as I pushed myself to my feet and ran down the empty aisle. That was it. I had to get out of here. I'd been right about Joha all along. He not only dressed like a scarecrow, he had as much heart as one too. My musings of apologies leading the way to a lifelong friendship flew out the window with the stench of horse dung. If I could have borne to touch it, I would have picked some up and thrown it at him. Horrible man. Whoever this Erynn woman was who'd hurt him, I applauded her. No doubt he'd been as rude to her as he was to me, only she had the audacity to do something about it.

How dare he say that about me? Here I'd been coming to apologize and ask if we might be friends, and he thought I was dirt. No, worse than dirt. Dirt had a purpose. I was simply "too prissy to be of use to anyone and too pretty to care." Heat scorched my face as if the words themselves had been seared there.

So what if I knew more about satin and lace than how to bridle a horse? I'd never had a single person hold it against me before. Peverell loved me. Hodenia too. I was their perfect darling of a princess, just like Mother had been.

I kicked at the grass, almost as furious at myself for letting his words get to me as I was him for saying them. Why did I care what he thought? Prince Marcos liked me. He thought me an acceptable choice for a wife, and he was going to be king of Hodenia one day. He'd never asked me to touch an animal, wear second-hand rags, or be someone I wasn't.

I held my left hand up in front of me, letting the sunlight dance over my ring, mesmerized again by the rainbow inside each of the diamonds surrounding it. *Yes, Joha Samson, Prince Marcos is marrying me. And he thinks I'm wonderful.*

A movement beyond my hand caught my attention. I froze.

Standing a mere three feet from where I fumed was a duck. And no small, cute, fluffy duck either. Gleaming black, with a crooked beak sharper than most knives I'd seen, it stood almost to my knee.

Feathers.

I'd seen the duck wandering about, even laughed at the way

she ran to Malisa the second Malisa or anyone else opened the house door, acting more like a playful puppy than a duck. But that had been from a distance. A long distance. Not three feet away.

My heart began its familiar race again, the nausea swirling in my stomach. I tried not to imagine the damage that beak could do if it chose to charge me. Did ducks charge? Her feathers shone in the sun, smooth with an emerald sheen. She might have been beautiful, majestic even, if not for that killer beak. I could just feel it slicing through my skin. My limbs felt weak.

The house was on the other side of the duck. *What do I do now?* All I could think was how much I hated this place and its animals. Joha included. Forget apologizing, it was his fault I was in this mess.

Move, duck! Not surprisingly, Feathers didn't respond to my silent pleas. I brought my shaking hands up against my chest with painstaking slowness. How long had I been standing here? Seconds? Minutes? Hours? It felt like hours, though with the sun not even having reached the top of the trees yet, it couldn't have been. Surely, someone would come soon to help. If I waited long enough, there was always someone around.

I stood like a statue. No one came.

Arden? Malisa? Someone? Anyone! Except you, Joha. I'd rather face the wrath of Feathers than have you save me again. If ducks were deaf, I could have called for help. Arden was in the stables. He would have heard me. But even a whisper was more attention than I was willing to risk.

Feathers settled herself on the grass, tucking her talons deep under her wings. It should have comforted me, seeing her so relaxed, only I knew the size of those wings and had seen the crook in her beak. She may have been sitting, but that made her no less dangerous.

Five minutes passed. I counted every second of them. Would I truly meet my demise at the beak of a duck? *Here lies Alina, Princess of Peverell, Queen of Hodenia, gored to death by a duck.*

No, that wasn't right. I'd die before I married Marcos and became queen. The morbid thought didn't help.

Come on, Alina. It's a duck. Just a little duck. So what if it has giant wings, talons of steel, and a beak which looks like it could carve strips from leather? You're bigger. And you are not going to let yourself be beaten by a duck.

Another six hundred seconds passed. Feathers didn't move. Neither did I. Where was everyone?

I counted another two minutes before finally giving in to the fact that no one was coming to save me. The duck wasn't moving, and I couldn't stay here forever. I took a miniscule step in the direction of the house. Feathers stayed still, so I took another, and another. The duck's lungs moved further than I did with each step, but at least I was moving. One more step, two, three—thirty seconds frozen because Feathers moved her head—four, five. Two steps more and the house would be closer than the duck. Dare I risk it?

I looked from the door to my position, trying to figure out if I could make it, rehearsing in my mind how I'd do it. *Sprint four steps to door, left hand to handle, right hand push door open, one step inside, close door. You can do this. You really can. You're a princess. You're strong and beautiful and*—I sighed—*a complete fake.* Brought down by a duck.

No. You can do this. You have to do this. Ready, set...

Cradling my arms over my head, I ran.

My hand was on the door when I heard it, the slow clap which sealed my fate. I knew without looking who it would be. I should have just gone inside. Instead, like a fool begging for trouble, I looked back.

There was Joha, leaning against the side of the stable, clapping. I didn't need the duck to gore me to death, I'd die of humiliation long before that.

"How long have you been standing there?"

He shrugged. "Long enough."

My face flamed, as much in anger as mortification. "And you didn't think to help?"

"I thought about it." He walked over to Feathers, picking her up, and cradling her like a baby. "I just didn't think you'd need help walking past a sleeping bird. The way you were acting, one would think you were face to face with an angry bull."

Stalking inside, I slammed the door in his smirking face before running up the stairs to my room. My pink heels thudded against the back of the wardrobe as I pegged them into the top shelf's dark expanse. It wasn't enough that I'd heard his true opinion of me, scathing as it was. No, then I had to prove to him how accurate he'd been in his assessment. Bested by a duck. I really was as weak and pathetic as he'd said. I shoved my feet into the slightly scuffed boots Nicola had brought over.

I'll show you I can be useful, Joha Samson.

"Malisa!"

My shout brought her running from the kitchen, dough-covered hands dripping bits of mixture on the carpet. "What? What is it? Are you injured? In pain?"

"I need your help."

TWENTY-FIVE

"Now, the flour goes in next. Four cups."

I scooped up a cup of the white powder, doing my best not to tip too much over the side of the container. I was quickly coming to realize why Malisa was always covered in the stuff. It floated around the room and stuck to everything. Scraping a knife across the top of the cup, I held it up to Malisa. "Like this?"

"Perfect. Oil next."

I looked down at my hands, speckled with flour, and tried to ignore Malisa's grin when I went to wash them. Again. I was doing my best to change and be less prissy, as Joha so kindly labeled me, but even normal people washed their hands when they were dirty.

Hands once again clean and dry, I walked back to the bowl, adding in first the oil then the jug of warm, yeasty water. The butter knife Malisa handed me to stir the floury mess with surprised me.

"I thought you'd use a spoon to mix it."

"Anything else and I would have, but dough is tough and running a knife through it works better. Of course, that's just to mix it. Most of the work is done when you knead it. You might want to take off that ring before you start that, though. Wouldn't want dough between those diamonds."

"Knead it?"

She wanted me to put my hands in that mess? No way. I couldn't do it. I'd already suffered through flour and oil on my hands—and oil wasn't the easiest thing to wash off, as I'd found out. My ring, I could take off. But what about my nails? I'd have to soak them for hours to get the dough out from under them. That was if they survived that long.

With a sympathetic smile, Malisa took the knife from me, using it to cut the dough together before plonking the whole mess out on a large glass board. I dubiously slid my beloved ring off my finger, placing it on the shelf above me.

Come on, Alina. You can do this. Don't you want to prove to Joha you're more than an ornament? It's just flour and water and—

I put my hands in. It was as disgusting as I'd expected it to be. At least it was warm. I'm pretty certain I would have gagged had it been cold.

"That's it. Use your palms to push the dough against the board and your fingers to roll it back. You'll get the rhythm of it in no time."

"It's too sticky." I held up a hand coated in doughy goo and told myself not to cry. I couldn't even turn the tap on to wash them with this much goop on them.

"Add some more flour. Here." Malisa threw another half cup of flour on top of the mess. "No, don't wash your hands. Keep going. It'll get better. The more you knead it, the less there will be on your hands." I didn't want to believe her. More than anything, I wanted to give up. But the memory of Joha's voice goaded me on. *Too prissy to be of use to anyone and too pretty to care.* I slammed the dough against the board again and again. He was wrong. Wrong, wrong, wrong.

"That's it. All done."

I looked down at the mess in front of me, surprised to see it wasn't a mess anymore but a smooth ball of dough. Had I done that? My hands were cleaner too, though my fingernails still looked like I'd dipped them in glue. "That's it?"

"For now. We'll put it in this bowl here, cover it with wrap, and let it rise. Come back in a couple of hours and it'll be twice the size it is now."

"And then we make it into pizza?"

"Yep. You can help me cut all the toppings."

"Okay. Can I wash my hands now?"

She smiled. "Yes. Wash your hands. You did well, sweetie."

Two hours to the minute later, I walked into the kitchen. Two seconds later, I considered walking straight back out again.

"What are you doing here? Where's your mother?"

"At Delia's."

Joha whipped the dough out of its bowl, kneading the sticky mass into a nice even ball. I tried not to notice how comfortable he seemed doing it. "Who's Delia?"

"Delia Mills. You haven't met her. Lives the next farm over. She's pregnant and just went into labor. One of the workers came to ask if Mom could stay with her until the doctor came since Mom was a trained nurse back in Peverell. She asked me on her way out to make sure you got fed, so here I am."

"How magnanimous of you."

"She also said you were helping, but I didn't think she was serious."

Of course he didn't. What were his words again? Too prissy to be of use to anyone? *Prove him wrong, Alina. How hard can topping a pizza be?* "What do you want me to do?"

"You're actually going to help? Won't it ruin your nails?"

I tucked my hands behind my back before he could see the mess the dough had already made of them. Soaking might have removed the dough from the beds of my nails, but it did nothing to budge the goop stuck underneath them. In a bout of frustration, I'd found some scissors and cut the nails short. The results had been less than impressive. I told myself again that it didn't matter. There weren't any dignitaries here bowing over my hands, and the nails would grow again before my wedding.

"Yes, I'm actually going to help." I picked up a knife in the hope that it would convince him. "Now are you going to give me a job or shall I find one myself?" *Give me a job. Please, give me a job. I don't know how to find one myself.*

"Okay. You can dice the bell peppers. They're in the fridge. Half red, half green. Fill this bowl."

He handed me a bowl from the stack on the counter. I wished he'd handed me the peppers instead. I looked from the bowl to the knife in my hand to the fridge.

"You don't know what a bell pepper is, do you?"

"Of course, I do." I walked to the fridge and stuck my head inside, searching for the mysterious peppers. *Half red, half green.* It was the only clue I had. *What's half red and half green?* The only foods I could see which fit that description were a bag of apples and the few tomatoes which hadn't quite ripened yet, neither of which I'd been asked to dice.

And dice? What did that mean, anyway? Perhaps I'd wash my hands first. That was a good thing to do before preparing food, wasn't it? And while I was doing so, maybe inspiration would strike. *Peppers, peppers...*

"Here."

I spun from the sink just in time to catch the object Joha threw at my head. It was smooth, green and, while clearly a food, shaped like nothing I'd ever seen. Was this a bell pepper? He placed another one along with two red versions of the same on the cutting board.

"Thanks."

I walked back to the chopping board I'd claimed, considering the object I held. I had two options—put a knife to it and cut it best I knew how, which was not at all, or ask Joha for help. Neither option had me smiling.

"Maybe I should cut something else."

"Cut the top off, slice down the sides, dispose of the seeds, and dice the rest. You do know what dicing is, don't you?"

"Of course," I lied, holding the pepper up to try to figure out which end was the top. The stalk? Like an apple? That would be right, wouldn't it? I tried to ignore the fact that Joha was still watching me and gingerly cut off the stalk. When the rebuke I anticipated didn't come, I let myself smile. I'd done it.

"You're cutting it too thick."

Somehow, probably due to years of deportment training, I kept my groan to myself, but that didn't stop me from sending a glare in Joha's direction. He should have known better than to give me a knife in my current mood. I wasn't normally a violent person but then, neither had I previously known Joha. He'd already laughed at me for not knowing what a bell pepper was to start with.

How was I supposed to have known? I'd only ever seen them in stews and salads, and they looked nothing like the oddly shaped thing Joha passed me. Even that was giving him more grace than he deserved. If I hadn't been watching, it would have hit me in the head. And he would have laughed.

I will cut every single one of these bell peppers, Joha Samson, and I will stand here on this spot until they're done. They'll be so thin you won't even be able to tell if they're red or green.

"That's too thin."

Placing my knife neatly beside the board, I walked out of the kitchen.

Dear Marcos,
       You have to come and save me. Please. I can't
   live like this a day longer. Pat and Malisa, the
   owners of the place and my current guardians, are
   nice enough but their son—

A knock at the door of my bedroom interrupted my self-imposed sulk. I dared it to be Joha, having spent the past hour planning exactly what I would say to him. None of it kind. None of it appropriate language for a princess. *Too prissy to be of use to anyone and too pretty to care.* Well, I cared. And look where it had gotten me.

"Come in."

It wasn't Joha who opened the door. It was Malisa. My bravado faltered at the look of concern on her face. "Are you okay, sweetie? Joha told me what happened. I'm sorry I wasn't there to help you. In my rush to go, I forgot to tell Joha you'd never been in a kitchen before."

"It's fine. I'm fine."

"I'd understand if you weren't, you know. Joha said you looked pretty upset when you left."

She said it like he cared. "Did he also mention he all but told me I was a complete waste of space? Three times. In one day."

"He said that?"

I closed my eyes against the anger. It would serve him right if I lied and said yes. But I couldn't do it. Why had I thought I could impress him? "Not in those words exactly, but I don't have to be able to read his mind to know he was thinking it."

"Oh, sweetie." Malisa walking inside, claiming the edge of the bed for her seat. "I'll talk to him. I don't think it's you he's upset with."

"Sure seems like it." I closed the blank journal, trapping Marcos's letter inside. A creak came from the other side of the room as Malisa shifted on the bed, making herself a little more comfortable.

"Can I be honest with you?" she asked.

I nodded. Everyone else certainly had no qualms doing so.

"I think you remind him of Erynn."

"His old girlfriend?" Really? That was his problem with me? All this time I'd thought it was me he hated when, really, he was just mad at someone else? And he thought I was the immature one.

Malisa nodded. "She was first girl he loved, if it truly was love. A reporter, and a very good one from what Joha said. She was a lot like you—stunningly beautiful, never a hair out of place, lived in her heels and designer clothes. Joha met her on a rare week away with friends and fell hard and fast. He'd travel the two and a half hours into the city every second weekend to see her.

"They'd been together for six months when he proposed, having spent almost all of his savings on a ring fit for his designer girl. She laughed in his face. From the scant bit of information I dragged out of Joha—and believe me, wrangling a calf from its mother is easier—she'd only gone out with him in the first place on a dare from a friend."

"Truly?" Such information should have made me feel better, Joha getting what he deserved. Only no one deserved that. How did one even come back from something like that? I would have hidden away for years after such humiliation. No wonder he was so bitter.

"He sold the ring for far less than he'd bought it, came home, and threw himself into the farm and the chapel build. That overnight trip we took to see Ben and Kenna last month was the first time he's been away from The Well since. That girl really hurt Joha and, unless I miss my guess, he determined the second you arrived that you'd be just as shallow as she was. He's wrong, you know."

"About Erynn?"

"About you. You're beautiful, sure, but you're nothing like her. Give Joha time, he'll see that just as surely as the rest of us have."

It had been almost a month already. How much time did a person need? "I guess I can try."

"Thanks. I know he's been tough on you, but I think the two of you could be good friends."

Nicola had said the same thing. I'd even begun to believe it, until today when his words had crushed that hope from diamonds to dirt. "Maybe."

Malisa stood, smoothing the bedspread back to perfection before smiling at me. "Are you hungry? There's pizza. And Joha's gone back to work so it'll just be the two of us."

I was hungry, but—

"Or if you don't want pizza, there's some leftover roast from last night's dinner which would go well on sandwiches."

"A sandwich would be lovely. Oh, how is Dana? Was that her name? The neighbor you went to help?"

"Delia, and she's good. False alarm, it turns out. I left her eating cheesecake while moaning about the fact that this baby is never going to come out. Speaking of which, we should make one of them next."

"A...baby?"

Malisa's laugh jiggled her whole body. "No, sweetie," she said when she finally caught her breath. "A cheesecake. I have a great recipe for one. No baking, messy hands, or peppers involved. And I promise, I'll be by your side the whole time this time."

Cheesecake? I loved cheesecake. Against better judgment, I felt myself capitulating. "I don't suppose it's chocolate?"

"Mmm-hmm. And caramel."

TWENTY-SIX

Did the Samsons always eat their dinner this slow? I'd never noticed it before, but my plate had been empty for ten minutes already. My stomach rolled, likely as much from the food I'd barely chewed in my haste to swallow as it was the nervous anticipation.

"Arden said he'd be by later to talk with you," Malisa told Pat. "Did I tell you that already? Around seven, I think he said."

"Is he all right?"

"Far as I know."

"Maybe he's finally gotten around to realizing he's in love with Nicola," Joha offered with a half-grin.

I should have been interested in the conversation bouncing back and forth across the table—especially since it involved Nicola and the man she was hopelessly in love with—but all I could think about was the chocolate cheesecake drizzled with caramel sauce sitting in the kitchen. Would it hold together when I released it from its tin, or collapse in a soggy heap? And if it did hold together, would they like it? Would the three slowest eaters in the universe ever get around to finishing their dinners so I could find out?

Joha put the final bite of chicken into his mouth, chewing it as he stood. "If you'll all excuse me, I have to check on Knight. He was a bit fussy when I put him away earlier."

"But—" I clamped my mouth shut around the word, holding back my protest. It still caught Malisa's attention.

"Oh, that's right. You can't go yet, Alina made dessert."

Joha let out a laugh. "Alina baked? Thanks, but if it's all the same to everyone else, I'd rather live to see tomorrow. I'll pass."

There was silence for a space of seconds before my chair clattered on the floor. Tears pricking at my vision, I didn't even stop to pick it up before running from the room. Not even wearing donated clothing had humiliated me as much as Joha had right then. I'd spent two hours making that cheesecake, following Malisa's recipe to perfection, and the rest of the afternoon stressing about it. It was the first thing I'd ever truly made all by myself—and in one single laugh, Joha had shattered every bit of pride it had given me.

A rush of night air cooled my tear-soaked cheeks as I wrenched open the back door, stumbling out into the darkness. Neither the door nor the walls could contain Malisa's angry voice, spilling out into the night.

"Joha Samson, how dare you!"

"What? It was a joke."

"Not to her. She worked hard on that cake, and you will give her the respect of trying it. *After* you apologize. And it had better be a good apology because rudeness like that is inexcusable."

"Fine."

I wiped the tears from my face with a sleeve and tucked myself in against the side of the house, fortifying myself for the storm which was to come. Joha might have been a grown man, but he wouldn't dare disobey his mother when she used that voice.

Sure enough, the door slammed open, his familiar frame appearing in the doorway as he searched for me. I stayed silent, refusing to make his search any easier. It didn't take him long. Three large strides and he was in front of me, though his face looked anything but contrite. I crossed my arms and waited.

"I'm sorry," he finally said. "I shouldn't have said that. You just get on my nerves."

"So it's my fault you're rude?"

"No, that's not what I meant. Look, I'm sure you're nice and the sweet princess everyone else thinks you are—"

"But not you."

His silence was an answer in itself. I looked up at the night sky, searching for stars through the tears which continued to well. After talking with Malisa this afternoon, I'd actually considered forgiving him for his insensitive remarks in the stable. And for his behavior making pizza. Even for his comment regarding my baking. Any man who proposed to the woman he loved only to have her laugh in his face deserved a bit of grace.

But the man couldn't even apologize without being rude.

"I thought as much. 'Too prissy to be of use to anyone and too pretty to care.' Isn't that what you told Arden? Guess you have me all figured out."

"Alina—"

"Save it. I don't need your apology any more than I do your pity or disdain. Just go away. Please."

"I really am sorry."

"I said go. I meant it."

"You're not—"

I didn't even bother opening my mouth this time, my glare saying everything I needed to say. He held up his hands in surrender and backed away, leaving me standing alone in the darkness. Right where I wanted to be. Alone to be strong and make a statement and—Who was I kidding? I was sulking. Mrs. Adeline would have pulled me up for it and, no doubt, Malisa also.

I'd been so excited about that cheesecake. Though I hadn't tasted it finished, I had licked a spot of mixture off the edge of the bowl, the cream coating every taste bud I possessed with chocolatey goodness.

But more than just the taste, it had looked beautiful. Smooth across the top with lashings of caramel sauce drizzled over, it could have come from the palace kitchens and been complimented by the king. And not just because he was my father and had to like it.

I'd wanted Joha to like it. I hadn't realized how much until he'd made that comment. I cared whether Malisa and Pat liked it too, but I hadn't hung my whole heart on their opinions like I had Joha's. They would have been judging the cheesecake. Joha judged me.

And, much as I hated it, I wanted to impress him. I ached to impress him. I wanted to hear him, just one time, tell me I'd done a good job. He told everyone else enough.

You're doing great, he'd told Kate over and over again as she rode Bluebelle around the ring that first time. *You've found a true treasure,* he'd told Arden, in front of Nicola. He even complimented Feathers, terror that that stupid duck was.

It didn't seem to matter who he was talking to, Joha had a word of encouragement for everyone. Except me. Me, he held to a higher standard. One I already knew I'd never measure up to. And yet, I still tried. It shouldn't have mattered. I hated him. His opinion should have meant nothing to me.

Instead, it meant everything.

Nicola and Arden came over after dinner along with Darrick and a few other friends. I escaped to my room before they could ask me to join them. I'd woken before dawn with such great hopes, only to have them dashed against rocks of pain and humiliation time and time again today. It wasn't a lack of sleep which drew me to my bed but rather a weariness reaching to my bones.

Marcos, please. Thoraben, even. Someone, come save me from this place.

I was almost asleep when I heard it—the music. *My* music. I would recognize that guitar playing anywhere. After six nights of silence, he was playing again. And this time, I couldn't let him go. I had to know who he was. Had to tell him how deeply he'd impacted me.

My heart thumped in time with the music as I wrenched my hair into a ponytail and pulled on some jeans. My hand shook on the doorknob. Was I really doing this? The mystery musician had been a dream in my heart for almost four weeks now. If I walked down those stairs, the dream would be forced into reality. What if it was Darrick whose music had captured my heart?

What if it wasn't?

The music stopped.

"No." The word tore from my throat before I could hold it in. I couldn't miss him. Dream man or not, I had to know who he was. Or she. It could be Malisa. Nicola even. I ran down the stairs into the brightly lit living room, my gaze skittering from person to person searching for my musician until they landed on the only person in the vicinity holding a guitar.

It wasn't a she.

It was a he. And he wasn't tall. Neither were his eyes blue—dark, light, or otherwise.

Even without being close enough to see, I knew. I'd seen them before. They were green. As green as they'd been the day he rescued me from the river, after daring me to go in in the first place.

"It's you."

Tears started running down my face. I swiped them away, but to my horror they kept coming. Sobs quickly followed. I walked straight back up the stairs, throwing myself into bed as I wept into my folded arms. I'd found him. I'd finally found him. Only it wasn't supposed to be him.

It wasn't supposed to be Joha.

TWENTY-SEVEN

My rubber boots were too big. Still, there was something unexpectedly satisfying about stomping around in them, knowing not a single speck of the mud or apple rotting on the ground could touch my feet, and something beautiful about picking apples on such a clear day. A breeze blew through the branches, asking the leaves to dance in a ball of their own. Kate was coming over later, come to visit with Malisa and I while her mom enjoyed a couple of child-free hours, but for now, this bliss-filled moment, I was alone. And happily so. Yesterday had been one disaster after another. If I could avoid anyone and everyone today—Malisa and Kate aside—I would be one happy princess.

I tugged an apple from its hold in the tree, placing it in the bucket at my feet before searching out another one. The apples themselves weren't hard to find, every branch holding several with what seemed like hundreds more scattered across the ground. It was the finding of perfection that proved a challenge.

Malisa had promised she'd teach Kate and me to make apple pie using the recipe which had been Mother's favorite. If we were going to make an apple pie using such a special recipe, every piece of fruit in it was going to be perfect. No spots, no odd shapes, certainly no bugs or bruises.

I pushed aside a branch, ducking my head to see past it. There. A cluster of three fruits, almost glistening in their perfection. And just out of my reach. I pulled at some leaves in the hope that the branch would lower enough for me to grab the apples, but the leaves came off in my hand. I reached up again, stretching as high as I could. My fingers grazed their red skin but weren't quite long enough to grasp them.

"Want some help?"

A sweat-stained hat ducked its way into my vision, sitting on the head of the last person I wanted to see. Ever again. Especially after the fool I'd made of myself last night. What was it with Joha that he kept turning up everywhere? Sure, he lived here, but he had horses to train, a farm to run, and a chapel to build. Why did he insist on irritating me? Hadn't he gotten the message that I didn't want him around?

"No." A twang in my stomach reminded me how rude such an answer was. I ignored it and walked to the other side of the tree. "Go away."

"I brought a ladder."

I picked up the half-filled bucket and moved two trees down. Joha picked one of the three perfect apples I'd been trying to reach and took a bite of it before following me.

"I'm not leaving. So you might as well let me help."

"I don't want help. Especially not from you."

"Of course you don't. You're prickly, perfect Alina, terrified someone might get close enough to see your flaws. But, unfortunately for the both of us, you're also the princess with a brother who'd happily kill me if anything happened to you. You shouldn't be in any danger here, but if a reporter could get to you at the palace, someone eager enough could get to you anywhere. Until Mom gets here, you're stuck with me."

I crossed my arms. He was right, much as I hated to admit it. "Fine." I picked two apples, putting one in the bucket and the other on the ground. "And I'm not prickly, or perfect."

"So I see." He pointed to the apple I dropped. "You missed."

"I meant to. It had spots."

"Which will come off when you peel it."

I stared at him, my forehead wrinkling in confusion.

"You take the skin off the apples to make pie," he said. "That's what you're making, isn't it? Didn't you know?"

I pursed my lips, biting back a cry of frustration. No, I didn't know. I didn't know anything about cooking apple pie, or pizza, or any other type of meal. I didn't know what dicing was or how to wash my own clothes or why on earth it mattered that this man think me anything more than a complete fool. I was the princess. He was a stable boy turned amateur builder. He had nothing on me. And yet I was the one constantly coming off second best.

The ladder clunked against the trunk of the tree. In two strides and one leap, he was halfway up it, straddling one of the thick branches as he reached for another cluster of apples. I would have had to be made of marble not to appreciate his skill. Marble, I was not.

An attack of butterflies pirouetted in my stomach. I sent them away with a reminder that he was the same man who'd laughed at my ineptitude, called me useless, and crushed me last night with his words before offering the worst apology in the history of man. He might as well have thrown the cheesecake at my face. It would have been just as mortifying, but at least I would have had the chance to taste it. It had been gone this morning when I came down for breakfast. I didn't ask whether it had been eaten or thrown out. My shattered ego didn't want to know.

"Want to come up?"

I almost laughed before realizing Joha was serious. Crazy too, apparently, though that shouldn't have surprised me. "Me? Climb a tree?"

"Sure. Have you done it before?"

An insect of some kind buzzed near my nose. I flicked it away. "Princesses don't climb trees."

"That written in a manual somewhere?"

It might as well have been with as many times as I'd heard it said during my childhood. Every time we'd gone on a picnic or played outside, I'd asked.

"Come on. I'll help you. There's a couple of branches that twist around each other up here to form a pretty decent seat."

The bliss of the day around me belied the war of what-ifs inside me. What if I fell? What if someone saw me? What if I got stuck up there? What if Joha failed me? Again. But then, another—what if I loved it? Hadn't I always wondered as a child what the world would look like from the top of a tree?

It was that realization that had me putting a hand on the trunk, testing its strength, ignoring the ladder on the other side. I *wanted* to climb the tree—without the ladder. Wanted to know what it would be like to sit on a branch, hidden from the world by a cavern of leaves and—more—know that I'd been courageous enough to do it. Even if I had to trust Joha to do it.

I nodded up at Joha, not sure I could find a voice to talk with what felt like half of my stomach stuck in my throat. Was I really doing this?

"One hand on that branch and the other on that one," Joha instructed, pointing them out in turn. "Right foot into that crevice there. See it? Near your knee?"

My oversized boot fell off when I lifted my foot. I reached around for it, trying to slide my foot back in before he noticed the holes in my sock. My faced heated when Joha told me not to worry about it. "Leave the other one there too. It'll be easier to climb without them."

"But my socks..." Already threadbare, the bark would rip them apart.

"I'll personally buy you some new ones."

That was an offer too good to pass up. And he was right. It was much easier to slide my foot into the crevice he'd pointed out without the cumbersome boot around it. From there, it was easier than I expected to part pull, part push myself upward. I'm certain I looked like a complete fool, grinning like I was, but the satisfaction of having done even that much felt like absolute bliss. I'd done it. I'd climbed a tree. So what if I was only a foot and a half off the ground? It was more courage than I'd shown in a long time.

"What next?" I asked.

Joha climbed one branch higher, settling himself on another

perch before pointing out my next hand and foothold. Giddy, I took another step up. Then another, copying his movements.

Before I knew it, I was perched on the branch-made seat he'd mentioned, sheathed amongst the leaves, the world and its worries unable to penetrate this bubble of peace. I looked up, turning my face to where the sunlight peeked through. So many shades of green.

"So, how does it feel?"

I shook my head, smile still firmly on my face. There were no words. One day in the future, when Marcos and I had a daughter old enough, I'd make certain she knew that princesses *did* climb trees. Maybe I'd even bring her here to show her this one.

"You look a bit like a queen, sitting there on your throne. All you're missing is a crown."

The tree's whimsy captivated me. Before my proper side could convince me otherwise, I plucked some leaves, tucking them into my hair in a circle around my head. "How's that?"

His grin was worth it. "Perfect. I hereby dub thee Alina of the Apple Tree." He punctuated his proclamation with a jaunty bow, complete with twirling hand. My laughter mingled with the still dancing leaves. Had I met this Joha before the grumpy one, I might have fallen in love.

Love? Joha?

My body jerked, taking my balance with it. I grabbed blindly at the spindly branches near my hand, coming away with only a handful of leaves instead of the stability I craved. I tried to scream but only a yelp made it past the tightness of my throat. I was going to fall. I knew it. I'd fall and break every bone in my body, if I didn't spear myself on a branch on the way down. My vision dotted with black despite my furious blinking to displace it.

"Alina."

My heart pounded, trying to hammer its way out of my chest, the blood rushing past my ears so loud it was deafening. This was it. The end. I was going to die. Any second now the tenuous hold I had on the branch above me would slip and I'd go plunging the last few yards to my death.

"Alina!" Joha grabbed my shoulders, ripping terror-filled thoughts aside as he wrenched me upright and into his arms. I stared at him, blindly blinking as I tried to understand. Had he caught me? Was I safe? "Alina, hey, there you are."

I wasn't falling. I wasn't even moving. Joha's hands moved to my upper arms, holding me steady as he stared into my eyes. "Hey, it's okay. I've got you." His voice was calm, soothing. Like honey over the grated edges of my fear. I blinked the last vestiges of panic away, grasping onto his words and clinging to them as tightly as I did his arms. "I've got you. I might even forgive you for knocking off my hat."

My vision slowly cleared. His hat was missing. Had I really knocked it off? I didn't want to look down to see. Not that I could have looked away from him even if I had wanted to. This close, I could see the starburst shapes in his irises. His very green irises. Had they always been this green? Not iridescent or mossy or emerald but green like the color of a centuries-old book cover. Gentle. Comfortable. Welcome.

I took a breath, wishing it didn't sound so shuddery. "Thanks."

He shook his head, pain on his face. "Alina, I'm so sorry. I had no idea."

"That I couldn't climb trees? I told you I'd never done it before."

"That your anxiety was still so bad."

"What?" I leaned back slightly, my hand grabbing at the thick branch beside me, this time finding it. *Breathe, Alina. Focus. You're safe. You're in control.* "I'm fine."

"I called your name four times before you noticed just now. It was like you weren't even here anymore, even though you were looking right at me. You'd gone into your head, fighting or something. You were terrified, and I couldn't do anything to help you."

"You helped."

He shook his head again. "I laughed at you with Feathers. I thought you were so ridiculous to be scared of a little duck, but you were really terrified, weren't you? And of the cows. Mom said you wouldn't have gotten over the anxiety as fast as the palace said you did all those years ago. I should have believed her. I just—You were so different this time. Nothing like that scared little girl who came here as a child. But you're still fighting it, aren't you?"

I might have tried to answer had I not been trying so hard to stop my lips trembling. I flinched as his hand went to my shoulder, anticipating the way I usually fell apart when someone touched me. Only it didn't come. Instead, it was as if he shared his strength.

"Alina, I'm sorry. I shouldn't have laughed at you. All this time, I thought you were arrogant, but that's not it at all, is it? You were just trying to hold yourself together. Is it always this bad? Why didn't you say anything?"

"And have the world know I'm a fraud and wish Mother had been the one to live?" I sighed, my gaze dropping to his shoulder. I could have denied it, claimed this was a once-off occurrence, but I was so tired of hiding. It was nice to drop the perfect act, even for a few moments. "A quivering princess might be good fodder for the papers, but no one really wants a royal so broken they can't run a country. Or support the man who one day will."

"Hey." The hand on my shoulder moved to my jaw as Joha moved my gaze back to his. "You're not broken."

My breath caught in my throat again, this time for an entirely different reason. Surely my face where he'd touched it was as red as the apples around us. As red as the lips I found myself captivated by. Lips surrounded by the scruff of a beard which suddenly didn't seem as repulsive as it once had, or as far away.

"I'm engaged to Prince Marcos."

I wondered as I whispered the words which of the two of us I was reminding.

Joha's smile faltered but stayed. "Yes, you are."

"I should go."

His almost imperceptible sigh cracked another piece of my heart and made me wish that, somehow, we could stay up here in the apple tree forever. But that was as ridiculous as a princess falling for a penniless, bearded farmer when she was engaged to a handsome prince.

"I'll help you down."

The slight rustling of the wind in the leaves was the only noise as we made our way down the tree, Joha checking each step to make sure I was following. I appreciated both his consideration and his silence.

He kicked my boots out of the way before jumping the last foot to the ground. I waited for him to move away from the ladder so I could do the same. He didn't. Neither did he look up, his focus entirely captivated by something beyond the tree. I was about to tell him to move when he spoke a single, strangled word.

"Erynn."

TWENTY-EIGHT

A sharp intake of breath had me covering my mouth with my hand as I stood—one foot on the tree, one on the ladder—frozen in place. Erynn? The woman who'd laughed in Joha's face at the thought of marrying him? Here? At The Well?

"Does Prince Marcos know you and Princess Alina are together?" she asked in lieu of a greeting. Actually, demanded was probably closer to the truth, the way she bit out the question. I wished I could see her.

"What are you doing here?" Joha stepped away from the ladder. Only the bottom half of his body was in my line of vision now. Should I come down? Stay hidden? Joha swished a hand behind him. Stay hidden then. But, maybe—

"Really, Joha? You have to ask? I'm a reporter. This is a story, and about as big as they come. The darling princess of one country, engaged to the crown prince of another, dallying with a farmer?"

"She's not—We're not—" His hands moved out of sight. Had he put them in his pockets? Crossed his arms? Was he staring her down like he'd done me so many times? "How did you know Alina was here?"

"I didn't, until now. Thank you for confirming my suspicions."

"Erynn..."

There was that long-suffering tone I knew so well. I moved my head around, trying unsuccessfully to find a gap to see Erynn through the leaves.

"I was at the press conference the day Princess Alina disappeared, to my utter annoyance. Imagine, wasting my skills on a placatory pre-written speech from a girl who clearly didn't believe a word of it. No thank you. But then she fainted and all of a sudden it got a whole lot more interesting when your mother, of all people, was the one to whisk her away. It wasn't all that difficult to figure out she'd been brought here when she didn't show up again. 'Took a step back from public engagements.' Ha. As if any of us believe that story. She's been hiding. Here. With you, Mr. Paragon himself."

Joha let that snide comment pass. I wouldn't have been so generous. Although she'd been right about my speech.

"You've suspected Alina was here all this time and you're only writing your story about us now?"

"No one would have believed me then."

"No one will believe you now."

"Of course they will."

"They won't, because it's not true."

"Still so trusting, Joha Samson. Do you really think people will believe she's been here, all this time, living with a single man like yourself and *nothing* has happened between the two of you?"

"She's *living* with my parents and, as you've already said, she's engaged to Prince Marcos."

"That never stopped royalty before."

Joha's anger was instant. "How dare you."

"What," the woman said with a bitter laugh, "it's not like I'm wrong. She's photographed flirting with a different man every week. She's probably kissed at least half of them, if not done more."

"You're wrong. Very wrong. Princess Alina is kind, generous, compassionate, honorable—nothing like the woman you're describing. She's been through more in her life than you could ever imagine and come through it only stronger and more beautiful."

Oh...Joha...

"Well, that answers that question. You're in love with her."

His scoff was immediate. "Don't be ridiculous. I told you, she's engaged."

"So? You're under her spell and you don't even know. You're a fool, Joha Samson."

"I think it's time you left."

"What, no inside story? Not even a hint of one to make the career of the woman you used to love?"

"I told you, there's nothing between Alina and me. Please, don't write that story. You know it's not true."

"And if I don't write it? What's it worth to you? Money? Oh, that's right, you don't have any. Put it all into this charming place." She laughed, a noise as devoid of warmth as the woman herself. "The Well, where criminals come to find themselves again."

I didn't need to see Erynn's face to hear the disdain dripping from her words.

"Please, Erynn."

"You know, a few months after you proposed, I found a photo of the two of us and wondered if I'd made the wrong choice saying no to you. You're a handsome man, Joha Samson, and were always good for a laugh. But now? I am so glad I didn't marry you.

"I might have been able to ignore the dirt, the stench of horse, the fact that you have no money and maybe even your complete lack of ambition, but I could never love someone so delusional as to spend his whole life trying to serve some higher power no one's even proven exists. I knew when you started telling me about that silly chapel build of yours that it would never work. What kind of man builds a chapel before his own house? It's—"

I dropped down the last few rungs, unable to stand and listen to Joha's character be maligned any further, even at the risk of my own. Stalking over to the woman, who really was strikingly beautiful, I stuck out my hand. "Hi, I'm Alina."

A number of emotions crossed Erynn's perfectly made up face before it finally settled into a sneer. She ignored my hand, turning instead back to Joha. "Alina and Joha, sitting in a tree.

Want to try again to deny there's nothing between you and her?" She laughed, short and bitter. "I can see why you like her. She's a scruff like you. I should have brought my camera. The paper's going to love this. Peverell's pristinely perfect princess dressed in rags, hiding in trees with her new lover while Prince Marcos pines his loss."

With another bite of laughter, she turned on her tall green heels and walked away. Joha's hand on my arm was the only thing that stopped me following her. "It's not worth it."

"But she called you—"

"It doesn't matter."

"But she'll write that story."

He sighed. "Probably."

We watched until Erynn was out of sight.

"And that doesn't worry you at all?" It worried me. Though more for Joha's sake than mine. Like she said, it wouldn't be the first time I'd been in the gossip columns. But Joha's reputation—

"I don't like it, if that's what you're asking."

"Then let me go after her. I'll talk to her."

"She won't listen, and the more the two of us protest, the more she's going to believe we have something to hide."

He was right, much as I hated to admit it. The best—and only—thing we could do now was wait.

I turned back to him, surprised to realize I had to look up. "You're taller than me."

He looked pointedly at my feet. Oh, of course. No heels. I'd always had those three extra inches of height before. I wiggled my big toe, its bright pink toenail visible through the hole. I no longer minded that he saw it, nor that he knew my real height, diminutive as it was. Not after the way he'd defended me just now. He'd called me beautiful, but more than that, he'd called me strong. For that I could forgive him anything.

Plenty of people over the course of my life had called me beautiful. Joha was the only one who'd ever called me strong. I liked it, and whether it felt true or not right now, I wanted it to be.

"Thanks," I told him, even knowing he wouldn't understand why I said it. It was more than thanks for defending me, more than thanks for helping me be brave and climb the tree and understanding that it was important, more than thanks for stopping me from yelling at a woman I didn't even know and making the problem even bigger. It was thanks for seeing something in me that I couldn't yet see—and believing it could be true.

"That was Erynn, my...uh..."

I placed a hand on his forearm, saving him from trying to find the words. "I know. Your mom told me."

He took a moment to let that sink in. I couldn't tell whether he was upset about it or not, his face stoic but showing little else. He reached up to adjust his hat before realizing it wasn't there and rubbing a hand across his hair instead. I crossed my arms before I gave in to the temptation to do the same.

"Before she came," he said, "when you said you felt like a fraud? I know what you mean."

"You?"

"The night you walked out of the thanksgiving service, I wanted to do the same. It was such a relief when Mom said you wanted to leave. I've always liked hearing people's stories, but that night, it was like every one of them was pounding a spear through my chest. I'm the biggest fraud there is."

"You're not a Follower?"

"Oh, I'm a Follower, that's for sure. But not a Rebel. I've never paid anything for my faith. Mom and Dad left Peverell disgraced and branded as traitors, others have left families behind, friends, good careers. You heard the stories. Everyone who's come through The Well for the past fifteen years has had a story like it. They've paid for their faith and have the criminal record and heartache to prove it. And here I sit, living this easy life."

"I should have thought that a good thing."

"Sure. It is. Only everywhere I look are people who've made huge sacrifices for God. Whereas I've given, what? Nothing."

"You've put up with me for a month," I said, trying to lighten the mood.

With a hand as steady as his gaze, Joha brushed aside the piece of hair flicking across my face. His hand rested on my cheek for a moment before falling back to my arm. "That, Alina of the Apple Tree, has been a pleasure."

There were socks outside my door when I came back to my room later. Brand new, still with a cardboard label on, perfectly pink to match my toenails, socks. My laugh turned into a sob as I held them close, breathing in their new smell. My first new clothes in four weeks, and they'd come from the man I loved to hate. The man I wondered when I'd stopped hating. The note underneath them was short and smudged with dirt but as precious as if it was written on Father's personal stationery.

To Alina, Queen of the Apple Tree. Hope these fit. Joha.

TWENTY-NINE

The campfire threw stars into the air, crackling as it swayed and danced. It was as beautiful as it was dizzying. Had it not been for Kate and Joha sitting either side of me, I'm certain I would have fallen off my log seat by now, lulled into a trance by its warmth. As it was, every nerve in my body stood to attention—all due to the man beside me. The man who'd refused to listen to a single word of my paranoid protests that he shouldn't sit beside me. The man I couldn't ignore no matter how adorably Kate snuggled up against me or how worried I was about Erynn's potential story or how interested I tried to be in what Nicola was saying.

"—sure enough, I turned around and there was Feathers, on the wrong side of the duck house door again. She's like a mischievous little kid, the way she plays around. All the other ducks walked into their house for the night but no, not Feathers. I swear she was laughing as she dodged my arms."

Laughter spilled around the fire as others recounted their stories of the infamous Feathers jumping out at them or stealing their food. I smiled along with them, hoping my uneasiness wasn't showing. When Malisa had invited me to join the group around the fire tonight, I'd been hesitant, even more than the first few times she'd invited me. The last meeting I'd spent with the Followers had ended with me cowering in the hall. But the thought of another night battling loneliness and fear in my room while trying to block out their camaraderie was too much to bear. And, though he'd yet to play it, Joha had brought his guitar.

"I have a story, although it's not about Feathers." The hesitance in Arden's voice surprised me, almost as much as the way he stood, uncertain of what to do with his hands. After wringing them in front of him, tucking them into his pockets and dangling them at his sides, they ended up behind his back. "I wanted to share it at the thanksgiving service but, well..." His hands came forward again, his chest heaving in a breath I couldn't hear but felt within me.

"I'm Arden, and two years ago I left Peverell. Unlike many of you, though, I came of my own free will." His face scrunched into a grimace before clearing again. "No, that isn't true. I told myself I'd be completely honest tonight. The truth is, I came because I was afraid. I'd come to know God, made the choice to become a Follower, but didn't have the courage to stand up for it. I was a coward."

He looked down at the ground, staring at his shoes as he scuffed the grass with one. I don't know what he found there, I saw only shoes, but when he looked back at the crowd, there was something different about him.

"I left Peverell before I could be thrown out because I couldn't face the thought of being exiled. My pride at not having a criminal record warred every day with the failure I felt at not being strong enough to defend the God I'd come to believe in. Worthless was one of the better things I called myself.

"And then, by chance, I heard about The Well. They needed an architect and some building done, and I had the skills to do both. I worked here every day for a month, never once admitting I, too, believed. Until the day someone walked up to me and asked me outright—and refused to accept a word of my self-deprecation."

My curiosity over where Arden's story was going turned to amazement as he faced Nicola, pulling her to her feet. His hands finally found a place in Nicola's, grasped tightly as they were. She beamed through the tears dribbling down her face, her eyes never leaving his.

"Nicola, you changed my life. You took me as I was, a fledgling in my faith, and gave me the courage to be so much more. You believed in me when I didn't believe in myself. You introduced me to Pat, who's become like the father I never knew, and to Joha, who became my brother. I was an orphan who, within the walls of The Well, found a family."

Cheers erupted around the assembled group, their applause drowning out Nicola's words and Arden's answering response. It went until Arden held up a hand. He waited until the last few claps died away before speaking again. "There's more." A few people laughed. Arden wasn't one of them.

"Not only did I find a family within these walls, but I found love." Another deep breath. "With this woman." Without meaning to, I found myself leaning forward along with the rest of the group, desperate to hear every word and whisper of the love story unfolding in front of us. There were gasps and then a whole lot of shushing as Arden knelt down on one knee. The expression on his face as he stared up at her couldn't be mistaken for anything but the purest love. "Nicola? Will you marry me?"

I stumbled off the log, the sword in my heart too painful to stay and hear Nicola's answer, though, by the cheer that erupted seconds later, I assumed it was yes. She was probably muffling her delight against Arden's shoulder as they embraced and spoke of happy days to come. Everyone would be congratulating them, asking to see the ring.

I looked down at my ring, remembering the night Marcos had proposed to me. Had it truly only been four months ago? With all that had happened, it felt like years.

He hadn't needed to propose. Thanks to the alliance our fathers had made, we were already engaged. The wedding date had been set. All that was left was to announce the happy news to the world. I'd stood proudly beside Marcos as Father called for the attention of the revelers at the Midsummer's Ball and began to speak. And speak. And speak. I was wondering if he'd forgotten the two of us altogether when Marcos, not only my prince but clearly my savior, broke every rule of protocol known to royalty and interrupted the king's speech.

And then, there on the stage, under a spotlight so warm sweat trickled down the side of his face, he asked me to be his wife. Just like tonight, the crowd held their breath as, heart bursting with excitement, I said yes.

"You okay?"

Joha. He'd followed me, standing a respectful distance away, ever my bodyguard. Only the compassion on his face didn't feel very body-guardish. More like a caring friend, or—something. I shrugged, nodded, slowly shook my head.

The two of us stood there together, watching from the shadows as Nicola bounced on her toes, her face so bright with joy I was certain any moment she'd burst out of her skin. Person after person came to embrace her while Arden stood proudly beside, accepting his own share of back slaps and handshakes.

"She's engaged," I finally said.

"Yeah."

"She's so happy."

"You'd know."

He sounded sad. Maybe I wasn't the only reason Joha had walked over here. Was he hiding too? *Oh.* He'd proposed once too. Probably gotten down on one knee just like Arden had. Only Erynn had laughed in his face.

"She was wrong to laugh at you," I said softly.

He didn't reply, barely even flinched. Maybe I was wrong. Maybe he wasn't thinking about Erynn. Maybe—

"I'm glad she did. We were never right for each other. Seeing her again? I don't know why I ever thought I loved her."

Probably because she was beautiful.

He nodded toward Nicola, proudly showing off her ring. "I guess you're pretty excited to be engaged, too."

Was I? I'd been both ecstatic and charmed when Marcos had proposed, but we'd both already known the alliance was decided. Would he still have chosen me if the choice had been his? We'd barely even spoken before that night. We'd barely spoken since.

"Sure. It's wonderful," I said, my voice as flat as my emotions felt.

"Not very convincing."

"It's just..."

Another cheer rose up around the campfire as Arden pulled Nicola in for a kiss. And another. "Save it for the wedding," someone called out, gaining a round of laughter.

"Just?"

So many fears and doubts filled me I couldn't put a name to them, only feel them like a boulder, sitting in my stomach, pressing tight against my lungs. "What if he snores?"

"Are we talking about Arden or Marcos?"

"Either. Both. What if he snores so loudly I can't sleep?"

"You get earplugs."

"What if he takes things too seriously? Or spends all his time fooling around rather than running a kingdom? What if he prefers brunettes over blondes? Or I hate the way he kisses me? Does he like being the center of attention or hate it?"

"You're marrying a man you know nothing about?"

"It's not as if I have a choice. Our fathers decreed it."

"But you agreed."

"He's Prince Marcos, every girl's prince charming. And he picked me. Of course, I agreed. Plus, he's handsome."

"You're basing your whole future on the way he looks?"

"I never had a problem with it before."

"But you do now."

I sighed. More than I'd realized.

"It's not too late, you know. You could still ask him those questions, get to know him."

And have him ask me the same? No way. I wrapped my arms around me, the chill of the night seeping into my skin now I'd left the warmth of the fire. Or was it fear chilling me to the bone? *You're the princess. Be the princess.*

Doing so had never before seemed so difficult.

"It doesn't matter," I said.

I was marrying Prince Marcos whether I wanted to or not.

And I did want to. He had the build of a warrior, the hands of a pianist, and the heart of a poet. He couldn't have been more perfect if I'd designed him myself. What was I thinking, letting my mixed-up emotions second guess his affections for me? He was Prince Marcos, future king. The desire of every woman in his kingdom. And he was mine.

"Sure it does," Joha said. "Everyone should have the chance to marry for love." He glanced my way. "You do love him, don't you?"

Did I?

"Alina?"

"He's Prince Marcos. How could anyone not?"

I left before he could challenge me again, picking my way through the crowd to offer Nicola my congratulations. I was happy for her, truly. She'd found her prince. The question was, had I?

THIRTY

I'm pregnant. I suspected as much, but the doctor confirmed it this morning. A baby! It's almost too fantastic to be real. We've tried for so long— over two years now of hoping every month only to have those hopes dashed when my time came and I knew it wasn't to be. Over two years of smiling to the press and dodging the question every time it came up of when we'll give Thoraben a sibling. As if every time someone asked that question it didn't shatter my fragile heart again, leaving me, yet again, in tears behind the closed doors of my bedroom.

But, Faithful One, you've given us a miracle. Another child. You promised me you would, and you have. Forgive my doubt. Thank you that you are faithful when I am not. Thank you for this child. Our miracle.

I traced my finger over the messy words, so different from Mother's usual flawless script. Was it excitement which made her rush? Did her hand shake with fear and the enormity of what was to come? She called me a miracle. Would she still have had she known I would end her life? She'd prayed, she'd believed in a promise, she'd smiled when she wanted to cry—all for me. And I'd killed her. Where had her faithful god been then?

I flipped the pages forward, skipping over details of her gown fittings for the King's Ball and deliberation over which events to cut back on now her strength was limited. I stopped at my name.

It's a girl! Three months from now, Thoraben will have a little sister. My heart feels like it could explode with gratitude. I know already what we will name her—Alina, meaning "light." For in giving her to us, you have brought light into our lives. Our little Princess Alina. Faithful One, you are so good to us.

She might as well have thrust her pen through my heart, the way it ached. No, ache was too mild a description. My heart felt as if it bled, pulsing hot anger from my chest to my lungs before spreading out across the rest of my body. My fingers tingled with it. Mother loved me. She'd called me the light in her life. I, who'd been the one to snuff it out.

I spent the day with Malisa today. She brought little Joha with her. He asked why my stomach was so big and seemed a bit dubious when Malisa told him there was a baby in there. I don't think I'll ever forget the look of wonder on his face when he placed his tiny hand on my stomach and Alina kicked it. "Ba-by?" he said, eyes wide open. I'll probably have a bruise on my skin from where he pushed his hand against my stomach, trying desperately to feel the baby again, but I don't mind. There's something so precious about the wonder of a child.

Everson is already in discussion with King Dorien about arranging a marriage between Alina and their son, Marcos, forging a permanent alliance between our two kingdoms, but I can't help but think how sweet it would be if Joha and Alina married one day. Call it the fanciful thought of an overly pregnant mother, but it would make my heart smile for them to find love.

Of course, it will never happen. Alina is a princess and with privilege comes responsibility. I can only pray that Marcos will cherish her as I do, my precious baby girl. It won't be long now until I meet her. I cannot wait for that day, not only because I'm tired of being tired and of all the complications that come with being pregnant, but because I yearn to see her face. This child, this daughter I am already in love with. To hold her in my arms and place a kiss on her soft cheek. Faithful One, bless this child within me. Keep her safe and well.

I threw the book on the bed, stalking to my feet, the pain too much to take sitting down. I wanted someone to lash out at. Preferably Erynn.

Almost a week had passed since she threatened to write her story. Every day since, I'd waited for it. Every day it didn't show, I'd become more tense. It should have made me less so, but somehow, I knew it was only a matter of time. A good reporter didn't let a scoop like that pass them by, especially when there was enough truth in the story to make it fly.

I'd almost burst into tears when Malisa asked after breakfast today how I was doing. She'd hugged me tight for all of five seconds before I'd made some flimsy excuse I couldn't even remember now and fled to the safety of my room. It was as if I could feel every nerve in my body, twenty-four hours a day. And every one of them buzzed like a fly caught on the wrong side of a window.

Mother's journals were supposed to have calmed me down. Only they'd had the opposite effect.

She'd loved me, named me, cherished me—and never got the chance to know me. Had she seen me before she'd died? Held me even once? I'd never asked the details, not wanting to know, and no one had ever offered them. I wasn't certain I wanted to know

now. I *was* certain that any more time spent reading that journal and either my heart would tear in two or the book would.

I pulled on boots and stomped down the stairs. Was it the height of desperation or my world finally shattering beyond repair that I would consider time with the calves a happy diversion? Anything to get away from the knowledge that the woman who'd written this journal and gushed in her excitement over my life was about to die. I'd been so excited when Malisa had given me Mother's journals, wanting so badly to know her. But now—

I sighed when I reached the pen, running a hand over the head of the calf closest to me. Its hair was different than it looked from a distance, more coarse than soft and downy. They'd been on the other side of the pen when I'd come out the door but butted up against me now in their eagerness to be fed. Did that mean they hadn't? Or did they simply hope for more? Perhaps I should offer to feed them.

With a promise to the calves that I'd be back soon—did I really just talk to two calves? —I wandered back toward the house intent on finding Malisa. A car drove up as I was about to open the door, Nicola barreling out of the passenger's side before Arden had even stopped the engine.

"Alina, have you seen? The papers. Here, look."

My heart thudded to a stop before racing fast enough to send my head spinning. For the second time in as many months, a pile of royal scandal-filled magazines was thrust into my hands. Erynn's story. She'd finally written it. Sold it to every paper in Hodenia, it seemed. There was her byline, front and center. Only the story wasn't about me. Or Joha.

PRINCE'S SECRET SON! One paper's headline proclaimed.

WHO IS PRINCE MARCOS'S MYSTERY FLING? Another wondered.

A NEW HEIR FOR HODENIA'S THRONE?

This was the story Erynn had decided to go with? My legs turned to rubber as the buzzing nerves of far too much tension gave way. Joha was safe. She'd left him out of it. Gone with a ridiculous story trying to ruin Marcos and me instead. As if she was the first reporter ever to try it.

One by one I handed the papers back to Nicola. They were lies, of course. Every one of them. Marcos would never have done what they insinuated. He hadn't even so much as kissed me. I, his fiancée. And I'd begged.

It was five papers down that I saw my own face. This creative editor had taken our official engagement photo and torn it down the middle, a giant question mark hovering between the two halves, Is THE ROYAL ENGAGEMENT OFF? I rolled my eyes at that one. *No, Erynn Symonds, the engagement is most definitely not off.*

I looked over at Nicola, still wringing her hands, unable to take her eyes off me. "Oh, come on. You know better than to believe the papers. According to them I've been engaged three times, pregnant twice, and still cry myself to sleep every night over the loss of my mother—all of which are complete lies. The reporter probably saw a boy who resembled Marcos in some way and thought it would make good news."

Or made the entire thing up out of spite. Was Erynn really that desperate for a moment of fame? Still, at least she hadn't put Joha in there. Maybe she wasn't completely heartless. I handed the papers to Nicola and walked inside, weary of this day already.

Nicola barreled in after me.

"But what if it's true? Do you know what that would mean?"

I shrugged. "It's not, so what does it matter?"

There was no way Marcos had a son. He was far too honorable for that. A man who wouldn't even kiss his fiancée until his wedding day wouldn't go out and get a girl pregnant. It was laughable.

"The papers are wrong." I was as certain of that as I was my own name. "This happens all the time. The palace will have the papers print a retraction by the end of today, if they even deem such rubbish worth the effort."

"But it's in all the papers."

"They feed off each other. Really, Nicola. It's nothing to worry about. Please, can we talk about something else? Your wedding, perhaps. Have you picked a date yet? Do you have a theme in mind? Casual? Formal? Indoor or outdoor? Ooh, I'm sure I could talk Mrs. Rosina into designing your gown. She makes the most spectacular creations."

Nicola refused to be distracted. "I can't believe you're dismissing this so quickly. I know he's your fiancé and you want to believe the best of him, but you have to at least wonder."

"No, I don't. It's lies, and that's all I need to know. If you want to feel sorry for anyone, consider the royal publicists and the mess they're dealing with this morning."

I walked into the kitchen, picking up one of the warm muffins sitting in a basket on the table, breathing in the aroma of apple and cinnamon. *Thank you, Malisa, for your love of baking.*

Nicola, frown still firmly etched in her face, had walked back to Arden, hands flying about as she gestured first to the papers then to me. I poured myself a glass of juice. She'd been away from the palace too long. The royal family dealt with this kind of censure all the time. She'd see. Two days and it would pass over, three and it would be all but forgotten.

Arden pulled a still ranting Nicola into his arms. She pushed him away, holding out a paper, pointing to its headline. I took two more muffins from the basket and went back outside, handing them to the couple, taking Nicola's stack of papers in return. Without another glance at them, I walked over to a bin and dropped them in.

"Arden, good to see you. How is the chapel build going?"

If relief could have made a man fly, Arden would have soared. "It's coming along really well. Would you like to see it?"

Leave the craziness of the paper headlines, the tension of the past week, Nicola's stress, and my melancholy behind to escape to the peace of the chapel? He had no idea how much. "I'd love to."

I kept Arden talking about the chapel and its build the whole walk there. Nicola continued to stew, but at least she did it in silence. Hopefully soon she'd let it go altogether.

"And the design? You're the architect, right? Did you base the design for the chapel off another building or create something new? Were there others involved in the process?"

That should keep him going for a while. It did. I half listened for the next ten minutes to him describe certain architectural styles and how he'd overlaid two of them, after deciding against another, to create the final blueprints. I hoped I nodded at the right times since I understood very little of it.

Would the palace take these claims seriously? What would this mean for our wedding? I had no doubt Marcos was innocent of all this, but clearing him of it in the public's eye, were they to be swayed against him, would take months, if not years. There would be character references to find, phone trails to follow, DNA testing. They'd not only have to prove the boy wasn't his, but also that a relationship resulting in a child hadn't occurred in the first place.

"And here it is."

Caught up in my musings, I hadn't even noticed we'd arrived. I looked from one side of the building to the other, remembering it as it had been five weeks ago. It wasn't difficult given how little it had changed.

"I thought—" I stopped, swallowing back the words before they embarrassed me. Or worse, offended Arden. The walls of the chapel still only reached my shoulders. I'd expected them to have been higher by now, if not finished. Not that I knew a lot about construction, if anything, but the buildings at home always seemed to rise at a rapid rate.

"As you can see, it's coming along well. We hope to have the walls finished by early next month so we can get the roof on before storm season."

"It's just the few of you working on it?" Pat and Joha had full-time jobs already with the farm, and if Arden worked as an architect, he likely did too. I had yet to find out what Darrick did, but he was rarely out here during the day. "Can't you hire a crew or some other professionals to assist you?"

"Sure, if we had the money. Pat refused to start work on it at all until we had all the funds in hand for the materials themselves, so they're sorted, but what's leftover doesn't stretch far enough to hire anyone. Other Followers come and help when they can. It's slow going, but it's going to be worth every drop of sweat and aching muscle we have to see The Well have a chapel of its own."

"A lighthouse," I said, remembering. "To welcome people home."

"Yeah."

"Could we help?" I asked, heat filling my face as Arden's eyebrows rose. No, of course they wouldn't want me. I couldn't even make a pizza without ruining it. Why would they want someone with my ineptitude assisting in the building of their precious chapel? "Don't worry. Silly question. We'll go back. Leave you men to your work."

"You're sure? Because you're welcome to stay. The first thing I have to do this morning is move a huge pile of bricks so we can keep going with the walls. It's not a glamorous job by any means, but it would go a lot faster if I didn't have to do it alone."

"Truly? You'd actually let us help?" The resident butterflies in my stomach took flight, hope and excitement unfurling their wings, making me want to bounce on my toes.

Arden grinned. "Come on. The bricks are over here."

THIRTY-ONE

My shoulders ached, my body so tired I was certain I'd melt into the seat if I sat here much longer. And yet, I relished the feeling. The pain. The simple beef sandwiches in front of me—even if it did take twice the amount of strength as usual to raise each bite to my mouth.

My family would have been shocked to see me lugging bricks—or doing any type of menial labor. Joha certainly had been. His mouth had dropped open when he spotted me. He'd promptly tripped over a brick, catching himself just shy of falling onto another one. I'd waited for him to say something, perhaps even send me away, but he hadn't. He hadn't said anything, offering only a nod before turning away. I hadn't known whether to be disappointed or relieved. After a few more minutes, I hadn't cared. Was lugging bricks around something a princess should have done? Probably not, but I harbored no regrets.

One day, when the chapel was finally finished, I'd be able to say I'd been part of its build. Even if it had only been piling bricks in and out of a wheelbarrow. For three hours, I'd been part of something bigger than me. Something which would—hopefully—stand long after I'd died.

"More water?" Malisa asked. I pushed my glass toward her, eyes drooping, almost hypnotized, as I watched the water flow from jug to glass. "And a rest, I think, for you, sweetie."

"I was going to help you with the roast for dinner."

"At this rate, you won't even make it to dinner. Go on. Have a rest. The roast will still be here later."

My mind couldn't think fast enough to formulate an argument against her, or remember why I wanted to. How did Joha and Pat do this day after day? I should have showered before I fell into bed, sticky and coated in grime as I was, but couldn't even find the strength for that. My last thought before I fell asleep was of the calves. I'd promised them breakfast.

I woke with a groan of pain, hardly believing I could possibly feel any worse than I had at lunch. I did. My stomach and back joined my shoulders in their protest as I heaved myself out of bed. *Shower. Now.*

I felt somewhat better after a pounding of steaming water on my back. Enough, at least, to attempt the stairs without landing in a heap at the bottom of them. Falling would have been faster than the snail's pace I took them, even if it did result in more bruises than I cared to count.

"Oh good, you're up," Malisa said, meeting me at the bottom of the stairs. "I was just going to come and wake you."

"What is it? What's wrong?"

"Prince Marcos is here."

She might as well have dropped one of those bricks on my chest. "Here? At The Well?"

"Yes. He's waiting for you in the garden. Said he has to speak with you urgently."

My hands fluttered from my clothing to my hair, as uncertain as the butterflies in my stomach of where to land. Marcos was here? "Why?"

"You'll have to ask him." She caught one of my hands in hers, squeezing it before pushing me toward the front door. "Go on. Dinner will wait."

The short walk outside wasn't nearly long enough to get my racing emotions into order. It felt like so long since I'd seen him, although it had only been five weeks. For that first week, I'd spent every moment I wasn't arguing with Joha silently begging Marcos to come and save me. And here he was. No, *there* he was.

His back was to me as he stood near one of the heavy garden benches, arms behind his back, hands locked together.

"Prince Marcos."

He turned at the sound of his name. All thoughts of Mother, Joha, Followers, and how sore I was flew from my mind as I ran to him, throwing myself in his arms. He smelled of lemon, lime, and something leathery. So strange a combination and yet so wholly him. My heart raced. Whether it was reacting to the surprise and excitement of seeing him or the thrill of being in his arms, I didn't know. Neither did I care. Marcos was here. He'd finally come. Everything would make sense again now.

I raised a hand to his neck, stroking the short hair above his collar, marveling at how easy it would be to bring him closer still. Our lips were mere inches apart. One tug would be all it took.

"Alina..."

His whisper of my name was all the encouragement I needed. Pulling his head closer, I lined up my mouth with his. At the last moment, he turned his head, my lips grazing his cheek before I pulled back, grinning. I should have been annoyed—he'd all but rejected me—only a large part of me had been expecting it. We might have been engaged but he was a stickler for propriety.

"You'll have to kiss me eventually, you know. You can't avoid me forever."

He didn't laugh. Didn't even smile. I let my arms fall and took a step back. "Marcos?" Did I smell? Was that it? Surely not. I'd had a shower, rinsed the sweat and grime from my hair even if my arms had been too tired to wash it. Perhaps it was the clothes. They were definitely not the usual formal fare he saw me in, scuffed and dusty as they were. Though, surely, he could forgive me that. I was living on a farm.

"Marcos?" I tried again, ducking my head around, trying to catch his gaze. My heart skidded almost to a halt when I did. Foreboding crept down my throat, capturing my breath in its grip. "What is it?"

"I'm sorry. So sorry. I never meant for this to happen. I never thought it would—" He broke off, turning his gaze to the shrubs beside us, finding their greenery captivating. I told the feeling of unease tiptoeing up my body to go away. It disobeyed and continued its trek. Marcos had always been serious, but his manner was beginning to scare me. "You saw the papers?"

A snort of a laugh which would have sent my deportment teacher into horrified hysterics burst from my mouth, my uncertainty washed away in its wake. "Sure, I did. Ms. Symonds's talents are wasted on papers. She should be writing novels with an imagination like that."

He still didn't smile. If anything, he became more dejected. What was going on? The answer hit me a second later.

"Wait, *that's* why you're here? You thought I believed those lies? Surely you don't think I'm that foolish. I might be naïve, but even I know it takes more than a handshake to create a child. Tell the papers there's no possibility it could ever be true and be done with it. Better yet, ignore it altogether. They'll move on soon enough."

With a shake of his head, Marcos let out a sigh that set the hem of my shirt dancing. "I can't."

"Why not?"

Another sigh. A cringe. A shake of his head. "Because it might be true."

"No!" The word tore from my throat so fast I wasn't even sure an instant later if I'd said it aloud or it had come from somewhere else. My hand dropped from his arm, hitting the bench behind me with enough force to leave my fingers stinging. I sat, cradling the hand in my lap as I willed myself to focus on the pain and not the thudding of my heart. The all-too-familiar shaking began in my stomach, radiating out until I felt as if my whole body vibrated.

Can't...breathe...

It couldn't be true. That would mean—

"There was a girl. Once." Marcos pursed his lips again, to hold back words or self-recrimination I wasn't certain. He closed his eyes, shaking his head before opening them again. "I was seventeen and furious at my father and all the rules that came with being a prince. She was a friend of a friend who was foolish enough to care. It only happened that one time. We were both so ashamed that we never saw nor spoke to each other again. I don't know if that night resulted in a child. I suppose I assumed she would have come forward long before this if that were the case."

I slumped back against the bench, earning more silent lectures from my old deportment teacher. I swept them aside, wishing I could claim back my innocence as easily. Prince Marcos, a father. And...lover. I shook my head, trying to rid it of the words. The image of him embracing another girl. I wanted him to laugh and tell me it was all a grand joke, sick as it was. He didn't laugh. The lines crumpling his face were pure torture. "No," I whispered into the pain-charged air.

"I'm sorry."

I hadn't realized how high a pedestal I'd put Marcos on until this moment. Marcos, my perfect prince. The man who could do no wrong. He hadn't just teetered on that pedestal, he'd crashed off it altogether. And I didn't have the strength to put him up again. He was the one who was supposed to be strong and hold me together, not the other way around.

"It was her who came forward?"

"I don't know. All Father will tell me is that there is a woman claiming me to be the father of her son. He and his advisors are investigating, of course. How the papers got hold of the story is anyone's guess. Father has told me to keep my silence and speak of this to no one until the investigation is complete. But I had to tell you."

I supposed I should have been grateful for that, but it took all my concentration to keep from throwing up all over my jeans. I had more respect for the faded, ill-fitting denim right now than the man beside me.

"Did you love her?" I was torturing myself asking, but I had to know. He was my fiancé. I might not have been certain of my feelings toward him at this moment, but the thought of someone else having him—

"I barely knew her."

And yet he'd given her everything. Including, possibly, a son.

"What happens now?" My words were flat, far devoid of the emotion I'd always felt toward Marcos before.

"We wait, I suppose, until the truth is discovered."

"And how long will that take?"

"I don't know." Marcos sighed. "I'm so sorry, Alina. It was only one night. One stupid mistake of a night. I never thought anyone would ever have to know."

If his revelation had been a knife in my chest, that would have been the moment it twisted. All around us, life went on as usual—insects buzzed, leaves danced, a horse whinnied somewhere in the stables, the sun dropped its last few inches to the horizon—every one of them oblivious to the fact that I was bleeding out inside. Marcos had never planned to tell me. I, who if not for Thoraben's wedding postponing my own, would have been his wife by now. It was the ultimate betrayal.

"And our wedding? The alliance?"

The silence following my question was deafening, ringing so loud in my ears I wasn't certain I would even hear Marcos's answer if he found one. His eyes were closed, brow wrinkling as he searched for control. I could all too easily empathize. But I had to remain in control, if only on the outside. I had to prove to Marcos, and myself, that I was strong enough to make it through this. *You're the princess. Be the princess.*

"I can't marry you now."

I nodded calmly, though the voice inside continued to scream, every nerve in my body lit on fire. At least, sitting down, I was spared the humiliation of collapsing in a heap on the ground.

"The boy might not be yours."

"Even if he's not—" Marcos ran a hand through his hair before sighing again. It seemed the height of irony that, with everything else falling apart around me, his hair would remain perfect. "I have to make things right. I've regretted for years that night and the way I walked away. I can't help but think this is my chance to make it right. I owe her."

He'd chosen the girl. Over me. Even without knowing for certain whether it was her or not. Marcos looked the same as he always had and yet, nothing about him drew me. Not anymore.

I spun my beautiful ring around my finger twice before slipping it off and handing it to him. He took it without a word.

"Thank you for coming, Prince Marcos. You'll understand, I hope, if I ask you to leave."

THIRTY-TWO

It was difficult to believe on nights like this that the moon's light was merely a reflection. The shadows cast through the trees made me almost certain it beamed on its own. It should have been eerie. Instead, the moonlight welcomed me. Beckoned me to join in its melancholy. I, too, had lost my shine, if I'd ever had one at all. The only glow I had came from what people made of me. Anyone could play the part of a beautiful princess if they had enough stylists around them.

Clothing designers, speech writers, hair stylists, photo editors—the perfection was nothing but a façade. Like the moon, I was simply a hard, dry rock, reflecting the light of those around me.

And I couldn't even do that anymore.

Prince Marcos was gone. Even if our fathers ruled we marry and he became my husband, the man I thought I knew was gone forever. The naïve girl I'd been was too.

I wanted to wipe the conversation from my mind. I couldn't tell anyone even if I'd wanted to but apart from that, I didn't want to think about it. Marcos had been with another woman. Whether it had been one night or a hundred, he had. The more I tried not to think about it, the deeper it planted itself. And the more reality shook me.

I wandered along the path toward the gazebo, thankful for the lateness of the hour and the silence it offered. I'd lain on my bed all afternoon, staring blankly at the ceiling before picking at dinner and skipping dessert altogether. No one had questioned me when I'd excused myself from the table, claiming tiredness, nor had they asked about Marcos's visit, though they had to have been wondering why he'd come. And, just as quickly, gone. I'd come outside, too proud to let them hear my tears through the thin walls of my room. Only the tears I'd expected hadn't come. My eyes felt as dry and brittle as my soul.

My whole life, I'd thought the emptiness inside me stemmed from the loss of my mother and the desperate hope to be good enough to justify my life over hers. Now, I knew it was simply a lacking in me. Stripped of the frills and frivolity I hid behind, who was I even? Take the title of princess away and all that was left was a girl lacking in any skill with no thoughts or opinions of her own. I'd been so quick to defend myself against Joha's criticism, but he'd seen me clearer than I saw myself.

"You know you shouldn't be out here alone. Even a half-trained enemy could pick you off a mile away exposed as you are in this moonlight."

As if my thoughts had conjured him here, Joha appeared in the gazebo's doorway.

"I hope they do."

"Really? That's your answer? After all your family and country has done to protect you all your life?"

"They needn't have bothered."

Joha walked inside, stopping just short of where I sat. I didn't even need to look up to know he was frowning. "What's wrong with you?"

"Nothing."

This time he did sit down, crossing his legs in front of him as if he planned on staying a while. "Clearly it's something, or you wouldn't be sitting out here all alone looking like the world just landed on your shoulders. So, come on. Spill."

Anyone else, and I would have put up my defenses. Smiled. Brushed aside their concern with a flick of my carefully straightened hair. Anyone else and I probably would have gotten away with it, too. But anyone else wasn't Joha, who'd already forced his way through every defense I'd raised. I didn't have the strength to try any more. And my hair hadn't seen a straightener in weeks.

"I wish Mother had lived," I said quietly, finally admitting the truth. "Instead of me."

"And deprive the world of Princess Alina Ciera Georgia whatever-your-other-name-was of Peverell?"

"If it meant Mother lived."

"What about your life?"

"What about it? She was beautiful, caring, confident, full of faith. She could have changed the world."

"And you don't think you can? You don't think God has a purpose for you too?"

"Hardly. You've been saying it yourself since the day I arrived—I'm useless."

"Hey, I—"

I held up a hand, stopping him. "I know. You apologized, but it was the truth, even if I didn't want to hear it. I can't milk a cow or make a cheesecake. I don't know how to groom a horse or put it away. I didn't even know what a pepper was until you threw one at my head."

"I thought you were watching, and you're wrong about the cheesecake. It was good. And I mean, *really* good. I had two pieces before losing a fight to Dad for the last one. You should make it again, but not tell anyone but me."

He was trying to cheer me up, but I couldn't even find a fake smile. I might have been the one to make the cheesecake, but Malisa had been standing beside me the whole time coaching me.

"Didn't I see Prince Marcos here before? I would have thought he'd cheer you up. You've been begging to see him since the day you arrived."

"He called off the wedding." My voice broke on the last word, the tears I'd refused to allow since the Feathers incident breaking through my stubborn resolve. "The papers were right, for once. I don't know how Erynn found out, but it's true. He has a son.

Or, at least, could have. I suppose we'll find out for certain in the coming days. He won't kiss me but with that girl..."

Joha frowned. "Marcos cheated on you?"

This time it was my sigh which broke through the moonlight. "No. It was years ago, before we were officially together."

"Still."

I shrugged in lieu of words, pursing my lips in an effort to contain the tears which continued to fall. The piece of cloth Joha fished out of his back pocket smelled like he'd used it to rub down one of his animals, but I took it gratefully. "I shouldn't be talking about it. He wasn't even supposed to tell me. See? Yet another reason I'm a complete failure as a princess. Can't keep my mouth shut. Feel free to add that one to your ever-growing list."

"Come on, don't be ridiculous. I don't have a list. And you're not a failure."

"No? Marcos certainly thinks so. First chance he has to walk away and he takes it. Claims he plans to marry the girl."

"Some would call that honorable."

"He's had six years to be honorable. Instead, he's brushed it aside until now, like it didn't even happen. He wouldn't have even mentioned it to me if Erynn hadn't forced his hand. She might as well have brought her camera along that day and shared the picture of me in my raggedy clothes. It's how the world will see me now anyway."

I missed the word Joha said under his breath, which was probably for the best given how his hands clenched beside him. I stared down at mine instead, so still where normally they'd be trembling.

"The boy might not even be his," I whispered.

"And if he is?"

I closed my eyes against the pain ripping through me. The fear—even stronger than the pain—that I wasn't enough. That I never would be. And now, everyone would know. "Then I hope that sniper is watching."

Joha's huff would have put his horses to shame. "Seriously? That's how much you value your life? Look, I get it. He broke the engagement and your trust. Maybe even your heart. You're hurt and, believe me, you have a right to be. I've never even met the man and I want to hit him right now. But you're acting like it's the end of the world. Sure, hurt for a while, get angry, throw some stuff, but sooner or later you'll move on and see that this isn't the end. God has a purpose for you. There are plenty of other things you could do."

I gritted my teeth against the childish anger screaming at me to send him away. It wasn't his fault. He didn't mean to belittle my pain. He just didn't understand. How could he? Sure, he'd had his heart trodden on by Erynn, but he'd never stood in a kitchen, waves of humiliation crashing over him at the knowledge that he didn't even know what a simple bell pepper looked like. Or stood beside a five-year-old, wishing for even a portion of her courage. I could charm a crowd and wear beautiful clothes but take that away...

"No, there are plenty of other things *you* could do. I only know how to be a princess, as you've pointed out more than once."

"I told you, I was wrong. You can do far more than smile and wave."

"Like what? We've already established I'm no good at cooking, cleaning, being around children, or anything to do with animals. I can't make my mind remember being here as a child. I can't even walk across a log without needing to be rescued."

"That cheesecake was incredible, your pizza didn't kill anyone, Kate absolutely adores you, and you might remember one day but who cares if you don't? The rest of us can fill in those missing memories. As to the animals, you're improving. But even if you weren't, they're all just skills. Anyone can learn skills. Things like kindness, compassion, and courage—they're a lot harder to learn. And you have them in bucketfuls. Not to mention influence. Just think of all you could do."

I stared at him, dumbfounded. Had he just given me a compliment?

"I'm not courageous."

"No?"

"You saw me in the river that day. And in the tree. And with Feathers. Those weren't one-off occurrences. That's my life. The fear, the terror. It's there, every single day. I might look brave, but you don't see how much I shake inside."

"What I see is a girl who refuses to give in to that fear. A girl who fights it, every single minute of every single day. A girl who has a whole country in love with her smile because she finds the strength to smile and be out there with them even when she's scared. Sounds like courage to me."

I frowned into the muted light, wondering at his words. Wanting to accept them but not sure they were mine to claim. Was that really courage?

A breeze rustled the trees around us, branches scratching across the gazebo's roof in a sound that might have been eerie had I been alone. I twisted the piece of cloth Joha had given me around my hand, tucking it between my fingers before pulling it out again. Maybe that *was* courage, and maybe I was strong, like he'd told Erynn that day under the apple tree. Maybe I was even beautiful, like Kate had said. But none of it changed anything. Marcos was still gone.

Joha's hand covered mine, stilling their twisting. "Alina?" His hand was so warm, fire against my worry-chilled ones. "It'll get easier. I promise."

Maybe. For him. He had work to throw himself into—a farm, the chapel build, friends, his faith. I had family and friends I'd pushed away and a handful of broken dreams.

"You don't get it. If a prince rejects me, no one else is ever going to want me. Men are either intimidated by the princess title or gold-diggers after the money they think I have. I was going to be a queen. Now, I'll forever be the princess who wasn't enough. The failure. No man will want that."

And just like that, his warm hand was gone, wrenched from mine as he stood and crossed his arms, glaring down at me. "You know what? Maybe you are a loser."

"What?" I blinked up at him, silhouetted by the moonlight, wondering if I'd heard him wrong. It was one thing to call myself one but another entirely to be called it to my face. Admittedly, it was Joha, who'd never had a problem with being blunt, but then—

"Only a loser would think so poorly of themselves. See, this is what really bugs me. You have all this going for you—family, friends, girls who want to be you, beauty, kindness, perfect health, more influence than most people would know in a lifetime. You could do anything, be anything, and you're moping about how miserable you are and how you have nothing to live for.

"Are you really so blind that you can't see the difference you make? Just by being you. You have this way about you which just, I don't know, glows. It warms people. Their lives are better off for having known you. I wish you'd wake up and see yourself as the rest of us do. You're...you're...arghh!"

With a growl of frustration, Joha pulled me to my feet and into a kiss I was completely unprepared for. I'd been kissed before, but nothing like this. My hands grabbed at his back to keep my balance as he wove his fingers into my hair, loosening my bun, holding my mouth captive against his. His beard tickled my face, but it wasn't irritating, as I'd expected. More...just...Joha. Wholly Joha. My heart thudded, beating its way up my throat. Joha Samson was kissing me.

If he meant to shock me, he'd succeeded. And beyond. But what began in frustration gentled until all I felt was cherished. His lips brushed against mine, taking every rational thought from my mind and replacing them with a desperate wanting for more. His thumb stroked my jaw, leaving behind it a wave of longing. I could have walked away, I should have, but that would have meant leaving the circle of his arms. This kiss. His kiss. Tearing my heart out would have been less painful.

Long before I was ready, his hands dropped to my arms and Joha pulled away. Far enough to break the kiss, close enough to feel his shuddering breath still colliding with mine. Could he feel my hands trembling against his back?

"Alina." His whisper was barely louder than a breath.

"Mmm?"

With a sigh that said far more than words ever could, Joha dropped his arms altogether and walked to the middle of the gazebo. His gaze when he met mine was tortured. "I'm going for a ride. Please, go inside the house. I couldn't bear it if something happened to you."

I nodded, letting loose the tears I'd done so well to stop earlier as he strode toward the stables. I wished he'd stayed as much as I was thankful he'd gone.

Joha had kissed me. The man I'd told myself I hated all this time. And I'd enjoyed every single second of it.

THIRTY-THREE

For the second time in a week, I watched, impatient, as the sun crept its way above the edge of the horizon before fleeing my room to find Joha. There'd been no point in staying in bed, not with my emotions as muddled as they were. He'd done that. Him and his God, the one Mother called Faithful One. Could it be true? Could their God be real? Could it be he did have a purpose for me, like Joha had said?

I'd always thought myself so levelheaded and certain, at least on the outside. Now, I wasn't sure about anything, except that I needed to speak with Joha. He'd have the answers. Even if I didn't quite know what I was asking.

He wasn't in the stable, nor were any of the horses missing. It was a rhythmic clanging in the distance which sent me toward the chapel, where to my relief I found him, already having raised a sweat despite the coolness of the morning. Had he been here all night? Surely not, and yet, I envied him if he had. I'd tossed and turned for hours, my mind too full of questions and what all this might mean to fully rest. Menial labor would have been a relief, knowing at least something productive was coming from my restlessness.

"Joha?"

He kept hammering. "What are you doing here?"

"I could ask you the same question."

"Working." A nail slammed into the triangle of wood I assumed would be part of the roof. Another followed it, and another. Was he really going to ignore me? After what happened last night?

"Hiding is more like it."

The hammering stopped but he still didn't look at me. "You think I'm hiding?"

"I know you are. You're hiding from me and the fact that everything has changed between us."

"You're wrong. Nothing has changed." Another nail. Another slam of the hammer. This one left a dent in the wood.

"Nothing?" If he hit the wood any harder, he'd crack the whole piece. I hoped it wasn't my face he was imagining under it.

"Nothing."

No. I couldn't accept that. I wouldn't. I walked over to him, pulling at his arm, forcing him to stand and face me. "You kissed me. Are you telling me that meant nothing to you?"

"Don't be ridiculous. Of course it didn't."

Oh.

Right.

Well, good. At least he'd admitted it. "Then it's me. I knew it. First Marcos rejects me, now you."

He took off his hat, wiping the sweat from his forehead before replacing it again. His angry frown didn't change, although his eyes may have softened a bit. Possibly. It was difficult to tell with him refusing to meet my gaze. "I'm not rejecting you."

"Certainly looks that way."

"What do you want from me, Alina? For all we both know, you're still engaged to Prince Marcos, no matter what he said. And even if, by chance, he does have the power to break off your engagement without the approval of King Dorien and your father, I'm a farmer. I live above a stable. I could spend my whole life here at The Well and be content. You're a princess used to ball gowns and maids and the best of everything. It wouldn't work between us. You don't fit here. You never did and you never will."

Tears bit at my vision, but I refused to let them fall. This moment was too important to have him brushing me off as an emotional, irrational female. "I could change. I *have* changed. Because of you and your family and—" *The Rebels. Your God.* For the first time in my life, I felt as if there might be hope and a reason I'd lived. He'd given me that. Was he seriously going to take it away? Just like that? "You told me last night that I could be anything. What if I want to be here? With you? Please, Joha, give me a chance."

"No." He turned back to his task, pounding another nail into the wood. It might as well have been my heart. "Go back to your prince."

"That's it? You're not even going to look at me?"

"It's better that way."

I stalked away before the urge to slug him got the better of me. All night, I'd kept coming back to the moment when he kissed me and time stood still under the Hodenian moon. All would be well, I'd dared to tell myself. Joha cared for me. This time at The Well hadn't been for nothing. I'd found a true friend, maybe even more. I'd imagined walking up to him, running my hand along the wiry smoothness of his beard, and kissing the smile blooming beneath it at the sight of me.

He hadn't been smiling. No talk of what now or if we might figure out a relationship between us. He'd barely even looked at me. At least he hadn't seen the way I fought for control.

I stopped at the edge of the stable, leaning back against it as I tried to even out my breathing. I hadn't asked for a marriage proposal or any commitment at all, only the acknowledgement from him that the relationship between us had changed. Because, for me, everything had.

"Oh, thank God, here you are. I've been looking everywhere."

I raised my chin, blanking my face of emotion as I turned to Malisa.

"Forgive me. I woke early so I went for a walk." *Only to be thoroughly demoralized by your son, who I can't believe I thought might be God's gift to me. Was it all lies?* "It's such a beautiful morning." *Smile, change the topic.* "Did you feed the calves yet? I could help, if you like."

"Actually, your maids are here. That's why I came to find you."

"My maids?"

"Yes, all four of them. Lovely girls. Offered to help me find you but I assured them you wouldn't have gone far. They're waiting up in your room. Bring them down for breakfast when you're ready."

I nodded, already heading toward the house, my mind rushing to figure out what they were doing here. Had they come with a message? Perhaps my wardrobe? To take me home?

The door to my room stood open. I stopped at it, staring at the four women waiting in there before they had the chance to turn. I'd missed them, certainly, but couldn't help but wish they'd stayed away a few days more. For weeks, all I'd wanted to do was go home but now?

I'm not ready to go home.

Christi was the first to see me. She wasn't fast enough to cover the shock on her face nor the nudge she gave Tayma. I glanced down at my jeans—the same ones I'd worn yesterday—and my pale blue t-shirt. They'd seemed fine when I pulled them on in the pre-dawn hours of the morning. Now, I wished I'd taken a little more time to dress. It didn't say much for my status as princess that my maids were better dressed than me.

"Princess Alina," Laure said, "good to see you again."

"What are you doing here?"

"We've come to take you home, of course. The King's Ball is tonight. Your father wants the whole family present. The kingdom and its neighbors need the show of solidarity having you there would offer, especially with all that's happened since the last ball and the rumors of Prince Marcos's son."

The King's Ball. Held once a year, its sole purpose was for Peverell to show off its grandeur and elegance to visiting dignitaries and royals and ensure the small kingdom and its power were not forgotten. I usually spent weeks preparing for it.

Usually.

In the past six weeks, I hadn't even thought about it once. If my maids hadn't showed up, I wouldn't have even remembered it was today.

"Marcos will be there?"

"Of course. The Hodenian royal family always come to the King's Ball."

I walked to the window, staring out at the empty field, blocking out my maids and their enthusiastic chatter about what needed to be done before we departed.

I was going home.

I should have been thrilled. I hated this place, with its smelly animals, lumpy furniture, and shared bathroom. And the clothes—I picked at a smudge on my sleeve, wondering where it had come from—they were not only lacking in style but a poor fit. I was finally going home to my oversized wardrobe full of gowns and outfits made to my precise measurements.

But Joha wouldn't be there. Something I would have thought a good thing—before last night happened. Or Malisa and Pat. I had so many more questions for them about my mother and the decisions they'd made. Even little Kate, the girl who'd challenged my view of beauty. I'd promised I'd watch her ride Bluebelle before having lunch with her today. She was going to bring some of her mother's chocolate chip biscuits. If I left now, would she understand?

And what about Prince Marcos? Could I pretend everything was the same between us when we both knew it wasn't? Everyone would have heard the rumors. Did anyone but the two of us know the truth?

"Princess Alina?" Christi asked quietly, waiting until I turned to continue. "We brought outfits for you to travel home in. Which would you like to wear?"

Three outfits were laid out on my bed, now made to perfection. A silky fuchsia pantsuit and matching hat, a magenta sun dress accented with white piping, and a floor-length gown, rippled with roses. A pile of clutches sat beside them, five pairs of heels lined up on the floor beneath. Tayma held one of my large jewel boxes, ready to accessorize whichever outfit I chose. I couldn't help but wonder what Joha would think of this profusion of pink.

The memory of his kiss assaulted me again. It was a wonder my face didn't turn as bright as the sun dress. I had to talk to him. I had to try again. Maybe if he knew I was leaving, he'd be more willing to put down his hammer and talk. I put a hand on the door, steadying myself as I forced a smile for the waiting maids. "Excuse me. I have to see someone."

"Now? But there's no time. As soon as you're dressed, we have to go."

My hand stilled on the doorknob. "We're leaving now?"

"The King's Ball is tonight. We're already running behind schedule, Your Highness."

I dropped my hand, mind once again racing. "But—"

Laure took my arm, guiding me back to the bed. "There will be plenty of time for chatting once you're home. Oh, you're not wearing your ring." She held up a hand before I could think up a good reason why. "Never mind. We'll find one similar enough that no one will notice tonight. In the meantime, how about this dress? You're looking a little pale, the color should bring a bit more life to your face should any reporters be present."

Thirty minutes later, my hair straightened and styled, face made up, and gowned in a dress which felt tight and starchy after having worn jeans and shirts for so long, I was ready to go. At least, my maids told me I was. My heart told quite a different story.

Taking one last look at the room which had become my sanctuary, I pasted on a smile and followed my maids down the hall.

"Wait, there's one more thing I have to do before we leave. I promise, it'll only take a minute."

"Hurry, then. We have a strict schedule to keep."

Of course we did. I was the princess again, with schedules and protocols and not a minute to myself. Well, I was taking this one.

I rushed back to the room I'd called mine, grabbing a stool

from the bathroom on the way, using it to reach to the back of the top of the wardrobe. My fingers skittered back and forth until I found what I was looking for. My pink jeweled heels. I pulled them down, brushing the dust off them with a shirt. I wished I had a box or something to put them in, but there was no time to find one. I told myself it didn't matter as I walked back past my confused maids and down the stairs. Kate wasn't here yet, but Malisa would be in the kitchen. The tears began when I saw her there, spoon in hand, making waffles by the dozen. How had I ever thought this woman anything less than a saint?

I swiped at the tears as I plonked the shoes on the counter.

"Alina, honey, are you okay?"

No. I wasn't. But I had neither the time nor the emotional energy to tell her that. "I have to go. Father wants me home today. That's why the maids are here. Will you tell everyone goodbye for me?"

"Sure, but do you have to go right now? You can't sit down, at least eat breakfast? I made enough for everyone."

"I wish we could."

"I'll send it with you. Let me just find something to put them in. I'll put some berries in too. They're your favorite, aren't they?"

I nodded, gratitude filling my heart. "These shoes, will you give them to Kate? Tell her—" I bit my lip, shaking my head to try to dispel the tears intent on breaking me. It was no use. They fell with abandon. I took a breath, determined to get the words out. "Tell her she's already a princess."

"Oh, honey."

My tears soaked into Malisa's well-worn cardigan as she embraced me. My maids were waiting in the hall, no doubt a bunch of guards and official transport somewhere close also, but I selfishly ignored them, drinking in this one final moment with the woman who'd been a mother to me when I'd needed one most.

"I'll see she gets them."

"Thank you."

"All will be well, sweetie. Don't you forget that."

Footsteps at the door reminded me the moment couldn't last forever, and I pulled away. With a final farewell, and a smile of gratitude for the still-steaming waffles passed my way, I walked out the door and back into the life I'd been born into.

THIRTY FOUR

We weren't going to the palace. I could have asked why but, to be honest, I welcomed the reprieve. Three hours in the car to prepare myself and I still wasn't ready. The car turned twice more before I recognized the direction.

Mrs. Rosina's. Of course. A gown, a schedule, the King's Ball—it was as if my six weeks at The Well were nothing but a blink in time. Had it even happened?

I touched a finger to my lips, remembering the warm softness of Joha's against them, the expression in his eyes as he'd said my name, him and me and the Hodenian moon. Yes, it had happened.

The memory carried me through the next two hours of trying on gown after gown. While I'd been away, Mrs. Rosina had created nine gowns for me to choose from. They were exquisite, every one of them from the dreamy baby pink one with its bell skirt and delicate butterflies to the striking magenta satin A-line gown accented from shoulder to waist to floor with a line of gold fabric roses. Just what I had dreamed of wearing to the state dinner on my birthday. Perfect, every one of them.

For the old Alina.

"No? Not that one either?"

I stepped out of the eighth gown, careful not to catch my heels on the voluminous mass of tulle making up the skirt. It was stunning, just like the seven before it had been, but I couldn't wear it. It was too much, just as I knew the ninth would be without even trying it on.

"They're beautiful. You've outdone yourself."

"And yet none of them please you." Mrs. Rosina clicked her tongue, muttering to herself as she hung back the gown, smoothing a loving hand across the roses. I didn't want to think how long they'd taken to create.

"I was simply hoping for something more—"

"More flowers? More pink? More diamonds? They do not sparkle enough for you?"

"More simple."

"Simple." She looked at me as if I'd lost my mind. She wasn't far off. I could barely believe the words coming out of my mouth were mine. "But...you ask for diamonds! More frills, more roses, more pearls, more flounces!" Her arms rose higher, punctuating each word she spoke.

I let my gaze roam around the room, jumping from table to fabric rolls to each of the nine gowns hung before me. All I had to do was choose one and this painfully long fitting session would be over. Was it not the gowns at all but the reality of being princess again which had me hesitating? I had neither the will nor the energy to analyze my tumble of emotions right now. The ball started in less than five hours, and I didn't even have a gown yet.

"What's that one?" Four sets of eyes turned to the gown I pointed out. "The purple one, there in the corner."

Mrs. Rosina walked over to the mannequin, pulling it to where I stood. Now in the light rather than shadows, the fabric was closer to burgundy than purple. The color of a deep red wine. "It was an early version of that rose-colored one with the capped sleeves, the base from which we created what you now see in all its fullness there."

I touched the chiffon, marveling at its luster.

"May I try it on?"

Though she looked at me as if I'd lost my senses, Mrs. Rosina nodded. "Certainly. Every gown in my collection is available to you."

The instant I turned and saw my reflection in the mirror, I

knew I'd found my gown for the ball. It was perfect. No one else in the room dared comment, but I knew it.

Made entirely of burgundy chiffon, rather than my usual satin, it was by far the least ornate gown I'd ever worn. The tiny cap sleeves, a single layer of the delicate fabric, fluttered over my shoulders like butterfly wings. The bodice, with its simple yet flattering v-shaped neckline, tucked in to a two-inch thick band of fabric at my waist. But it was the skirt that had me captivated.

Flowing from waist band to floor were layer upon layer of the floaty fabric. They rustled against each other and swished as I moved, creating the image in my mind of a flower, its petals dancing in the breeze.

"Petticoats will add fullness to the skirt. Perhaps two or three? A few hundred crystals splayed across the bodice, with a spray of them down the skirt, would look wonderful, but I'm afraid there simply isn't time to add them all. If we used the crystal-studded belt from the baby pink gown, though, and overlaid the skirt with the silver chiffon."

"No. No changes. It's perfect."

"But—"

"Time is short, is it not?"

Mrs. Rosina huffed. "Not too short that we can't make it into a gown befitting the Princess of Peverell. Verity, get the belt. Faye, the crystals. We have work to do."

"No." I stopped the assistants running about with a shake of my head. "I'll wear this gown as is."

There was silence for all of five seconds and then, "Are you certain? There is time."

I swished the skirt again, captivated by its graceful movement. "I am. It reminds me of a flower, whose beauty comes not from primping or sparkles but from its striking simplicity. Tonight, I'll be that flower."

The ball began at eight that evening. I made my entrance at seven-thirty, relieved no one but the string quartet tuning their instruments and a few servants were there to see it. I'd have to find the strength to face people somewhere, but I had no idea where. I loitered at the side of the ballroom, taking one of the seats provided and focusing on breathing.

If only Malisa was here. I yearned for her wisdom. Just a few nights ago, I'd been sitting at their dinner table, wishing they would eat faster, terrified my cheesecake would fall apart before I had the chance to serve it. Now, I worried it was me who would collapse.

In the space of twenty-four hours, I'd been betrayed by Marcos, kissed by Joha, and wrenched home. Only nothing about this place felt like home. Not even the suite I'd called mine all my life and decorated to my heart's content.

My heart wasn't content. It ached, and I had no idea how to fix it or even what was wrong with it. It wasn't broken, just confused, perhaps. Shaken. Bruised.

Had it been unfaithful of me to kiss Joha last night? I could have argued that it was him who started it and take none of the blame, but it would have been a lie. Certainly, Joha had shocked me with his kiss, but I'd been an all-too-willing participant. If my engagement to Marcos had been a normal one, none of this would have bothered me. He'd broken off the engagement and, subsequently, our relationship. There was nothing stopping me from kissing another man.

Nothing except the marriage alliance that still stood between our two kingdoms. Did Marcos have the power to break that? Did I? Despite his words and sentiments, was I still engaged to Marcos, as Joha had wondered? Had I kissed one man while being engaged to another?

I stared down at my silver heels, ignoring the increasing bustle of servants around me as the questions ate at my mind. Questions and guilt. I'd enjoyed Joha's kiss. No, more than enjoyed. I'd relished it. Wanted another. And another.

My first night back at the palace, back in the public eye, on a night when everyone in two kingdoms would be watching Marcos and me in particular—and I couldn't stop thinking about another man.

The grand doors opened, my moment of stolen solitude at an end as several dignitaries walked into the ballroom. I stood, straightening my shoulders and lifting my chin, the familiar smile I didn't feel pressed firmly on my face.

You're the princess. Be the princess.

On the heels of that admonition came another, Malisa's parting words, the ones I ached to believe.

All will be well.

THIRTY-FIVE

"Princess Alina, what a pleasure to see you this evening. And looking so well."

"It is a pleasure to be here, Minister Jordan, as always. Are you enjoying your stay in Peverell? I heard you and your wife took in the theatre last night. The show is a wonder, is it not?"

"Indeed it is, Your Highness."

"Perhaps you will have the chance to visit the public gardens, also, while you are here. They are a spectacular sight at this time of year."

The conversation felt as shallow as my emotions were fragile. Both of them held together by good intentions and pride rather than any strength of character. I took another sip of lemonade before excusing myself to move on to the next dignitary. Three more and I would have spoken with them all, no mean feat given the ballroom boasted fifty-seven of them this evening.

Father had greeted me earlier and complimented me on my appearance but been interrupted by one of his advisors before I could ask about the status of my betrothal. Much as I wanted answers from him, tonight was neither the time nor the place to confront him. The King's Ball might have seemed like a frivolous dance to anyone looking in, but in reality, it was a showcase of all Peverell had to offer—its dignitaries, resources, wealth. A calculated reminder to neighboring kingdoms that, though Peverell was small in size and strength, its people were not to be trifled with.

Father had his role to play and I had mine—smiling, caring, regaining the trust I'd lost last month when those articles had come out. It was more important tonight than ever that I play my part to perfection. Even if, tonight more than ever, I rued it. The fraudulence of it all grated on me, making me wonder who I was really doing this for. What was the point in showing strength when none of it was real?

Or, like Joha had said, was that strength in itself?

Music swirled around me as I watched couples take the dance floor, mesmerized by the swishing colors of the women's gowns. Muted colors, nothing gaudy at the King's Ball. Striking yet simple, each woman dressed to show the opulence of their own kingdoms and titles while ensuring no disrespect to anyone else's. They, like me, walked the careful line between showing just enough power to instill in their people confidence and just enough humility to keep them reachable. Part of the people, yet separate. Rulers, yet friends.

What did my people think of me? Did they, like Joha, see past my smiles to the trembling girl within? Did they think me strong? Arrogant? Weak? A smile in a pretty dress? How could I show them I was more than that? That I loved them? Fiercely.

"Alina?"

Thoraben. A smile rose unbidden across my lips at the sound of his voice. It felt like forever since I'd heard it. His steps were uncertain as he walked closer, not surprising given the last time we'd spoken I'd stalked out of dinner, as furious with him as I was the world in general. I owed him the grandest apology I could find. But first...

I closed the gap between us, not caring who saw as I threw myself into his arms. "Thoraben." I held tight to his back, relishing the feeling when he held me just as close. "I'm so sorry. So, so sorry. I never should have said—"

"Hey," he said, lifting my gaze to his, "it's okay. Truly. I'm sorry I didn't realize how much you were struggling. When I saw you curled up at the bottom of that lectern, oblivious to everything around you as you hid inside yourself, I just about died.

I knew you'd hate The Well and probably never forgive me for sending you there, but I had to get you away."

"No, it was...thank you."

We shared a smile. One day I'd tell him exactly how much I appreciated what he'd done for me, sending me there—perhaps even ask about his faith, but, like my conversation with Father, all that had to wait. Tonight, we needed to present a unified family, not put worries in the minds of anyone who might overhear us speaking of Rebels and exiles.

"Dance with me?"

It was the lifeline I'd been searching for. I walked out onto the floor on Thoraben's arm, thankful for all the dance lessons I'd been forced to endure over the years. If the steps hadn't been so ingrained in my mind, I'm certain I would have forgotten every one of them as I focused on trying to keep my legs from collapsing with relief.

"You doing okay?"

I nodded, wondering yet again if it was a lie.

"I heard you had a run in with Feathers."

My head flung up so fast I rammed Thoraben in the chin, making him stumble even as he laughed. He recovered far faster than I did. "Who told?"

"You didn't think I'd send you off to another country and not keep track of what you were up to, did you? I also know that you climbed a tree, learned how to make pizza, befriended Kate, wore jeans with three-inch pink heels, and overheard a conversation between Joha and Arden which he's been trying to figure out a way to apologize for ever since."

"You talked to Joha."

"I called him every couple of days to check on you."

"But you never asked to talk to me?"

"Would you have wanted me to?"

I opened my mouth to say yes before remembering what those first few weeks had been like. "Probably not."

Our conversation lapsed into silence as we waltzed our way around the room. Dignitaries watched on—some smiling, some not. Marcos's parents, King Dorien and Queen Galielle, were noticeably absent from their esteemed place beside Father on the dais, though Father's advisors had tried to hide the fact by removing the extra chairs there. Even with the bad publicity and ongoing investigation of Marcos's alleged son, I'd thought they'd be here. It spoke volumes that they weren't. Nicola had been right to worry.

The song finished before I realized it, and Thoraben led me back to the edge of the dancefloor. I held on to his arm, reluctant to let go. The ballroom, once my favorite stage, felt overwhelming tonight. The crush of people in their finery and fraudulent smiles, so far from the wide, open spaces of The Well and its quiet stillness. And Joha. "I have to talk to you," I told Thoraben. "Not tonight, but soon."

"We will," he said. "By the way, you look really beautiful."

I nodded, breathing in what little air I could, willing the panic batting at my heart to flee. My lips trembled with the effort.

The room swayed. Thoraben frowned. "Hey, you okay? Want to leave? You've only just arrived home. People would understand."

People might, but I wouldn't. I was the princess. This was my role. Father would expect it and Mother—I thought back to her journal, the number of times she'd faced the crowds and shown strength in her character even if she didn't feel it inside her. If she could be strong, so could I. "I'll be fine."

"You're sure?"

"Certain."

"I'll send Kenna over."

Thoraben, ever my protector. But this time I didn't mind. "Thanks."

The world swayed again. I closed my eyes against the dizziness and leaned back against the wall, gulping in as much air as I could force down my panic-clogged throat. It wasn't enough. My head still pounded, lights dancing against the back of my eyelids. The quartet's music, the tapping of heels on the wooden floor, a hundred different conversations—it all swirled together, bouncing and echoing off the wall behind me in a distorted cacophony of sound. I had to get out of this room.

I chanced opening my eyes, avoiding the glare of color as I searched the walls. There, to my right. A side door. With a nod to the two uniformed men who guarded it, I slipped out before duty could open its mouth and convince me to stay. *Five minutes, that's all. Five minutes to breathe. Then I'll go back in, find Kenna, and the last three dignitaries. Just five minutes...*

Crouching down in the blissfully empty hallway, I let the silence renew me. Out here, there were no people wanting or offering answers, no lights burning headaches into my eyes, no expectations. Just air. Stillness. Space. Slowly, the dizziness began to fade.

The ball was spectacular. They always were. Lights, flowers, the string quartet's music echoing from polished wood floor to painted ceiling. I'd always reveled in the palace balls before, flitting from person to person, drinking in compliments like they were the oxygen which kept me alive. Perhaps they were. My ego, at least.

A light caught my eye through one of the hall's many windows. No, not a light. The moon. White and brilliant in its fullness. The same moon Joha and I had stood under last night when he told me I was more than a title. The same moon sending streaks of silver through Joha's hair as he wrenched me to my feet. The same moon looking on in wonder as he'd kissed me.

"Alina?"

A wave of latent dizziness—or was it guilt?—almost leveled me as I spun around, searching for the voice. There, three feet away, every imposing inch of him, the man who should have been my husband. Only, he didn't seem all that imposing tonight. More uncertain. Defeated, perhaps. His shoulders slumped a little, his hair flat on one side as if he'd been sitting with his head in his hands for a while, his suit jacket gaped open underneath the hands tucked in his pockets. I'd never seen him any less than perfect, even when he'd come to The Well.

And his eyes... Even from this distance, they looked sad. I

considered running to him as I had Thoraben but in the end just stood. With Thoraben, I'd been certain of my welcome. I didn't know where I stood with this man.

"Prince Marcos? What's wrong? Why are you standing out here in the hall?"

THIRTY-SIX

Marcos took two steps forward but even they were small, lacking the confidence I'd always admired in him. Had the two days since the story broke truly been this hard on him? He was like a different man. Not that I was the same person I'd been either.

"My parents and advisors thought it best I attend the ball."

That made sense. Appearances and all. "But why—?" I gestured toward the ballroom with my hand. The ball had started almost two hours ago. Had he been out here all this time?

"Did you ever wish you had the option of saying no?" He crossed his arms, sighing into the moonlit hall. "I'm here. You can vouch for me, but I can't go in there. They'll all want answers and I don't have any to give. I wish I did."

I nodded, understanding all too well his reluctance to face the crowd. "The investigation isn't going well?"

Another sigh, this time accentuated by a shrug. "I don't know that either. They're hiding information from me and rather than admit it, they sent me here to be the representative of Hodenia's royal family. 'Too close to be objective' was Father's official line, but I've spent enough time with publicists spinning stories to see past that. They're worried."

"And you?"

"I worry too, but for a different reason. I fear they'll cover it all up before I have the chance to meet my son."

"They wouldn't."

"You have far more faith in them than I do. Come on, Alina. It's a scandal of the highest order. An unexpected heir who could change the future of Hodenia? The easiest way forward would be to cover it all up. Pay the woman off. Pretend she never existed. Tell the papers it was merely a hoax or another silly gossip piece. They're printed so often, people would believe it."

Like I had. He was right, much as I hated to admit it. I wanted to believe the best of both my father and his, but sometimes being a ruler meant choosing what was best for the country over the comfort of an individual. And it wasn't like the woman was being killed or sent away. She'd come out of it a wealthy woman, the son's needs provided for for the rest of his life in return for her silence.

"Easier for you, also."

"Easy, yes, but not right. I want it all to be over but not at the expense of a child. Or Rachana."

I felt the name like a tear across my chest. Until this moment, the woman had been nameless. I could almost convince myself she wasn't real while she had no name. Now I had no option but to accept it. "It was her?"

"I don't know. They still won't tell me."

"You could find out though. You know her name."

"It's a common name. It would only increase the scandal if I tried to find her. There are too many people watching me. My only recourse is to wait. Has your father said anything?"

"We've barely spoken. I arrived back from Hodenia this afternoon with just enough time to be sewn into my gown before the ball began."

"Oh."

He looked so dejected there, wringing his hands as if he didn't know what to do with them. The strong man brought low. I didn't know if I could help him—I was probably the last person in the world he wanted to try—but I had to do something. "Come inside. Ask me to dance."

I walked a step forward, holding out a hand, leaving the decision to him whether he took it. Close now, I could see the fatigue pulling at his eyes, resting in the lines across his forehead. Had he slept at all since the story broke?

"I don't know."

"One dance, that's all I'm asking. Show them all you're here, that you're still the man they know you are."

"But I'm not."

"No, but you could be again." Something Mother had written in one of her journals came back to me. A line about courage and capability. "Someone far wiser than me told me that our greatest strength as leaders is shown through what we do with our weakness. You made a mistake, but who hasn't? It's what you do next that matters."

He considered my words for a moment. Though my hand grew tired, I kept it out, hoping he'd take it. It felt right to offer it, and the forgiveness that came with it. Like something Mother would have done.

"And you'd still dance with me, even knowing—?"

That he'd been with another woman? That he had no plans to marry me? That we'd have every person in the room and beyond talking about us? I didn't know how Marcos planned on finishing that question, but it didn't matter. If he could find the courage, so could I.

"You're not the only one with regrets. Six weeks ago, it was me in the papers. Now, it's you. We'll get through this."

"I can't marry you."

"We'll get through that too."

Conversation ceased as we walked through the door together, dancers faltering as those around them craned their necks to see what was happening. A wide channel grew through the middle of the ballroom ending at our feet. The river at The Well with its improvised log bridge had been less treacherous. At least there, I'd only had an audience of four—two of whom had been far more interested in the food than a silly girl trying to cross a log. Here, half the world watched. I took a deep breath and started forward determined to ignore, best I could, the whispers starting up again. *All will be well. All will be well.*

The words repeated in my head as I gently tugged Marcos forward, sounding so natural that we were almost at the middle of the ballroom before I thought to question them. When had the Rebel's catchphrase become my mantra? And what's more, did I actually believe it?

I had no time to think of that now. Not standing in front of Marcos, his hand on my waist, my heart racing the music.

It was our engagement dance all over again—the floor empty except for us—only instead of staring into Marcos's face, giddy with the realization that this man would be mine for the rest of my life, I was letting him go. I still wasn't sure how I felt about that. First, I'd felt anger, then when the flash burn of anger subsided, there had been hurt. Betrayal. But seeing him tonight, the strong man broken, it was difficult to feel anything but compassion.

The dance finished with the same flourish it started, both of us knowing our parts too well to defer. Marcos might be a father, our countries and their alliance hung on a tottering balance, and then there was Joha and my attraction with him to consider—and yet we danced. Smiled. Talked about the weather, the room's decorations, my gown, and a score of other inconsequential things. At the end of the song, he bowed over my hand and took me to where Kenna and Wenderley stood together.

He thanked me for the dance. I thanked him in reply. Then he walked away, through the crowd to the other side of the ballroom.

"You should have gone with him," Wenderley said, nudging me with her shoulder. "Ask him for another dance."

Once upon a time, I would have. But he'd broken our engagement and was fighting battles none of us could help him with. Especially not me. The only thing that would help him now was answers, and even they were likely to bring more trouble before peace.

"Not this time," I hedged.

"Then I will," Wenderley said, oblivious—or simply ignoring—the tension radiating out from Hodenia's prince. "Someone has to let him know we don't all hate him."

She wound her way through dancers and dignitaries, her sights set on the man hiding behind his glass of lemonade, a trick I'd used all too often. Don't want to make eye contact? Take a sip. Admirer getting too close? *I'm feeling parched. Would you mind getting me a drink?* Don't want to dance? *Actually, I was just thinking of getting a drink. It's rather warm in here. Join me?*

Of course, it didn't work if your partner was as determined as Lady Wenderley Davis and simply took the glass out of your hand, placing it on a table before she pulled you on to the dance floor. *Good on you, Wenderley.*

"How are you?" Kenna asked, turning her gaze back to me. "Feeling any better?"

"I'm fi—" I stopped myself just short of spouting out the lie which came so naturally. No more. Not with family. And Kenna was family, even if it had taken me a while to admit it. "Actually, no. Not really. It's been a long few weeks."

"I can imagine." She placed a hand on my arm. "If you need someone to talk to..."

"You'll be first on my list. Every time. Promise."

Kenna's smile was watery, her blinking too fast to be anything but trying to hold back tears. If we'd made up anywhere else, I might have hugged her, but that would set us both off, and then we'd both be crying. Far better for now to change the subject. Wenderley and Marcos waltzing past proved perfect timing. They were smiling, both of them. His was small but definitely there. *Thank you, Wenderley.*

Thoraben came to claim Kenna for a dance then, leaving me alone to my thoughts. I probably should have gone to find those three dignitaries I still hadn't talked to, but it was nice to stand in the shadows for a few moments and simply watch the dancers. Thoraben winked and said something to Marcos as they passed on the dancefloor. Marcos's smile grew as Wenderley blushed and Kenna shook her head.

"Poor girl."

I flinched at the woman's words. She wasn't the first person tonight to offer her opinion on Marcos and me. Though everyone had been careful to stay well away from the topic to my face, I'd heard the whispers as I passed, seen the sympathy in their eyes. The best thing about hiding in the shadows was that no one saw you. Unfortunately, the worst thing about hiding in the shadows was the same.

"Don't you think, Princess Alina?"

I turned, slightly confused. Was she talking to me? Mrs....*Lu-ellen Eggins, that's her name. Wife of Mr. Martin Eggins, Peverellian minister of...of...Oh bother, was he agriculture or infrastructure? Two children, though. Warren and another boy starting with H. Hugh? Harold? No, Harry. That was it. Warren and Harry.*

"Mrs. Eggins, I—"

"Oh, I know, it wasn't her fault. None of us blame the poor girl. After all, the heart does what the heart wants and hers fell for your brother hard."

She was talking about Wenderley, not me. "I think—"

"And now she's torturing herself dancing with another prince she can never have. The poor girl, just going to get her heart broken all over again."

"She's not—"

"Well, if it isn't the prince himself," Mrs. Eggins said suddenly, all smiles and cheer as Marcos and Wenderley came back. "What a pleasure to see you here tonight, Prince Marcos. And Wenderley, dear. So good of you to come and find a smile for us all, even though—well, I won't mention it, but you know..." She bustled off then, muttering a few more "poor dear's" under her breath. Marcos bowed awkwardly before taking leave himself. I didn't blame him. There were enough unwarranted opinions here to drown us all.

"Wenderley—"

"Forget it. I'm fine."

"You don't have to be. She was rude. I'm sorry."

"It's not your fault."

"But—"

"Thanks for caring, but it's fine. I can handle it. Move on, right?" She bunched her skirt in one hand and flicked hair out of her face. "I'm going to dance. Someone will want me."

Her mouth teetered in a smile no doubt supposed to assure me. It didn't even come close. *Oh, Wenderley...*

It was almost impossible to stand detached after that. For the first time ever, I looked out on the people around me—most of whom I'd known most of my life—and wondered what their stories were. Beyond the names and titles on the pages I studied before each event. What had brought them here tonight, beyond an invitation asking them to. What made them laugh. What worries they tried to hide. And, more than anything, how many of them—like Marcos, like Wenderley, like me—were crying on the inside.

THIRTY-SEVEN

L aure, has my father asked to see me yet?"

"No. Would you like to send him a message?"

I looked at the clock again, trying to remember what Father would usually be doing at this time. Twelve-thirty. Lunch time at The Well. Had Joha and Pat come back for lunch or worked through as they far too often did? I shook my head, annoyed at the direction my thoughts had taken. *Forget them. Forget The Well. Forget Joha. Forget the kiss—*

"No message. I'll wait. Thank you."

If Laure noticed the extra heat in my cheeks, she didn't say anything. I breathed a sigh of relief when the door closed behind her, leaving me alone, even if it was only a temporary reprieve. They'd be back in half an hour to style my hair and ensure I was ready for the opening of the ballet this afternoon, before dinner with the Minister of the Arts, his wife, and several of the ballet's greatest contributors. My dusky pink gown, a sleek one-shoul-dered design, hung waiting in my dressing room. Beautiful as it was, all I could think was how constricting it would be to wear for hours on end.

Five weeks and six days. That's all the time I'd been away, and yet I'd changed. My room seemed overly large, my maids overly loud, and my thoughts overly distracting. I would have to get those thoughts in order before seeing Father. When he eventual-ly called for me.

I twirled a pen around my finger and tried again to focus on the schedule on the desk in front of me.

Ballet and dinner tonight, junior school visit tomorrow morning, lunch meeting at the Community Center, speech at the opening of a new garden planted in honor of my eighteenth, dinner with Father's advisors and their families—at least Thoraben and Kenna would be at that one—then hairdresser appointment first up the next morning and—

I closed the thick binder. Too much, too soon. I should have been thrilled to be back. I was the princess again. Clothed in pink, my hair straight and styled, jewels around my neck—I looked the part, but I didn't feel it. By all accounts, I was home. Only nothing about this place felt like home anymore.

Tayma had found me sleeping on the window seat when she came in this morning. She assumed I'd woken early and moved over there to watch the sunrise, falling asleep again before it rose. I didn't bother to correct her. What would I have said? My bed was too soft to sleep in? I missed the plain simplicity of my borrowed room at The Well?

It had been almost embarrassing to walk back into the gaudiness of my suite. I'd thought it so beautiful once. Walls patterned with pink flowers, great swaths of curtains pulled with thick gold ropes at each of the eight bay windows, the four-poster bed with its velvety canopy which in itself was almost as large as my room at The Well had been, the pristine sitting room with its ornately hand-woven rug.

Come on, Alina. You're home now. You should be excited. This is what you've been begging for since the day you left.

But that was the thing, I didn't know what I wanted anymore. I didn't even know who I was.

I'd surrounded myself with pink because it reminded me of Mother, but it wasn't the strongest reminder I had of her anymore. She'd been so much more than the beloved queen of Peverell. She'd been a mother, a wife—and a Follower. It wasn't her clothes or jewels which most summed her up, it was her faith in God. Faithful One, she'd called him. Giver of Miracles.

I pulled out her last journal, tucked beneath the photo album in my desk drawer, holding it for a moment before opening it to the page I'd read so many times yet still felt like an axe to my chest.

> *Faithful One, I pray my children will know you. Thoraben and Alina and however many others you may bless us with in the future. I pray they know you. Not just as God but as their God. The one who loves them more than they'll ever know, the one who would do anything for them. Faithful One, Giver of Miracles. May they not just know your name but know your heart. If I only had one request in the whole of my life, it would be that. May my children know and love you.*

All my life, I'd yearned to know her heart, and here it was. Her greatest wish. She wanted me to believe so much she ached with it. Cried tears as she wrote it. They pock-marked the paper even almost twenty years later. She didn't ask for riches or that we'd be healthy, strong, or beautiful. She asked that we'd know her God. Thoraben did. But me? I wavered. Back and forth like a flower thrown about by a breeze, certain only of one thing—I was going to fail. And maybe that was the crux of it all.

Because to make her greatest wish come true, I would have to break Father. His enemy or his daughter. I couldn't be both. Whatever I chose, I couldn't make them both happy.

All my life, I'd tried—been the best daughter and princess I could be in the hope they'd be proud of me. I'd stood and waved when I wanted to hide and presented a front no one could fault. And all for nothing. If I chose Mother's God, Father would disown me, and if I chose to deny God—

But that was it, I couldn't deny him. Every day at The Well, I'd seen proof of his existence and care, not only in the kindness and acceptance of the Samsons but in the strength of Nicola and Arden, the exuberance of Kate, Joha's achingly beautiful music.

I'd never heard anyone play like that before and doubted I ever would again. That kind of talent could only come as a gift from someone greater than music itself. I believed in God. But did he believe in me? More, if I chose his way, would I have the courage to deal with the consequences?

Maybe it wasn't Father's reaction stopping me. Maybe it was the fear that I'd never be enough. Any god worth his adoration would be a fool to accept anything less than perfection. Father certainly demanded it, and he was just a man. If the Rebel's god was as powerful as they claimed, and as worthy, he would know how far I strayed from that standard.

What if I came to him, offered him all I had, and he laughed, like Erynn had Joha? Broken pieces, shattered dreams? What did I have to offer him?

How did Thoraben do it?

I closed the journal, returning it to the drawer before walking out of my suite. Alina, before The Well, had needed two hours to prepare for an event. The woman I was today needed answers far more than a facial. And the two people I hoped might have them were right down the hall. Albeit a long one.

"Kenna?" I knocked softly on the door to the Princess Suite, wondering if she was even in there. Desperately hoping she was. I hadn't been to her room before, refusing to come anywhere near it out of spite after Kenna and Thoraben married. It had been too much of a reminder of everything that had been taken from me. I knocked louder, calling again. "Kenna?"

Shock was written across her face when she opened it. "Alina?"

"Can I come in?"

"Sure. You know you're always welcome. But I should tell you, I'm about to go out. Ben and I are going to the village to serve dinner."

The feast the day after a Feast. I'd forgotten. The day after every palace ball, Thoraben and Kenna took a feast of leftovers to the village to feed those who struggled. I'd gone too—once.

The people had overwhelmed me—their dirtiness, their gratitude, their smiles. The instant the food I was serving had run out, I'd demanded to be driven back to the palace. I'd never gone back.

"Did you ever feel like your world was falling apart?" I blurted out, all the careful questions I'd rehearsed on the way here bypassed. "Like everything you knew was true, all the plans you had for your life, were suddenly taken away and you had no idea what to do next or even who you were anymore?"

Kenna stared at me, a grin slowly appearing on her face. "Better than you'd realize."

Of course, she knew. What was I thinking? In the space of a night, she'd gone from commoner to future queen. Something I'd held against her for way too long.

"I'm sorry, Kenna. I should never have blamed you."

"You were hurt."

And she was overly gracious, but it was more than that. "I was selfish. All my life, you'd been my companion. By my side but half a step behind. You were the sister I never had and my best friend, but still, I was the princess and you weren't. And then you married Thoraben and all that changed. You outranked me both in status and popularity, the wedding I'd been counting down to was postponed, my birthday all but forgotten, and I realized our family would never be the same. You were the change, so I blamed you. But I was wrong. Could you ever forgive me?"

"I already have."

I shook my head, overwhelmed by such an unexpected gift. Unexpected, and undeserved. I'd treated her worse than an enemy. "Thank you."

"Did something happen at The Well? Is that where this question's come from? I know you hated Ben for sending you away, but you're back now. Aren't you happy?"

"Yes." Part of me, at least. Just not the part pressing against my patched together heart.

"But?"

I thought talking to Kenna about Joha and The Well and all the mixed-up emotions related to them would help, but now I was here, I couldn't find the words. Kenna was right. I was home. I should have been thrilled. Maybe it would just take a few days to adjust. That was it.

"Alina?"

"Never mind. I'd better go. My maids will be wondering where I am."

"Sure, if that's what you want."

What I wanted was for someone to make my decisions for me. But that would never happen. Neither, at the very heart of me, beneath the fear and perpetual overthinking, did I want them to.

You're the princess. Be the princess.

All will be well.

It was the second admonition which almost broke me. How I ached for it to be true.

"Alina?"

I should have known I was too fragile right now to talk to anyone. One harsh word, one incorrect assumption, one embrace or touch from someone who cared, and I knew I'd fall apart. Until I'd sorted out my feelings and spoken with Father, I'd be better off keeping my mouth shut. "Enjoy your outing."

With a small smile, I let myself out of the Princess Suite and returned to my own.

THIRTY-EIGHT

The scent of lavender rose up around me, filling my senses and smoothing over my battered emotions. This I'd missed— my oversized bathtub, soothing music playing while I whiled away the hours. No one knocking on the door to hurry me up or timed showers to conserve water. No slippery, greasy cakes of soap or thin towels better suited to an animals' stall. No odd smells I knew better than to question. Just me, my thoughts, and as much time as I wanted to spend in my tub full of water.

Two minutes later, I was out of the bath and wrapped in a thick towel. My maids turned in shock when I walked back into the main room.

"Out already? Was the water too warm? Too cold?"

"The lavender," Christi said to Tayma. "I told you not to put so much in."

"No, no," I assured my bickering maids. "It was great. Perfect, really. But I'd like to dress now, if that's not too much to ask."

"Of course not. What would you like to wear? Your rose gown?"

I shook my head, trying my best not to cringe at the thought of it. Baby pink with layer upon layer of frills and roses, tied at the waist with a giant bow—it was better suited to a spring parade float than anyone's wardrobe. Immature child was not the impression I wanted to make when I confronted Father, and a confrontation was what it was going to take. I'd been home four days, and he still hadn't mentioned the alliance or my wedding.

Or lack of. It was difficult to focus on anything while my future hung in such a precarious position.

"No, thank you. I'm going to see my father, so perhaps..." I wandered into the wardrobe, rejecting outfits as quickly as I considered them. Too many frills, too pink, too childish, too small. Had I nothing appropriate for a simple meeting with Father?

It was right at the back of the wardrobe that I spotted them, a pair of cream linen pants. I pulled them toward me, running my finger down the ironed-in crease, so sharp I would have cut myself had the fabric been any less soft. I didn't know how long they'd been there, I didn't even know *why* they were there given I'd never once worn anything but dresses and gowns before my time at The Well, but they were perfect. A silky turquoise blouse, slightly off the shoulder, and a pair of black heels finished off the ensemble.

"Princess Alina, you look—" I waited as Tayma searched for words, wondering how she planned on finishing her description. Bland? Older? I would have been content with different. "Fabulous!" I breathed out a smile. That description I would cling to as I confronted Father. "You should wear that color more often. It's exceptional on you. It makes your eyes so blue they glow."

I looked closer at my eyes in the mirror. Tayma was right. Usually an unremarkable mix between blue and green, today they were almost bursting with mesmerizing color. "Thank you. I quite like it."

And I had more important things to do than stare at myself in the mirror. Father hadn't called for me, but I couldn't wait any longer. Sleep was hard fought each night as it was without the added worry of a future so unresolved.

I hesitated at his door, that in itself unsettling me as much as the size of my room had. I'd never hesitated there before, always barging in whether or not a guard was posted. This time, I knocked.

"Come in."

Father sat as his desk, Mr. Grant-Hartley and Mr. Watts, his two closest advisors, across from him. I acknowledged each of them with a nod before turning my attention to Father. He held out a hand to welcome me in. I took it gratefully, drinking in the approval in his smile.

"Alina. It's good to have you home again. I don't know why Thoraben insisted you needed to be removed from the palace, but I am thankful to see you looking so well."

"Thank you."

"You look nice," Father said. Mr. Watts nodded in agreement, before catching himself and remembering his place as an observer. "Older."

"Thank you."

I rubbed the hem of the blouse between two fingers as I considered my next words. Father's attention was already straying back to the papers strewn across his desk. If I waited too long, I'd lose him altogether. His two advisors had no such qualms, watching the interplay between us, ever vigilant to their role in Father's life. Had I interrupted something important? Was that why they were staring at me?

Should I ask them to leave? The matter of Marcos and myself was a personal matter, best discussed only with Father. Unless, of course, the alliance was what the men were meeting to discuss with him. In which case, it was probably better that they stayed. The silence stretched as I looked from the men to Father, desperately hoping wisdom might fly through the window and into my heart and mind.

"Was there something you wanted?" Father asked, pen scratching at the paper in front of him. I wished he'd look up. He'd seemed pleased to see me and not ordered me from the room, but neither did he seem all that interested in my presence.

"You never asked to see me."

"Was I supposed to?" he asked, crossing out a line on his page and writing a sentence in its place. I'm certain my mouth gaped open.

"I would have thought you'd want to discuss the dissolution of my engagement and how it affects the alliance."

Finally, he looked up. Only instead of the apology I was hoping for, or perhaps even compassion, he looked confused. "Your wedding hasn't been called off. Why would you think that? It will go ahead as planned. We're in the final stages of settling on a date as we speak, something you will be alerted of as soon as it is decided."

So, Joha had been right. Marcos and I were still engaged. "But what about the child? Marcos's son—"

"Will not be a problem, if he even is proven to be Prince Marcos's, which is highly unlikely. Far more likely a dying woman's attempt to secure a life better than she had for her son."

I grabbed at the wall behind me, thankful when my hand connected. "Dying?" *Marcos...*

"What? You thought an anonymous woman coming forward with claims for the throne would dissolve all King Dorien and I have worked toward all these years?"

"No, of course not but... The woman is dying?" It couldn't be true.

"It's why she came forward now, apparently, though I still think it rather *providential,* shall we say, that she would come forward right around the time when Prince Marcos is to marry. She hopes that Prince Marcos, as her boy's alleged father, will care for the boy after she's gone."

"Does Marcos know this?"

"If he doesn't, he soon will."

Poor Marcos. What he must be going through to hear the shocking news that he has a son only to be compounded by the fact that the boy's mother is dying. "And you're still expecting us to marry? While he is dealing with all this? Do you not even care?"

"This will all blow over, same as scores of other such scandals which have touched the palace over the years. They are of no consequence to us."

He crossed out another line on his paper, writing a note in the margin beside it, drawing an arrow linking the paragraph to another further down. That was it? End of conversation? *No. It can't be. Marcos deserves better. I deserve better.*

When he made another note and turned to confer with Mr. Watts and Mr. Grant-Hartley, I stormed forward, tearing the paper out of his hand, forcing him to look up.

"No consequence? That's all you have to say? They are real people. Marcos told me himself that he and Rachana had a relationship, short and unconsidered as it was. Whether or not tests prove the boy is his, he plans to do the honorable thing and marry her."

"The honorable thing, *Alina*, would be to marry the woman he is engaged to. He proposed to you in front of every person of importance in my kingdom and even if he hadn't, papers have been signed."

"He doesn't want to marry me. He came to The Well himself to break off the engagement."

"He has no authority to do such a thing."

"It's his life and future which has been thrown into turmoil—"

"His fault—"

"—and I will not marry a man who has no wish to marry me."

"Don't be ridiculous. You *will* marry Prince Marcos."

"Not if he doesn't wish to."

"You would dare defy me and the decisions I make? In front of my advisors?"

I glanced at the two men, their attention captivated by our conversation. I should have asked them to leave, but it was too late now. I'd started this, I couldn't back down now. "If that is what it takes then yes, I will. It's my life, my future, and should, at least in part, be my decision."

"It's my country!" he roared, hands pressed against the desk as he rose out of his chair. I took a step backward before forcing myself to stand my ground. "This attitude of yours is Malisa's fault. Six weeks in her presence and you come back with a complete lack of respect for those in authority, just like her. I should never have agreed to let you stay. I suppose I should be thankful she hasn't turned you further and made you—"

He stopped, swallowing back the words. I had no such qualms.

"What, Father? A Follower? One of the hundreds of people whose lives you've destroyed?"

"Alina, don't."

There was warning in his tone, but I was too angry at him to care. He'd gone too far this time, belittling first Marcos, desperately trying to find the honorable thing to do in an impossible situation, and every single friend I'd made at The Well and far more afield. Including, whether he knew it or not, his own son.

"Too late, Father. I am a Rebel. You can do what you like to me, but I no longer answer to you as my highest authority."

THIRTY-NINE

A thousand scenarios batted against me as I ran down the halls, each fighting another for supremacy. I pushed them all aside, refusing to dwell on a single one of them. I couldn't control the future, but I knew someone who could. Or, at least, I wanted to. The desperation clawed at my insides, begging for answers.

"Thoraben!" I pounded on his door. "Ben, Ben, you have to help me." *Please be in there. Please be in there.* A burst of pain shot up my arm as I continued to thump my fist against the wood. I ignored it, refusing to believe that he might be somewhere else. Not now, when I needed him so much. Where else would he be? The dining room? A meeting? The marketplace? *Please, not the marketplace. I need him here, now, before word spreads, before Father—No, don't think about that. You know this is right, whatever the consequences. God of the Rebels, please...* "Thoraben—"

The door swung open. I fell forward into my brother's arms, relief draining the last of my strength. He was here. All would be well.

"Alina, what is it? Are you hurt?"

I shook my head against his chest, messing my hair in the process. It should have bothered me, but I couldn't make myself care. There was so much more at stake right now than my hair.

"No, not me." I choked the words out, the weight of what I'd done—and was about to do—squeezing the air from my lungs. "But Father, he's...I...in his office just now. In front of his advisors...both of us angry and—" I closed my eyes, grabbing at control.

All will be well. All will be well.

Seconds passed in silence as the words soaked into my panic-ridden mind, a blanket of peace over the fear, anger, pain, and each worsening scenario trying to break me. When I opened my eyes and spoke again, my heart still thudded but my words were clear.

"Ben, I told him I was a Rebel."

A clock ticked somewhere behind me. A door closed nearby—Kenna returning to her side of the adjoining suite? Thoraben stood so still I would have wondered if he'd heard me if not for his expression. He stared at me, his eyes wide, in them a mixture of pain, confusion, worry, and—was that hope?

"But you're not."

"No. Not yet anyway. He told me my insolence came from Malisa, and I got so angry that I just said it. Only, it's true. I mean, I want it to be. I want what they've got—Joha, Malisa, Nicola. You. I want the faith you all have and the belief that all will be well. I want to know your God."

His hands moved to my shoulders as he put a step of space between us. Yes, that was definitely hope in his expression. And love. So much love. It softened his deep brown eyes, wet with tears.

"You want to be a Rebel?"

"Yeah. Are you crying?"

"Learned it from Kenna."

"What?"

With a small laugh, he swiped a hand across his eyes. "Never mind. Yes, I am. But you have no idea how long I've prayed for this. Me and so many others. Mother would have been so happy." His voice cracked on the last word, a few more tears falling down his cheeks.

His approval, his words, his emotion, it was too much for my shaky, sure yet terrified heart. I twisted away from his embrace and walked further into the room, stopping in front of a painting on the wall, pretending to examine it. The colors swirled as I fought to get my emotions in check. A tissue appeared over my shoulder. I took it from Thoraben gratefully, wiping the tears that, now released, refused to stop.

"Mother, yes, but Father's going to disown me. Thoraben, you should have seen his face. Putting a knife through his chest would have been kinder—and more likely to be forgiven. He's never going to talk to me again."

"Even if he doesn't, would you still choose our God?"

Wrecked as I felt, it didn't take more than a few seconds to find the answer. "Yes. Absolutely."

The words sealing my fate were barely out of my mouth before I was bowled over by an embrace so tight it forced the air out of me. Thoraben's shout of joy brought Kenna running from the other room. Her bemused expression was so comical Thoraben and I both burst into laughter, only confusing her more. I didn't blame her. The two of us must have been quite a sight—laughing while tears rolled down our faces, my hair a mess, his grin unshakeable.

"Alina believes," Thoraben said.

It wasn't much of an explanation, but it was enough for Kenna. Her hand instantly came to her mouth, her eyes wide with delight. Then she was the one reaching for the box of tissues as she, too, began to cry. "Truly?"

Thoraben was pushed aside as Kenna wrapped her arms around me before pulling me over to the sitting area of their suite. Thoraben followed close behind. We were just getting comfortable when there was a knock at the door. My heart skidded, certain it was Father, come to send me to prison or something of the like. I opened my mouth to beg Thoraben to ignore it when it opened without him, Mrs. Adeline poking her head through the gap. Spotting the three of us, she came inside, closing the door carefully behind her.

"Is it true?"

I didn't need to ask what she meant. One only had to look at her face to know. It held the same mix of hope, love, and concern which had been on Thoraben's. None of us answered her. I guess we didn't need to.

"Oh, sweetie." Her warm, comfortable embrace was so much like Malisa's that I started sobbing. I hadn't even done anything yet—just told them I wanted to believe—and yet, here they were, three of the people most precious to me in the world, humbling me with their unrestrained delight. "Brock said as much. He came straight to me with the news, but I didn't dare believe it. Oh, oh, honey."

"Brock? Mr. Grant-Hartley?" Why would one of Father's advisors go straight to Mrs. Adeline? Unless—

"He's a Follower too," Thoraben answered, before I could ask. I shook my head in wonder. Thoraben and Kenna, Kenna's parents, one of my father's closest advisors—so many Rebels, right under Father's nose. Believing. Praying. And now me.

Maybe.

Hopefully.

"What if God doesn't want me? I'm not good like Mother and Malisa or kind like Nicola. I'm not perfect. I'm so broken, sometimes I wonder..." *How anyone could love me.* I didn't say the words. They'd just refute them—they had to, they were family—but it was the truth. Etched in my heart and mind for as long as I could remember. *They love the girl they see, the princess, the smiling, perfect girl, but what if they really knew me? Would they still love me if they saw the girl inside? Would they think I was worth Mother's sacrifice?*

Was I?

"It doesn't matter."

I frowned at Thoraben's answer. "How could it not? Father expects perfection. What kind of god would accept anything less?"

His answer was quiet but certain. "The one who loves you. The one who made it so that none of this depends on us."

"Nothing?" I sank into the cushioned seat behind me, stunned by his words. Desperate to believe them as much as I knew they couldn't be true. The seat dipped as Mrs. Adeline sat beside me.

Kenna snuggled up next to Thoraben, tucking her feet under her, contentment wrapping around her like a blanket. Any other time, I probably would have envied her peace. As it was, I could barely breathe for the desperation welling inside me. "But how? He deserves everything."

"Deserves it, absolutely. But he knows us. He knows how often we fail and how weak we are. God knew we'd never be good enough to deserve his love or favor, so he took us out of the equation. It's not a matter of being good enough or knowledge-able enough or rich enough, just about being willing."

"To what?"

"Accept him. Accept his love."

It still sounded too good to be true. But I had to try. "Do you truly think he'd want me?"

Mrs. Adeline laid a hand on my arm. "Sweetie, he's been wait-ing for you your whole life."

"But why? I've done nothing to deserve such love. I'm far from perfect."

"We all are. That's what makes his offer so precious."

I looked around the circle of family, from one tear-stained, smiling face to another. In my mind, there were others here too—Malisa, Nicola, Joha. People who'd believed in me before I'd giv-en them any reason to do so. Malisa, who'd called me back when I'd tried to run away and loved me when I'd fought against it. Nicola, who'd stayed by my side though I'd called her a criminal. Joha, who'd seen through the mask I hid behind and accepted me anyway. Who'd admitted he fought with his own doubts and let me see his heart. Who'd called me strong. I'd need that strength in the days to come.

"Are you willing to accept it?"

Faithful One, you'll hold me, won't you?

On top of that desperate prayer, almost before I'd finished forming the words, came the answer.

I've got you. I love you. All will be well.

I took a deep breath and wiped away the last of my doubts along with my tears. I couldn't deny the wanting anymore. I'd tried so hard to push it aside, telling myself it didn't matter. Only it did. Even if Father disowned me, even if their god laughed at me, I had to try.

"Yes. I want to be a Follower."

I didn't go to bed until close to three in the morning and was wide awake by six, my heart full of wonder and my mind full of nerves. The window was cold against my cheek as I leaned against it, staring out at the pink and orange sky beyond, pondering the God who'd painted it. Who was he, truly, that he would be so great and yet take an interest in me?

Mrs. Adeline said God had been waiting all my life for me to come. For eighteen years, he'd been orchestrating events and sending the right people my way to bring me to his side. It was almost too fantastic to be real. Certainly too much for me to take in but—*Thank you. Faithful One, for accepting me. I know I'm not much and I make a lot of mistakes, but for as long as you want me, I'm yours.*

"You're up early," Tayma said as she breezed through the door.

"Couldn't sleep."

Tayma looked both behind her and around the suite before closing the door and walking toward me. She stopped directly in front of the window seat, fingers playing with a frill on the sleeve of the dress she carried. That she had something on her mind was clear.

"Tayma?"

"Is it true? Are you one of us?"

"One of you?"

She looked around the room again before whispering, "A Rebel."

"You're a Rebel?" My heart swelled to overflowing at her nod. I stared at the woman before me, wondering if I'd truly known her. She'd served as my maid for the past eleven years, and I'd never once suspected her true allegiance lay anywhere but to my father. It felt like such an act of love on the Rebel God's behalf that the first person I encountered this tumultuous morning would be one of his Followers. "Yes, yes I am."

The expensive dress dropped to the floor as Tayma rushed to embrace me. Her arms were tight around my shoulders. Two months ago, I would have admonished her for being so familiar, but today I held on to her just as tightly. She pulled back, eyes wet with tears. Was every Follower I met from now on going to burst into tears when they saw me? Perhaps I should start carrying around a box of tissues.

"Tayma?"

"Forgive me, Your Highness. I just can't believe it. These are happy tears. We've prayed for so long." Tears continued to fall, wetting her cheeks along with her smile. "I almost gave up hope. Adeline told me not to, but it seemed so impossible that you would ever come to know him and yet, here you are. A Follower."

I shrugged, lost for words, overcome again by the wonder of the God who'd waited. "The other maids? Do they believe also?"

Tayma shook her head. "No. Only me. Please, don't tell them, Your Highness. I couldn't bear for them to have to choose between protecting me and respecting your father. You know what a stickler for rules Laure is. It would break her to have to report me, and I really want to keep serving you."

I sighed into the early morning. "It may not matter. Father hasn't said anything about my decision yet—I think I surprised him—but I have no doubt he'll have plenty to say when I see him next. None of it good. We may both be looking for work after today." Or I might be sitting in prison.

Tayma picked up the dress, smile still on her face as she brushed invisible dust off the back of it. "Yesterday, I would have worried about that, but overnight, God gave me a miracle. He's brought you this far. He'll lead you through this too. All will be well."

I smiled at the phrase I'd heard so many times but now not only understood but believed. "Yes. All will be well."

FORTY

I lost count of the number of times I reminded myself of that promise while I waited for Father's summons. I knew it would come. Had his advisors not been there, he might have ignored my claims or put them down to a temper tantrum, but there were witnesses present. Witnesses too righteous to bribe. Sooner or later, Father would have to confront me. I prayed I would have the strength to stand.

Had it not been for Tayma, I might have given in to the fear. But there she was, smiling at me from across the room as she tidied my clothing and, in the mirror, while Laure dressed my hair. More than once, I caught her wiping wet eyes. It was a wonder the other three maids didn't notice and question it. Tayma's delight at my decision and tears on my behalf gave me strength. This was real. And it was true.

The knock came just after lunch. I thought it would be another servant, delivering a message. Instead, it was Father himself. My maids dropped what they were doing, excused themselves, and left the room.

I walked to the door, silent as I gestured for him to come in. For the first time ever, I didn't know how to greet him. He was my father, yet he was also my king. And I'd just admitted before him and two of the most powerful men in Peverell that I was a criminal. It might have been a lie at the time, but it was the truth now.

Would he send me away? Make an example of me? Put it

down to a case of the frivolous Princess Alina being her usual childish self? The girl who wore pink to a Black and White Ball and frittered away money on bows and flounces while others lived in near poverty.

"I haven't been in here since you were a little girl."

I looked around the suite, trying to see it as he might, hoping he wouldn't tiptoe around the topic for too long. My nerves couldn't take it. Already, I felt light-headed.

"It is good to see you, Father."

"And you. Did you sleep well?"

I thought about lying, but what was the point? Not even Laure's magic had been able to hide the tired lines of my eyes. "No."

He sighed. "Me neither."

"Father?"

"You've put me in a difficult position, you know, declaring your faith so openly."

"I know. I'm sorry."

I held my hands tight together in front of me, telling them not to shake as Father stalked from one side of the room to the other, glancing out a window before stalking back again. He paused in front of Mother's portrait on the wall. "What am I supposed to do now?"

Was he asking me or Mother? Uncertain, I answered with the only words I could. "I don't know."

He turned back to me then, considering me as if seeing me for the first time, taking in my hair, the blue and green swirls on my dress, my bare feet, the hands turning white with the effort it took to keep them still. Though he smiled when he finally met my gaze, it was sad, his eyes blinking back more emotion than I'd ever seen in them. "You're so like your mother."

"Truly?"

"She would have stood up to me too." He walked back to me, sitting on one of the rose-patterned couches. Though there was plenty of room left on it for me to sit beside him, I took the chair opposite, perching right on the edge, back as straight as I could hold it.

Thoraben had offered to be with me when Father's summons came. Kenna and Mrs. Adeline too. Though none of them had announced it as publicly as me, all of them shared my crime. They'd assured me they'd stay at the palace today, ready to come and stand with me the second I called. But, though I appreciated their support more than I could say, I didn't call for them. They would have their moment. This one was between Father and me.

"Father—"

"I was wrong," he said, shocking me into silence. "I should never have said that about Marcos's son nor about you. You're not a child anymore, and it's time I accepted that. You're right, it is your life, your family, and your future. If you and Marcos wish to call off the engagement, so be it."

My hands stilled, as still as the breath caught in my lungs. *Breathe, Alina, breathe.* "You would do that?"

"I will."

"What about the alliance?"

"If I cannot find a way to keep the peace between our country and another without using my daughter as collateral, then I'm not a very good king, am I?"

Though my heart ached to tell Father about Joha and the feelings I had for him, my head, for once, wisely stopped me. True, Joha's kiss had evoked emotions I still couldn't put words to, but this wasn't a decision to take lightly, and it certainly couldn't be ruled by emotions. There was so much more at stake.

"Thank you."

"As to the other matter, that of you calling yourself a Rebel."

Here it came. The condemnation. The moment I'd been dreading. "Yes?"

"Is it true? Are you one of them?"

As I sat there, staring into the face of the man I'd looked up to all my life, usually so happy looking at me but now filled with pain, I realized I could wipe that angst away with just one word. One denial. It wouldn't be difficult. Tell him no and see his smile again. Believe in secret, as so many in the palace did.

But I couldn't do it. Was this what the Rebels had felt when they stood before him at their trials? Fear, uncertainty over the future, pain—and yet, peace. That even despite those things, they'd made the right choice. There was no other. Come what may, I couldn't go back. Not even for this man I adored and had spent my life revering.

"Yes."

"Why?"

There was a softness in Father's voice I'd never heard before. His question wasn't a challenge, it was a plea. The desperate cry of a man searching for truth. He wasn't asking to condemn me, he truly wanted to know. Because *he* needed a reason.

"Because I had no choice."

"You were coerced?"

"No!" I couldn't have him thinking that. But how could I explain the peace I felt when I knew so little? I hadn't had time to learn the right words or what to say to defend my new faith, especially to a king.

No, not a king. He set that role aside when he entered my suite. He could have summoned me to his throne room. Instead, he met me here. Waited to be welcomed in. The man sitting before me was simply my father.

"While I was in Hodenia, I stayed with some Rebels."

Father's eyes closed, but not before I saw the flash of pain. When he opened them again, it was gone, hidden behind decades of practiced control. "Malisa and Pat Samson. I know."

Of course he did. That was what had made me confess in the first place. *Just tell the story, Alina.*

"I didn't know at first that they were Followers, as they call themselves, only that they were kind to me when I gave them no reason to be. When I learned what they were, I was terrified and determined to stay as far away from them as possible. Them and all their Rebel friends. Only I couldn't do it. The longer I stayed, the harder it was to stay away.

"I envied their closeness and the peace they had. The Samsons live in a house so old and dated it should be in a museum and their clothes are just as worn—probably because they put all their money into helping others—and yet, they were happy. They had a joy I couldn't understand. How could they be so content when they had so little? I wanted what they had."

"You chose their way."

"Not while I was there. It was—" Honesty, I'd promised myself to be honest— "when I told you I was one of them."

Father frowned. "You lied to me?"

"Yes. And no. I wasn't when I said it. I was furious at you for being so rude to Marcos and wanted to hurt you, so I said the one thing I knew you'd hate. But, as soon as the words were out of my mouth, I realized how much I wanted them to be true. I believe in their God and, by some miracle of love, he believes in me too.

"I don't know if any of that makes any sense to you or what will happen to me now for saying it, but it's the truth and, no matter what, I won't change my mind. If you have to send me away now, I'll understand."

Though my heart thumped triple time as I waited for his reply, my hands didn't shake. I'd laid my heart out on the floor for Father to crush, my life too, should he choose to do so, and yet, I wasn't afraid. There was no panic—no shaking, no nausea, no forcing myself to breathe. Whether he sent me away or allowed me to stay, I'd made the right choice. All would be well. Was that what gave the Followers peace? The knowledge that, no matter what happened, one day everything would work out because the God of the universe was in control?

The silence stretched. I chanced a glance at Father only to find him staring at me, his chin resting on steepled hands.

"Your mother believed in God."

I blinked, surprised by the turn of the conversation. I'd been steeling myself for judgment and he offered none.

"He was everything to her, so much so that I envied him. She loved me, I never once doubted that, but her God she adored. He was a part of her, as much as an arm or leg or even the oxygen she breathed."

I nodded, knowing that already from her journals. Every page confirmed it. He'd been not just a part of her life but life itself.

"She prayed over you when you were born."

"Truly?" My voice cracked over the word.

Tears gathered at the corners of Father's eyes. "It was the last thing she said. 'Faithful One, bless my Alina. May she know you.'"

He broke down then, sobbing into his hands. There was wetness on my own cheeks as I watched my strong father, the man who'd always been in complete control, lose control completely. I ached to go to him and wrap him in my arms, but I stayed still. This was a private pain no embrace could fix. He grieved for the woman he'd lost. Did he also grieve for the faith he'd lost? Malisa had said he believed once, before Mother's death had crushed him. He spoke of Mother's joy. Did he remember what it felt like? Were the tears as much for himself as they were for her?

"Father?" I waited until his tears were back under control and he looked at me, the question in my heart too much to ignore. Who knew when, if ever, we'd have a chance to talk like this again? "Why did you do it?"

The silence stretched long enough for me to second-, third-, and tenth-guess my boldness in asking. I should have left it, but I had to know. "Why did you make them criminals?"

Father's eyes were sad, his tears wrenching my heart in a way nothing before ever had. "Malisa didn't tell you?" I shook my head. "I'm surprised. I thought she'd be all too happy to tell everyone she met how I ruined her life."

If only he knew. "None of the Rebels I met ever said a word against you. All they could talk about was God's faithfulness."

"Malisa wasn't just a Rebel. She was the first one. The first Follower I ever exiled."

"What?" Disbelief burst out of me, shock begging him to take it back. He didn't. I knew he wouldn't, but still—

"My wife's best friend. Ciera would have been horrified."

Malisa had never even mentioned it. None of them had. She'd said Mother's death started it all, but really? She'd been the first?

"It was eight months after your mother died. Malisa came to the palace to confront me. I will never forget the sight of her storming into my office like an avenger and ordering me to put down my work and go to the nursery to see my children. She told me I could mourn for as long as I liked but, with two children to care for, I didn't have the luxury of doing it alone.

"Looking back now, I know she told the truth, but at the time, I was so angry and bitter that all I saw was a do-gooder telling me I wasn't good enough. She'd been hinting at similar things for weeks, but that day she outright told me off. Her honesty was more than I could take. I was furious. I didn't just want her out of the palace, I wanted her out of the kingdom. I had her hauled out of my office and straight to trial, where I told everyone she was trying to destroy the royal family and exiled her."

"But you made Rebels of them all, not just Malisa."

"You have no idea how helpless I felt sitting beside my dying wife, knowing there was nothing I could do to save her. I hope you never know the feeling. She had faith, even to the end. I tried. I begged God to save her, told him I couldn't do this alone. But he didn't. He let her die. What kind of heartless, cruel God does that? You were just hours old. You never even had the chance to know her. I couldn't follow a God like that."

"But to purge him from Peverell?"

"Do you know what it's like to have your failure thrown in your face time and time again? Every chapel, every prayer, every Follower I saw was yet another reminder that God hadn't saved her. I couldn't let them stay and convince more people to believe in this god who failed me and would, in time, fail them all, so I outlawed it. I thought I was doing what was best for my people. Saving them, such as it was. It was easy enough, after Malisa, to convince myself Followers were dangerous. Deluded, even. I thought I'd rid the kingdom of them, but now I see they were around me all the time. Ciera had made sure of it."

"Adeline and Nate?" I guessed.

He nodded. "I didn't know Adeline was Malisa's sister when I brought her to the palace, only that she was Ciera's choice to care for you. By the time I found out, and that she held the same faith, you'd become so attached to her that I couldn't bear to take another mother from you, such as she was. I let her stay, on the condition that neither she nor Nate ever said a word to you about their God. I had no idea my decision back then would impact our family forever."

"Because Thoraben married Kenna."

"I did everything I could to separate them and make Thoraben marry someone else but, in the end, it was for nothing. They still married."

"He loved her."

"I know."

"He believes too."

Father's sigh held more pain than I could take. "I know."

He looked up then. Opened his arms to me. I didn't wait for another invitation, flinging myself into his embrace. His still-flowing tears wet my neck as he held me tight.

"I'm so sorry, Alina. I've made some terrible decisions as king of this country. Even at the time, I knew they were wrong, but your mother was gone and, with her, my light."

"You could change. It's not too late. You could ask for their forgiveness and bring them all home. They'd understand."

"Even if by some miniscule chance they did, it wouldn't matter. I can never forgive myself."

He held up a hand when I opened my mouth to refute him again. "No, Alina. Don't. Perhaps one day I'll have the strength to do what you have but, right now, the repercussions of my hypocrisy are more than I can consider. Just know you needn't be afraid. Not of me. I could no more take away the joy of your faith than I could that of your mother."

"It's real, Father. *He's* real."

His smile was strained, but it was there. Though he didn't understand the decision I'd made, he would support me in it. It was more than I could have hoped. *Thank you, God of the Rebels.*

FORTY-ONE

The letter in my hand shook as I wandered the garden paths, unable to see anything but the words in front of me, and even they were blurry. Though I'd opened it in my suite, my engagement ring falling out into my hand, it had taken only a paragraph to know I couldn't stay there—not with three of my four maids staring at me, not even bothering to pretend they weren't. I'd come to the gardens half an hour ago and still had yet to sit. Neither had I finished the letter, a direct reply to the one I'd sent Marcos after speaking with Father three days ago.

Read the rest, Alina. The truth can't be any worse than the unknown.

I'd told myself that for the first time as I passed Mother's favorite rosebush, then again as I'd waved to a gardener pruning, and as I'd stared at my reflection in the fish pond, and read the inscription long ago memorized on the plaque at the entry to the garden.

I hadn't expected a reply from Marcos so soon. He'd left right after the ball, too anxious of what decisions might be made in his absence to be away from the investigation for long. I'd gotten the impression the investigation would be a lengthy process, giving me plenty of time to settle in my own heart what it was I wanted before hearing the details which could change all that. Was this how Kenna had felt the day after the whirlwind? Like everything was moving too fast, leaving her with neither the power to stop it nor the strength to keep up?

No. You are not Mackenna. You are Princess Alina Ciera Georgia May the First, daughter of King Everson and the late Queen Ciera of Peverell. You have the power to stand and the strength to surrender. No matter what this letter holds, all will be well.

Taking a deep breath, I perched myself on the armrest of a marble garden bench and tried again.

> *Dear Alina,*
>
>   *Thank you for your letter. It was a welcome surprise amidst the craziness of this past week, especially to have someone care enough to ask how I am faring, as opposed to telling me. Though the investigation is ongoing, tests came back yesterday with the confirmation that Ryan is my son. I'm still trying to make myself believe it. All these years, I've had a son, and I didn't know.*
>
>   *I've not yet been allowed to meet him nor speak with Rachana. As I feared, Father is intent on covering up my "indiscretion," as he is calling it. However, despite the pressure both he and his advisors are placing on me to do otherwise, I plan to formally acknowledge Ryan as my son and heir as soon as possible.*
>
>   *As to what to do after that—I have never before struggled so strongly to find the right and honorable course of action. I made a public commitment to you and your Father, pledging my future to you—something that, despite my rash actions the day I came to see you in Hodenia, I take very seriously. And yet, how can I ignore my responsibility to Rachana and our son? I have done precisely that for six years already.*
>
>   *Though she isn't asking me to marry her, only acknowledge our son, I still feel as if marrying Rachana would be the right thing to do. However, as Father daily reminds me, I cannot think only of*

*my own interests at this time. As heir to the throne
of Hodenia, I must consider what is best for the
kingdom, which would be to marry you and there-
by cement the alliance between our two kingdoms.*

*I hate to put the decision on you, knowing full
well the overbearing weight of it, but as it is your
future affected as well as mine, and Ryan will
henceforward be part of my—our—lives, I must
ask. What would you have me do? Do you still
wish to marry me?*

The ring is yours, no matter what you decide.

*I await your reply. And again, forgive me. I
regret so much the way I've hurt you.*

Marcos

The letter shook in my hand, my heart aching for the prince
brought low. He hadn't mentioned Rachana dying, so his father
must have hidden that from him. Perhaps that was the reason
they hadn't allowed him to see her. I couldn't help but think it
might make his decision easier if he knew. He could marry us
both if he wanted to. Marry Rachana, see her through her final
days, and then marry me. If Father was right and Rachana as
ill as he claimed, it wouldn't be a long wait. Practically, it made
sense. Emotionally, it would wreck us all.

Still, the option remained. If I chose it.

How am I supposed to choose? Marcos was supposed to have
decided. It's what I'd hoped he'd tell me. *"No, Alina, I won't marry you,"* or *"Yes, I choose you."* He wasn't supposed to have raised
more questions. Tell him to marry Rachana? Beg him to marry
me?

The pressure...too much pressure.

Father, Marcos, Joha. The three most influential men in my
life. Two were royalty. One, a farmer. Two could give me the life
I wanted, one could give me the life I craved. If he chose me.

And in that lay my dilemma. Joha hadn't chosen me. Unlike

Marcos, he'd made no promises. I wasn't even certain he liked me. And yet—

"That's a serious look you've got there."

I blinked twice, torn from my pondering by Mrs. Adeline's voice. Where had she come from?

"You've been out here a while. Are you okay?"

No. Not even close.

"Father wants me to marry Prince Marcos and Marcos said he will marry me if I still want him to."

"I don't see the problem."

"I don't know if I want to marry him."

Mrs. Adeline sat in the chair across from me, picking a tiny purple grass flower the gardeners had missed from the ground as she did so. The bloom spun as she twirled the stem between her fingers, a half smile on her face. "Joha's pretty special, isn't he?"

"How did you—?" We were talking about Marcos. Weren't we? I hadn't said anything about Joha.

"Malisa said he's been moping about too."

I shook my head, not believing it. Joha didn't mope. Least of all over a princess he'd told in no uncertain terms to leave him alone.

"I don't think so. Joha doesn't even like me. He spent most of the past six weeks angry at me." Except for our time in the apple tree. And that kiss. I touched a hand to my burning cheek. Was it hot out here? I hadn't noticed it before, but I had been out here a while.

"Something tells me you like him though."

"He grows on a person." Though I tried to be nonchalant, I knew she saw through it. Malisa might have been observant, but Mrs. Adeline had known and mothered me since the day I was born. There was no point in hiding anything from her. I abandoned my perch and sat on the bench. "He kissed me."

"Did he now?"

"Yes, but you can stop smiling like that because it wasn't a real kiss. I don't even think he meant to do it. He was angry at me for calling myself worthless and in the middle of the lecture he just—he kissed me."

"And?"

I shrugged, feeling as if to speak the details aloud would negate them somehow, stripping the moment of its magic. "And then he told me to go inside. Like a child." Only it hadn't been an order as much as a plea, his breath whispering across my face as he said it.

"He cares for you."

Did he? Never once in the weeks I stayed at The Well did I ever think Joha cared about me. Despised me and put up with me, certainly, but not cared. And then, that night, moonlight in our hair...*I couldn't bear it if something happened to you.* Was it his protective attitude kicking in or something more? "Maybe."

"Do you love him?"

"How would I know?"

"Do you care what he thinks? Admire him? Want to be the first person he runs to when he has news, good or bad? Does he have the ability to make you feel like the most cherished woman in the whole world one moment and so angry the next that you wonder what could have possibly drawn you to him in the first place, and yet it would break your heart to be with anyone else?"

"Yes." Could it truly be? "To all of them."

"Sounds like you're in love."

I folded Marcos's letter and placed it on the seat beside me, unconvinced. Love was supposed to be happy all the time. Airy, fairy, daffodils, diamonds, and roses. Sweet kisses and warm toes and feeling such strong affection that you might just melt into a puddle—and not even care so long as the one you loved was with you.

This was none of those things.

What I felt for Joha was strong and fierce. An ache, not a comfort. I desperately wanted him to see me, not as the princess everyone else knew and the papers frequently commented on, but as a woman. As me. I wanted him to see me and—I sighed—I wanted him to want me. To kiss me again and look at me like he had that night in the gazebo, as if I was the most precious thing in the world.

I wanted him to see past the selfishly rude person I'd been when he first met me to the woman I'd become and know that my opinion of him had changed too. I was so ashamed of the things I'd called him. They were the immature notions of a silly, spoiled brat of a princess who'd had someone stand up to her for the first time in her life. I'd love him forever for that. He'd changed my life, whether or not I was ready for it or appreciated it at the time.

"But what if I do but he doesn't love me? With the exception of that kiss, which I'm certain was just to shut me up, he's never once shown a shred of evidence that he holds any affection for me, even a little." Except perhaps, that day in the apple tree. I couldn't put words to it, but there had been something there. Perhaps the first moment of respect, perhaps love in its infancy, but something.

"Well, of course he hasn't. You were engaged to Prince Marcos. The man who will one day be his king. He knew that, even if you've forgotten."

I stared down at Marcos's ring, back on my finger where it had delighted me since the night he'd proposed. I'd loved it on sight. Ran halfway through the palace to show it off to Kenna before Marcos and I were even officially engaged. It was the most sparkly, beautiful thing I'd ever seen with its enormous pink diamond in the center and smaller white diamonds interspersed with sapphires surrounding it and the gold band.

It had been beautiful.

Now it just felt big. Big and heavy. Not just on my finger but in my heart. Far more than just a ring, it was a commitment and responsibility. And a representation of the girl I'd once been—the girl who'd been slowly disappearing since the day I arrived at The Well.

I was engaged to Prince Marcos, heir to the throne of Hodenia.

I was in love with Joha Samson.

I hadn't meant to. I hadn't even realized I was until Mrs. Adeline had pointed out the truth.

The marriage between Marcos and me would cement the alliance between Hodenia and Peverell forever. Two kingdoms becoming one. It had been decided years ago and counted on for even longer.

And now, I'd been given the chance to walk away from it all and choose to marry whoever I wanted. I'd thought the responsibility of marrying into another country was heavy. It was nothing compared to this decision.

The man I'd committed to or the man I loved?

It should have been simple. Marcos had everything—wealth, influence, the title of Crown Prince and all its privileges. If I married him, all that would be mine. I'd have even more maids than I did now, a greater wardrobe, two kingdoms of people swooning at a simple wave from my hand. Our children would have the best of everything, a secure future. Instead of merely a princess, one day I'd be queen, just like my mother.

And, as much as Father played it down, Peverell needed this. We were a small country, vulnerable to attack because of size and traditionalist beliefs. Landlocked on three sides by Hodenia, it was imperative they stay an ally. The alliance between our countries, symbolized by our marriage, ensured their protection.

I shook my head, wishing I was anywhere but here having to make this choice.

I'd thought having someone else tell me what to do every day of my life was tiresome. It was so much worse to have to make the decisions for myself. What if I made the wrong decision? What if I chose the wrong man? The wrong life? The wrong future? My chest ached. *Calm down, Alina. You can do this. You asked for this. You wanted the choice, now make it. It's only your life...and Marcos's...possibly Joha's...and every person in Peverell.*

What if I chose Joha and Peverell paid for my decision, losing Hodenia's protection? But then, what if I chose Marcos and he never learnt to care for me? Or worse, I him. Could I live a loveless life, knowing my sorrow had bought my country's future? I pressed a hand against my chest, trying to force back the building panic. *You can do this.*

"I can't do this." The words tumbled out before I could think the better of them.

"Oh honey." Mrs. Adeline came over to my side, wrapping an arm around me. I lay my head on her shoulder, leaning into her embrace. "Forget Peverell and your father for a moment. What do *you* want?"

But therein lay the problem. I wanted it all—to save Marcos, love Joha, protect Peverell, help The Well, stay my Father's little girl, have faith like Mother. But choosing one meant denying another, and I could never forget who I was.

Marrying Marcos was the logical choice in every way. Neither Peverell, I, nor our children would ever want for anything.

Except the man I loved. The man who had no title, no wealth, not even a home of his own. The man who was more comfortable on the back of a horse than in a room full of people. The man who climbed trees instead of hierarchies and had little to no tact. The man whose faith determined every decision he made and who had, sometime in the past six weeks, gained every bit of respect and admiration I had within me. And more.

I spun the ring around my finger.

Marcos or Joha? Ball gowns or jeans? Father's alliance or Mother's dreams? Honor or love?

God of the Rebels, Faithful One, I need you. Help me as you helped Nicola, Arden, Pat, and all the others. Show me what to do.

The news broke the next day.

Prince Marcos Claims Son as His Own.

Hodenia's New Heir, Prince Ryan the First.

Though the papers lay beside my place at the breakfast table, I didn't do any more than glance at the headlines. Marcos had already told me the true story. I didn't need a sensationalized version from the media. I was more worried about the empty seat at Father's place. He'd missed breakfast again, for the third day in a row. Was he busy or avoiding me? At least Thoraben and Kenna had come. Solitude would have left far too much room for the doubts to overwhelm me.

"How are you doing with all this?" Thoraben asked, nodding toward the papers. "I had no idea. Marcos always seemed so—"

"Perfect?" So much for counting on Thoraben and Kenna to provide a distraction from the decision I was trying to avoid. I took a bite of my toast, chewing it almost to the point that there was nothing left to swallow.

"Well, no one's perfect, but yeah. Upright. It's come as a bit of a shock that he has a son."

"Ryan." I pushed my plate away, the weight of the decision I had to make lying so heavy in my stomach that it didn't leave room for more than a few bites, tiny as they had been. "I can't do this."

"Eat breakfast? Hey, I'll take yours," Thoraben said, pulling my plate toward him. "Save me getting more." Three forkfuls of scrambled eggs made it into his mouth before he noticed the silence around him. The compassion on Kenna's face was almost my undoing.

"I don't think she's talking about breakfast," she told her husband.

My lips trembled against the glass I tried to drink from. I put it down before I choked on the lump in my throat. "I know I should marry Marcos. It's what's best for everyone. Peverell needs me to, but—" I blinked furiously, trying to stop the tears before they fell. One escaped anyway, trickling its way down my cheek. I swiped it away. "I just—I mean—I feel as if I don't even know him anymore, let alone trust him. He kept this from me, what other secrets might he have?"

"I doubt he has another son hidden away," Thoraben said, earning a frown and quick shake of the head from Kenna. His teasing didn't bother me like it normally would have. How could it, when there was so much else on my mind?

"I always wanted to marry Marcos. I thought him the most

wonderful man I'd ever met and was thrilled when Father told me the betrothal had been made official. But now..."

"You're having second thoughts?"

"It's just, Marcos isn't the only one who's changed. What if I don't want to be queen anymore?"

"Then you don't marry him," Thoraben said pragmatically. "Neither Marcos nor Father would have given you the choice if they hadn't meant it."

"But Peverell—"

"Has survived perfectly well without a marriage between the two of you for centuries already and will go on doing so in the future should you choose not to. Despite what it may feel like, it's not your job to save Peverell."

"I wish I could believe you."

"Believe it."

"It's not as easy as you think."

"It's also not as difficult as you're making it. What do *you* want, Alina?"

There it was. That question again. The one I still had no answer to.

The one I needed an answer to by tomorrow.

FORTY-TWO

"I've come to a decision." My heart raced in my chest as I stood before Father, sitting at his desk. His face was blank, his attention solely on me and what I was about to say, having put down his pen and papers the instant I walked through the door. As much as I appreciated his attention, I wouldn't have minded if he wasn't quite so focused. I'd have more chance of convincing him I felt confident about my decision if he couldn't see the way my hands were shaking.

You made the right decision, Alina. Really, you did. The sooner you tell him, the sooner you can escape his scrutiny.

The sooner you can go back to your room and fall apart.

"I will marry Prince Marcos, as soon as arrangements can be made."

"You're certain of this?"

Unbelievably, yes. Three days of sitting in my room, begging Mother's God to show me what to do, and I'd finally found peace. Marcos. There was still so much about the future that had me uncertain, but who I'd face it with was sure.

"You've always told me that the princess is the heart of the kingdom. Much as I might wish at times to be in not so bright a spotlight, the truth is, I am a princess and with that comes the obligation to do what is best for the people. I've been reading Mother's journals and, time and time again, she chose her people over her own comfort."

"She also married for love."

I stared at Father, unable to comprehend what he was doing. He'd wanted me to marry Prince Marcos. It was the reason we'd fought in the first place and why I'd told him I was a Rebel. And now he was questioning my decision?

Hold on to the peace. Marcos is the right choice.

"Do you love Prince Marcos?"

"No, not yet, but—"

"Duty to one's country is a heavy weight to bear. A princess *is* the heart of her people, but a heart is of little use if it is crushed beneath such a burden."

"I will not be crushed." I had to believe it. If I didn't, no one else would. I could be strong, even if I currently felt like any second I might shatter into a thousand pieces. The God of the Rebels, now my God, would help me. Hadn't Mother said that in her journal? Every second page it seemed was a plea for her God to help her. Every other page was a prayer of gratitude that he had. He would help me too. "Prince Marcos is a good man, and he cares for me. I believe, together, we can lead the people of Hodenia into a wonderful future."

"If you're certain."

"I am."

"Very well, then. I'll speak with King Dorien and see to arrangements."

"Thank you."

I walked out of the room before Father could change my mind. Maybe if Joha hadn't sent me away that day, my decision might have been different. But he had. Joha didn't want me. He'd made that clear. It was time I stopped thinking about him and stepped into the future I'd been born into.

Did I love Prince Marcos? No. Not like I'd once thought. Not even close to how much I loved Joha. But I cared. About him. About his son. About the future of our kingdoms. And, for now, that would have to be enough.

Pure white satin draped my frame, twenty feet of lace overlay clutched in my hand as I stared out the window and pushed down the panic. *Not now. It's too late for regrets. You made the right choice. The only choice. Your people need this.* I needed this. Marriage to Prince Marcos meant security, honor, a future, and the power, influence, and resources to make a difference.

Yes, I'd made the right decision. If only I could make it official.

"Where's Father? He should be back by now."

We'd been waiting in the vestry of Peverell's chapel for forty-five minutes now, our car having been rushed around the back on arrival rather than to the front doors as planned. All the driver had been able to tell us was that he'd been ordered to, the wedding party not yet ready for my arrival. Father had left at once to see what the matter was. The wedding was supposed to have started an hour ago. The press weren't the only ones getting restless.

"Why don't you sit," Kenna said. "I'm sure it'll only be a few more minutes."

I shook my head, too jittery to sit. I'd believed Kenna's reassurances the first time she'd offered them. Now, I was beginning to wonder. "No, something's wrong."

Kenna exchanged a glance with Wenderley before looking back at me. Though she assured me everything was fine—again, not for the first time—I could see the two of them were beginning to worry.

I'd originally planned on having three bridesmaids—Kenna, Wenderley, and Wenderley's sister, Jade, in lieu of Nicola, but Jade was out of the country on a belated honeymoon. I hadn't replaced her. I was thankful for that now. Less people to see me fall apart.

I forced another breath, wrenching my focus from my fear. *Think about something else. Anything else...*

Mrs. Rosina had done exquisite work with our gowns, Kenna and Wenderley's being the same style as mine only tea-length and made from the palest of pink satins instead of white. No diamonds, no pearls or rosettes, simply satin overlaid with lace. And yet, I couldn't have imagined any design more beautiful. Like my gown from the King's Ball, the gowns' beauty lay in their simplicity. I'd loved them on sight.

A sob escaped my throat. Kenna was instantly at my side. "Hey, it's going to be fine. Any second, your father is going to come back through that door, and you'll be on your way down the aisle. You'll see." The handle rattled. "Oh look, here he is now."

But the man who walked through the door wasn't Father.

"Thoraben?"

My heart took a dive to join the butterflies swirling in my stomach at the expression of sympathy on my brother's face. He ignored his wife, walking straight to me, taking my hands in his. His lips pursed so tight they lost their color as he looked my gown up and down before turning his gaze to mine. When he shook his head, everything in me stilled. "I'm sorry. So sorry."

My heart pounded along with every other nerve in my body. Was the world tipping? Was I? A chair materialized behind me, Kenna's—or was it Wenderley's?—hands at my sides, guiding me into it. Spots blurred my vision as Thoraben knelt down in front of me.

"I'm not getting married," I whispered, closing my eyes against the dizzying blackness. A hand rubbed circles across my back, another pulled the veil from my hair. I hadn't realized how heavy it was until it was removed.

"No," Thoraben said, confirming my fear. "Prince Marcos eloped yesterday with the mother of his son."

I sat up suddenly, sending my head and the room into a spin. He couldn't be married to Rachana. He was marrying me. He'd told me. We'd agreed it was the right decision.

And I'd prayed. *Faithful One, I asked. You said Marcos. I was so certain. Was I wrong?*

Had I just made the biggest mistake of my life?

"Marcos isn't even here?"

"Not him or his parents. He didn't tell anyone what he was

doing or where he was going. His Head of Security found the notes this morning—one for his parents and this one for you."

Thoraben held out a folded piece of paper. My hand trembled as I took it. Though I opened it, the black writing blurred and bounced so much I couldn't make sense of the few lines. I handed it back to Thoraben. "Please?"

His voice was gentle as he read, as apologetic as I'm certain Marcos felt as he wrote it.

> *Alina,*
>   *I thought I could marry you, but I can't. I have to do what's right for my family, and that means marrying Rachana. I hope one day you can forgive me.*
>   *Marcos*

I nodded as Thoraben refolded the paper, wondering what I should have been feeling. Anger? Distress? Was that what one was supposed to feel when her fiancé left her at the altar, with two countries standing witness? Perhaps that would come later. Right now, all I felt was numb.

"What happens now?"

"Father has gone to Hodenia to see King Dorien, but as for you, home. There are guards waiting outside the door to escort you to the car and see you safely back to the palace. The driver has been directed to take back roads and stay well clear of the crowds. Wenderley will go with you. Kenna, you'll stay with me."

"What about the guests? The press?" I closed my eyes again as the weight of so many people's hopes crashed down on me. They were all there, waiting. For a wedding which was never going to happen. I pressed a hand against my forehead.

"Kenna and I will sort all that out. We'll make a speech, let them all know. You won't need to worry about it."

I nodded again. It seemed all I could do. My heart must have kept its beat somewhere within my body, but I couldn't feel it. The butterflies lay still too.

"Are you ready?" Thoraben asked. I blinked down at him. Ready? For what? "You should go before news spreads."

News. Right. That Marcos had left me. Again.

And this time, he wasn't coming back.

FORTY-THREE

I walked to the window, running my hand along the edge of the sill. Father had come home this morning after a week spent with King Dorien with little more information than that Marcos truly had married. He and Rachana hadn't returned to the palace yet but they would, soon, to begin their life together. The numbness had passed, but instead of the anger I expected, it was restlessness and confusion which filled me.

I'd chosen to marry Marcos. I'd known even despite my feelings for Joha that it was the right choice. For me and for Peverell. I'd agonized over it, pushing aside the what-ifs and focusing instead on what our marriage would mean for the future of our countries. All that agonizing, praying, begging God to show me what to do. I'd been so certain his answer was to choose Marcos.

But now?

Had I gotten it wrong? I was so new to this faith thing. Maybe I'd mistaken God's answer and the peace I felt about it. Easy enough to do. And yet. *No. It was right.* Choosing Marcos had been the only choice. Even knowing it meant giving up Joha.

But Marcos hadn't chosen me. And now I'd lost them both.

You don't fit here. You never have and you never will. Joha's words hurt as much today as they had almost two months ago when he said them. Mostly because they were wrong. I might not bake as well as Malisa, swing a hammer like Arden, or ever be comfortable milking a cow, but I wanted to believe there was a place for me at The Well. If nothing else, I could move bricks from one place to another.

A vision of the finished chapel skittered through my mind, looking as it had in my dream that night all those months ago. Tall, stately, welcoming. Home. And Joha, standing at the front, eyes closed, head lifted heavenward as he played his guitar. Worshiping the Faithful One who'd given them the time, the funds, and the passion to see it built.

I walked to my desk and pulled out Mother's journal, sliding out the paper I'd slipped inside it. The words to that song Joha had sung the night of the thanksgiving service. I'd asked Malisa for the words later on before copying them down.

> *Because of Him I know*
> *No matter where I go*
> *If I'm with Him and He with me*
> *All will be well.*

All would be well. How I ached to believe that.

I could serve God just as well here in the palace as I could at The Well. Thoraben, Kenna, and her parents had proven that. For eighteen years, they'd prayed and believed that one day our whole family would come to know God's love. Thoraben had used his position and influence to do what no one but him could have, assisting and ensuring not one of the exiled Rebels was lost or forgotten. Who knew what I could do with my influence?

Joha did.

The thought stuck in my heart even as I admitted it wasn't entirely true. God was the only one who saw me completely, but Joha had seen something in me that I was only just beginning to realize. I could make a difference, not only in what fashions were popular each season but in people's lives.

I wanted that. Not to be in the spotlight, but to make a difference. To believe in others as the Samsons and Nicola had believed in me. As Joha had.

Joha...

What was he doing right now? What did he think of my non-marriage to Marcos? Was he relieved? Disappointed? Happy? Did he care at all? If only I could talk to him, even just for a moment. Of course, he'd made it clear he didn't want that, but what if he regretted what he'd said that morning? He had said our kiss meant something to him. Well, to be exact, it was more along the lines of it hadn't meant nothing, but that was something, right?

Oh, this was ridiculous.

I couldn't invite myself to The Well, it would be highly improper, even if I hadn't been under strict instructions not to leave the palace until the media circus settled down but... I put Mother's journal back in its drawer and pulled out some paper.

> *Dear Joha,*
>
> *You would have heard by now that Prince Marcos has married. It came as a shock to me, though I suppose it shouldn't have. He told me that day he came to The Well that he felt as if this was his chance to redeem the worst choice he'd ever made. I guess now he has that chance. I'm not as hurt by his decision as I would have expected. He's a different man now than the one I thought I knew.*
>
> *You asked me the night Nicola and Arden got engaged if I loved Marcos. I can't remember exactly what I said, but it was probably some glib answer about how everyone did. The truth is, I don't think I even knew that night what love was. I do now, and no, it's not what I ever felt for him.*
>
> *But enough about Marcos. What I really want to do is thank you. I've changed so much since that day you found me trying to escape The Well and, while I still have a long way to go, I'd like to think it's for the better. Your parents helped with that, Mrs. Adeline and other Rebels too, even Marcos*

leaving me to a degree, but much of it was because of you.

You saw past the image I've spent my whole life perfecting to who I really was—and you didn't hate me for it. When I felt so weak, you said I was strong. I just wanted to thank you for that. I hope one day to have the chance to see you again and tell you in person how much your words meant to me.

Until then,

Alina

P.S. I miss hearing you play guitar. I've been surrounded by music all my life but never had any of it impact me as deeply as your playing. It's like you don't just play notes or chords, you play God's heart.

A week later, Marcos and his new family came home. Two days after that, official portraits were published in all the papers. I'd thought I was handling the situation so well until Tayma handed me the glossy magazine with their smiling faces plastered across the front of it. Somehow, deep at the heart of me, underneath the smiles and assurances to everyone that I was okay—something I'd truly believed until this moment—I'd still been holding on to the hope that this was all a big misunderstanding.

Now, even that hope was gone.

The photo blurred as I dropped the magazine onto my dressing table, hung my head, and let the sobs come. It was all true. Marcos was married. To the beautiful, slim, striking woman beside him. The proof was there in front of me, in Marcos's and Rachana's smiles and the stoic face of the young boy standing with them. My grand, faith-filled sacrifice in choosing him over Joha had been for nothing. I'd failed, not only myself but Peverell. I couldn't save them.

The room began to close in on me until the giant suite of

rooms felt like a wooden box, pinning me on every side. I gasped in a breath and willed my head to stop spinning. My hands shook.

Failure. That's what you are. You gave it all up—and for what? Nothing. No Marcos. No Joha.

No. I could fight this. I could. It hadn't been for nothing. I'd found faith, and purpose, and strength, and—

Purpose? Strength? You, the girl who's barely been out of her room in the past week. You, the girl who was so certain God would honor her sacrifice of honor over love. Where's that God of yours now? Laughing? You're a fool.

The room was going to suffocate me, if the voice inside my head didn't first. I had to get out of here. The Well was out of reach but—

The stables. I could go there. No one would bother me. No one would even think to look for me there. It wasn't The Well or the comforting arms of Joha lending me his strength like he had that day in the apple tree, but it would smell the same. That strange mix of straw, manure, horses, sweat, and life. I'd plugged my nose the first time I smelled it, gagging as it caught in my throat, certain I'd never be clean again. Now, it was all I wanted. To be surrounded by that smell.

The grooms looked at me strangely when I entered, immediately asking if I wished to ride and offering to saddle a horse. I shook my head, thanking them before walking further in, poking my head over every stall till I found an empty one.

God, you're here, right? Not literally in this stall but with me? Like you were with Mother? Because I think I messed up. And now? A piece of straw skittered across the room as I sighed. *I don't know what to do.*

The tears came then, quiet ones, slowly meandering their way down my cheeks. They didn't come with answers, but neither did they hold condemnation. I sat down, there in the straw, and let them fall.

It was Kenna's father who found me an hour later, curled up in that empty horse stall, wrapped in a blanket I'd found there. He took one look at me, nodded, and walked away. I was so glad he didn't ask the requisite "Are you okay?" question that a few more tears fell. Wasn't it clear to everyone that I wasn't? Every time someone asked, I felt like I had to assure them I was. Or would be. It was what a princess did. Stayed strong. Even when she was as broken as me.

You're not broken.

I sighed into the empty stall. Joha had said that. That day in the apple tree. I'd believed him that day. Why was it so difficult to believe it now?

The door swung open. I sat up quickly before letting myself slump back into the straw. It was just Mr. Nate, back again. He handed me a glass of water. I took it gratefully. I thought he'd walk straight out again but he sat down instead. Right there on the dusty, hay-strewn floor. I might have been embarrassed to have him watching me except he didn't. He stretched out his legs, leaned back against the wall, pulled an apple out of his pocket, and began to eat. I swallowed another few mouthfuls of the water, as content as he was to sit in silence. He finished the apple around the same time I finished my water.

And then we just sat, each on our own side of the stall, caught up in our own thoughts as the noise of the stable washed around us. Horses being taken out and brought back by stable hands. The slosh of buckets full of water being carried to their stalls. Shovels grating over cement as empty stalls were cleaned.

But in this stall, silence.

"More?" Mr. Nate finally asked, gesturing toward my empty glass.

I shook my head. "Thank you, though."

He nodded, then stood and walked the few steps to the door. It was probably time I stopped hiding too, much as I hated to go back. My maids would be turning the palace inside out looking for me.

Mr. Nate held the door open for me as I walked out it. Then he took the glass from me and placed a hand on my arm. He was so gentle, his movements so slow, like he was caring for a spooked horse. Perhaps I looked that way to him.

"I'll be okay." I found myself telling him, the lie coming all too easily.

"I wasn't going to ask."

Oh. "Thank you."

"I just wanted to say..." He stopped. Dropped his hand but continued to gaze at me in that strong but gentle way. Waiting. For me to answer?

"Yes?"

"You have a lot of names, Alina. And I don't only mean Georgia and Ciera and that long list. You're princess, sister, inspiration, someone people look up to. I'm pretty sure I've even heard your father call you the Heart of Peverell." He smiled at that. "You're so many things to so many people, but did you know God has a name for you too? You know what he calls you?"

I shook my head.

"*Mine.* He calls you his. He looks at you with an expression of absolute delight, his heart so full of love that it can't help but break into song. Even on those days when you feel like everyone else has abandoned you, God never will. When you start feeling like everything is falling apart, remember that. God calls you his. He's proud of you. You will always have a place in his arms."

He left then, walking up the stable's aisle, checking in on horses and grooms as if he hadn't just dumped a giant jewel of wisdom in my lap. One far more precious than all the jewels I owned.

He calls you mine. He's proud of you.

How had Mr. Nate known how desperately I needed those words? Was it possible the same God who held Mother when she was weak had put the words in the usually-so-silent Mr. Nate's mind just for me?

Truly?

Mine.

The words echoed in my heart as I walked back to the palace, up the long flight of stairs and down the hall to my suite. They echoed in my mind as I reassured my maids I hadn't run away nor been abducted by eager news reporters. They stayed with me long into the night as I wrestled fear and regret back into submission and were still playing on my mind when I woke.

God hasn't abandoned you. He never will. God calls you his. All will be well.

It wasn't until I went to breakfast that they faltered.

Father's seat was empty. Again.

God hadn't abandoned me, but I was starting to think Father had. He rarely came to meals anymore, choosing instead to take them in his office or suite where he spent the vast majority of his time. Though my relationship with Thoraben and Kenna was closer than ever, it came at the expense of the one I'd always shared with Father. My choice to believe in the God of the Rebels wrenched our family unevenly in two—with Thoraben, Kenna, Mother, and I on one side of the crevice and Father standing alone on the other.

Still, if God could reach into my self-centered life and capture my heart, then he could certainly claim Father's heart too.

Couldn't he?

FORTY-FOUR

Cream cheese, eggs, vanilla, sugar. I was missing something. Cream? No. Malisa had called it something else. *Sugar cream? Curdled cream? Sour cream.* That was it. Sour cream. I wrote it down beside the other ingredients and told myself again that my decision to raid the kitchens today had nothing to do with Joha telling me I should make another cheesecake. For him.

Seriously, Alina, what are you going to do? Post it? Like the letter he still hasn't replied to?

Twenty-three days and counting. I'd told myself not to expect a reply—he'd made his view of a relationship between the two of us more than clear, and sitting down to write a letter didn't really seem his style—yet, against all logic, I'd hoped he would. Every day that went by without an answer felt like a year. Our locations didn't change, and yet with each passing hour, we moved further apart.

He frequented my dreams almost nightly, in those few hours I managed to stop wrestling the sheets long enough to sleep. In some of the dreams, he held me close. Others, he pushed me away. I cherished them all. I would have taken him pushing me away in person if it meant seeing him again.

Perhaps it was better to let it—and him—go. He didn't want me. But my heart couldn't be convinced, refusing to give up that tiny scrap of hope. *Maybe,* it argued. *He hasn't replied yet but neither has the letter been returned. Maybe he cares. Maybe he didn't mean what he said, the morning after the kiss. Maybe there's hope for us. Maybe Marcos marrying Rachana wasn't the end for you.*

"Here you are. Finally."

"Thoraben? What are you doing in the kitchens?"

He looked around, taking in my apron, the mess of ingredients on the counter, the pair of chefs pretending not to pay me any attention while no doubt wondering whether or not letting me in would cost them their jobs.

"Looking for you, though it took asking three quarters of the palace staff to find you. What are you doing here?"

I shrugged. "Making a cheesecake? Malisa showed me how."

To his credit—and my eternal gratitude—Thoraben neither laughed nor looked completely stricken, though neither did he ask to taste some when it was done. Probably a good choice, given I'd be completely guessing on the amounts for each ingredient. I was pretty certain I remembered, but this was my first solo attempt.

"You were looking for me?"

"Yes. They finished the chapel," Thoraben said. "A sizeable donation allowed them to employ enough workers to get it done within weeks rather than months." He crossed his arms, shaking his head at me. "How did you do it? I've offered time and time again to fund the rest of the build, but Joha refused to accept it, wanting it to be a work of the Followers as a whole rather than one person."

"I didn't just send money."

When I'd tried to give Marcos back my engagement ring, he'd refused it, saying it was mine to do with whatever I thought best. I could think of no better use for it than to sell it and use the funds to send workers to finish the chapel, their wages and expenses paid for as long as it took. Joha might have been too proud to accept money, but he couldn't send away Followers in need of jobs.

It pleased me no small amount to know it had worked.

"They've invited me to come and speak at its dedication next week. Would you like to come? I'll clear it with Father if you do."

My heart flew to my throat, butterflies instantly filling my stomach. "To The Well?"

"Yes."

"Yes." My answer was soft but certain. "Please." I didn't know if Joha would want me or if he even wanted to see me, but I had to find out. I couldn't live my life wondering what might have been if I'd only had the courage to go.

"Good. I'll see to the details. You be ready early Sunday."

He was gone as quickly as he'd come, leaving me standing, holding a hand against the butterflies threatening to escape my stomach. I was going to see Joha again. Soon.

The butterflies were my constant companions over the next five days. It didn't seem to matter how hard I tried to distract myself. The little voice at the back of my head, as excited as it was anxious, kept repeating the news. *You're going to see Joha. You're going to see Joha.* Sunday couldn't come fast enough.

I don't think I said a single word to Thoraben during the three-hour drive to The Well. He tried to engage me in conversation numerous times before giving up, turning his attention to the speech he was preparing. I stared out the window and tried to stop my mind from exploding from the force of emotions pounding it.

I was no closer to conquering them when we turned into The Well's long driveway.

Faithful One, if ever I needed the peace Kenna speaks of you giving, it's now.

The car stopped.

"Ready?" Thoraben asked me. I shook my head, wondering if coming back had been the worst idea I'd ever had. Had Thoraben told them I was coming with him? Did they even want me here?

God calls you "mine." You will always have a place in his arms.

I wanted to cling to the comforting words, but they bounced off my fears before they could settle. What if this was supposed to be a family-only celebration? I hadn't seen the invite. It might have been.

What if—?

"Alina." Thoraben laid a hand on my knee. "Breathe."

He stepped out of the car. I hadn't even taken my seatbelt off yet. Was I not breathing? That would explain the light-headedness.

A place in his arms. A place in his heart. A song he's written just for me. Because he loves me. He accepts me. Even cowering in a ball. I'm not alone.

I gulped back two breaths, then, deeper, another three. Then I forgot to breathe altogether.

"Ben, good to see you."

Joha. There he was, shaking Thoraben's hand, patting him on the back. Grinning at something Thoraben said. Looking a thousand times better in real life than he ever had in my dreams. He'd been in every single one of them this past week—walking beside me, sending me away, laughing with me over something Kate said, carrying me out of the water, telling me I could never be enough, holding me so close I could feel his heart beating against mine. Sometimes I woke furious at him, sometimes I didn't want to wake at all. None of them had done him justice.

"Alina, are you coming?"

While I'd been staring at Joha through the window, Thoraben had ducked his head back down to look at me through the door. "Yes." I shook my head to clear aside the dream-images. "Yes, of course." The seatbelt tugged tight against my chest when I tried to stand. My face burned as I clicked it off. Thoraben didn't hide his grin quite fast enough for me to miss it, but I did appreciate the expression of sympathy he replaced it with. And the hand he offered to assist me out of the car, it being the only reason I didn't fall on my face in front of both men.

You're the princess. Be the—

No, don't be the princess. Be Mine. Be the woman I created you to be. The woman who brings me such delight. Whether you wear gowns or jeans, stand strong or fall to pieces, you will always have a place in my heart.

This time, I was ready, catching the words before my fears

sent them flying. The butterflies stilled, peace settling over the fear like a blanket over fire. A smile began in my heart, spreading to my face. I let it come. Was this the peace Kenna spoke of?

All will be well.

Yes, Faithful One, all will be well.

"I'll leave you two to catch up, shall I?" Thoraben said. "I have to go see Pat, check some details for the dedication." He was half-way to the house before I could decide whether he deserved my gratitude or a slug to the arm. Probably both. Still, I'd wanted the chance to speak alone with Joha. I just hadn't expected it the second I stepped out of the car. There were so many things I wanted to say to him.

"I wondered if you'd come," Joha said.

Not, "I hoped you'd come," or "I wish you hadn't," but "I wondered..." Was that good? Bad?

"Thoraben invited me."

He nodded, letting the silence stretch so long I wondered if it would snap. A bird flew past, both of our gazes following its path until it dipped out of sight, forcing our attention back to each other.

All will be well.

I took another breath and tried again. "I sent you a letter."

"I got it."

Time traveled at a snail's pace between us as we stood there. Was that all he was going to say? I got it? Had he read it? What had he thought of it? He crossed his arms, moving his weight from one foot to the other as I waited. Was he going to say anything? What was going on inside that head of his?

"Mom told me about your decision." The left side of his mouth tugged upward the tiniest bit. "You Rebel."

I grinned. I hadn't thought of it like that, but I was now, wasn't I? Even if Father hadn't exiled me. Which suddenly wasn't sounding as terrifying as it once had. Not if it meant another stay at The Well. "Joha, can we talk? So much has changed in my life since I last saw you and—"

His half grin disappeared back into his beard, a tortured expression taking its place. "Alina, I..." He looked away, his gaze skittering from my hair to the car to the tree line before landing on the stable. A sigh took the place of the thoughts he held inside, a shake of his head confirming their prison sentence. Whatever he'd been about to say, he'd thought better of it. "You should get inside before it rains. Mom's in the kitchen. She'll be thrilled you're here."

His back as he walked to the stable, closing himself inside, told me more than any words he could have offered. Malisa would be thrilled, but not him.

I swallowed back the hurt and focused instead on the peace, letting it saturate my disappointment until the sadness was all but washed away. *Faithful One, thank you for taking me just as I am. Help me to remember that my hope and happiness doesn't rest in anyone's hands but yours.*

And help me to let him go.

It was just as it had been in my chapel dream all those weeks ago—the people, the building, the welcome, the peace. The instant I walked through the door of the newly finished chapel, I knew I was home. A seat had been reserved for me in the front row alongside Thoraben, but I didn't take it, instead slipping into a chair in the back. Overwhelmed by emotion, my legs wouldn't have carried me that far, but it wasn't only that. I simply wanted to savor it. Out of the spotlight.

Here, the presence of God wrapping around me like the softest of silks, I could simply be. Not a princess, not a Rebel, not a Follower—just me. In God, I'd finally found the strength to stand, and all I wanted to do was kneel.

I closed my eyes to people still finding their seats and the music beginning up in the front and dropped to my knees, hands covering my face.

I had no words to say. All my years of deportment training and speeches and studying the right protocols in every situation, and I couldn't find a single word to encapsulate the gratitude my heart felt toward this God who'd not only found me but given me a place to belong. A family. A home. His heart. "Thank you" didn't even come close.

Music swirled around me as I knelt there, letting my heart speak what my mind couldn't comprehend. God's goodness. God's grace. God's compassion. God's patience. God's majesty. More than a word or title, it was who he was. Not simply King but everything. Above everything. Part of everything. My everything.

I stayed there until the music faded away and my feet went numb. I wished I could have stayed forever.

"Hi everyone, I'm Ben." A trickle of laughter swirled its way around the room at Thoraben's casual introduction, so against protocol—he should have at least used his whole name even if he deigned to leave off the title—and yet, it was so perfect for this group of people. Like Joha had told me the first day I met him, they were family.

"I know you're all as thrilled as I am to be here today—and that Malisa has catered enough food to last us three days at least—so I won't keep you long. But since I have the stage for a few minutes, I want to talk to you about dreams. Not the ones occupying your mind while you sleep, but the ones God puts in your heart."

What? That wasn't his speech. He'd shown me his speech yesterday, asking my opinion on it. It had been about finding hope in the middle of life's challenges. Not something as namby-pamby as dreams. Had he rewritten it on the way here? Was that what he'd been asking me about when I'd been too caught up in my nerves to think?

Thoraben stepped out from behind the lectern, notes left behind as he walked to the wall and placed a hand on the brick.

"This chapel was a dream God placed in the heart of one man—Pat Samson. A dream to build a place on this property where people could come and meet with God. Where they'd feel welcome and at home. At first, it probably seemed as impossible to reach as our sleeping dreams. It had taken all the money he had just to buy the property, leaving nothing left for such a large building project. But he held on to the dream, knowing if God planted it there, God would see it through.

"Along the way, it became the dream of others—Malisa, Joha, Arden, and so many others who found hope here at The Well. A decade on from that first spark, though he had nothing physical to show for it, the dream was becoming a reality. God was bringing the right people along to make it happen and building the strength of those already here.

"It was another five years before the foundation of the building you're sitting in today was laid. Fifteen years of holding on to that dream before a single brick was laid. Another eleven months of work to finish it. But in all that time, Pat never let go of that dream. And tonight, that dream has become reality. Pat's reality, our reality, God's reality. You're sitting in a dream come true."

I stared at the back of Pat's head, my respect for the man rising even further than the heights it had already scaled. Fifteen years? With not a single thing to show for it? That was almost as long as I'd been alive. I let my gaze roam around the room, taking in the high ceilings with their dangling lights, the rough brick walls, the way the sun's late afternoon rays lit up the single stained-glass window behind Thoraben.

"So, let me ask you, what's your dream? What dream has God placed in your heart?"

I looked down at my hands, fighting against the answer which immediately came to mind. *To marry Joha and live here at The Well, helping people like they helped me.* It was ridiculous. Not only completely and utterly selfish but impossible. Joha didn't want me. He'd made that more than clear.

"Don't worry if it seems impossible right now or the practicalities of seeing it through overwhelm you. It wouldn't be a God-dream if you could do it alone."

Was Thoraben talking to me alone? No, other people were nodding too. Some wiping away tears even as they considered his words. I wanted to throw my thoughts out the window. That couldn't be my dream.

Why not? It honors God, doesn't it? Marriage to a good, faith-filled man. Using your influence to help others.

But it's impossible, I argued myself. Pat's dream didn't depend on anyone else but him. I couldn't make Joha love me.

What if you're his dream too?

I swung my head around, guiltily checking that no one else had heard the voice which seemed so loud in my heart. Me? Be Joha's dream? Now I knew the voice was wrong. I was nobody's dream. No one's but God's. He'd accepted me, flaws and all. His approval was all I needed.

"Don't let fear or doubt tug loose your hold on that dream. If God's placed it in your heart, you can be certain he'll see it through. May this chapel be a reminder of that."

Thoraben walked back to his seat. The band stood, claiming their instruments as the music began again. No, not all the band. Joha still sat. With barely a glance at him, Darrick came forward, easily slipping into the lead position as if it was nothing out of the ordinary. Voices raised around me as people lifted their gratitude to God. Joha walked down the side of the chapel, through the door, and out of sight.

What if you're his dream too?

My heart thudded against my throat. What if I was? What if it wasn't such an impossible dream that we be together? My legs shook as I stood, clutching the back of the chair in front of me until I was certain they'd hold. The need to follow Joha was like a hunger inside me, one that neither food nor water could quench.

Faithful One?

Go.

FORTY-FIVE

I was halfway back to the house when the sky let loose the rain it had been threatening all afternoon. Within seconds, I was soaked, wet skirts slapping against my legs with each step I took. I stopped only long enough to pull off my heels and throw them aside before continuing on, the certainty that I was doing the right thing growing with each step. Had my quest to find Joha been a whim, the rain would have crushed it for sure. Instead, the hunger only increased.

The stable was the first place I looked, sure he'd be here. Horses nickered as I ran past their stalls, searching. He wasn't. Not in any of the stalls or in his one-roomed apartment I guiltily checked. I thrust dripping hair out of my eyes and ran to the house instead, mentally promising Malisa I'd clean up the trail of water left from one room to the next as I checked every one. Not here either. I pushed aside the disappointment ushering in failure and peered out the kitchen window, straining to see through the rain. He wouldn't have taken Knight out for a ride in this, would he? Maybe, but...no, Knight had been in his stall. All the stalls had been full. So then, where...?

There. In the gazebo. Someone was sitting there. It had to be Joha. And if it wasn't, I was desperate enough to be wrong. One hand shading my eyes, I ran back out into the rain.

"Joha!"

It only took one shout of his name for the figure to turn his head. It was him. Relief had me trembling and my bare foot skidded on the wet ground, pitching me forward. My hands hit soft grass an instant before Joha was there, pulling me upright again, his arm on mine holding me steady.

"Alina! What are you doing here? Don't you know it's raining?"

I looked up at him, his face so dear. Water dripped off his beard, his hair not yet plastered to his head as mine was but certainly close. How had I ever thought this man not handsome? My heart sped to triple time. All I could think about was the last time we'd been here together at the gazebo. The night he'd kissed me.

"I had to see you."

"And you chose running through the rain to do it? At least come under here where it's dry, if not warm. Silly girl."

Maybe you're his dream too.

"Wait." I had to know before any more time passed. I'd waited too long already. I had to know if he cared. "Kiss me."

"What? Come out of the rain."

"Please?"

"Alina..."

"Don't you want to?"

"That's not fair."

I shook my head, hot tears burning their way down my icy face. He didn't want me. I'd gotten it wrong. Again. First my certainty that God wanted me to choose Marcos, only to have Marcos choose Rachana. Now, running out here, begging Joha to love me, so sure God had told me to come. As if Joha would ever choose a girl like me.

"I'm sorry," I said, taking a step back, missing instantly the warmth of his hand on my arm. "You're right, of course. I just— What's so wrong with me that no one wants me? Marcos refused to kiss me too. Did you know that? I asked him, more than once. We should have been married, and he wouldn't even kiss me. And now you, the man I love, refusing me just like he did. Is it because I'm a princess? I know I was useless when I first arrived here, but I've changed, I really have. I—"

My words were swallowed up in Joha's kiss, my rain-chilled body instantly warm as one strong, calloused hand cradled my face and the other at my back pulled me closer. Time stopped altogether as Joha Samson kissed me. Just like he had in my dreams, only a million times better because it was real. When he finally pulled back, my breathing was ragged. I laughed in quiet wonder as I realized his was too.

"You kissed me."

"You asked me to." He frowned slightly, the hand on my face dropping to my shoulder. "If you didn't mean it..."

"No. I did."

"And the bit about loving me?"

My heart thudded erratically—racing at the thought of him knowing the truth, skipping beats as I worried over his reaction. I hadn't meant to tell him. Not so bluntly nor so soon. But now that the truth was out there, I refused to hide from it either. "I meant that too."

Joha shook his head. My heart almost stopped. Words tumbled out of my mouth as I tried to fill the silence.

"It's okay if you don't. Love me back, that is. I mean, I want you to, especially after that kiss. Woah, that kiss. But I'm not forcing you or anything. I mean, I made you kiss me just now, but I promise I won't do it again because—"

He was kissing me again. Apparently, he thought that the best way to stop me talking. Not that I was complaining. At all. My hands came up behind his neck, pulling him in closer, if that were even possible. *Joha...*

He pulled back, just enough to kiss my cheek and tuck his head in against my neck. I wasn't sure whose heartbeat it was thudding against my chest.

"You kissed me again."

A deep laugh rumbled near my ear. "Making up for lost time."

"What?"

With a shake of his head and a tender smile which turned my now-racing heart to mush, Joha pulled me under the gazebo. He took my hands in his, turning them over, rubbing his thumbs over the backs of them. When he looked at me, I wondered how I'd ever find the will to look away.

"Alina." He breathed out my name, letting it dance around the gazebo and fall to the ground before continuing. "Do you know what I was doing out here?"

"Hiding?"

"Trying to get over you."

I couldn't stop the smile that spread across my face. "Truly?"

"Yeah. Obviously, I failed."

I didn't want to assume, but him saying that after a kiss that still had me reeling... "Then, you like me?"

His laugh was short. The grin that followed it rueful. "Like doesn't even begin to cover it."

I laid a trembling hand against the side of his beard, so soft under my fingers. Words failed me as, for the second time today, gratitude overwhelmed my heart. He liked me. Couldn't get over me any more than I could him.

"You're shivering."

Was I?

"Come with me."

I took the hand he offered, content to follow him wherever he led, be it the house or all the way back to Peverell. It wasn't either. It was back through the rain to the stable. I laughed, feeling almost giddy with joy. Of course, it was the stable. We stopped just inside the door. Joha grabbed a horse blanket from a hook on the wall, wrapping it around me before kissing me on the nose.

"Wait here," he said. "I have something for you." He ran up the stairs leading to his apartment. A shiver raced from my neck, down my spine, to my bare toes. I looked down at them, noticing for the first time the mud splashed across my shins and the front of my skirt. I should have been horrified to have Joha see me like this. Three months ago, I would have been, but here now, wrapped in a scruffy horse blanket, my hair messy from the rain, I'd never felt more beautiful.

Joha reappeared, something held behind his back. His grin as he came to stand in front of me might as well have been a direct challenge to find out what. I waited a whole ten seconds before trying to peek.

"Uh-uh." He twisted away, keeping whatever he held a secret no matter which way I ducked. "Not yet."

"Joha Samson..."

"Alina...uh, do you have a last name?"

"No."

"Oh. Well. How's this then. Alina, Princess of the Apple Tree and Queen of My Heart, I don't just really like you, I love you. I have since the moment you took my dare and stepped up on to that log bridge, despite how hard I tried to deny it."

No way. "That long?"

He grinned. "Maybe longer."

"But you said—"

"I lied. Truth is, I was scared."

"Of me?"

"You, what I felt for you, what that might mean, the fact that it shouldn't have meant anything. You were engaged to Prince Marcos, supposed to be married already. I had no right to be falling for you. And really, I still have no idea how this will work with us being from such different worlds or if it's even possible your father would give his permission or why you would want a poor farmer like me, but—"

My breath caught in my throat. "But?"

He laid a hand against my cheek. I fought the urge to close my eyes and drown in the swirl of emotions it caused. Was this real?

"I can't lie anymore. To either of us. I love you, and I want you in my life. Don't tell Ben, but I have no idea what he said in there earlier because the minute he started talking about dreams, all I could think about was you."

Tears threatened at his words. *Maybe you're his dream too.*

"I know they're not a pink diamonds from halfway across the world but..." From behind his back, Joha pulled out a pair of bright pink boots, bedazzled along the edges with tiny white gems in the shape of diamonds. "Alina, will you marry me?"

He'd made me my own boots—pink, sparkly, perfectly clean boots. No diamond could have been more perfect. I threw my arms around his neck, barely holding back a squeal which would have terrified every horse in the stable. "Yes. Absolutely, yes."

The boots dropped to the ground, sending up a waft of dust. "Really? You mean it? Even knowing we only have one shower here and I might occasionally smell like horse?"

"You always smell like horse, and we would definitely be getting another shower. But yes. I really do mean it. I love you, Joha Samson, and there's no other man I'd rather spend the rest of my life with. But—" I pulled myself out of his arms, hating that I had to ask. "Are you sure? You know I will never be able to walk away entirely from the title and responsibilities of being a princess. We'd have to attend the four balls each year at least, and I'd still have to make appearances sometimes and speeches and attend certain functions and—"

"We can do that."

"—I still have a lot to learn about being a Follower and letting God be in charge rather than me, and I don't know how to bake very well or—"

Joha's hand landed on my arm. "Alina. Stop." I closed my mouth, dropping my gaze to the boots sitting at our feet. Hating the fact that I'd moved so quickly from bliss to fear and doubt. "Look at me."

The boots blurred. I gritted my teeth together in a desperate attempt to gain control. Joha's hand touched my chin, tugging my tear-filled gaze back to his. "Hey, it's okay. You don't have to be perfect. God and you both know, I'm not. And yes, there are a lot of things we need to figure out, I'm not denying that, but I want to do it with you. We can figure it out together. Will you let me?"

His hands on my shoulders were strong, his gaze steady, just as it had been that day in the apple tree. And like that day, I found my anxiety slipping away, forced aside by the strength he lent me.

Faithful One. Giver of Dreams. Fulfilment of Hopes. You did it.

I bent down and slipped my feet into the boots, the extra height when I stood again bringing me perfectly in line with Joha's face. His eyes searched mine, a smile reaching them the instant before I leaned in and kissed him. Though it was brief, for now, it was enough.

"Yes."

ACKNOWLEDGMENTS

Some stories are harder to write than others. This one almost broke me. Maybe it was because Alina had so many layers and kept doing things I didn't expect, or maybe simply because I, like Alina, far too often let my doubts and anxiety get the better of me. The fact that you're holding *Heart of a Princess* in your hands today is due to some pretty incredible people I'm thrilled to be able to publicly thank.

Firstly, my mum, Jacqui. Not only were you the first one to ask for Alina's story—back when it hadn't even crossed my mind to write more about Peverell—but you were the one who encouraged me time and time again when I just couldn't get the story right, or wrote five thousand words one day only to delete ten thousand the next. You believed in me, and Alina, when I'd given up on us both. Thank you, times a million, for that. And for always being my first reader. And second. Third. Two-hundredth. Your support means the world to me.

My friend, Tricea. There's a moment in the writing of every story where the book suddenly comes to life for me. With this story, it was when I changed the hero's name to Joha. In an instant, he went from shallow and one dimensional to alive and full of heart. Thank you for letting me use your son's name and imagine, in the smallest part, what he might have been like. He will never be forgotten.

My husband, Brett. Thanks for being so supportive and giving me the space to dream big. Also for having a beard. So I could write accurately what kissing a man with a beard felt like. There are far too few fictional romance heroes with beards.

My amazing kids. You have no idea how much it makes me smile when you proudly recommend my books to your friends (even though you're all still too young to read them) or write stories "just like Mummy." Thanks for your encouragement, your excitement, your hugs, your patience when "just a sec" turns into quite a few more, the way you talk about my characters like they're real people, and for making even the worst writing day good because I got to spend it with you.

My dad, David. From the day I was born, you've been supporting my dreams. Thanks for reading and praying over my princess books, even though they're a long way from what you'd normally read.

My sister, Cherith. I don't think I could ever thank you enough for ensuring I don't have thirteen months in one year, or people meeting before they were born, or changing eye color, or attending nine full events in one day. You constantly amaze me with your attention to detail and the things you pick up. I love that you have such an analytical brain (and will try my best not to take total advantage of it...). Thank you!

David and Roseanna White and the team at WhiteFire Publishing. From the start, you have been so incredibly encouraging and amazing to work with. Thanks for all you do, both seen and unseen. David, thanks for reading, liking, and championing my books, even though you might never understand why girls find princess books so appealing. (I love that you try!) And Roseanna, I still can't believe I get to work with one of my favorite authors! (Eek! One day, that might sink in.) Thank you for your emails and excitement and for designing yet another stunning cover. It's so beautiful!

Karryn, Georgia, Jeshanah, and Petra. Thank you for praying, cheering, sending cards, and proudly buying my books even when I was already planning on giving you one. Friends like you mean the world to me. You have no idea how many times your random messages (and smiley heart emojis) made my day.

Melissa Tagg and Kara Isaac. Thank you for not only writing amazing books but taking the time out of your crazy, busy lives to send a note of encouragement and support to a just-starting-out author like me. You have no idea how much those simple words meant coming from authors I've admired for years. I hope one day I can be as much an encouragement to another fledgling author as you've both been to me.

And, God. Faithful One. Without all the above people, this book wouldn't have made it into anyone's hands, but without God, there wouldn't even be a story. He is the one who gives me worth and reason, who loved me first, who knew I would never be enough so took out the need for me to be. He's the one who picks me up, time and time again, when I don't have anything left, and reminds me that I don't have to, because He will always be enough. Like the Rebels, I can sing that because of Him I know no matter where I go, if I'm with Him and He with me, all will be well.

To God be the glory.

THE DAUGHTERS OF PEVERELL SERIES

Heart of a Royal
Daughters of Peverell, Book 1

Everyone wanted her to be their princess...
except the ones who mattered most.

YOU MAY ALSO ENJOY

Gone Too Soon
by Melody Carlson

An icy road. A car crash.
A family changed forever.

Seeing Voices
by Olivia Smit

Skylar Brady has a plan for her life—
until an accident changes everything.

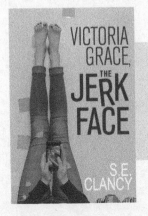

Victoria Grace, the Jerkface
by S.E. Clancy

A sassy teen, a woman born before
sliced bread.
Just add boys...and homework.